Spirit Quest

Native American Indian Legends Stories and Fables

Written and Edited by
G.W. Mullins
With Original Art by C.L. Hause

LIGHT
OF THE
MOON
PUBLISHING

The following book represents a collection of Native American works which are public domain. You may have read the stories before. In true story telling fashion, the stories have been left as close to the original form as possible. In Native American culture, in order to pass the stories along with all information intact, they had to be told pretty much word for word, to keep the legends alive. Many of these stories were translated directly from original Native language texts. With that in mind, please be aware that some spellings and word usage may vary from one tribe to another. For instance, the spelling of "teepee", as used in this book, can also be written as "tipi", and "tepee". All are correct. Also when using words like "someone", in most native cultures, it would be "some one". So keep in mind, these are not necessarily misspellings. They are simply dialect and translations.

Also Available From G.W. Mullins And C.L. Hause

Walking With Spirits Volume 1 Native American Myths, Legends, And Folklore
Walking With Spirits Volume 2 Native American Myths, Legends, And Folklore
Walking With Spirits Volume 3 Native American Myths, Legends, And Folklore
Walking With Spirits Volume 4 Native American Myths, Legends, And Folklore
Walking With Spirits Volume 5 Native American Myths, Legends, And Folklore
Walking With Spirits Volume 6 Native American Myths, Legends, And Folklore
The Native American Story Book - Stories Of The American Indians For Children
The Native American Story Book Volume Two - Stories Of The American Indians
For Children
The Native American Story Book Volume Three - Stories Of The American Indians
For Children
Cherokee A Collection of American Indian Legends, Stories And Fables
Creation Myths - Tales Of The Native American Indians
Strange Tales Of The Native American Indians
Spirit Quest - Native American Indian Legends Stories and Fables
Animal Tales Of The Native American Indians
Medicine Man - Shamanism, Natural Healing, Remedies And Stories Of The Native
American Indians
The Native American Cookbook
Native American Cooking - An Indian Cookbook With Legends And Folklore
Native American Legends: Stories Of The Hopi Indians Vol. One
Native American Legends: Stories Of The Hopi Indians Vol. Two

Available From C.L. Hause With Graphic Design And Layout By G.W. Mullins

The Native American Art Book – Art Inspired By Native American Myths And
Legends

WALKING WITH SPIRITS & THE NATIVE AMERICAN STORY BOOK

This book is dedicated to
Vince Mullins, my
Grandfather (Pawpaw).
A tall red man who I
loved so much. I think
he would have liked this.

G.W. Mullins

The beauty of the trees, the softness of the air,
the fragrance of the grass speaks to me.
The summit of the mountain, the thunder of the sky,
The rhythm of the sea, speaks to me.
The faintness of the stars, the freshness of the morning,
the dewdrop on the flower, speaks to me.
The strength of the fire, the taste of salmon, the trail of the sun,
and the life that never goes away, they speak to me
And my heart soars.

...Chief Dan George (1899-1981)

Chief Dan George, (July 24, 1899 – September 23, 1981) was a chief of the Tsleil-Waututh Nation, a Coast Salish band located on Burrard Inlet in North Vancouver, British Columbia, Canada. He was also an author, poet, actor, and an Officer of the Order of Canada. At the age of 71, he was nominated for an Academy Award for Best Supporting Actor in Little Big Man.

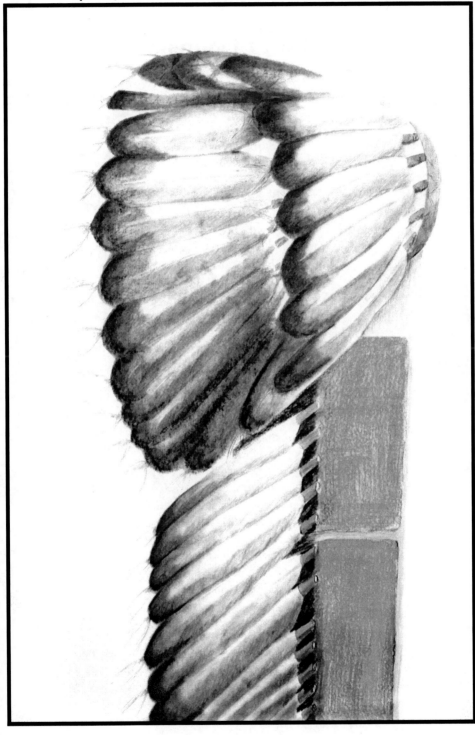

Table of Contents

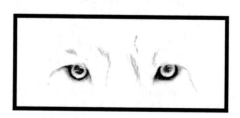

Introduction

Before the time of books, computers, tablets and recording devices, the history of many cultures was passed down, from person to person, by word of mouth. The rich histories of so many people were told in songs, chants, poems and stories. This was and still is the way of Native American tribes. Each in its own way enriching their stories with their own experiences. By reliving these stories and songs, we have the opportunity to bring life back to the ancient spirits that created them. We have a chance to walk with the spirits of the past.

Native Americans used their stories to teach the children the traditions of their grandfathers. It was in this way that local customs were passed down and lessons were taught about how to live off the land and track animals. It was with stories they learned to grow crops and thrive in their natural environment.

When foreign men entered and settled upon Indian sacred lands, the Native Americans were often forcibly removed. They were sent to areas unfamiliar. If it were not for their customs, language and tradition passed down through stories, they would have lost connection with who they were. These songs and myths were their way of keeping their legacy alive.

Today Native Americans still keep their tribal languages alive. The myths and legends are still passed down from generation to generation.

Mythology

Mythology has always played a huge role in Native American stories. Of the stories told, those of Creation are often best known. Nature has always been looked at as an unfolding mystery. And in the stories of Native Americans, they sought to explain everything from natural occurrences, to animals, plant life, and weather related events. It was a way to express their ideas of their own beginnings.

Among all the stories told, each tribe had their own views of creation and how life came into this world. While some themes were similar, others could not be more different. In their stories, they explored the importance of Native American culture but also the individuality of each tribe and it's believes. These myths pay respect to the ancient ones that came before them and how nature has shaped their lives.

Songs, Poems and Music

Story telling didn't just involve words, or simple retelling of history. It included chants, poems, songs and music. Much set to the sound of a drum. The drumming invited everyone into the dance. After all, these stories and history were meant to be shared by all. It has been and still is custom to share stories and music at pow-wows.

Legacy

Through storytelling, the rich history of the Native American tribes is alive and well today. It has been shared and preserved and still pays tribute to fallen heroes of the past. Often, Native Americans have been misrepresented as violent people. It is through the glimpses into the past, and these stories much like the ones that are contained in this book, that you can see what a proud heritage they possess and how in tune with the Earth Native Americans really are.

Being there were so many different tribes with countless beliefs and customs, the only way to understand their ways is through understanding their stories. In this book I have endeavored to show a wide landscape of different tribes and hopefully present a true look at their beliefs.

With this book I hope you understand the Native American people a little better and understand where they have come from and what they can offer the world. By exploring these stories, I offer you a glimpse into an often forgotten past. The past of my people. I was born Cherokee and as a child heard many of these stories. These stories were passed to me in the old traditional way by my grandfather. And now I give these stories to you, to carry forward for younger generations to explore and learn.

The mythology of the North America Indians is a cultural treasure trove, but many of these myths and legends are hidden away in many old books and documents. So this vast body of wisdom lies out of reach of most people... until now.

Origin Tales

The Story of the Drum

An Abenaki Legend

It is said that when Creator was giving a place for all the spirits to dwell who would be taking part in the inhabitance of Mother Earth, there came a sound, a loud BOOM, from off in the distance.

As Creator listened, the sound kept coming closer and closer until it finally it was right in front of Creator. "Who are you?" asked Creator. "I am the spirit of the drum" was the reply. I have come here to ask you to allow me to take part in this wonderful thing." "How will you take part?" Creator questioned." I would like to accompany the singing of the people. When they sing from their hearts, I will to sing as though I was the heartbeat of Mother Earth. In that way, all creation will sing in harmony. "Creator granted the request, and from then on, the drum accompanied the people's voices.

Throughout all of the indigenous peoples of the world, the drum is the center of all songs. It is the catalyst for the spirit of the songs to rise up to the Creator so that the prayers in those songs reach where they were meant to go. At all times, the sound of the drum brings completeness, awe, excitement, solemnity, strength, courage, and the fulfillment to the songs. It is Mother's heartbeat giving her approval to those living upon her. It draws the eagle to it, who carries the message to Creator.

It changes people's lives!

Peace and happiness are available in every moment.
Peace is every step. We shall walk hand in hand.
There are no political solutions to spiritual problems.
Remember: If the Creator put it there, it is in the right place.
The soul would have no rainbow if the eyes had no tears.
Tell your people that, since we were promised we should never
be moved,
we have been moved five times.

An Indian Chief, 1876

The Origin of Corn

A Jicarilla Apache Legend
Frank Russell, Myths of the Jicarilla Apaches, 1898

An Apache who was an inveterate gambler had a small tame turkey, which followed its master about everywhere. One day the Turkey told him that the people were tired of supporting him, as he gambled until he lost everything that they gave him.

They had decided to give him one more stock of supplies, and if he made away with that he should be killed.

Knowing that he could not resist the temptation to gamble if he had any property in his possession, he decided to leave the tribe before their wrath should overtake him.

The next day he began to chop down a tree from which to build a boat.

The Woodpecker, Tsitl-ka-ta, commanded him not to cut the tree; the woodpeckers must do that for him.

They also cut out the inside of the trunk, so that he could get into the cylinder, after which the spider sealed him in by making a web over each end. The woodpeckers carried the log, thus prepared, to the Rio Grande River, and threw it in. The faithful Turkey followed along the shore.

In the whirlpool above San Juan the log left the main current, and spun round and round until the Turkey pushed it on into the channel again. Farther down the river the log caught in the rocks in an upright position above a fall, but the Turkey again started it on its journey.

At the pueblo of Isleta, the boys hauled out the log with others for fuel. The Turkey' rescued the log and placed it in the water, and again, at another pueblo far down the river, the log was returned to the stream.

Far to the southward the log drifted out of the channel into a grove of cottonwoods. The man came out of the log and found a large quantity of duck feathers lying about. That night he had no blanket in which to sleep, so he covered himself with duck feathers.

He killed a duck, and with the sinews of its legs made a bowstring.

After he landed, the Turkey soon overtook him, and they remained there for four days. During this time the man cleared a small space and leveled it.

"Why do you clear this place?" said the Turkey. "if you wish to plant something you must make a larger field." Then the Turkey ran toward the east, and the field was extended in that direction: toward the south, the west, and the north he ran, until the field was large enough.

Then he ran into the field from the east side, and the black corn lay behind him; from the south side, and the blue corn appeared; from the west, and the yellow corn was made; from the north, and the seeds of every kind of cereal and vegetable lay upon the ground.

The Turkey told the man to plant all these seeds in rows. In four days the growing plants appeared.

The Turkey helped his master tend the crops, and in four more days everything was ripe. Then the man took an ear of corn and roasted it, and found it good.

Go Forward With Courage

When you are in doubt, be still, and wait;
when doubt no longer exists for you, then go forward with courage.
So long as mists envelop you, be still;
be still until the sunlight pours through and dispels the mists
-- as it surely will.
Then act with courage.

Ponca Chief White Eagle (1800's to 1914)

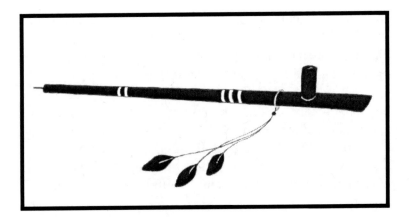

The Legend of the Peace Pipes
An Arikara Legend

The people came across a great water on logs tied together. They pitched their tents on the shore. Then they thought to make for themselves certain bounds within which they were to live and rules which should govern them. They cleared a space of grass and weeds so they could see each other's faces. They sat down and there was no obstruction between them.

While they were holding a council, an owl hooted in the trees near by. The leader said, "That bird is to take part in our council. He calls to us. He offers us his aid."

Immediately afterward they heard a woodpecker. He knocked against the trees. The leader said, "That bird calls to us. He offers us his aid. He will take part in our council."

Then the chief appointed a man as servant. He said, "Go into the woods and get an ash sapling." The servant came back with a sapling having a rough bark.

"We do not want that," said the leader. "Go again and get a sapling with a smooth bark, bluish in color at the joint where a branch comes." So the servant went out, and came back with a sapling of the kind described.

When the leader took up the sapling, and eagle came and soared about the council which was sitting in the grass. He dropped a downy feather; it fell. It fell in the center of the cleared space. Now this was the white eagle. The chief said, "This is not what we want," so the white eagle passed on.

Then the bald eagle came swooping down, as though attacking its prey. It balanced itself on its wings directly over the cleared space. It uttered fierce cries, and dropped one of its downy feathers, which stood on the ground as the other eagle's feather had done. The chief said, "This is not what we want." So the bald eagle passed on.

Then came the spotted eagle, and soared over the council, and dropped its feather as the others had done. The chief said, "This is not what we want," and the spotted eagle passed on.

Then the imperial eagle, the eagle with the fantail, came, and soared over the people. It dropped a downy feather which stood upright in the center of the cleared space. The chief said, "This is what we want."

So the feathers of this eagle were used in making the peace pipes, together with the feathers of the owl and woodpecker, and with other things. These peace pipes were to be used in forming friendly relations with other tribes.

When the peace pipes were made, seven other pipes were made for keeping peace within the tribe. One pipe was to prevent revenge. If one man should kill another, the chief took this pipe to the relatives and offered it to them. If the relatives of the dead man refused to accept it, it was offered again. It was offered four times. If it was refused four times, the chief said, "Well, you must take the consequences. We will do nothing, and you cannot now ask to see the pipes." He meant if they took revenge and any trouble came to them, they could not ask for help or for mercy.

Each band had its own pipe.

Certain things catch your eye,
But pursue only those
that capture your heart.

Old Native Saying

How a Piegan Warrior Found the First Horses
A Blackfoot Legend

A long time ago a warrior of the Piegan Blackfoot dreamed about a lake far away where some large animals lived. A voice in the dream told him the animals were harmless, and that he could use them for dragging travois and carrying packs in the same way the Indians then used dogs. "Go to this lake," the dream voice told him, "and take a rope with you so that you can catch these animals."

When the Piegan awoke he took a long rope made from strips of a bull buffalo's hide and travelled many miles on foot to the shore of the lake. He dug a hole in the sandy beach and concealed himself there. While he watched, he saw many animals come down to the lake to drink. Deer, coyotes, elk and buffalo all came to quench their thirsts.

After a while the wind began to blow. Waves rose upon the lake and began to roll and hiss along the beach. At last a herd of large animals, unlike any the Piegan had ever seen before, suddenly appeared before him. They were as large as elks, and had small ears and long tails hanging to the ground. Some were white, and some black, and some red and spotted. The young ones were smaller. When they reached the water's edge and bent their heads to drink, the voice the man had heard in his dream whispered to him: "Throw your rope and catch one."

And so the Piegan threw his rope and caught one of the largest of the animals. It struggled and pulled and dragged the man about, and he was not strong enough to hold the animal. Finally, it pulled the rope out of his hands, and the whole herd ran into the lake and sank out of sight beneath the water.

Feeling very sad, the Piegan returned to camp. He went into his lodge and prayed for help to the voice he had heard in his dream. The voice answered him: "Four times you may try to catch these animals. If in four times trying you do not catch them, you will never see them again."

Before he went to sleep that night the Piegan asked Old Man to help him, and while he slept Old Man told him that he was not strong enough to catch one of the big animals. "Try to catch one of the young animals," Old Man said, "and then you can hold it."

Next morning the Piegan went again to the shores of the big lake, and again he dug a hole in the sand and lay hidden there while the deer, the coyotes, the elk and the buffalo came to drink. At last the wind began to rise and the waves rolled and hissed upon the beach. Then came the herd of strange animals to drink at the lake, and again the man threw his rope. This time he caught one of the young animals and was able to hold it.

One by one he caught all the young animals out of the herd and led them back to the Piegan camp. After they had been there a little while, the mares--the mothers of these colts-- came trotting into the camp. Their udders were filled with milk for the colts to drink. Soon after the mares came, the stallions of the herd followed them into the camp.

At first the Piegans were afraid of these new animals and would not go near them, but the warrior who had caught them told everybody that they would not harm them. After a while the animals became so tame that they followed the people whenever they moved their camp from place to place. Then the Piegans began to put packs on them, and they called this animal po-no-kah- mita, or elk dog, because they were big and shaped like an elk and could carry a pack like a dog.

That is how the Piegan Blackfoot got their horses.

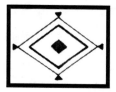

Humankind has not woven the web of life.
We are but one thread within it.
Whatever we do to the web, we do to ourselves.
All things are bound together.
All things connect.

Chief Seattle, 1854

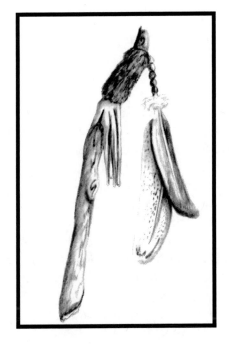

Traditional Talking Stick

Eastern Band of Cherokee Indians enrollment # 1009

The Talking Stick is a tool used in many Native American Traditions when a council is called. It allows all council members to present their Sacred Point of View. The Talking Stick is passed from person to person as they speak and only the person holding the stick is allowed to talk during that time period.

The Answering Feather is also held by the person speaking unless the speaker addresses a question to another council member. At that time, the Answering Feather is passed to the person asked to answer the query. Every member of the meeting must listen closely to the words being spoken, so when their turn comes, they do not repeat unneeded information or ask impertinent, questions.

Indian children are taught to listen from age three forward; they are also taught to respect another's viewpoint. This is not to say that they may not disagree, but rather they are bound by their personal honor to allow everyone their Sacred Point of View. People responsible for holding any type council meeting are required to make their own Talking Stick. The Talking Stick may be used when they teach children, hold council, make decisions regarding disputes, hold Pow-Wow gatherings, have storytelling circles, or conduct a ceremony where more than one person will speak.

Since each piece of material used in the Talking Stick speaks of the personal Medicine of the stick owner, each Talking Stick will be different. The Qualities of each type of Standing Person (Tree) brings specific Medicine. White Pine is the Peace Tree, Birch symbolizes truth, Evergreens represent the continued growth of all things. Cedar symbolizes cleansing. Aspen is the symbol for seeing clearly since there are many eye shapes on the truth. Maple represents gentleness. Elm is used for wisdom; Mountain Ash for protection; Oak for strength; Cherry for expression, high emotion, or love. Fruit woods are for abundance and walnut or pecan for gathering of energy or beginning new projects.

Each person making a Talking Stick must decide which type of Standing Person (Tree) will assist their needs and add needed medicine to the Councils held. The ornamentation of each stick all have meaning.

In the Lakotah Tradition, red is for life, yellow is for knowledge, blue is for prayer and wisdom, white is for spirit, purple is for healing, orange is for feeling kinship with all living things, black is for clarity and focus. The type of feathers and hide used on a Talking Stick are very important as well. The Answering Feather is usually an Eagle Feather, which represents high ideals, truth as viewed from the expansive eye of the eagle, and the freedom that comes from speaking total truth to the best of one's ability.

The Answering Feather can also be the feather of a Turkey, the Peace Eagle of the south, which brings peaceful attitudes as well as the give and take necessary in successful completion of disputes.

In the Tribe that see Owl as good Medicine, the Owl feather may also be used to stop deception from entering the Sacred Space of the Council.

The skins, hair or hides used in making a Talking Stick brings the abilities, talents, gifts and medicine of those creatures-beings to council in a variety of ways. Buffalo brings abundance; Elk brings physical fitness and stamina; deer brings gentleness; rabbit brings the ability to listen with big ears; the hair from a horse's tail or mane brings perseverance and adds connection to the earth and to the spirits of the wind.

If an illness of heart, mind, spirit, or body has affected the group gathering, snake skin may be wrapped around the Talking Stick so that healing and transmuting of those poisons can occur. The Talking Stick is the tool that teaches each of us to honor the Sacred Point of View of every living creature.

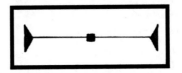

Like the grasses showing tender faces to each other,
thus should we do,
for this was the wish of the Grandfathers of the World.

Black Elk

The First Fire

A Cherokee Legend
Myths of the Cherokee,
James Mooney, 1900

In the beginning of the world, there was no fire.

The animal people were often cold. Only the Thunders, who lived in the world beyond the sky arch, had fire. At last they sent Lightning down to an island.

Lightning put fire into the bottom of a hollow sycamore tree.

The animal people knew that the fire was there, because they could see smoke rising from the top of the tree. But they could not get to it on account of the water. They held a council to decide what to do.

Everyone that could fly or could swim was eager to go after the fire. Raven said, "Let me go. I am large and strong."

At that time Raven was white.

He flew high and far across the water and reached the top of the sycamore tree. While he sat there wondering what to do, the heat scorched all his feathers black.

The frightened Raven flew home without the fire, and his feathers have been black ever since.

Then the council sent Screech Owl. He flew to the island. But while he was looking down into the hollow tree, a blast of hot air came up and nearly burned out his eyes. He flew home and to this day, Screech Owl's eyes are red.

Then Hooting Owl and Horned Owl were sent to the island together. But the smoke nearly blinded them, and the ashes carried up by the wind made white rings about their eyes. They had to come home, and were never able to get rid of the white rings.

Then Little Snake swam across to the island, crawled through the grass to the tree, and entered it through a small hole at the bottom.

But the smoke and the heat were too much for him, too. He escaped alive, but his body had been scorched black. And it was so twisted that he doubled on his track as if always trying to escape from a small space.

Big Snake, the climber, offered to go for fire, but he fell into the burning stump and became as black as Little Snake. He has been the great blacksnake ever since.

At last Water Spider said that she would go. Water Spider has black downy hair and red stripes on her body. She could run on top of water and she could dive to the bottom. She would have no trouble in getting to the island.

"But you are so little, how will you carry enough fire?" the council asked.

"I'll manage all right," answered Water Spider. "I can spin a web." so she spun a thread from her body and wove it into a little bowl and fastened the little bowl on her back. Then she crossed over to the island and through the grass. She put one little coal of fire into her bowl and brought it across to the people.

Ever since, we have had fire. And the Water Spider still has her little bowl on her back.

You have noticed that everything an Indian does is in a circle,
and that is because the Power of the World always works in circles,
and everything tries to be round.

In the old days all our power came to us from the sacred hoop
of the nation and so long as the hoop was unbroken the people
flourished. The flowering tree was the living center of the hoop,
and the circle of the four quarters nourished it. The east gave peace
and light, the south gave warmth, the west gave rain and the north
with its cold and mighty wind gave strength and endurance. This
knowledge came to us from the outer world with our religion.

Everything the power of the world does is done in a circle.
The sky is round and I have heard that the earth is round like a ball
and so are all the stars. The wind, in its greatest power, whirls.
Birds make their nests in circles, for theirs is the same religion as ours.
The sun comes forth and goes down again in a circle. The moon
does the same and both are round. Even the seasons form a great
circle in their changing and always come back again to where they
were.

The life of a man is a circle from childhood to childhood, and so it is
in everything where power moves. Our teepees were round like the
nests of birds, and these were always set in a circle, the nation's hoop,
a nest of many nests, where the Great Spirit meant for us to hatch our
children.

Black Elk, Holy Man of the Oglala Sioux 1863-1950

The Origin of Game and of Corn

A Cherokee Legend
Myths of the Cherokee,
James Mooney, 1900

Long ages ago, soon after the world was made, Kenati, a Cherokee Indian hunter and his wife Selu, lived on Looking-glass Mountain in North Carolina. They had a little son named Good Boy.

Whenever Kenati hunted in the woods, he always brought back all the game his family needed. His wife cut up the meat and washed it in the river not far from their lodge. Good Boy played near the river almost every day. One day his parents thought they heard laughing in the bushes, as if there were two children playing there.

That evening Kenati asked his son, "Who were you playing with today down by the river?"

"He is a boy who comes out of the water and calls himself my elder brother," replied Good Boy.

When Selu washed game in the river again, the parents thought the water boy must grow from the animal blood. She never saw the water boy, because as she approach ᵈ ʰᵃ disappeared.

One evening, Kenati said to his son, "Tomorrow when your playmate comes out of the water, wrestle with him and hold him down and call me, so we can come and see him." Good Boy promised to do as his father asked.

Next day a wrestling match took place between the two boys. Kenati and Selu were not far away, and at the first call from their son, they ran to see the boy from the river. Compared with Good boy, the other one looked wild.

"Let me go! Let me go!" he cried out. Good Boy held him down until his parents arrived. They took the water boy home with them.

The family kept the wild one in the house form some time, trying to tame him. But he was always disagreeable in his disposition and tried to lead Good Boy into mischief. The family discovered that wild one possessed some magic powers, so they decided to keep him. They named him Wild Boy.

Always Kenati came home from hunting with a large fat deer on his back. Always he was lucky with game. One day, Wild Boy said to his brother, "I wonder where our father finds so much game? Let's follow him next time."

In a few days, Kenati took his bow and arrows and went hunting. Shortly afterward the boys followed. Staying out of sight, they saw their father go into a swamp where some strong reeds were growing. With these, hunters usually made arrow shafts. Wild Boy changed himself into a puff of bird's down. A little wind carried him up and onto Kenati's shoulder. There he watched where Kenati went and what he did. The father was not aware of Wild Boy's presence on his shoulder as he gathered reeds and fitted them with feathers.

"I wonder what those things are for?" thought Wild Boy to himself. Kenati came out of the swamp and went on his way into the woods. The wind carried the down off Kenati's shoulders and soon Wild Boy was his normal self again. Still keeping out of sight of their father, the two brothers followed him into the mountains.

When Kenati reached a certain place, he stopped and lifted a large rock. At once, a large buck deer came running out of the hole. Kenati shot it and lifted it upon his back, starting home with his prize.

"Oho!" said the boys. "He keeps the wild animals shut up inside a cave until he needs them. He then kills the game with those things he made in the swamp." They hurried to reach home before their father arrived with his heavy load.

The very next day, the boys wanted to see if they could do as their father had done. First, they went to the swamp and made some arrows. When they came to the big rock, they lifted the cover and instantly a deer ran out, but they forgot to replace the cover.

As they made ready to shoot the deer, another deer came out of the hole, then another, and another--the boys became so confused they forgot what to do next.

Long ago, a deer's tail stuck straight out from his body. When Wild Boy struck at a deer's tail with an arrow, the tail stood straight up. The boys thought it great fun. As another deer ran by, Good Boy swung at it with an arrow so hard that the tail curled over the deer's back. Since that time most deer's' tails curl at the end.

All of the deer in the cave came out and disappeared into the forest. Following them were raccoons, rabbits, and all the other four-footed animals. Last came turkeys, partridges, pigeons, and other winged creatures. They darkened the air as they flew away. Such a noise arose that Kenati heard it at his lodge. To himself he said, "I must go to see what trouble my boys have stirred up."

Kenati went to the mountain, to the place of the large rock. There stood the two boys, but all the animals and birds were gone. Kenati was furious with them, but said nothing. He went into the cave and kicked off the covers of four large jars that stood in the back corner.

Out of the jars swarmed bedbugs, lice, and gnats that attached the two boys. they screamed from terror as they tried to beat off the insects. Bitten and stung, the boys dropped to the ground from exhaustion. When Kenati thought they had learned their lesson, he brushed away the pests. "Now you rascals," he scolded them. "You have always had plenty to eat without working for it. When we needed game, all I had to do was to come up here and take home just what we needed. Now you have let all of the game escape. From now on when you are hungry, you will have to hunt throughout the woods and mountains and then not find enough game."

The two boys went home and asked their mother for something to eat.

"There is no more meat," said Selu. "I will go to the storehouse and try to find something."

She took her basket and went to the two-story provision house set upon poles high above the ground, out of reach of most animals.

Every day before the evening meal, Selu climbed the ladder

to the one opening. She always came back with her basket full of beans and corn.

"Let's go and see where she gets the corn and beans," urged Wild Boy to his brother. They followed Selu and climbed up in back of the storehouse. They removed a piece of mud from between the logs and looked through the crack. There stood Selu in the middle of the room with her basket on the floor. When she rubbed her stomach, the basket was half-filled with corn. When she rubbed her legs, the basket was full to the top with beans. Wild Boy said, "Our mother is a witch. Maybe her food will poison us."

When Selu came back to the house, she seemed to know what the boys were thinking. "You think I am a witch?"

"Yes, we think you are a witch," Wild Boy replied.

"When I die, I want you boys to clear a large piece of ground in front of our lodge. Then drag all of my clothes seven times around the inside of the circle. If you stay up all night and watch, next morning you will be rewarded with plenty of corn."

Soon thereafter Selu became ill and died suddenly. The boys set to work clearing the ground as she had said. But instead of the whole piece of ground in front of the lodge, they only cleared seven small spots. This is why corn does not grow everywhere in the world.

Instead of dragging Selu's clothing seven times, they only went around the circle twice, outside and inside the circle. The brothers watched all night, and in the morning there were fully grown beans and corn, but only in the seven small spots.

Kenati came home from a long hunting trip. He looked for

Selu but could not find her. When the boys came home, he asked them, "Where is your mother?"

"She turned into a witch and then she died," they reported. Kenati was saddened by the news.

"I cannot stay here with you any longer. I will go and live with the Wolf people," he said.

He started on his journey. Wild Boy changed himself into a tuft of bird's down and settled upon Kenati's shoulder to learn where he was going.

When Kenati reached the settlement of the Wolf people, they were having a council in their town-house. He went in and sat down with the tuft upon his shoulder. Wolf Chief asked Kenati what was his business.

"At home I have two bad boys. In seven days, I want you to go and play a game of ball with them."

The Wolf people knew that Kenati wanted them to punish the boys and promised to go in seven days. At that moment the down blew off of Kenati's shoulder and the smoke carried it up and through the smoke hole in the roof. It came down to the ground outside, where Wild Boy resumed his own shape and ran home fast to tell his brother. Kenati did not return but went on to visit another tribe.

The two brothers prepared for the coming of the wolves. Wild Boy the magician told his brother what to do. Together they made a path around the house, leaving an opening on one side for the wolves to enter.

Next, they made four large bundles of arrows. These they placed at four different points on the outside of the circle.

Then they hid themselves in the woods nearby and waited for the wolves.

At the appointed time, a whole army of wolves surrounded the house. They came in the entrance the boys had made. When all were within, Wild Boy magically made the pathway become a high fence, trapping the wolves inside.

The two boys on the outside began shooting arrows at the wolves. Since the fence was too high for the wolves to jump over, they were trapped and most were killed.

Only a few escaped through the entrance and made their way into a nearby swamp. Three or four wolves eventually survived. These were the only wolves left alive in the world.

Soon thereafter, some strangers came from a great distance to learn about the brothers' good grain for eating and making bread. Only Selu and her family had the corn secret.

The two brothers told the strangers how to care for the corn and gave them seven kernels to plant the next night on their way home. They were advised that they must watch throughout the night, then the following morning they would have seven ears of corn. This they should do each night, and by the time they reached home, they should have enough corn for all their people to plant.

The strangers lived seven days' distance. Each night they did as the brothers had instructed them. On the last night of the journey, they were so tired that they fell asleep and were unable to continue the whole night's watch. Next morning, the corn had not sprouted and grown as on the previous six nights.

Upon arriving in their own village, they shared all the corn they still had left with their people. They explained how the two brothers told them the way to make the corn prosper. They watched over the planting with care and attention. A splendid crop of corn resulted. Since then, however, the Cherokee Indians needed to tend their corn only half the year to supply their people.

Kenati never came back to his home. The two brothers decided to search for him. Wild Boy sailed a magic disk to the north wind and it returned. He sailed it to the south wind and it returned, but it did not return from the east wind. They knew that was where their father was living. They walked a long, long time and finally came upon Kenati with a dog walking by his side.

"You bad boys," rebuked Kenati. "Why have you followed me here?"

"We are men now," they replied. "We plan to accomplish what we set out to do." Wild Boy knew that the dog was the magic disk that had not returned, and had become a dog only a few days ago.

Kenati's trail led to Selu, waiting for him at the end of the world where the sun comes up. All seemed glad to be reunited for the present.

Their parents told the two brothers that they must go to live where the sun goes down. In seven days, the two boys left for the Land of the Setting-Sun. There they still live, overseeing the planting and the care of corn.

The brothers still talk about how Selu brought forth the first corn from her seed. Since that time, the Cherokee tribe refer to her as the "Corn Woman."

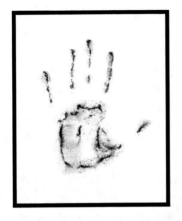

Crossing the Red Sea

A Cheyenne Legend
Dorsey, Field Museum:
Anthropological Series, ix,
37, No. 15

Many thousands of years ago the Cheyenne inhabited a country in the far north, across a great body of water. For two or three years they had been overpowered by an enemy that outnumbered them.

They were about to become the enemy's slaves, and they were filled with sorrow. Among their number was a great medicine-man who possessed a wooden hoop, like those used in the games of to-day. On one side of the hoop were tied magpie feathers, while opposite them, on the other side of the hoop, was a flint spear head, with the point projecting toward the center of the hoop. One night the great chief told the people to come to a certain place.

When they were assembled he led them away. He kept in advance of them all the time, and in his left hand he held a long staff, and in his right hand he held his hoop horizontally in front of him, with the spear head of the hoop pointing forward. No one was allowed to go in front of him. On the fourth night of their journey they saw, at some distance from the ground, and apparently not far in front of them, a bright light.

As they advanced the light receded, and appeared always a little farther beyond. They traveled a few more nights, and the fire preceded them all the way, until they came to a

large body of water. The medicine-man ordered the
Cheyenne to form in a line along the edge of the water, and
they obeyed. He then told them that he was going to take
them across the water to another land, where they would
live forever. As they stood facing the water the medicine-
man asked them to sing four times with him, and he told
them that as they sang the fourth time he would lead them
across the water.

As he sang the fourth time he began to walk forwards and
backwards and the fourth time he walked directly into the
water. All the people followed him. He commanded them
not to look upward, but ever downward. As they went
forward the waters separated, and they walked on dry
ground, but the water was all around them. Finally, as they
were being led by night the fire disappeared, but they
continued to follow the medicine-man until daylight, when
they found themselves walking in a beautiful country.

In the new country they found plenty of game to live on.
The medicine-man taught the Cheyenne many things, but
they seemed to be of weak minds, though they were
physically strong. Out of these Cheyenne there sprang up
men and women who were large, tall, strong, and fierce,
and they increased in number until they numbered
thousands.

They were so strong that they could pick up and carry off
on their backs the large animals that they killed. They
tamed panther and bear and trained them to catch wild
game for them to eat. They had bows and arrows, and were
always dressed in furs and skins, and in their ignorance
they roamed about like animals. In those days there were
very large animals. One variety of these animals was of the
form of a cow, though four times as large; by nature, they
were tame and grazed along the river banks; men milked

them.

Boys and men to the number of twenty could get upon their backs without disturbing them. Another variety of these large animals resembled in body the horse, and they had horns and long, sharp teeth. This was the most dangerous animal in the country.

It ate man, had a mind like a human being, and could trail a human being through the rivers and tall grasses by means of its power of scent. Of these there were but few. In the rivers there were long snakes whose bodies were so large that a man could not jump over them.

The Cheyenne remained in the north a long time, but finally roamed southward, conveying their burdens by means of dogs. While they were traveling southward there came a great rain and flood all over the country. The rivers rose and overflowed, and still the rain kept falling. At last the high hills alone could be discerned. The people became frightened and confused.

On a neighboring hill, and apart from the main body of the Cheyenne, were a few thousand of their number, who were out of view, and had been cut off from the main body by the rising water. When the rains ceased and the water subsided the part who were cut off looked for their tribesmen, but they found no sign of them; and it has ever since been a question among the Cheyenne whether this band of people was drowned, or whether it became a distinct tribe.

Long afterward the Cheyenne met a tribe who used many of their words, and to-day they believe that a part of their people are still living in the north. Nearly all the animals were either drowned or starved to death. The trees and fruit upon which the people had formerly subsisted were destroyed. A few large gray wolves escaped with them, for they had crossed with the tame dogs. The dogs were so large that they could carry a child several miles in a day.

After the flood had subsided the senses of the Cheyenne seemed to be awakened. They became strong in mind but weak in body, for now they had no game to subsist on. They lived on dried meat and mushrooms, which sustained them for a long time.

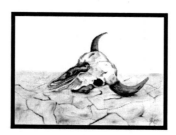

Thanksgiving

We return thanks to our mother, the earth,
which sustains us.
We return thanks to the rivers and streams,
which supply us with water.
We return thanks to all herbs,
which furnish medicines for the cure of our diseases.
We return thanks to the moon and stars,
which have given to us their light when the sun was gone.
We return thanks to the sun,
that has looked upon the earth with a beneficent eye.
Lastly, we return thanks to the Great Spirit,
in Whom is embodied all goodness,
and Who directs all things for the good of Her children.

Iroquois

Story of the Red Fox Clan

A Chickasaw Legend

John R. Swanton, 44th Annual Report of the Bureau of American Ethnology, 1926

Red Fox (Tcula) was once found in a cave asleep by a hunter. The hunter crept up to him and saw that it was Tcula. As he lay there asleep he looked red all over, and in consequence the hunter called him Red Fox.

From that time on his descendants have been known as the Red Fox clan.

Some time after this Red Fox took up with a woman belonging to the Wildcat clan. Their descendants were known as Tcula homa iksa, and they lived only in the woods. They made a living by stealing from other people, and that was why they wanted to live in the timber continually. If this clan had been handed down through the women, it would have been numerous to-day; but since it depended on the father's side it did not last long.

They kept on stealing until about 1880, when the other people got tired of them and killed nearly all, so that there are now only a few remaining among the Choctaw and Chickasaw.

A person of the Red Fox clan did whatever he liked.

Once a man of this clan went hunting. He did not return that day nor the next day after. In fact, he was gone for several days, and presently the people thought something had happened to him and chose three men to send in search of him.

These men at length reached a place where they expected to find him, but when they got close to it he was not there. They discovered that he had taken up with a woman of the Bird clan; that was why he had not returned home. When they at length came to the place where he was living, he told them that he did not think it was harmful to take any woman, whether she was of the same clan or not.

Therefore, when he met this woman and found that he liked her and that she liked him, they lived together. The men told him that it was against the will of his people and contrary to their customs, but he could not be persuaded and after a while they left him. Before he left his people he had already been married. Afterwards he wanted to go back to live with them as he had before, but they would not listen to him.

It was the belief of the people of the Red Fox clan that one should not marry outside, and it was their law that if one did so they would not have anything to do with him. They would not help him in any way but he who obeyed their customs was held in respect among them. They believed that things moved on as was intended by the Creator, but some people did not have any regard for this and did not care what happened to them. The customs and habits of the Red Fox clan are different from those of any other, and the same was true of those of the Double Mountain people. Anyone who wanted to learn their ways must marry one of their women (which, judging by what was said in the last paragraph in the case of the Red Foxes, would seem to have been difficult).

When winter was approaching and these people wanted to go on a hunt, they began their preparations a considerable time in advance. Some of them would get together and decide how many were to go and how long they would be gone.

Then these persons would fast for four days and meanwhile the women would cook food for them to take, enough to last for the time determined upon. They made sacks into which to put cold flour (banaha). While the men were fasting they would not sleep with their wives, for if one did he thought that luck would abandon him and he would kill no deer.

Some would not observe these rules and in consequence they were usually excluded from the party. If such a person were permitted to go, the deer would see him first and run off. But those who obeyed the regulations would have good luck and kill many deer and bear to bring home.

When they killed a deer they dried the meat to last them through the winter. When they went after bear they hunted about until they discovered his lair and then one of the hunters went into it bearing a pine torch.

Origin of the Raven and the Macaw

A Zuni Legend
Katharine Berry Judson,
Myths and Legends of
California and the Old
Southwest, 1912

The priest who was named Yanauluha carried ever in his hand a staff which now in the daylight was plumed and covered with feathers -yellow, blue-green, red, white, black, and varied. Attached to it were shells, which made a song-like tinkle. The people when they saw it stretched out their hands and asked many questions.

Then the priest balanced it in his hand, and struck with it a hard place, and blew upon it. Amid the plumes appeared four round things-mere eggs they were. Two were blue like the sky and two dun-red like the flesh of the Earth-mother.

Then the people asked many questions; "These," said the priests, "are the seed of living beings. Choose which ye will follow. From two eggs shall come beings of beautiful plumage, colored like the grass and fruits of summer. Where they fly and ye follow, shall always be summer. Without toil, fields of food shall flourish. And from the other two eggs shall come evil beings, piebald, with white, without colors. And where these two shall fly and ye shall follow, winter strives with summer. Only by labor shall the fields yield fruit, and your children and theirs shall strive for the fruits. Which do ye choose?"

"The blue! The blue!" cried the people, and those who were strongest carried off the blue eggs, leaving the red eggs to those who waited. They laid the blue eggs with much gentleness in soft sand on the sunny side of a hill, watching day by day. They were precious of color; surely they would be the precious birds of the Summer-land. Then the eggs cracked and the birds came out, with open eyes and pin feathers under their skins.

"We chose wisely," said the people. "Yellow and blue, red and green, are their dresses, even seen through their skins." So they fed them freely of all the foods which men favor. Thus they taught them to eat all desirable food. But when the feathers appeared, they were black with white bandings. They were ravens. And they flew away croaking hoarse laughs and mocking our fathers.

But the other eggs became beautiful macaws, and were wafted by a toss of the priest's wand to the faraway Summer-land.

So those who had chosen the raven, became the Raven People. They were the Winter People and they were many and strong. But those who had chosen the macaw, became the Macaw People. They were the Summer People, and few in number, and less strong, but they were wiser because they were more deliberate. The priest Yanauluha, being wise, became their father, even as the Sun-father is among the little moons of the sky. He and his sisters were the ancestors of the priest-keepers of things.

Origin of Light

A Gallinomero Legend
Katharine Berry Judson,
Myths and Legends of
California and the Old
Southwest, 1912

In the earliest beginning, the darkness was thick and deep. There was no light. The animals ran here and there, always bumping into each other. The birds flew here and there, but continually knocked against each other.

Hawk and Coyote thought a long time about the darkness. Then Coyote felt his way into a swamp and found a large number of dry tulle reeds. He made a ball of them.

He gave the ball to Hawk, with some flints, and Hawk flew up into the sky, where he touched off the tulle reeds and sent the bundle whirling around the world.

But still the nights were dark, so Coyote made another bundle of tulle reeds, and Hawk flew into the air with them, and touched them off with the flints.

But these reeds were damp and did not burn so well. That is why the moon does not give so much light as the sun.

Wakiash and the First Totem Pole

Kwakiutl
Based on a version reported by Natalie Curtis in The Indian's Book, 1907.

Wakiash was a chief named after the river Wakiash because he was open-handed and Howing with gifts, even as the river Howed with fish.

It happened once that the whole tribe was having a dance. Wakiash had never created a dance of his own, and he was unhappy because all the other chiefs had fine dances. So he thought: "I will go up into the mountains to fast, and perhaps a dance will come to me."

Wakiash made himself ready and went to the mountains, where he stayed, fasting and bathing, for four days. Early in the morning of the fourth day, he grew so weary that he lay upon his back and fell asleep. Then he felt something on his breast and woke to see a little green frog.

"Lie still," the frog said, "because you are on the back of a raven who is going to fly you and me around the world. Then you can see what you want and take it." The raven began to beat its wings, and they flew for four days, during which Wakiash saw many things. When they were on their way back, he spotted a house with a beautiful totem pole in front and heard the sound of singing inside the house. Thinking that these were fine things, he wished he could take them home.

The frog, who knew his thoughts, told the raven to stop. As the bird coasted to the ground, the frog advised the chief to hide behind the door of the house.

"Stay there until they begin to dance," the frog said. "Then leap out into the room."

The people tried to begin a dance but could do nothing-neither dance nor sing. One of them said, "Something's the matter; there must be something near us that makes us feel like this." And the chief said, "Let one of us who can run faster than the flames of the fire rush around the house and find what it is." So the little mouse said that she would go, for she could creep anywhere, even into a box, and if anyone were hiding she would find him. The mouse had taken off her mouse-skin clothes and was presently appearing in the form of a woman. Indeed, all the people in the house were animals who looked like humans because they had taken off their animal-skin clothes to dance.

When the mouse ran out, Wakiash caught her and said, "Ha, my friend, I have a gift for you." And he gave her a piece of mountain goat's fat. The mouse was so pleased with Wakiash that she began talking to him. "What do you want?" she asked eventually. Wakiash said that he wanted the totem pole, the house, and the dances and songs that belonged to them. The mouse said, "Stay here; wait till I come again."

Wakiash stayed, and the mouse went in and told the dancers, "I've been everywhere to see if there's a man around, but I couldn't find anybody." And the chief, who looked like a man but was really a beaver, said, "Let's try again to dance." They tried three times but couldn't do anything, and each time they sent the mouse to search. But each time the mouse only chatted with Wakiash and returned to report that no one was there. The third time she was sent out, she said to him, "Get ready, and when they begin to dance, leap into the room."

When the mouse told the animals again that no one was there, they began to dance. Then Wakiash sprang in, and at once they all dropped their heads in shame, because a man had seen them looking like men, whereas they were really animals.

The dancers stood silent until at last the mouse said: "Let's not waste time; let's ask our friend what he wants."

So they all lifted up their heads, and the chief asked the man what he wanted. Wakiash thought that he would like to have the dance, because he had never had one of his own. Also, he thought, he would like to have the house and the totem pole that he had seen outside. Though the man did not speak, the mouse divined his thoughts and told the dancers. And the chief said, "Let our friend sit down. We'll show him how we dance, and he can pick out whatever dance he wants."

So they began to dance, and when they had ended, the chief asked Wakiash what kind of dance he would like. The dancers had been using all sorts of masks. Most of all Wakiash wanted the Echo mask and the mask. of the Little Man who goes about the house talking, talking, and trying to quarrel with others. Wakiash only formed his wishes in his mind; the mouse told them to the chief. So the animals taught Wakiash all their dances, and the chief told him that he might take as many dances and masks as he wished, as well as the house and the totem pole.

The beaver-chief promised Wakiash that these things would all go with him when he returned home, and that he could use them all in one dance. The chief also gave him for his own the name of the totem pole, Kalakuyuwish, meaning sky pole, because the pole was so tall.

So the chief took the house and folded it up like a little bundle. He put it into the headdress of one of the dancers and gave it to Wakiash, saying, "When you reach home, throw down this bundle. The house will become as it was when you first saw it, and then you can begin to give a dance."

Wakiash went back to the raven, and the raven flew away with him toward the mountain from which they had set out. Before they arrived, Wakiash fell asleep, and when he awoke, the raven· and the frog were gone and he was alone.

It was night by the time Wakiash arrived home. He threw down the bundle that was in the headdress, and there was the house with its totem pole! The whale painted on the house was blowing, the animals carved on the totem pole were making their noises, and all the masks inside the house were talking and crying aloud.

At once Wakiash's people woke up and came out to see
what was happening, and Wakiash found that instead of
four days, he had been away for four years. They all went
into the new house, and Wakiash began to make a dance.
He taught the people the songs, and they sang while
Wakiash danced. Then the Echo came, and whoever made
a noise, the Echo made the same by changing the
mouthpieces of its mask. When they had finished dancing,
the house was gone; it went back to the animals. And all
the chiefs were ashamed because Wakiash now had the best
dance.

Then Wakiash made a house and masks and a totem pole
out of wood, and when the totem pole was finished, the
people composed a song for it. This pole was the first the
tribe had ever had. The animals had named it
Kalakuyuwish, "the pole that holds up the sky," and they
said that it made a creaking noise because the sky was so
heavy. And Wakiash took for his own the name of the
totem pole, Kalakuyuwish.

The Origin of Tobacco

A Hitchiti Legend
John R. Swanton, Myths
and Tales of the
Southeastern Indians, 1929

A man had lost his horses
and was looking for them.

A woman was also hunting
for horses.

They, the man and the woman, met and talked to each
other.

They sat talking together under a hickory tree which cast a
good shade.

The woman said, "I am hunting for some horses that have
been hidden away."

The man said, "I am also hunting for horses."

As they sat talking something occurred to the man and he
spoke to his companion as follows, "I am hunting about for
horses; you too are hunting about for horses. Let us be
friends, and lie here together, after which we will start on."

The woman considered the matter and said, "All right."

Both lay down, and when they got up the man went on his
way and the woman went on hers.

Next summer the man was looking for horses again and

happened to pass near the place where he and the woman had talked. The man thought, "I will go by that place just to look at it."

When he got there he saw that a weed had grown up right where they had lain, but he did not know what it was. He stood looking at it for a while and then started off.

He traveled on and told the old men about it. He said, "I saw something like this and this growing," and one answered, "Examine it to see whether it is good. When it is ripe we will find out what it is."

Afterwards the man started off to look at it. He saw that it had grown still bigger. He dug close about it to soften the soil and it grew still better. He took care of it and saw the leaves grow larger. When it blossomed the flowers were pretty, and he saw that they were big. When they ripened the seeds were very small.

He took the seeds from the hull, gathered leaves, and took them to the old men. They looked at these but did not know what the plant was. After they had looked at them in vain for some time they gave it up. Then one of them pulverized the leaves and put them into a cob pipe, lighted it and smoked it. The aroma was grateful.

All of the old men said, "The leaves of the thing are good," and they named it. They called it hitci (which means both "see" and "tobacco"), they say. Therefore, woman and man together created tobacco.

Origin of the Gnawing Beaver

Haida

Based on two versions of the same myth, reported by William Beynon in 1949 and Marius Barbeau in 1953.

The Haida of the Queen Charlotte Islands off the coast of British Columbia were great hunters of whales and sea otters.

There was a great hunter among the people living at Larhwiyip on the Stikine River. Ever on the alert for new territories, he would go away by himself for long periods and return with quantities of furs and food. He had remained single, although he was very wealthy and his family begged him to take a wife. As a true hunter, he observed all the fasts and cleanliness and kept away from women.

One day when he returned from a hunting trip, he said, "I am going to take a wife now. After that I will move to a distant region where I hear that wild animals are plentiful." So he married a young woman from a neighboring village who, like himself was clever and scrupulous in observing the rules. When the time came for them to go on their hunting trips, they both kept the fasts of purification, and the hunter got even more furs and food than he had before.

Some time later, he said to his wife, "let's go to a new country, where we'll have to stay a long time." After many days of traveling, they came to a strange land. The hunter put up a hut, where they lived while he built a house. When he had finished it, he and his wife were happy. They would play with each other every night.

Soon he said to her, "I'm going to my new hunting grounds for two days and a night. I will return just before the second night." In his new territory he made snares in his trapline, and when these were set, he went home just before sunset on the second day. His wife was very happy, and again they played together all through the night. After several days, he visited his snares and found them full of game. He loaded his canoe and came back, again before dark on the second day. Very happy, he met his wife, and they worked to prepare the furs and meat. When they had finished, he set out once more, saying, "This time I intend to go in a new direction, so I will be away for three sleeps." As he did, and rejoiced in being with his wife again when he returned.

To amuse herself when she was alone, the woman went down to the little stream flowing by the lodge. She spent most of her time bathing and swimming around in a small pool while her husband was away. As soon as he returned, she would play with him. No he said, "Since you've become used to being alone, I'm going on a longer trip." By then he had enlarged his hunting house, and it was full of furs and food.

The woman again took to her swimming. Soon she found the little pool too small for her, so she built a dam by piling up branches and mud. The pool became a lake, deep enough for her to swim in at ease. Now she spent nearly all her time in the new lake and felt quite happy. When her husband returned, she showed him the dam she had made, and he was pleased. Before going away once more, he said, "I'll be gone a long time, now that I know you are not afraid of being along."

The woman built a little house of mud and branches in the center of the lake. After a swim she would go into it and rest. At night she would return to the hunting house on land, but as soon as she would wake in the morning, she would go down to the lake again.

Eventually she slept in her lake lodge all night, and when her husband came back, she felt uncomfortable staying with him at the house. Now she was pregnant and kept more to herself, and she preferred to stay in her lake lodge even when her husband was home. To pass the time, she enlarged the lake by building the dam higher. She made another dam downstream, and then another, until she had a

number of small lakes all connected to the large one in which she had her lodge.

The hunter went away on a last long journey. He had enough fun and food to make him very wealthy, and he planned that they would move back to his village after this trip. The woman, whose child was due any day, stayed in the water all the time and lived altogether in the lodge. Buy now it was partly submerged, and its entrance was under water.

When the hunter returned this time, he could not find his wife. He looked all over, searching the woods day after day without discovering a trace of her. He was at a loss, unwilling to go back to his people without knowing her fate, for fear that her family might want to kill him. He returned sadly to his hunting house every night and each morning resumed the search.

One evening at dusk, he remembered that his wife had spent much of her time in the water. "Perhaps she traveled downstream," he thought. The next day he walked down to the lake that his wife had dammed and went around it, but he saw nothing of her.

After many days of searching, the hunter retraced his steps. When he came to the large lake, he sat down and began to sing a dirge. Now he knew that something had happened to his wife; she had been taken by a supernatural power. While he was singing and crying his dirge, a figure emerged from the lake. It was a strange animal, in its mouth a stick which it was gnawing. On each side of the animal were two smaller ones, also gnawing sticks.

Then the largest figure, which wore a hat shaped like a gnawed stick, spoke. "Don't be so sad! It is I, your wife, and your two children. We have returned to our home in the water. Now that you have seen me, you will use me as a crest. Call me the Woman-Beaver, and the crest Remanants-of-Chewing-Stick. The children are First Beaver, and you will refer to them in your dirge as the Offspring of Woman-Beaver."

After she had spoken, she disappeared into the waters, and the hunter saw her no more. At once he packed his goods, and when his canoe was filled, traveled down the river to his village.

For a long while he did not speak to his people. Then he told them what had happened and said, "I will take this as my personal crest. It shall be known as "Remnants-of-Chewing-Stick, and forever remain the property of our clan, the Salmon-Eater household." This is the origin of the Beaver crest and the Remnants-of-Chewing-Stick.

Why the Birch Tree Wears the Slashes in its Bark

This version of the legend comes from Frank Linderman's 1915 collection Indian Why Stories.

It was a hot day, and Old-man was trying to sleep, but the heat made him sick. He wandered to a hilltop for air; but there was no air. Then he went down to the river and found no relief. He travelled to the timberlands, and there the heat was great, although he found plenty of shade. The travelling made him warmer, of course, but he wouldn't stay still.

"By and by he called to the winds to blow, and they commenced. First they didn't blow very hard, because they were afraid they might make Old-man angry, but he kept crying:

"'Blow harder -- harder -- harder! Blow worse than ever you blew before, and send this heat away from the world.'

"So, of course, the winds did blow harder -- harder than they ever had blown before.

"'Bend and break, Fir-Tree!' cried Old-man, and the Fir-Tree did bend and break.'Bend and break, Pine-Tree!' and the Pine-Tree did bend and break.'Bend and break, Spruce-

Tree!' and the Spruce-Tree did bend and break.'Bend and break, O Birch-Tree!' and the Birch-Tree did bend, but it wouldn't break -- no, sir! -- it wouldn't break!

"'Ho! Birch-Tree, won't you mind me? Bend and break! I tell you,' but all the Birch-Tree would do was to bend.

"It bent to the ground; it bent double to please Old-man, but it would not break.

"'Blow harder, wind!' cried Old-man, 'blow harder and break the Birch-Tree.' The wind tried to blow harder, but it couldn't, and that made the thing worse, because Old-man was so angry he went crazy. 'Break! I tell you -- break!' screamed Old-man to the Birch-Tree.

"'I won't break,' replied the Birch; 'I shall never break for any wind. I will bend, but I shall never, never break.'

"'You won't, hey?' cried Old-man, and he rushed at the Birch-Tree with his hunting-knife. He grabbed the top of the Birch because it was touching the ground, and began slashing the bark of the Birch-Tree with the knife. All up and down the trunk of the tree Old-man slashed, until the Birch was covered with the knife slashes.

"'There! that is for not minding me. That will do you good! As long as time lasts you shall always look like that, Birch-Tree; always be marked as one who will not mind its maker. Yes, and all the Birch-Trees in the world shall have the same marks forever.' They do, too. You have seen them and have wondered why the Birch-Tree is so queerly marked. Now you know.

Animal Tales

The Beaver and the Old Man

A Jicarilla Apache Legend
Frank Russell, Myths of the Jicarilla Apaches, 1898

There was once an old man who was very fond of beaver meat. He hunted and killed beaver so frequently that his son remonstrated with him.

His son told him that some misfortune would surely overtake him as a punishment for his persecution of the sagacious animals, which were then endowed with the magic powers of the medicine-men.

The old man did not heed the warning, but continued to kill beaver nearly every day.

Again the son said, "If you kill them, they will soon catch and kill you." Not long afterward the old man saw a beaver enter a hole in the bank.

Disregarding his son's advice, he plunged head foremost into the burrow to catch the animal. The son saw him enter the hole, and went in after him. Catching the old man by the heels, he pushed him farther in.

Thinking another beaver had attacked him, the old man was at first too frightened to move, then he cried for mercy. "Let me go, Beaver, and I will give you my knife."

He threw his knife back toward the entrance, but received no reply to his entreaty. "Let me go, Beaver, and I will give you my awl." Again no answer. "Let me go, and I will give you my arrows."

The young man took the articles as they were handed to him, and hastened away without making himself known.

When the old man returned to the tipi, he said nothing of his adventures, and his son asked no questions. As soon as the old man left the tipi, the son replaced the knife and other articles in his father's fire-bag.

"Where is your knife?" said the son when the old man returned. "I gave it to the beaver to induce them to let me escape with my life."

"I told you they would catch you," said the son.

The old man never hunted beaver again.

I am poor and naked, but I am the chief of the nation.
We do not want riches but we do want to train our children right.
Riches would do us no good. We could not take them with us to the other world.
We do not want riches. We want peace and love.

Red Cloud, Oglala Lakota Sioux (1822-1909)

Turtle Gets a Shell

An Anishnabe (Anishinabe) Legend

It was one of those days when Nanaboozhoo was in a strange mood. He had just awakened from a deep sleep that was disturbed by the noisy quarreling and scolding of the blue jays. He was a bit cranky; his sleep was disturbed and besides that, he was hungry. His first thought was to down to the village and find something to eat.

Entering the village, he came across some men cooking fish. They had their camp located close to the water and Nanaboozhoo spied many fish cooking over a fire. Now, being very hungry, he asked for something to eat. The men were happy to give him some, but cautioned him that is was hot. Not heeding their warning, he quickly grabbed the fish and burned his hand. He ran to the lake to cool it off in the water. Still unsteady from his deep sleep, he tripped on a stone and fell on Mi-she-kae (turtle) who was sunning on the beach. At that time, Mishekae was not as we know her today. She had no shell and was comprised of soft skin and bone.

Turtle complained loudly to Nanaboozhoo to watch where he was going. Now, Nanaboozhoo felt ashamed of his clumsiness and apologized to Mishekae. He wondered, "what can I do to make it up to her?" He wanted to do something to help his friend. "I'll have to sit and think it over," he thought, as he followed the path back to his wigwam.

Sometime later, he returned to the beach and called for Mishekae. Turtle poked her head through the soft beach mud. Nanaboozhoo picked up two large shells from the shore and placed one on top of the other. He scooped up Mishekae and put her right in the middle, between the shells.

Nanaboozhoo took a deep breath and began. "You will never be injured like that again." he said slowly. "Whenever danger threatens," he continued, "you can pull your legs and head into the shell for protection"

Nanaboozhoo sat beside his friend on the beach and told Mishekae his thoughts. "The shell itself is round like Mother Earth. It was a round hump which resembles her hills and mountains. It is divided into segments, like martyrizes that are a part of her; each different and yet connected by her."

Mishekae seemed very pleased with and listened intently. "You have four legs, each representing the points of direction North, South, East and West." he said. "When the legs are all drawn in, all directions are lost. Your tail will show the many lands where the Anishnabek have been and your head will point in the direction to follow. "You will have advantages over the Anishnabek," he went on. "You will be able to live in the water as well as on land and you will be in your own house at all times."

Mishekae approved of her new self and thanked Nanaboozhoo for his wisdom. Moving now in a thick shell, she pushed herself along the shore and disappeared into the water.

So, ever since that accident long ago, Turtle has been special to the Anishnabek. To this day, she continues to grace Mother Earth, still proudly wearing those two shells.

The True Peace

The first peace, which is the most important,
is that which comes within the souls of people
when they realize their relationship,
their oneness, with the universe and all its powers,
and when they realize that at the center
of the universe dwells Wakan-Taka (the Great Spirit),
and that this center is really everywhere, it is within each of us.
This is the real peace, and the others are but reflections of this.
The second peace is that which is made between two individuals,
and the third is that which is made between two nations.
But above all you should understand that there can never
be peace between nations until there is known that true peace,
which, as I have often said, is within the souls of men.

Black Elk, Oglala Sioux & Spiritual Leader (1863 - 1950)

The Fox and the Deer

A Jicarilla Apache Legend
Frank Russell, Myths of the Jicarilla Apaches, 1898

As Fox was going along he met a Deer with two spotted fawns beside her. " What have you done," said he, "to make your children spotted like that?"

"I made a big fire of cedar wood and placed them before it. The sparks thrown off burned the spots which you see," answered the Deer.

Fox was pleased with the color of the fawns, so he went home and told his children to gather cedar wood for a large fire.

When the fire was burning well, he put the young foxes in a row before the fire, as he supposed the Deer had done.

When he found that they did not change color, he pushed them into the fire and covered them with ashes, thinking he had not applied sufficient heat at first.

As the fire went out, he saw their white teeth gleaming

where the skin had shriveled away and exposed them. "Ah, you will be very pretty now," said he.

Fox pulled his offspring from the ashes, expecting to find them much changed in color, and so they were, -- black, shriveled, and dead.

Fox next thought of revenge upon the Deer, which he found in a grove of cottonwoods. He built a fire around them, but they ran through it and escaped. Fox was so disappointed that he set up a cry of woe, a means of expression which he has retained from that day to this.

In our every deliberation, we must consider the impact of our decisions on the next seven generations.

- *Iroquois Maxim (circa 1700-1800)*

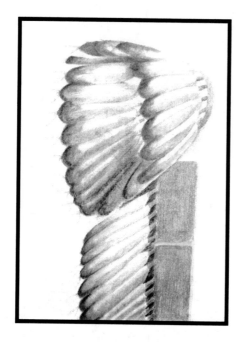

The Fox and the Kingfisher

A Jicarilla Apache Legend
Frank Russell, Myths of the Jicarilla Apaches, 1898

As Fox went on his way he met Kingfisher, Kêt-la'-i-le-ti, whom he accompanied to his home. Kingfisher said that he had no food to offer his visitor, so he would go and catch some fish for Fox. He broke through six inches of ice on the river and caught two fish, which he cooked and set before his guest.

Fox was pleased with his entertainment, and invited the Kingfisher to return the call. In due time the Kingfisher came to the home of the Fox, who said, " I have no food to offer you;" then he went down to the river, thinking to secure fish in the same manner as the Kingfisher had done.

Fox leaped from the high bank, but instead of breaking through the ice he broke his head and killed himself.

Kingfisher went to him, caught him up by the tail, and swung Fox around to the right four times, thereby restoring him to life. Kingfisher caught some fish, and they ate together.

"I am a medicine-man," said Kingfisher; "that is why I can do these things. You must never try to catch fish in that way again."

After the departure of Kingfisher, Fox paid a visit to the home of Prairie-dog, where he was cordially received. Prairie-dog put four sticks, each about a foot in length, in the ashes of the camp-fire; when these were removed, they proved to be four nicely roasted prairie-dogs, which were served for Fox's dinner.

Fox invited the Prairie-dog to return the visit, which in a short time the latter did. Fox placed four sticks in the fire to roast, but they were consumed by it, and instead of palatable food to set before his guest he had nothing but ashes. Prairie-dog said to Fox, " You must not attempt to do that. I am a medicine-man; that is why I can transform the wood to flesh." Prairie-dog then prepared a meal as he done before, and they dined.

Fox went to visit Buffalo, I-gûn-da, who exclaimed, "What shall I do? I have no food to offer you. Buffalo was equal to the emergency, however; he shot an arrow upward, which struck in his own back as it returned. When he pulled this out, a kidney and the fat surrounding it came out also. This he cooked for Fox, and added a choice morsel from his own nose.

As usual, Fox extended an invitation to his host to return the visit. When Buffalo came to call upon Fox, the latter covered his head with weeds in imitation of the head of the Buffalo. Fox thought he could provide food for their dinner as the Buffalo had done, so fired an arrow into the air; but when it came close to him on its return flight, he became frightened and ran away.

Buffalo then furnished meat for their meal as on the previous occasion. "You must not try this," said he; "I am a medicine-man; that is why I have the power."

Some time afterward, as Fox was journeying along, he met an Elk, Tsês, lying beside the trail. He was frightened when he saw the antlers of the Elk moving, and jumped to avoid what seemed to be a falling tree.

"Sit down beside me," said the Elk. "Don't be afraid."

"The tree will fall on us," replied Fox.

"Oh, sit down; it won't fall. I have no food to offer you, but I will provide some." The Elk cut steaks from his own quarter, which the Fox ate, and before leaving Fox invited the Elk to return the visit.

When Elk came to see Fox, the latter tried unsuccessfully to cut flesh from his own meager flanks; then he drove sharpened sticks into his nose, and allowed the blood to run out upon the grass. This he tried in vain to transform into meat, and again he was indebted to his guest for a meal.

"I am a medicine-man; that is why I can do this," said Elk.

The Fox and the Mountain Lion

A Jicarilla Apache Legend
Frank Russell, Myths of the Jicarilla Apaches, 1898

Fox could find nothing to eat for a long time, so that he grew weak and thin.

While on a journey in search of food he met the Mountain Lion, who, taking pity upon his unhappy condition, said, "I will hunt for you, and you shall grow fat again."

The Fox agreed to this, and they went on together to a much frequented spring. Mountain Lion told Fox to keep watch while he slept; if a cloud of dust was to be seen arising from the approach of animals Fox was to waken him.

Fox presently beheld the dust caused by the approach of a drove of horses.

Fox wakened Mountain Lion, who said, "just observe how I catch horses." As one of the animals went down to the spring to drink, he sprang upon it, and fastened his fangs in its throat, clawing its legs and shoulders until it fell dying at the water's edge.

Mountain Lion brought the horse up to the rock, and laid it before the Fox. "Stay here, eat, drink, and grow fat," said he.

Fox thought he had learned how to kill horses, so when the Coyote came along he volunteered to secure one for him.

Fox jumped upon the neck of the horse, as Mountain Lion had done, but became entangled in its mane and was killed.

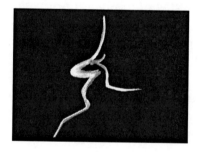

Out of the Indian approach to life there came a great freedom, an intense and absorbing respect for life, enriching faith in a Supreme Power, and principles of truth, honesty, generosity, equity, and brotherhood as a guide to mundane relations.

Black Elk, Oglala Lakota Sioux (1863-1950)

Coyote Steals Sun's Tobacco

A Jicarilla Apache Legend
Based on a tale reported by
Grenville Goodwin in 1939

One day Slim Coyote started out to Sun's house.

When he got there, Sun was not home, but his wife was. "Where is my cousin Sun?" he asked.

Sun's wife said that he had gone out and was not home yet.

Coyote saw Sun's tobacco bag hanging up on the side of the house. "I came to smoke and talk with my cousin," said Slim Coyote, "so give me a smoke while I'm waiting.

He won't mind, he's my cousin." Coyote was talking to Sun's wife as if she were his mother-in-law.

She handed him the tobacco bag, and he used it to fill his own little buckskin bag. Then he quickly hid his bag and rolled a cigarette, so that he actually got off with a lot of Sun's tobacco without her noticing. "Since my cousin hasn't come back yet, I guess I won't wait after all," Coyote told her, and started home.

Pretty soon Sun arrived. "Who's been here and gone again?" he asked, looking at his depleted tobacco bag.

"Somebody who said he was your cousin," answered his wife. She told him what had happened, and Sun was very angry.

"I'll get that fellow," he said. He went out front where he had Black Wind Horse tied, and saddled him up and set off after Coyote. Black Wind Horse could fly, and when he traveled he made a noise like lightening.

A light rain started to fall and covered up Coyote's tracks, but Sun could still follow the thief by the ashes from his cigarette.

It kept raining, and pretty soon the tobacco Coyote had with him started to grow. Soon it was putting out leaves then flowers. At last it ripened and dried, and the wind scattered the seeds everywhere.

When the Sun saw this, he gave up chasing Coyote and went home.

When Coyote got back to the Apache camp where he was living, he kept his tobacco for himself and wouldn't give any away.

The Apache held a council on how to get Coyote's tobacco away from him, and they decided to pretend to give him a wife.

"We're going to give you a wife," they told him.

Coyote said, "You're trying to fool me."

"No we're not," they said, "we're really going to give you a wife."

They set up a new wickiup for Coyote, dressed a young boy as a girl, and told the boy not to let Coyote touch him until just before dawn. They made a bed in the new wickiup, and Coyote felt so good that he gave them all his tobacco.

Just about dusk the boy dressed as a girl went over and sat down beside Coyote in his new wickiup. Slim Coyote was so excited he could not stand up but just crawled around on the ground. "why don't you come to bed?" he said to his bride. "Let's hurry and go to bed." But the boy just sat there.

After a while, when Coyote was more and more impatient, the boy lay down by him but not close to him. "I want you to lie close," Coyote said, and tried to touch the boy.

But the boy said, "Don't!" and pushed Coyote's hand away. This kept up all night, until just before dawn Coyote made a grab and caught hold of the boy's penis. He let go right away and jumped back.

"Get away from me, get back from me; you're a boy not a girl," he said. Then Coyote got up and called the people. "You lied to me," he said. "You didn't give me a wife at all. Give me my tobacco back!"

But no matter how loudly he yelled, they wouldn't do it. This is the way the people first got tobacco.

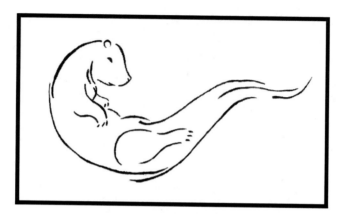

How The Rabbit Stole the Otter's Coat

A Cherokee Legend
Myths of the Cherokee, James Mooney, 1900

The animals were of different sizes and wore coats of various colors and patterns. Some wore long fur and others wore short. Some had rings on their tails, and some had no tails at all. Some had coats of brown, others of black or yellow.

They were always disputing about their good looks, so at last they agreed to hold a council to decide who had the finest coat.

They had heard a great deal about the Otter, who lived so far up the creek that he seldom came down to visit the other animals. It was said that he had the finest coat of all, but no one knew just what it was like, because it was a long time since anyone had seen him. They did not even know exactly where he lived--only the general direction; but they knew he would come to the council when the word got out.

Now the Rabbit wanted the verdict for himself, so when it

began to look as if it might go to the Otter he studied up a plan to cheat him out of it. He asked a few sly questions until he learned what trail the Otter would take to get to the council place. Then, without saying anything, he went on ahead and after four days' travel he met the Otter and knew him at once by his beautiful coat of soft dark-brown fur. The Otter was glad to see him and asked him where he was going.

"O," said the Rabbit, "the animals sent me to bring you to the council; because you live so far away they were afraid you mightn't know the road." The Otter thanked him, and they went on together.

They traveled all day toward the council ground, and at night the Rabbit selected the camping place, because the Otter was a stranger in that part of the country, and cut down bushes for beds and fixed everything in good shape. The next morning, they started on again. In the afternoon the Rabbit began to pick up wood and bark as they went along and to load it on his back. When the Otter asked what this was for the Rabbit said it was that they might be warm and comfortable at night. After a while, when it was near sunset, they stopped and made their camp.

When supper was over the Rabbit got a stick and shaved it down to a paddle. The Otter wondered and asked again what that was for.

"I have good dreams when I sleep with a paddle under my head," said the Rabbit.

When the paddle was finished the Rabbit began to cut away the bushes so as to make a clean trail down to the river. The Otter wondered more and more and wanted to know what this meant. Said the Rabbit, "This place is called

Di'tatlâski'yï (The Place Where It Rains Fire.) Sometimes it rains fire here, and the sky looks a little that way to-night. You go to sleep and I'll sit up and watch, and if the fire does come, a soon as you hear me shout, you run and jump into the river. Better hang your coat on a limb over there, so it won't get burnt."

The Otter did as he was told, and they both doubled up to go to sleep, but the Rabbit kept awake. After a while the fire burned down to red coals. The Rabbit called, but the Otter was fast asleep and made no answer. In a little while he called again, but the Otter never stirred. Then the Rabbit filled the paddle with hot coals and threw them up into the air and shouted, "It's raining fire! It's raining fire!"

The hot coals fell all around the Otter and he jumped up. "To the water!" cried the Rabbit, and the Otter ran and jumped into the river, and he has lived in the water ever since.

The Rabbit took the Otter's coat and put it on, leaving his own instead, and went on to the council. All the animals were there, every one looking out for the Otter. At last they saw him in the distance, and they said one to the other, "The Otter is coming!" and sent one of the small animals to show him the best seat.

They were all glad to see him and went up in turn to welcome him, but the Otter kept his head down, with one paw over his face. They wondered that he was so bashful, until the Bear came up and pulled the paw away, and there was the Rabbit with his split nose.

He sprang up and started to run, when the Bear struck at him and pulled his tail off, but the Rabbit was too quick for them and got away.

Wakinyan Tanka, The Great Thunderbird

Brule Sioux
Told by Lame Deer in 1969
in Winner, Rosebud Indian
Reservation, South Dakota,
and recorded by Richard
Erdoes.

John (Fire) Lame Deer, a Sioux medicine man, was about seventy when he told this tale and like "A Legend of Devil's Tower" it bears the hallmarks of his own crusty, evocative vision.

Wakinyan Tanka, the great thunderbird, lives in his tipi on top of a high mountain in the sacred Paha Sapa, the Black Hills. The whites call it Harney Peak, but I don't think he lives there anymore since the wasichu, the whites, have made these hills into a vast Disneyland. No, I think the thunder beings have retreated to the farthest end of the earth, where the sun goes down, where there are no tourists and hot-dog stands.

The Wakinyan hates all that is dirty. He loves what is clean and pure. His voice is the great thunderclap, and the smaller rolling thunders that follow his booming shouts are the cries of his children, the little thunderbirds. Four paths lead to the mountain on which the Wakinyan dwell. A butterfly guards the entrance at the East side. A Bear guards the West, a Deer the North, and a beaver the South.

There are four large, old Thunderbirds. The Great
Wakinyan of the West is the first and foremost among
them. He is clothed in clouds. His body has no form, but he
has giant, four-jointed wings. He has no feet, but enormous
claws. He has no head, but a huge, sharp beak with rows of
big, pointed teeth. His color is black.

The second Wakinyan of the North is red. The third
Thunderbird of the East is yellow. The fourth Thunderbird
of the South is white, though there· are some who say that
its colors are blue. That one has no eyes or ears, yet he can
see and hear. How that can be is a mystery. From time to
time a holy man catches a glimpse of a Wakinyan in his
dreams, hut always only a part of it. No one ever sees the
Thunderbird whole, not even in a vision, so the way we
think a Thunderbird looks is pieced together from many
dreams and visions.

The Great Wakinyan's tipi stands beside the tallest of all
cedar trees. That's why we use its foliage for the
"cedaring," the "smoking up," in our ceremonies which call
for sweet-smelling incense to purify our houses and
ourselves. Inside the Wakinyan's tipi is a nest made of dry
bones. In it lies the giant egg from which the little
thunderbirds are hatched. The egg is bigger than the whole
state of South Dakota.

You cannot see the Wakinyan because they are wrapped in
robes of dark clouds, but you can feel their presence. I have
often felt it. During a vision quest they may come and try to
frighten you, to see whether you have enough courage to go
through your "crying for a dream" your four days and
nights of fasting and listening and staying awake on top of
a lonely hill. They test you this way, but the Wakinyan are
good spirits. They like to help the people, even if they scare
you sometimes.

Everything in nature moves in a certain way that whites call clockwise. Only the thunder beings move in a contrary manner-counterclockwise. That's their way; they do everything differently. That's why, if you dream of the Wakinyan, you become a heyoka: an upside-down, hot-cold, forward-backward man. This gives you power, but you don't want to stay a heyoka for long, so we have a ceremony through which you can become your old self again.

The Wakinyan's symbol is the zig-zag lightning, forked at the ends, which I use in some of my rituals. It's a design I like and to which I feel in some way related, because a heyoka is also a sacred clown, and there is some of that clown nature within me.

The thunder beings are guardians of the truth. When you're holding the sacred pipe and you swear on it, you can say nothing but the truth. If you lie, the Wakinyan will kill you with their lightning bolts.

So thunderbirds stand for rain, and fire, and the truth, and as I said before, they like to help the people. In contrast, Unktehi, the great water monster, did not like human beings from the time they were put on this earth. lJnktehi was shaped like a giant scaly snake with feet. She had a huge horn corning out of the top of her head, and she filled the whole of the Missouri River from end to end. The little water monsters, who lived in smaller streams and lakes, likewise had no use for humans.

'What are these tiny, lice-like creatures crawling all over the place?" they asked. "What are these blood-clot people creeping out of the red pipestone? We don't want them around!"

The Great Unktehi could place her body and puff it up in such a way that it made the great Missouri overflow, and her children, the little water monsters, did the same with their streams and lakes. So they caused a great flood that spread over the whole country, killing most of the people. Only a few escaped to the top of the highest mountain, and even there the waves threatened to sweep them off.

Then the great thunderbird spoke: "What's to be done? I like these humans. They respect us; they pray to us. If they dream of us, they get a little of our power, and that makes them relatives of ours, in a way. Even though they are small, helpless, and pitiful, Grandfather put them on this earth for some purpose. We must save them from Unktehi!"

Then began the great battle between the thunderbirds and the evil water monsters. It lasted many years, during which the earth trembled and the waters burst forth in mighty torrents, while the night was like day because of the flashes of lightning. The Wakinyan have no bodies as we imagine them-no limbs or hands or feet-but they have enormous claws. They have no mouths, but they have big, sharp teeth. They have no eyes, but lightning bolts somehow shoot out of the eyes which are not there. This is hard to explain to a wasichu.

The Wakinyan used their claws, their teeth, their lightning to fight the water monsters. The Wakinyan Tanka grappled with the Great Unktehi and the little thunder children were pitted against the smaller water monsters. The battle was not only long but desperate, for the Unktehi had spikes at the tip of their powerful tails that could gouge out fearful wounds as they roared and thrashed.

At last the Wakinyan Tanka called to the little thunderbirds: "My children, the Unktehi are winning. This close body-to-body fighting favors them!"

All the thunder beings retreated to the top of their sacred mountain and took council together. The Great Wakinyan said: "Our country is the air. Our power comes from the sky. It was wrong to fight the Unktehi on their own ground, on the earth and in the water where they are all-powerful. Come, my children, follow me!"

Then all the thunderbirds Hew up into the sky. "When I give the signal," said the Wakinyan Tanka, "let's use our lightning and thunderbolts together!"

So the thunder beings shot off all their bolts at the same instant. The forests were set on fire, and Hames consumed everything except the top of the rock on which the humans had taken refuge. The waters boiled and then dried up. The earth glowed red-hot, and the Unktehi, big and small, burned up and died, leaving only their dried bones in the Mako Sicha, the Badlands, where their bones turned to rock.

Until then the Unktehi had represented the water power, and now this power was taken by the Thunderbirds. And the few humans who survived climbed down from their high rock, praising the Wakinyan for saving them. These few again peopled the earth, and all was well. The battle and the victory of the Wakinyan took place in the first of the great four ages-the age of Tunka, the Rock.

When I was young, hardly more than a boy, I went after some horses which had somehow got lost. Following their tracks into the Badlands, I searched for many hours. I lost all sense of time and was surprised by nightfall, sudden and pitch-black. The clouds that were covering the moon and stars split open in a thunderstorm. Hailstones as big as mothballs blanketed the ground with icy mush, and I thought that I might freeze to death in the summer.

I happened to be in a narrow gulch, where I was in danger of drowning from the rush of water. As best I could, I began scrambling up toward a high ridge. I couldn't see except when there was a flash of lightning, and the earth was crumbling under me. Somehow I made it.

The thunder never stopped, and the lightning became almost continuous. I could smell the wakangeli, the electricity, all around; it made my hair stand up. The thunder was deafening. I straddled the ridge as if I were riding a horse. I could see enough in the lightning to know that I was very high up and the canyon was a long way down, and I was afraid of being blown off the ridge and hurled into that black nothingness. My teeth chattering, my legs and hands clamped to the razorback ridge, I moved inch by inch as I tried to get out of there.

But I felt the presence of the Wakinyan, heard them talking to me through the thunder: "Don't be afraid! Hold on! You'll be all right."

At last the storm ended, and finally dawn came. Then I saw that I was straddling a long row of petrified bones, the biggest I had ever seen. I had been moving along the spine of the Great Unktehi. Stiff with cold, I waited until the sun warmed me. Then I scrambled down and ran toward home. I forgot all about the horses; I never found them. And I searched many times for the ridge deep inside the Badlands that formed Unktehi's spine. I wanted to show it to my friends, but I never found the ridge either.

The Snake Myth

A Hopi Legend
H. R. Voth, The
Traditions of the
Hopi, Field
Columbian Museum
Anthropological
Series, 1905

At Tokóonavi, north of the Grand Canyon, lived people who were then not yet Snake people. They lived close to the bank of the river. The chief's son often pondered over the Grand Canyon and wondered where all that water went to.

"That must certainly make it very full somewhere," he thought to himself. So he spoke to his father about it. "So that is what you have been thinking about," the latter said. "Yes," his son answered, "I want to go and examine it."

The father gave his consent and told his son that he should make a box for himself that would be large enough for him to get into, and he should arrange it so that all openings in the box could be closed. This the boy did, making also a long pole (according to others a long báho), with which he could push the box in case it became fast or tangled up anywhere.

When he was ready he took a lot of báhos and some food, went into the box, and allowed himself to be pushed into the water, on which he then floated along. Finally, he came to the ocean, where he drifted against an island. He found the house of Spider Woman (Kóhk'ang Wuhti) here, who

called him to come to her house. He went over and found
that he could not get through the opening leading to her
house. "How shall I get in?" he said; "the opening is too
small." She told him to enlarge it.

This he did and then entered. He told her a story and gave
her a báho, and said that he had come after beads, etc. She
pointed to another kiva away out in the water and said that
there were some beads and corals there. but that there were
some wild animals guarding the path to it. "If you had not
informed me, how could you have succeeded in getting
there and how would you have gotten back? But I shall go
with you," she said, "because you have given me a báho,
for which I am very glad."

She then gave the young man some medicine and seated
herself behind his right ear. He spurted the medicine over
the water and immediately a road like a rainbow was
formed from the dwelling of Spider Woman to the other
kiva. On this they went across the water. As they
approached the kiva to which they were going they first
encountered a panther, who growled fiercely.

The young man gave him a green báho and spurted some
medicine upon him, which quieted him. A little farther on
they met a bear, whom they quieted in the same manner.

Still farther on they came upon a wildcat, to which they
also handed a báho, which quieted the animal. Hereupon
they met a gray wolf, and finally a very large rattle-snake
(K'áhtoya), both of which they appeased in the same
manner as the others. They then arrived at the kiva, where
they found at the entrance a bow standard (Aoát nátsi).
They then descended the ladder and found in the kiva many
people who were dressed in blue kilts, had their faces
painted with specular iron (yaláhaii), and around their

necks they wore many beads.

The young man sat down near the fireplace, Spider Woman still being seated on his ear, but no one spoke. The men looked at him, but remained silent. Presently the chief got a large bag of tobacco and a large pipe. He filled the latter and smoked four times. He then handed the pipe to the young man and said: "Smoke and swallow the smoke."

The swallowing of the smoke was a test: any one not being able to do that was driven off. Spider Woman had informed the young man about this test, so he was posted. When he commenced to smoke she whispered to him: "Put me behind you." This he did in an unobserved manner, so when he swallowed the smoke she immediately drew the smoke from him and blew it away, and hence he did not get dizzy.

The men who did not observe the trick were pleased and said to him: "All right, you are strong; you are certainly some one. Thank you. Your heart is good: you are one of us; you are our child." "Yes." he said, and handed them some red nakwákwosis and a single green báho with red points, such as are still made in Shupaúlavi in the Antelope society.

They then became very friendly, saving that they were very happy over the báhos. On the walls of the kiva were hanging many costumes made of snake skins. Soon the chief said to the people: "Let us dress up now," and turning to the young man bid him to turn away so that he would not see what was going on. He did so, and when he looked back again the men had all dressed up in the snake costumes and had turned into snakes, large and small, bull-snakes, racers, and rattle-snakes, that were moving about on the floor hissing, rattling, etc.

While he had turned away and the snake People had been dressing themselves, Spider Woman had whispered to him that they were now going to try him very hard, but that he should not be afraid to touch the snakes; and she gave him many instructions.

Among those present in the kiva had also been some pretty maidens who had also put on snake costumes and had turned into serpents. One of them had been particularly handsome. The chief had not turned into a snake, and was sitting near the fireplace. He now turned to the young man and said to him: "You go now and select and take one of these snakes." The snakes seemed to be very angry and the young man got frightened when they stared at him, but Spider Woman whispered to him not to be a coward, nor to be afraid.

The prettiest maiden had turned into a large yellow rattle-snake (Sik'á-tcua), and was especially angry. Spider Woman whispered to the young man, that the one that acted so very angrily was the pretty maiden and that he should try to take that one. He tried, but the snake was very wild and fierce. "Be not afraid," Spider Woman whispered, and handed him some medicine. This he secretly chewed and spurted a small quantity of it on the fierce snake, whereupon it immediately became docile.

He at once grabbed it, held and stroked it four times upward, each time spurting a little medicine on it, and thus freeing it from its anger. The chief was astonished and said: "You are very something, thanks. Now, look away again." He did so and when he turned back he saw that all the snakes had assumed the forms of men and women again, including the maiden that he had captured. They now were all very good to him, and talked to him in the kindest manner, because they now considered him as initiated and as one of them.

He was now welcome, and the chief invited him to eat. The
mána whom the young man had taken got from another
room in the kiva some bread made of fresh corn-meal,
some peaches, melons, etc., and set this food before the
young man. Spider Woman whispered to the young -man to
give her something to eat too, which he did secretly. She
enjoyed the food very much and was very happy.

Now the chief asked the man why he came, etc. "I hunt a
lólomat kátcit (good life) and was thinking about the water
running this way, and so this way it runs. I have come also
to get Hopi food from here. I also heard that there lives a
woman here somewhere, the Hurúing Wuhti, from whom I
want beads." "What have you for her?" they asked. "These
báhos," he said. "All right, you will get there. But now you
sleep here." But Spider Woman wanted to get back. He told
them that he wanted to go out a little while.

Then he went and took Spider Woman home, and put her
down. She invited him to come and eat with her. She had a
pövö'lpik'i off which she lived and which never gave out,
but he left her and returned to the Snake kiva, where he was
welcomed and called brother and son-in-law
(möö'nangwuu), although he had not yet married, but only
caught the mana. So he remained there. That evening and
night the chief told him all about the Snake cult, altar, etc.,
etc., and instructed him how he must put this up, and do
that, when he would return. He did not sleep that night.

In the morning he again went out on the same excuse as the
previous evening, and went to Spider Woman, who went
out. She made a rainbow road into the ocean to a high bluff
where Hurúing Wuhti lived, and to which they ascended on
a ladder. They went in and found an old hag, but on all the

walls many beads, shells, etc. The woman said nothing.
The young man gave her the báhos, then she, said faintly,
"Áskwali!" (Thanks!)

At sundown she went into a side chamber and returned a
very pretty maiden with fine buffalo and wildcat robes, of
which she made a bed, and after having fed him, invited
him to sleep with her on the bed. Then Spider Woman,
whispered he should comply with her request, then he
would win her favor and get the beads. So he did as
requested.

In the morning he awoke and found by his side an old hag,
snoring. He was very unhappy, He stayed all day, the hag
sitting bent up all day. In the evening the change, etc., that
occurred on the previous day was repeated, but the hag
after this remained a pretty maiden. He remained four days
and nights with Hurúing Wuhti, who is the deity of the hard
substances.

After four days he wanted to go home, so she went into a
room on the north side and got a turquoise bead; then from
a room west the same: from a room South a reddish bead
(cátsni); from one east, a hard white bead (hurúingwa), a
shell. Then she gave him a few of all kinds of beads and
told him to go home now, but charging him not to open the
sack, because if he did they would be gone, and if he did
not they would increase. "You go to the Snakes, who will
give you clothes, food, etc."

He then returned to the Snake kiva. There he stayed four
days and four nights, sleeping with his wife. When he was
ready to go home the chief said: "Take this mana with you.
You have won us. Take it all with you, take of our food.
Practice the ceremonies there that I told you about. This
woman will bear you children and then you will be many

and they will hold this ceremony for you." So they started.
At Spider Woman's house he told his wife, "You stay here.
I will go to the rear." So he went to Spider Woman's house
and she asked: "Well, did you get the mana?" "Yes," he
said. "Well, you take everything along." But she forbid him
to touch his wife while they would be on the way, as then
his beads would disappear and also his wife.

So they started. The beads were as yet not heavy. During
the night they slept separately. In the morning they found
that the beads had increased, and they kept increasing as
they went along the next day. The next night they spent in
the same way. They were anxious to see whether the beads
and shells had increased, but did not dare to do so. The
third night was again spent, and the contents of the bag
increased the same as the previous two nights.

The bag with the beads and shells now became very heavy
and the young man was very anxious to see them, but his
wife forbade him to open the sack. The fourth night was
spent in the same manner, and when they arose in the
morning the sack was nearly full and was very heavy.
Spider Woman had also put some strings into the bag with
the beads, and the beads were strung onto these strings and
they kept increasing.

They now approached the home of the young man, and the
latter was very anxious to get home in order to see the
contents, of the sack, so they traveled on. When they had
nearly one more day's travel to make the sack had become
full. During the last night the man opened the sack,
although his wife remonstrated most energetically.

He took out many of the finest beads and shells and spread
them on the floor before them, put them around his neck,
and was very happy. So they retired for the night. In the

morning they found that all the beads except those which Hurúing Wuhti had given to the man had disappeared.

Hence the Hopi have so few beads at the present day. If that man had at that time brought home with him all the beads which he had, they would have many. So when they arrived at home they were very despondent.

At that time only the Divided or Separated Spring (Bátki) clan and the Pö'na (a certain cactus) clan lived at that place, but with the arrival of this young couple a new clan, the Snake clan, had come to the village. Soon this new woman bore many children. They were snakes who lived in the fields and in the sand. They grew very rapidly and went about and played with the Hopi children, whom they sometimes bit. This made the Hopi very angry and they said: "This is not good," and drove them off, so they were very unhappy.

The woman said to her husband: "You take our children back to my home and there we shall go away from here alone." Then the man's father made báhos, gave them to his son, who put all the snakes with the báhos into his blanket and took them back to his wife's home, and there told the Snake people why he brought their children and the báhos. They said it was all right. Hence the Snake priests, when carrying away the snakes from the plaza after the snake dance, take with them and deposit with the snakes some báhos, so that they should not themselves return to the village.

When the Snake man returned to his village lit and his wife traveled south-eastward, stopping at various places. All at once they saw smoke in the distance, and when they went there they found a village perched son the mesa. This was the village of Wálpi. They at once went to the foot of the

mesa on which Wálpi was situated and announced their
presence. So the village chief went down to them from the
mesa, and asked what they wanted.

They asked to be admitted to the village, promising that
they would assist the people in the ceremonies. The chief at
first showed himself unwilling to admit then), but finally
gave his consent and took them up to the village. From that
time the woman bore human children instead of little
snakes. These children and their descendants became the
Snake clan, of whom only very few are now living.

Soon also the Bátki and Pö'na clan came to Wálpi and
found admittance to the village. At Wálpi the Snake people
made the first Snake típoni, Snake altar, etc., and had the
first Snake ceremony. From here the Snake cult spread to
the other villages, first to Shongópavi, then to
Mishóngnovi, and then to Oraíbi. At the first Snake
ceremony the Snake chief sent his nephew to the north, to
the west, to the south, and to the east to hunt snakes.

He brought some from each direction, the chief then
hollowed out a piece of báho, made of cottonwood root.
Into this he put the rattles of three of the snakes and the
fourth snake entirely. He then inserted into it a corn-ear,
and tied to it different feathers of the eagle, the oriole, bluebird, parrot, magpie, Ásya, and topóckwa, winding a
buckskin String around these feathers. When he had made
this típoni, the first ceremony was celebrated, and
afterwards it took place regularly.

The Elk Spirit of Lost Lake
Wasco
Collected by Ella Clark in 1953

In the days of our grandfathers, a young warrior named
Plain Feather lived near Mount Hood. His guardian spirit
was a great elk. The great elk taught Plain Feather so well
that he knew the best places to look for every kind of game
and became the most skillful hunter in his tribe.

Again and again his guardian spirit said to him, "Never kill
more than you can use. Kill only for your present need.
Then there will be enough for all."

Plain Feather obeyed him. He killed only for food, only
what he needed. Other hunters in his tribe teased him for
not shooting for fun, for not using all his arrows when he
was out on a hunt. But Plain Feather obeyed the great elk.

Smart Crow, one of the old men of the tribe, planned in his
bad heart to make the young hunter disobey his guardian

spirit. Smart Crow pretended that he was one of the wise men and that he had had a vision. In the vision, he said, the Great Spirit had told him that the coming winter would be long and cold. There would be much snow.

"Kill as many animals as you can," said Smart Crow to the hunters of the tribe. 'We must store meat for the winter."

The hunters, believing him, went to the forest and meadows and killed all the animals they could. Each man tried to be the best hunter in the tribe. At first Plain Feather would not go with them, but Smart Crow kept saying, "The Great Spirit told me that we will have a hard winter. The Great Spirit told me that we must get our meat now."

Plain Feather thought that Smart Crow was telling the truth. So at last he gave in and went hunting along the stream now called Hood River. First he killed deer and bears. Soon he came upon five bands of elk and killed all but one, which he wounded.

Plain Feather did not know that this was his guardian elk, and when the wounded animal hurried away into the forest, Plain Feather followed. Deeper and deeper into the forest and into the mountains he followed the elk tracks. At last he came to a beautiful little lake. There, lying in the water not far from the shore, was the wounded elk. Plain Feather walked into the lake to pull the animal to the shore, but when he touched it, both hunter and elk sank.

The warrior seemed to fall into a deep sleep, and when he awoke, he was on the bottom of the lake. All around him were the spirits of many elk, deer, and bears. All were in the shape of human beings, and all were moaning. He heard a voice say clearly, "Draw him in." And something drew Plain Feather closer to the wounded elk.

"Draw him in," the voice said again. And again Plain
Feather was drawn closer to the great elk. At last he lay
beside it.

"Why did you disobey me?" asked the elk. "All around you
are the spirits of the animals you have killed. I will no
longer be your guardian. You have disobeyed me and slain
my friends."
Then the voice which had said, "Draw him in," said, "Cast
him out." And the spirits cast the hunter out of the water,
onto the shore of the lake.

Weary in body and sick at heart, Plain Feather dragged
himself to the village where his tribe lived. Slowly he
entered his tepee and sank upon the ground.

"I am sick," he said. "I have been in the dwelling place of
the lost spirits. And I have lost my guardian spirit, the great
elk. He is in the lake of the lost spirits."

Then he lay back and died. Ever after, the Indians called
that lake the Lake of the Lost Spirits. Beneath its calm blue
waters are the spirits of thousands of the dead. On its clear
surface is the face of Mount Hood, which stands as a
monument to the lost spirits.

The Fable of the Animals

A Karok Legend
Katharine Berry
Judson, Myths
and Legends of
California and
the Old
Southwest, 1912

A great many
hundred snows
ago, Kareya,
sitting on the Sacred Stool, created the world. First, he
made the fishes in the Big Water, then the animals on the
green land, and last of all, Man! But at first the animals
were all alike in power.

No one knew which animals should be food for others, and
which should be food for man. Then Kareya ordered them
all to meet in one place, that Man might give each his rank
and his power. So the animals all met together one evening,
when the sun was set, to wait overnight for the coming of
Man on the next morning.

Kareya also commanded Man to make bows and arrows, as
many as there were animals, and to give the longest one to
the animal which was to have the most power, and the
shortest to the one which should have least power.

So he did, and after nine sleeps his work was ended, and
the bows and arrows which he had made were very many.

Now the animals, being all together, went to sleep, so they might be ready to meet Man on the next morning. But Coyote was exceedingly cunning -he was cunning above all the beasts. Coyote wanted the longest bow and the greatest power, so he could have all the other animals for his meat.

He decided to stay awake all night, so that he would be first to meet Man in the morning. So he laughed to himself and stretched his nose out on his paw and pretended to sleep. About midnight he began to be sleepy.

He had to walk around the camp and scratch his eyes to keep them open. He grew more sleepy, so that he had to skip and jump about to keep awake. But he made so much noise, he awakened some of the other animals. When the morning star came up, he was too sleepy to keep his eyes open any longer.

So he took two little sticks, and sharpened them at the ends, and propped open his eyelids. Then he felt safe. He watched the morning star, with his nose stretched along his paws, and fell asleep. The sharp sticks pinned his eyelids fast together.

The morning star rose rapidly into the sky.

The birds began to sing. The animals woke up and stretched themselves, but still Coyote lay fast asleep. When the sun rose, the animals went to meet Man. He gave the longest bow to Cougar, so he had greatest power; the second longest he gave to Bear; others he gave to the other animals, giving all but the last to Frog. But the shortest one was left. Man cried out, "What animal have I missed?" Then the animals began to look about and found Coyote fast asleep, with his eyelids pinned together.

All the animals began to laugh, and they jumped upon Coyote and danced upon him. Then they led him to Man, still blinded, and Man pulled out the sharp sticks and gave him the shortest bow of all. It would hardly shoot an arrow farther than a foot.

All the animals laughed.

But Man took pity on Coyote, because he was now weaker even than Frog. So at his request, Kareya gave him cunning, ten times more than before, so that he was cunning above all the animals of the wood.

Therefore, Coyote was friendly to Man and his children, and did many things for them.

Honor the sacred.
Honor the Earth, our Mother.
Honor the Elders.
Honor all with whom we
share the Earth: -
Four-leggeds, two-leggeds,
winged ones,
Swimmers, crawlers,
plant and rock people.
Walk in balance and beauty.

Native American Elder

The Theft of Fire

A Karok Legend
Katharine Berry Judson,
Myths and Legends of
California and the Old
Southwest, 1912

There was no fire on earth and the Karoks were cold and miserable. Far away to the east, hidden in a treasure box, was fire which Kareya had made and given to two old hags, lest the Karoks should steal it. So Coyote decided to steal fire for the Indians.

Coyote called a great council of the animals. After the council he stationed a line from the land of the Karoks to the distant land where the fire was kept. Lion was nearest the Fire Land, and Frog was nearest the Karok land. Lion was strongest and Frog was weakest, and the other animals took their places, according to the power given them by Man. Then Coyote took an Indian with him and went to the hill top, but he hid the Indian under the hill. Coyote went to the tepee of the hags. He said, "Good-evening." They replied, "Good-evening."

Coyote said, "It is cold out here. Can you let me sit by the fire?" So they let him sit by the fire. He was only a coyote. He stretched his nose out along his forepaws and pretended to go to sleep, but he kept the corner of one eye open watching. So he spent all night watching and thinking, but he had no chance to get a piece of the fire.

The next morning Coyote held a council with the Indian. He told him when he, Coyote, was within the tepee, to

attack it. Then Coyote went back to the fire. The hags let
him in again. He was only a Coyote. But Coyote stood
close by the casket of fire. The Indian made a dash at the
tepee. The hags rushed out after him, and Coyote seized a
fire brand in his teeth and flew over the ground. The hags
saw the sparks flying and gave chase.

But Coyote reached Lion, who ran with it to Grizzly Bear.
Grizzly Bear ran with it to Cinnamon Bear; he ran with it to
Wolf, and at last the fire came to Ground- Squirrel. Squirrel
took the brand and ran so fast that his tail caught fire. He
curled it up over his back, and burned the black spot in his
shoulders. You can see it even to-day. Squirrel came to
Frog, but Frog couldn't run. He opened his mouth wide and
swallowed the fire.

Then he jumped but the hags caught his tail. Frog jumped
again, but the hags kept his tail. That is why Frogs have no
tail, even to this day. Frog swam under water, and came up
on a pile of driftwood. He spat out the fire into the dry
wood, and that is why there is fire in dry wood even to-day.

When an Indian rubs two pieces together, the fire comes
out.

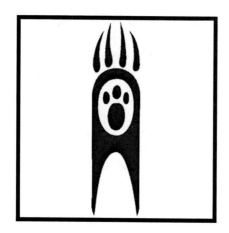

The Badger and the Bear

A Lakota Legend
Zitkala Sa, American
Indian Stories, 1921

On the edge of a forest there lived a large family of badgers. In the ground their dwelling was made. Its walls and roof were covered with rocks and straw. Old father badger was a great hunter. He knew well how to track the deer and buffalo.

Every day he came home carrying on his back some wild game. This kept mother badger very busy, and the baby badgers very chubby. While the well-fed children played about, digging little make-believe dwellings, their mother hung thin sliced meats upon long willow racks. As fast as the meats were dried and seasoned by sun and wind, she packed them carefully away in a large thick bag.

This bag was like a huge stiff envelope, but far more beautiful to see, for it was painted all over with many bright colors. These firmly tied bags of dried meat were laid upon the rocks in the walls of the dwelling. In this way they were both useful and decorative. One-day father badger did not go off for a hunt. He stayed at home, making new arrows. His children sat about him on the ground floor.

Their small black eyes danced with delight as they watched the gay colors painted upon the arrows. All of a sudden there was heard a heavy footfall near the entrance way. The oval-shaped door-frame was pushed aside. In stepped a large black foot with great big claws. Then the other clumsy foot came next. All the while the baby badgers stared hard at the unexpected comer. After the second foot, in peeped the head of a big black bear!

His black nose was dry and parched. Silently he entered the dwelling and sat down on the ground by the doorway. His black eyes never left the painted bags on the rocky walls. He guessed what was in them. He was a very hungry bear. Seeing the racks of red meat hanging in the yard, he had come to visit the badger family.

Though he was a stranger and his strong paws and jaws frightened the small badgers, the father said, "Hau, how, friend! Your lips and nose look feverish and hungry. Will you eat with us?"

"Yes, my friend," said the bear. "I am starved. I saw your racks of red fresh meat, and knowing your heart is kind, I came hither. Give me meat to eat, my friend."

Hereupon the mother badger took long strides across the room, and as she had to pass in front of the strange visitor, she said: "Ah han! Allow me to pass!" which was an apology.

"Hau, hau!" replied the bear, drawing himself closer to the wall and crossing his shins together.

Mother badger chose the most tender red meat, and soon over a bed of coals she broiled the venison.

That day the bear had all he could eat. At nightfall he rose, and smacking his lips together (that is the noisy way of saying "the food was very good!") he left the badger dwelling. The baby badgers, peeping through the door-flap after the shaggy bear, saw him disappear into the woods near by.

Day after day the crackling of twigs in the forest told of heavy footsteps. Out would come the shame black bear. He never lifted the door-flap, but thrusting it aside entered slowly in. Always in the shame place by the entrance way he sat down with crossed shins. His daily visits were so regular that mother badger placed a fur rug in his place. She did not wish a guest in her dwelling to sit upon the bare hard ground.

At last one time when the bear returned, his nose was bright and black. His coat was glossy. He had grown fat upon the badger's hospitality. As he entered the dwelling a pair of wicked gleams shot out of his shaggy head.

Surprised by the strange behavior of the guest who remained standing upon the rug, leaning his round back against the wall, father badger queried, "Hau, my friend! What?"

The bear took one stride forward and shook his paw in the badger's face. He said: "I am strong, very strong!"

"Yes, yes, so you are," replied the badger. From the farther end of the room mother badger muttered over her bead work: "Yes, you grew strong from our well-filled bowls."

The bear smiled, showing a row of large sharp teeth. "I have no dwelling. I have no bags of dried meat. I have no arrows. All these I have found here on this spot," said he, stamping his heavy foot. "I want them! See! I am strong!" repeated he, lifting both his terrible paws.

Quietly the father badger spoke, "I fed you. I called you friend, though you came here a stranger and a beggar. For the shake of my little ones leave us in peace."

Mother badger, in her excited way, had pierced hard through the buckskin and stuck her fingers repeatedly with her sharp awl until she had laid aside her work. Now, while her husband was talking to the bear, she motioned with her hands to the children. On tiptoe they hastened to her side.

For reply came a low growl. It grew louder and more fierce. "Wa-ough!" he roared, and by force hurled the badgers out. First the father badger; then the mother. The little badgers he tossed by pairs. He threw them hard upon the ground.

Standing in the entranceway and showing his ugly teeth, he snarled, "Be gone!" The father and mother badger, having gained their feet, picked up their kicking little babes, and, wailing aloud, drew the air into their flattened lungs till they could stand alone upon their feet. No sooner had the baby badgers caught their breath than they howled and shrieked with pain and fright. Ah! what a dismal cry was theirs as the whole badger family went forth wailing from out their own dwelling!

A little distance away from their stolen house the father badger built a small round hut.

He made it of bent willows and covered it with dry grass and twigs. This was shelter for the night; but alas! it was empty of food and arrows. All day father badger prowled through the forest, but without his arrows he could not get food for his children. Upon his return, the cry of the little ones for meat, the shad quiet of the mother with bowed head, hurt him like a poisoned arrow wound. "I'll beg meat for you!" said he in an unsteady voice.

Covering his head and entire body in a long loose robe he halted beside the big black bear. The bear was slicing red meat to hang upon the rack. He did not pause for a look at the comer. As the badger stood there unrecognized, he saw that the bear had brought with him his whole family. Little cubs played under the high-hanging new meats. They laughed and pointed with their wee noses upward at the thin sliced meats upon the poles.

"Have you no heart, Black Bear? My children are starving. Give me a small piece of meat for them," begged the badger.

"Wa-ough!" growled the angry bear, and pounced upon the badger. "Be gone!" said he, and with his big hind foot he sent father badger sprawling on the ground. All the little ruffian bears hooted and shouted "ha-ha!" to see the beggar fall upon his face.

There was one, however, who did not even smile. He was the youngest cub. His fur coat was not as black and glossy as those his elders wore. The hair was dry and dingy. It looked much more like kinky wool. He was the ugly cub.

Poor little baby bear! He had always been laughed at by his older brothers. He could not help being himself. He could not change the differences between himself and his brothers. Thus again, though the rest laughed aloud at the badger's fall, he did not see the joke. His face was long and earnest.

In his heart he was shad to see the badgers crying and starving. In his breast spread a burning desire to share his food with them. "I shall not ask my father for meat to give away. He would say 'No!' Then my brothers would laugh at me," said the ugly baby bear to himself.

In an instant, as if his good intention had passed from him, he was singing happily and skipping around his father at work. Singing in his small high voice and dragging his feet in long strides after him, as if a prankish spirit oozed out from his heels, he strayed off through the tall grass. He was ambling toward the small round hut. When directly in front of the entranceway, he made a quick side kick with his left hind leg. Lo! there fell into the badger's hut a piece of fresh meat. It was tough meat, full of sinews, yet it was the only piece he could take without his father's notice.

Thus having given meat to the hungry badgers, the ugly baby bear ran quickly away to his father again.

On the following day the father badger came back once more. He stood watching the big bear cutting thin slices of meat. "Give..." he began, when the bear turning upon him with a growl, thrust him cruelly aside.

The badger fell on his hands. He fell where the grass was wet with the blood of the newly carved buffalo. His keen starving eyes caught sight of a little red clot lying bright upon the green. Looking fearfully toward the bear and seeing his head was turned away, he snatched up the small thick blood.

Underneath his girdled blanket he hid it in his hand. On his return to his family, he said within himself: "I'll pray the Great Spirit to bless it."

Thus he built a small round lodge. Sprinkling water upon the heated heap of sacred stones within, he made ready to purge his body. "The buffalo blood, too, must be purified before I ask a blessing upon it," thought the badger.

He carried it into the sacred vapor lodge. After placing it

near the sacred stones, he sat down beside it. After a long silence, he muttered: "Great Spirit, bless this little buffalo blood." Then he arose, and with a quiet dignity stepped out of the lodge.

Close behind him some one followed. The badger turned to look over his shoulder and to his great joy he beheld a Lakota brave in handsome buckskins. In his hand he carried a magic arrow. Across his back dangled a long fringed quiver.

In answer to the badger's prayer, the avenger had sprung from out the red globules.

"My son!" exclaimed the badger with extended right hand.

"Hau, father," replied the brave; "I am your avenger!"

Immediately the badger told the sad story of his hungry little ones and the stingy bear. Listening closely the young man stood looking steadily upon the ground. At length the father badger moved away. "Where?" queried the avenger.

"My son, we have no food. I am going again to beg for meat," answered the badger.

"Then I go with you," replied the young brave. This made the old badger happy. He was proud of his son. He was delighted to be called "father" by the first human creature.

The bear saw the badger coming in the distance. He narrowed his eyes at the tall stranger walking beside him. He spied the arrow. At once he guessed it was the avenger of whom he had heard long, long ago.

As they approached, the bear stood erect with a hand on his thigh. He smiled upon them. "How, badger, my friend!

Here is my knife. Cut your favorite pieces from the deer,"
said he, holding out a long thin blade.

"Hau!" said the badger eagerly. He wondered what had
inspired the big bear to such a generous deed.

The young avenger waited till the badger took the long
knife in his hand. Gazing full into the black bear's face, he
said: "I come to do justice. You have returned only a knife
to my poor father. Now return to him his dwelling."

His voice was deep and powerful. In his black eyes burned
a steady fire. The long strong teeth of the bear rattled
against each other, and his shaggy body shook with fear.

"Ahow!" cried he, as if he had been shot. Running into the
dwelling he gasped, breathless and trembling, "Come out,
all of you! This is the badger's dwelling. We must flee to
the forest for fear of the avenger who carries the magic
arrow."

Out they hurried, all the bears, and disappeared into the
woods. Singing and laughing, the badgers returned to their
own dwelling.

Then the avenger left them. "I go," said he in parting, "over
the earth."

The Toad and the Boy

A Lakota Legend
Zitkala Sa, Old Indian
Legends, 1901

The water-fowls were flying over the marshy lakes. It was now the hunting season. Indian men, with bows and arrows, were wading waist deep amid the wild rice.

Near by, within their wigwams, the wives were roasting wild duck and making down pillows. In the largest teepee sat a young mother wrapping red porcupine quills about the long fringes of a buckskin cushion.

Beside her lay a black-eyed baby boy cooing and laughing. Reaching and kicking upward with his tiny hands and feet, he played with the dangling strings of his heavy-beaded bonnet hanging empty on a tent pole above him.

At length the mother laid aside her red quills and white sinew-threads. The babe fell fast asleep. Leaning on one hand and softly whispering a little lullaby, she threw a light cover over her baby. It was almost time for the return of her husband.

Remembering there were no willow sticks for the fire, she quickly girdled her blanket tight about her waist, and with a short-handled ax slipped through her belt, she hurried away toward the wooded ravine.

She was strong and swung an ax as skillfully as any man.

Her loose buckskin dress was made for such freedom.

Soon carrying easily, a bundle of long willows on her back, with a loop of rope over both her shoulders, she came striding homeward. Near the entrance way she stooped low, at once shifting the bundle to the right and with both hands lifting the noose from over her head.

Having thus dropped the wood to the ground, she disappeared into her teepee. In a moment she came running out again, crying,

"My son! My little son is gone!"

Her keen eyes swept east and west and all around her. There was nowhere any sign of the child. Running with clinched fists to the nearest teepees, she called: "Has any one seen my baby? He is gone! My little son is gone!"

"Hinnu! Hinnu!" exclaimed the women, rising to their feet and rushing out of their wigwams. "We have not seen your child! What has happened?" queried the women.

With great tears in her eyes the mother told her story. "We will search with you," they said to her as she started off. They met the returning husbands, who turned about and joined in the hunt for the missing child. Along the shore of the lakes, among the high-grown reeds, they looked in vain. He was nowhere to be found. After many days and nights, the search was given up. It was sad, indeed, to hear the mother wailing aloud for her little son. It was growing late in the autumn. The birds were flying high toward the south. The teepees around the lakes were gone, save one lonely dwelling.

Till the winter snow covered the ground and ice covered the lakes, the wailing woman's voice was heard from that

solitary wigwam. From some far distance was also the
sound of the father's voice singing a sad song.

Thus ten summers and as many winters have come and
gone since the strange disappearance of the little child.
Every autumn with the hunters came the unhappy parents
of the lost baby to search again for him.

Toward the latter part of the tenth season when, one by one,
the teepees were folded and the families went away from
the lake region, the mother walked again along the lake
shore weeping.

One evening, across the lake from where the crying woman
stood, a pair of bright black eyes peered at her through the
tall reeds and wild rice. A little wild boy stopped his play
among the tall grasses. His long, loose hair hanging down
his brown back and shoulders was carelessly tossed from
his round face. He wore a loin cloth of woven sweet grass.

Crouching low to the marshy ground, he listened to the
wailing voice. As the voice grew hoarse and only sobs
shook the slender figure of the woman, the eyes of the wild
boy grew dim and wet. At length, when the moaning
ceased, he sprang to his feet and ran like a nymph with
swift outstretched toes. He rushed into a small hut of reeds
and grasses.

"Mother! Mother! Tell me what voice it was I heard which
pleased my ears, but made my eyes grow wet!" said he,
breathless.

"Han, my son," grunted a big, ugly toad. "It was the voice
of a weeping woman you heard. My son, do not say you
like it. Do not tell me it brought tears to your eyes. You
have never heard me weep. I can please your ear and break

your heart. Listen!" replied the great old toad.

Stepping outside, she stood by the entrance way. She was old and badly puffed out. She had reared a large family of little toads, but none of them had aroused her love, nor ever grieved her. She had heard the wailing human voice and marveled at the throat which produced the strange sound.

Now, in her great desire to keep the stolen boy awhile longer, she ventured to cry as the Lakota woman does. In a gruff, coarse voice she broke forth: "Hin-hin, doe-skin! Hin-hin, Ermine, Ermine! Hin-hin, red blanket, with white border!"

Not knowing that the syllables of a Lakota's cry are the names of loved ones gone, the ugly toad mother sought to please the boy's ear with the names of valuable articles. Having shrieked in a torturing voice and mouthed extravagant names, the old toad rolled her tearless eyes with great satisfaction.

Hopping back into her dwelling, she asked: "My son, did my voice bring tears to your eyes? Did my words bring gladness to your ears? Do you not like my wailing better?"

"No, no!" pouted the boy with some impatience. "I want to hear the woman's voice! Tell me, mother, why the human voice stirs all my feelings!"

The toad mother said within her breast, "The human child has heard and seen his real mother. I cannot keep him longer, I fear. Oh, no, I cannot give away the pretty creature I have taught to call me 'mother' all these many winters."

"Mother," went on the child voice, "tell me one thing. Tell

me why my little brothers and sisters are all unlike me."

The big, ugly toad, looking at her pudgy children, said:
"The eldest is always best." This reply quieted the boy for a
while. Very closely watched the old toad mother her stolen
human son.

When by chance he started off alone, she shoved out one of
her own children after him, saying: "Do not come back
without your big brother." Thus the wild boy with the long,
loose hair sits every day on a marshy island hid among the
tall reeds.

But he is not alone. Always at his feet hops a little toad
brother.

One day an Indian hunter, wading in the deep waters, spied
the boy. He had heard of the baby stolen long ago. "This is
he!" murmured the hunter to himself as he ran to his
wigwam.

"I saw among the tall reeds a black-haired boy at play!"
shouted he to the people.

At once the unhappy father and mother cried out, "'Tis he,
our boy!" Quickly he led them to the lake. Peeping through
the wild rice, he pointed with unsteady finger toward the
boy playing all unawares.

"'Tis he! 'tis he!" cried the mother, for she knew him. In
silence the hunter stood aside, while the happy father and
mother caressed their baby boy grown tall.

Bear-Woman and Deer-Woman

A Lassik Legend Goddard, Journal of American Folk-Lore, xix, 135, No. 2

Grizzly Bear and Doe, the two wives of Chickenhawk, were pounding acorns. When they had finished, one of them said, "Let us go down to the creek and leach the meal."

While they were waiting for the meal to soak, they agreed to hunt one another's heads for lice. Doe looked first in Grizzly's hair. "You have no lice," she said. "Well then," said Grizzly, "I will look in yours." When in her search she reached the Doe's neck she sprinkled in some sand. "You have many lice," she said, "I will chew them." "Ukka! ukka!" cried Doe, "hold on there." Biting her head off, she killed her.

Taking Doe's head and both lots of acorn meal she went back to the house. She put the head in the fire and when the eyes burst with the heat she told the children it was only the white oak log cracking in the fire. "I think it is our mother's head," said one of the Doe's children. "Go a long way off and play," said Grizzly. "You won't be permitted to live long," they heard their mother's head so say to them.

The two bear children and the two fawns went out to play. "Let us play smoke-eachother-out in this hollow log," suggested the fawns. The bears agreed and the fawns went in first. "That's enough, that's enough," they cried. "Now you go in," they told the bears. The fawns fanned the smoke into the log until the bears were smothered.

Going back to the house, one of them held out what she had in her hand and said, "Here is a skunk we killed in a log." "Very well," said the bear mother. Then the other fawn held out hers and said, "Here is a skunk we killed in a log." "Thank you, my niece; after a while I will make a meal upon them," replied Grizzly.

"She is eating her children," she heard some one say. "What did you say?" she asked. "First you killed some one, and now you are eating your own children's hands." She ran after the children who had been taunting her. When she came near them she called in a pleasant voice, "Well, come home." They ran up on a ridge and barely escaped being caught.

Finally, they came to a place where Crane was fishing by the river. "Grandfather, put your neck across and let us go over on it. An old woman is after us. Put your neck across." They crossed over safely and running to the top of a ridge hid in a hole in a rock. When Grizzly came, Crane put his neck across again for a bridge, but when she was half way over he gave it a sudden twist. She went floating down the middle of the stream.

How the Fawn Got its Spots
A Dakota Sioux Legend

Long ago, when the world was new, Wakan Tanka, The Great Mystery, was walking around. As he walked he spoke to himself of the many things he had done to help the four-legged ones and the birds survive.

"It is good," Wakan Tanka said. "I have given Mountain Lion sharp claws and Grizzly Bear great strength; it is much easier now for them to survive.

"I have given Wolf sharp teeth and I have given his little brother, Coyote, quick wits; it is much easier now for them to survive.

"I have given Beaver a flat tail and webbed feet to swim beneath the water and teeth which can cut down the trees and I have given slow-moving Porcupine quills to protect itself. Now it is easier for them to survive.

"I have given the Birds their feathers and the ability to fly so that they may escape their enemies. I have given speed to the Deer and the Rabbit so that it will be hard for their enemies to catch them. Truly it is now much easier for them to survive."

However, as Wakan Tanka spoke, a mother Deer came up to him. Behind her was her small Fawn, wobbling on weak new legs.

"Great One," she said. "It is true that you have given many gifts to the four-leggeds and the winged ones to help them survive. It is true that you gave me great speed and now my enemies find it hard to catch me. My speed is a great protection, indeed. But what of my little one here? She does not yet have speed. It is easy for our enemies, with their sharp teeth and their claws to catch her. If my children do not survive, how can my people live?"

"Wica yaka pelo!" said Wakan Tanka. "You have spoken truly; you are right. Have your little one come here and I will help her."

Then Wakan Tanka made paint from the earth and the plants. He painted spots upon the fawn's body so that when she lay still her color blended in with the earth and she could not be seen. Then Wakan Tanka breathed upon her, taking away her scent.

"Now," Wakan Tanka said, "your little ones will always be safe if they only remain still when they are away from your side. None of your enemies will see your little ones or be able to catch their scent."

So it has been from that day on. When a young deer is too small and weak to run swiftly, it is covered with spots that blend in with the earth. It has no scent and it remains very still and close to the earth when its mother is not by its side. And when it has grown enough to have the speed Wakan Tanka gave its people, then it loses those spots it once needed to survive.

Lakota Instructions for Living

Friend do it this way - that is,
whatever you do in life,
do the very best you can
with both your heart and mind.

And if you do it that way,
the Power Of The Universe
will come to your assistance,
if your heart and mind are in Unity.

When one sits in the Hoop Of The People,
one must be responsible because
All of Creation is related.
And the hurt of one is the hurt of all.
And the honor of one is the honor of all.
And whatever we do effects everything in the universe.

If you do it that way - that is,
if you truly join your heart and mind
as One - whatever you ask for,
that's the Way It's Going To Be.

Passed down from White Buffalo Calf Woman

Song of the Buffalo
An American Indian Legend - Nation Unknown

When the Buffalo first came to be upon the land, they were not friendly to the people. When the hunters tried to coax them over the cliffs for the good of the villages, they were reluctant to offer themselves up. They did not relish being turned into blankets and dried flesh for winter rations. They did not want their hooves and horn to become tools and utensils nor did they welcome their sinew being used for sewing. "No, no," they said. We won't fall into your traps. And we will not fall for your tricks." So when the hunters guided them towards the abyss, they would always turn aside at the very last moment. With this lack of cooperation, it seemed the villagers would be hungry and cold and ragged all winter long.

Now one of the hunters' had a daughter who was very proud of her father's skill with the bow. During the fullness of summer, he always brought her the best of hides to dress, and she in turn would work the deerskins into the softest, whitest of garments for him to wear. Her own dresses were like the down of a snow goose, and the moccasins she made for the children and the grandmothers in the village were the most welcome of gifts.

But now with the hint of snow on the wind, and deer becoming more scarce in the willow breaks, she could see this reluctance on the part of the Buffalo families could become a real problem.

Hunter's Daughter decided she would do something about it. She went to the base of the cliff and looked up. She began to sing in a low, soft voice, "Oh, Buffalo family, come down and visit me. If you come down and feed my relatives in a wedding feast, I will join your family as the bride of your strongest warrior."

She stopped and listened. She thought she heard the slight rumbling sound of thunder in the distance. Again she sang, "Oh, Buffalo family, come down and visit me. Feed my family in a wedding feast so that I may be a bride."

The thunder was much louder now. Suddenly the Buffalo family began falling from the sky at her feet. One very large bull landed on top of the others, and walked across the backs of his relatives to stand before Hunter's Daughter.

"I am here to claim you as my bride," said Large Buffalo.

"Oh, but now I am afraid to go with you," said Hunter's Daughter.

"Ah, but you must," said Large Buffalo, "For my people have come to provide your people with a wedding feast. As you can see, they have offered themselves up."

"Yes, but I must run and tell my relatives the good news," said Hunter's Daughter. "No," said the Large Buffalo. No word need be sent. You are not getting away so easily."

And that with said, Large Buffalo lifted her between his horns and carried her off to his village in the rolling grass hills.

The next morning the whole village was out looking for Hunter's Daughter. When they found the mound of Buffalo below the cliff, the father, who was in fact a fine tracker as well as a skilled hunter, looked at his daughter's footprints in the dust.

"She's gone off with a Buffalo, he said. I shall follow them and bring her back."

So Hunter walked out upon the plains, with only his bow and arrows as companions. He walked and walked a great distance until he was so tired that he had to sit down to rest beside a Buffalo wallow.

Along came Magpie and sat down beside him. Hunter spoke to Magpie in a respectful tone, "O knowledgeable bird, has my daughter been stolen from me by a Buffalo? Have you seen them? Can you tell me where they have gone?"

Magpie replied with understanding, "Yes, I have seen them pass this way. They are resting just over this hill."

"Well," said Hunter, would you kindly take my daughter a message for me? Will you tell her I am here just over the hill?"

So Magpie flew to where Large Buffalo lay asleep amidst his relatives in the dry prairie grass. He hopped over to where Hunter's Daughter was quilling moccasins, as she sat dutifully beside her sleeping husband. "Your father is waiting for you on the other side of the hill," whispered Magpie to the maiden.

"Oh, this is very dangerous," she told him. These Buffalo are not friendly to us and they might try to hurt my father if he should come this way. Please tell him to wait for me and I will try to slip away to see him."

Just then her husband, Large Buffalo, awoke and took off his horn. "Go bring me a drink from the wallow just over this hill," said her husband.

So she took the horn in her hand and walked very casually over the hill. Her father motioned silently for her to come with him, as he bent into a low crouch in the grass. "No," she whispered. The Buffalo are angry with our people who have killed their people. They will run after us and trample us into the dirt. I will go back and see what I can do to soothe their feelings."

And so Hunter's daughter took the horn of water back to her husband who gave a loud snort when he took a drink. The snort turned into a bellow and all of the Buffalo got up in alarm. They all put their tails in the air and danced a Buffalo Dance over the hill, trampling the poor man to pieces who was still waiting for his daughter near the Buffalo wallow.

His daughter sat down on the edge of the wallow and broke into tears.

"Why are you crying?" said her Buffalo husband.

"You have killed my father and I am a prisoner, besides," she sobbed.

"Well, what of my people?" her husband replied. We have given our children, our parents and some of our wives up to your relatives in exchange for your presence among us. A deal is a deal."

But after some consideration of her feelings, Large Buffalo knelt down beside her and said to her, "If you can bring your father back to life again, we will let him take you back home to your people." So Hunter's Daughter started to sing a little song. "Magpie, Magpie help me find some piece of my father which I can mend back whole again."

Magpie appeared and sat down in front of her with his head cocked to the side. "Magpie, Magpie, please see what you can find," she sang softly to the wind which bent the grasses slightly apart. Magpie cocked his head to the side and looked carefully within the layered folds of the grasses as the wind sighed again. Quickly he picked out a piece of her father that had been hidden there, a little bit of bone. "That will be enough to do the trick," said Hunter's Daughter, as she put the bone on the ground and covered it with her blanket.

And then she started to sing a reviving song that had the power to bring injured people back to the land of the living. Quietly she sang the song that her grandmother had taught her. After a few melodious passages, there was a lump under the blanket. She and Magpie looked under the blanket and could see a man, but the man was not breathing. He lay cold as stone. So Hunter's Daughter continued to sing, a little softer, and a little softer, so as not to startle her father as he began to move. When he stood up, alive and strong, the Buffalo people were amazed. They said to Hunter's Daughter, "Will you sing this song for us after every hunt? We will teach your people the Buffalo Dance, so that whenever you dance before the hunt, you will be assured a good result. Then you will sing this song for us, and we will all come back to live again."

It was our belief that the love of possessions is a weakness to be overcome. Its appeal is to the material part, and if allowed its way, it will in time disturb one's spiritual balance. Therefore, children must early learn the beauty of generosity. They are taught to give what they prize most, that they may taste the happiness of giving.

Ohiyesa

Why Kingfisher Wears a War Bonnet

An American Indian Legend - Nation Unknown

One day in the winter-time when Old-Man and the Wolf were hunting. The snow covered the land and ice was on all of the rivers. It was so cold that Old-Man wrapped his robe close about himself and his breath showed white in the air. Of course the Wolf was not cold; wolves never get cold as men do.

Both Old-Man and the Wolf were hungry for they had traveled far and had killed no meat. Old-Man was complaining and grumbling, for his heart is not very good. It is never well to grumble when we are doing our best, because it will do no good and makes us weak in our hearts. When our hearts are weak our heads sicken and our strength goes away. Yes, it is bad to grumble.

When the sun was getting low Old-Man and the Wolf came to a great river. On the ice that covered the water, they saw four fat Otters playing.

"'There is meat," said the Wolf; "wait here and I will try to catch one of those fellows."

"'No! No!" cried Old-Man, "Do not run after the Otter on the ice, because there are air-holes in all ice that covers rivers, and you may fall in the water and die." Old-Man didn't care much if the Wolf did drown. He was afraid to be left alone and hungry in the snow--that was all.

"'Ho!" said the Wolf, "I am swift of foot and my teeth are white and sharp. What chance has an Otter against me? Yes, I will go," and he did.

Away ran the Otters with the Wolf after them, while Old-Man stood on the bank and shivered with fright and cold. Of course the Wolf was faster than the Otter, but he was running on the ice, remember, and slipping a good deal. Nearer and nearer ran the Wolf. In fact, he was just about to seize an Otter, when Splash!... into an air-hole all the Otters went. Ho! the Wolf was going so fast he couldn't stop, and Swow! into the air-hole he went like a badger after mice, and the current carried him under the ice. The Otters knew that hole was there. That was their country and they were running to reach that same hole all the time, but the Wolf didn't know that.

Old-Man saw it all and began to cry and wail as women do. Ho! but he made a great fuss. He ran along the bank of the river, stumbling in the snowdrifts, and crying like a woman whose child is dead; but it was because he didn't want to be left in that country alone that he cried, not because he loved his brother, the Wolf. On and on he ran until he came to a place where the water was too swift to freeze, and there he waited and watched for the Wolf to come out from under the ice, crying and wailing and making an awful noise, for a man.

Well, right there is where the thing happened. You see, Kingfisher can't fish through the ice and he knows it, too;

so he always finds places like the one Old-Man found. He was there that day, sitting on the limb of a birch-tree, watching for fishes, and when Old-Man came near to Kingfisher's tree, crying like an old woman, it tickled the Fisher so much that he laughed that queer, chattering laugh.

Old-Man heard him and--Ho! but he was angry. He looked about to see who was laughing at him and that made Kingfisher laugh again, longer and louder than before. This time Old-Man saw him and Swow! he threw his war-club at Kingfisher; tried to kill the bird for laughing.

Kingfisher ducked so quickly that Old-Man's club just grazed the feathers on his head, making them stand up straight.

"'There," said Old-Man, "I'll teach you to laugh at me when I'm sad. Your feathers are standing up on the top of your head now and they will stay that way, too. As long as you live you must wear a head-dress, to pay for your laughing, and all your children must do the same."

This was long, long ago, but the King-fishers have not forgotten, and they all wear war-bonnets, and always will as long as there are Kingfishers.

Man's law changes with his understanding of man.
Only the laws of the spirit remain always the same.

Crow

The Big Turtle's War Party
A Pawnee Legend

A turtle went on the warpath, and as he went along, he met Coyote, who said: "And where are you going Grandson?" The turtle said: "I am on the warpath." Coyote said: "Where are you going?" "I am going to a camp where there are many people," said the turtle. "Let me see you run," the turtle said. Coyote ran. The turtle said: "You cannot run fast; I do not want you."

The turtle went on, and he met a fox. "Well, brother," said the fox, "where are you going?" said the fox. "I am going where there are many people," said the turtle. "Can I go with you?" said the fox. The turtle said: "Let me see your run." The fox ran, and he went so fast that the turtle could hardly see him. The turtle said: "You cannot run fast; I do not want you."

The turtle then went on, and a hawk flew by him, and the hawk heard the turtle say: "I am on the warpath; I am looking for people to join me." The hawk said: "Brother, what did you say?" "I am on the warpath," said the turtle. "Can I join you?" said the hawk. "Let me see you fly your best," said the turtle. The hawk flew so fast that the turtle could not see him for a while. When the hawk came back, the turtle said: "You cannot fly fast; I do not want you."

Again the turtle went on, and kept crying: "I am on the warpath; I am looking for people to join me." A rabbit jumped up and said: "Can I go along?" "Let me see you run," said the turtle. The rabbit ran, and ran fast. The turtle said: "You cannot run fast; I do not want you."

The turtle went on saying: "I am looking for people to join me." Up jumped a flint knife and said: "Brother, can I join you?" "You may if you can run fast," said the turtle; "let me see you run." The knife tried to run, and could not. "You will do," said the turtle; "come with me."

They went on, and the turtle was saying: "I am looking for people to go on the warpath with me." Up jumped a hairbrush. "What did you say?" said the brush. "I am on the warpath," said the turtle. "Can I go along?" said the brush. The turtle said: "Let me see you run." The brush tried to run, but could not. The turtle said: "You will do; come with us."

They went on, and the turtle was saying: "I am on the warpath; I am looking for people to join me." Up jumped an Awl, and it said: "Can I join you?" The turtle said: "Let me see you run." The Awl tried to run, but could not. "You will do," said the turtle; "come with us."

So the four went on, and they came to a big camp, and the turtle sent the knife into the camp. The knife went into camp, and one man found it, took it home, and while trying to cut meat the man cut his fingers, and threw the knife at the doorway. The knife went back to the turtle and said: "I was picked up, and while the man was trying to cut meat, I cut his hand and he threw me at the doorway, so I came back."

The turtle said: "Very well. Now Brush, you go and see what you can do." So the brush went into camp, and a young girl picked it up and commenced to brush her hair. The brush pulled the girls hair out, so that the girl threw the brush at the doorway, and it came back. It said: "Brother Turtle, there is a young girl who has lovely hair. She used me on her head, and I pulled her hair, so she threw me away. See I have her hair here." "Well done," said the turtle.

"Now, Awl, go and be brave," said the turtle. The Awl went into camp, and an old woman picked it up. She began to sew her moccasins, and all at once she stuck the Awl in one of her fingers. The woman threw it away, and it came back and said: "Brother Turtle, I hurt a woman badly. She was using me while she was sewing her moccasins, and I stuck one of her fingers, she threw me away." "Well done, brothers, now it is my turn." said the turtle.

The turtle went into camp, and the people saw him and said, "What does this mean? Look at Turtle; he is on the warpath. Let us kill him." So they took him, and the people said: "Let us spread hot coals and put him in there." "All right," said the turtle, "that will suit me for I will spread out my legs and burn some of you. People said: "True let us then put a kettle over the fire, and when the water boils let us put him in." The turtle said: "Good! Put me in, and I will scald some of you." People said: "True! Let us throw him into the stream." The turtle said: "No, do not do that. I am afraid, I am afraid! Do not throw me in the water!" So the people threw the turtle in the water. The turtle came up to the surface and said: "I am a cheat. Heyru! Heyru!" poking his tongue out.

The people picked up the knife, awl and brush and used them. The turtle stayed in the water, and every time the people went to the water, Turtle would say: "I cheated you; water is my home." People would throw stones at it, and it would dive.

Mikmaq Legend of the Wild Goose

A Micmac Legend

When birds migrated to the south in the long, long ago, they came and left by themselves. Many of the little ones were killed by storms. This caused great sorrow to Kluskap, the great God of the Mikmaq. He asked the Wild Goose the largest bird and the last one to leave the north each fall, to care for all of the smaller ones. The Wild Goose called all the little birds together and told them of Kluskap's wonderful plan.

They agreed that the Wild Goose would lead them in their long flight to the south, shelter them in their far away homes, be with them during their journey back and protect them while they were in the North during the summer season.

Ever since the time of Kluskap the Wild Goose has been the guide and protector of all the small birds that come to our country each year.

Why the Owl has Big Eyes
Iroquois

Raweno, the Everything-Maker, was busy creating various animals. He was working on Rabbit, and Rabbit was saying: "I want nice long legs and ears like a deer, and sharp fangs and claws like a panther."

"I do them up the way they want to be; I give them what they ask for," said Raweno. He was working on Rabbit's hind legs, making them long, the way Rabbit had ordered.

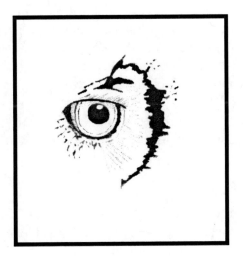

Owl, still unformed, was sitting on a tree nearby waiting his turn. He was saying: "Whoo, whoo, I want a nice long neck like Swan's, and beautiful red feathers like Cardinal's, and a nice long beak like Egret's, and a nice crown of plumes like Heron's. I want you to make me into the most beautiful, the fastest, the most wonderful of all the birds."

Raweno said: "Be quiet. Turn around and look in the other direction. Even better, close your eyes. Don't you know that no one is allowed to watch me work?" Raweno was just then making Rabbit's ears very long, the way Rabbit wanted them

Owl refused to do what Raweno said. "Whoo, whoo," he replied, "nobody can forbid me to watch. Nobody can order me to close my eyes. I like watching you, and watch I will."

Then Raweno became angry. He grabbed Owl, pulling him down from his branch, stuffing his head deep into his body, shaking him until his eyes grew big with fright, pulling at his ears until they were sticking up at both sides of his head.

"There," said Raweno, "that'll teach you. Now you won't be able to crane your neck to watch things you shouldn't watch. Now you have big ears to listen when someone tells you what not to do. Now you have big eyes--not so big that you can watch me, because you'll be awake only at night, and I work by day. And your feathers won't be red like cardinal's, but gray like this" --and Raweno rubbed Owl all over with mud--"as punishment for your disobedience." So Owl flew off, pouting: "Whoo, whoo, whoo."

Then Raweno turned back to finish Rabbit, but Rabbit had been so terrified by Raweno's anger, even though it was not directed at him, that he ran off half done. As a consequence, only Rabbit's hind legs are long, and he has to hop about instead of walking and running. Also, because he took fright then, Rabbit would have been an altogether different animal.

As for Owl, he remained as Raweno had shaped him with anger--with big eyes, a short neck, and ears sticking up on the sides of his head. On top of everything, he has to sleep during the day and come out only at night.

A Raccoon Story
A Seneca Legend

An uncle and nephew lived together. One day when the
nephew was in the woods, hunting, a handsome young
woman came to the cabin. She had a basketful of bread on
her shoulders.

Unstrapping the basket and putting it down in front of the
old man, she said, "Here is marriage bread, my father and
mother have sent me here to marry your nephew."

"Very well," said the uncle.

When the young man came home, his uncle said, "You are
married now."

"I am glad," said the nephew.

After this the young woman cooked and the men hunted. Each day the nephew returned with a heavy load of game. One day while hunting he came to a tree in which there was a large hole and in the hole was a litter of coons. He climbed the tree and threw one coon after another on to the ground.

All at once he heard a woman say, "Come down. Come down, you are tired," then she ran off through the forest.

When the young man went home, he told what had happened. His wife laughed, but said nothing. Not long after, when packing up his game ready to start for home, a woman came up behind him, took him by the arm and led him to a log. They sat down, she pulled his head on to her lap and began to look in his hair.

The man was soon asleep. The woman put him in a basket, put the basket on her back and went to an island in the middle of a lake. Then she took the man out of the basket and asked, "Do you know this place?"

"I know it. This is where my uncle and I used to fish," and giving a spring into the water the man became a bass and escaped.

When he went home, he told his wife what had happened. She laughed, but said nothing.

The man was so frightened that he stayed at home for several days. Then the feeling wore away and he started off to hunt.

As he was packing up his game to go home a woman said, right there at his side, "Stop, wait a while, you must be tired."

They sat down on a log. She drew his head to her lap and began looking in his hair. He was soon asleep. Putting him into a basket the woman carried him to a great ledge of rocks where there was only a foothold, then, taking him out of the basket, she asked, "Do you know this place?"

"I will tell you soon," said the man, looking around.

That minute the woman disappeared.

Soon he heard someone say, "I will fish a while."

A line dropped into the water below and a man began singing and pulling up fish.

At last he said, "I have enough, I'll rest and have something to eat. This is what we people eat when we are among the rocks," and he took a baked squash out of his basket.

The young man said to the rocks, "Stand back a little so that I can string my bow."

The rocks stood back; he strung his bow, and, saying, "Now boast again!" he shot the fisherman.

He heard a loud noise and looking in the direction it came from saw an enormous bat coming toward him. The bat passed a little to one side. The young man took a hemlock leaf from his pocket and dropping it over the rocks, sang, "A tree must grow from this hemlock leaf. A tree must grow from this hemlock leaf."

Soon a tree came in sight. Then the man talked to the tree, said, "Come near, and have many limbs."

As the tree came to a level with the place on the rocks where the young man was sitting, it stopped growing. He had seen that along the narrow shelf of rocks there were many men. He called to the nearest one to tell all to come and they could escape.

The men crept up, one after another, then went down on the tree. When all had reached the ground, the young man took a strawberry leaf from his pocket and dropping it said, "Grow and give berries." Then he sang, "Ripen berries. Ripen berries." The vines grew, were covered with blossoms. The blossoms became berries and the berries ripened.

When the men had eaten as many berries as they wanted, the young man picked a leaf from the vines, put it in his pocket and the vines and berries disappeared. Then he said to the men, "Let us go to our wife"--meaning the woman who had captured them.

When they had traveled some distance, the young man killed an elk. Taking the hide, he cut it into strings and made a baby board, but one large enough for a grown person. After a while they saw a house and in front of it a woman pounding something.

When she saw them, she began to scold and, holding up the pounder was going to strike them.

The young man said, "Let the pounder stop right there!"

The pounder stopped in the air, half raised.

They seized the woman, strapped her to the board, and, saying, "You must be cold," they set the board up in front of the fire. Just then the young man's wife came and, finding that they were about to roast the woman, she was angry.

She freed her, and said, "You are free now, and I will go home."

She went to the lake and called on Bloodsuckers to stretch across the water. They came and she walked over on them.

Each man went his own way. When the young man got home his wife was there.

The nephew and uncle were raccoons.

People Tales

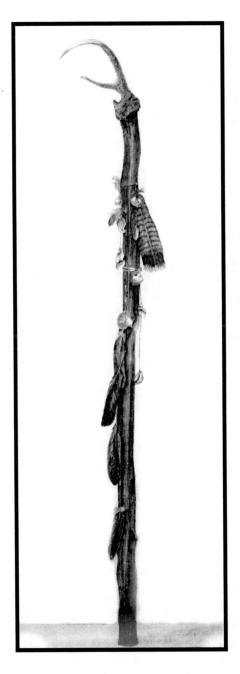

The Simpleton's Wisdom

A Sioux Legend
Marie L. McLaughlin, Myths and Legends of the Sioux, 1913

There was a man and his wife who had one daughter. Mother and daughter were deeply attached to one another, and when the latter died the mother was disconsolate.

She cut off her hair, cut gashes in her cheeks and sat before the corpse with her robe drawn over her head, mourning for her dead. She would not let them touch the body to take it to a burying scaffold.

She had a knife in her hand, and if anyone offered to come near the body the mother would wail, "I am weary of life. I do not care to live. I will stab myself with this knife and join my daughter in the land of spirits."

Her husband and relatives tried to get the knife from her, but could not. They feared to use force lest she kill herself. They came together to see what they could do.

"We must get the knife away from her," they said.

At last they called a boy, a kind of simpleton, yet with a good deal of natural shrewdness. He was an orphan and very poor. His moccasins were out at the sole and he was dressed in wei-zi (coarse buffalo skin, smoked).

"Go to the teepee of the mourning mother, " they told the simpleton, "and in some way contrive to make her laugh and forget her grief. Then try to get the knife away from her."

The boy went to the tent and sat down at the door as if waiting to be given something. The corpse lay in the place of honor where the dead girl had slept in life. The body was wrapped in a rich robe and wrapped about with ropes.

Friends had covered it with rich offerings out of respect to the dead.

As the mother sat on the ground with her head covered she did not at first see the boy, who sat silent. But when his reserve had worn away a little he began at first lightly, then more heavily, to drum on the floor with his hands.

After a while he began to sing a comic song. Louder and louder he sang until carried away with his own singing he sprang up and began to dance, at the same time gesturing and making all manner of contortions with his body, still singing the comic song. As he approached the corpse he waved his hands over it in blessing.

The mother put her head out of the blanket and when she saw the poor simpleton with his strange grimaces trying to do honor to the corpse by his solemn waving, and at the same time keeping up his comic song, she burst out laughing. Then she reached over and handed her knife to the simpleton.

"Take this knife," she said. "You have taught me to forget my grief. If while I mourn for the dead I can still be mirthful, there is no reason for me to despair. I no longer care to die. I will live for my husband."

The simpleton left the teepee and brought the knife to the astonished husband and relatives.

"How did you get it? Did you force it away from her, or did you steal it?" they asked.

"She gave it to me. How could I force it from her or steal it when she held it in her hand, blade uppermost? I sang and danced for her and she burst out laughing. Then she gave it to me," he answered.

When the old men of the village heard the orphan's story they were very silent. It was a strange thing for a lad to dance in a teepee where there was mourning. It was stranger that a mother should laugh in a teepee before the corpse of her dead daughter.

The old men gathered at last in a council. They sat a long time without saying anything, for they did not want to decide hastily. The pipe was filled and passed many times. At last an old man spoke.

"We have a hard question. A mother has laughed before the corpse of her daughter, and many think she has done foolishly, but I think the woman did wisely. The lad was simple and of no training, and we cannot expect him to know how to do as well as one with good home and parents to teach him. Besides, he did the best that he knew. He danced to make the mother forget her grief, and he tried to honor the corpse by waving over it his hands."

"The mother did right to laugh, for when one does try to do us good, even if what he does causes us discomfort, we should always remember rather the motive than the deed. And besides, the simpleton's dancing saved the woman's life, for she gave up her knife. In this, too, she did well, for it is always better to live for the living than to die for the dead."

It is better to have less thunder in the mouth and more lightning in the hand.

Apache

The Foster Child of the Deer

A Zuni Legend
Frank Hamilton Cushing,
Zuni Folk Tales, 1901

Once, long, long ago, at Háwikuh, there lived a maiden most beautiful. In her earlier years her father, who was a great priest, had devoted her to sacred things, and kept her always in the house secure from the gaze of all men, and thus she grew.

She was so beautiful that when the Sun looked down along one of the straight beams of his own light, if one of those beams chanced to pass through a chink in the roof, the skyhole, or the windows of the upper part of the maiden's room, he beheld her and wondered at her rare beauty, unable to compare it with anything he saw in his great journeys round about the worlds.

Thus, as the maiden grew apace and became a young woman, the Sun loved her exceedingly, and as time went on he became so enamored of her that he descended to earth and entered on one of his own beams of light into her apartment, so that suddenly, while she was sitting one noon-day weaving pretty baskets, there stood before her a glorious youth, gloriously dressed.

It was the Sun-father. He looked upon her gently and lovingly; she looked upon him not fearfully: and so it came about that she loved him and he loved her, and he won her to be his wife. And many were the days in which he visited her and dwelt with her for a space at noon-time; but as she was alone mostly, or as she kept sitting weaving her trays when any one of the family entered her apartment, no one suspected this.

Now, as she knew that she had been devoted to sacred things, and that if she explained how it was that she was a mother she would not be believed, she was greatly exercised in mind and heart. She therefore decided that when her child was born she would put it away from her.

When the time came, the child one night was born. She carefully wrapped the little baby boy in some soft cotton-wool, and in the middle of the night stole out softly over the rooftops, and, silently descending, laid the child on the sheltered side of a heap of refuse near the little stream that flows by Háwikuh, in the valley below. Then, mourning as a mother will mourn for her offspring, she returned to her room and lay herself down, poor thing, to rest.

As daylight was breaking in the east, and the hills and the valleys were coming forth one after another from the shadows of night, a Deer with her two little brightly-speckled fawns descended from the hills to the south across the valley, with ears and eyes alert, and stopped at the stream to drink.

While drinking they were startled by an infant's cry, and, looking up, they saw dust and cotton-wool and other things flying about in the air, almost as if a little whirlwind were blowing on the site of the refuse-heap where the child had been laid. It was the child, who, waking and finding itself alone, hungry, and cold, was crying and throwing its little hands about. "Bless my delight!" cried the Deer to her fawns. I have this day found a waif, a child, and though it be human it shall be mine; for, see, my children, I love you so much that surely I could love another."

Thereupon she approached the little infant, and breathed her warm breath upon it and caressed it until it became quiet, and then after wrapping about it the cotton-wool, she gently lifted it on her broad horns, and, turning, carried it steadily away toward the south, followed on either side by her children, who kept crying out "Neh! neh!" in their delight.

The home of this old Deer and her little ones, where all her children had been born for years, was south of Háwikuh, in the valley that turns off among the ledges of rocks near the little spring called Póshaan. There, in the shelter of a clump of piñon and cedar trees, was a soft and warm retreat, winter and summer, and this was the lair of the Deer and her young.

The Deer was no less delighted than surprised next morning to find that the infant had grown apace, for she had suckled it with her own milk, and that before the declining of the sun it was already creeping about. And greater was her surprise and delight, as day succeeded day, to find that the child grew even more swiftly than grow the children of the Deer. Behold! on the evening of the fourth day it was running about and playing with its foster brother and sister. Nor was it slow of foot, even as compared with those little Deer.

Behold! yet greater cause for wonder, on the eighth day it was a youth fair to look upon-looking upon itself and seeing that it had no clothing, and wondering why it was not clothed, like its brother and sister, in soft warm hair with pretty spots upon it.

As time went on, this little foster-child of the Deer (it must always be remembered that it was the offspring of the Sun-father himself), in playing with his brother and sister, and in his runnings about, grew wondrously strong, and even swifter of foot than the Deer themselves, and learned the language of the Deer and all their ways.

When he had become perfected in all that a Deer should know, the Deer-mother led him forth into the wilds and made him acquainted with the great herd to which she belonged. They were exceedingly happy with this addition to their number; much they loved him, and so sagacious was the youth that he soon became the leader of the Deer of the Háwikuh country.

When these Deer and the Antelopes were out on the mesas ranging to and fro, there at their head ran the swift youth. The soles of his feet became as hard as the hoofs of the Deer, the skin of his person strong and dark, the hair of his head long and waving and as soft as the hair on the sides of the Deer themselves.

It chanced one morning, late that summer, that the uncle of the maiden who had cast away her child went out hunting, and he took his way southward past Póshaan, the lair of the Deer-mother and her foster-child. As he traversed the borders of the great mesas that lie beyond, he saw a vast herd of Deer gathered, as people gather in council. They were quiet and seemed to be listening intently to some one in their midst.

The hunter stole along carefully on hands and knees, twisting himself among the bushes until he came nearer; and what was his wonder when he beheld, in the midst of the Deer, a splendid youth, broad of shoulder, tall and strong of limb, sitting nude and graceful on the ground, and the old Deer and the young seemed to be paying attention to what he was saying.

The hunter rubbed his eyes and looked again; and again he looked, shading his eyes with his hands. Then he elevated himself to peer yet more closely, and the sharp eyes of the youth discovered him. With a shout he lifted himself to his feet and sped away like the wind, followed by the whole herd, their hoofs thundering, and soon they were all out of sight.

The hunter dropped his bow and stood there musing; then picking it up, he turned himself about and ran toward Háwikuh as fast as he could. When he arrived he related to the father of the girl what he had seen. The old priest summoned his hunters and warriors and bade the uncle repeat the story. Many there were who said: "You have seen an apparition, and of evil omen to your family, alas! alas!"

"No," said he, "I looked, and again I looked, and yet again, and again, and I avow to you that what I saw was as plain and as mortal as the Deer themselves."

Convinced at last, the council decided to form a grand hunt, and word was given from the housetops that on the fourth day from that day a hunt should be undertaken--that the southern mesa should be surrounded, and that the people should gather in from all sides and encompass the herd there, in order that this wonderful youth should not escape being seen, or possibly captured.

Now, when the Deer had gone to a safe distance they slackened their pace and called to their leader not to fear. And the old foster-mother of the youth for the first time related to him, as she had related to them long ago, that he was the child of mortals, telling how she had found him.

The youth sat with his head bowed, thinking of these things. Then he raised his head proudly, and said: "What though I be the child of mortals, they have not loved me: they have cast me from their midst, therefore will I be faithful to thee alone."

But the old Deer-mother said to him: "Hush, my child! Thou art but a mortal, and though thou might'st live on the roots of the trees and the bushes and plants that mature in autumn, yet surely in the winter time thou could'st not live, for my supply of milk will be withholden, and the fruits and the nuts will all be gone."

And the older members of that large herd gathered round and repeated what she had been saying. And they said: "We are aware that we shall be hunted now, as is the invariable custom when our herd has been discovered, on the fourth day from the day on which we were first seen. Amongst the people who come there will be, no doubt, those who will seek you; and you must not endeavor to escape.

Even we ourselves are accustomed to give up our lives to the brave hunters among this people, for many of them are sacred of thought, sacred of heart, and make due sacrifices unto us, that our lives in other form may be spared unceasingly."

A splendid Deer rose from the midst of the herd, and, coming forward, laid his cheek on the cheek of the boy, and said: "Yet we love you, but we must now part from you. And, in order that you may be like unto other mortals, only exceeding them, accompany me to the Land of the Souls of Men, where sit in council the Gods of the Sacred Dance and Drama, the Gods of the Spirit World."

To all this the youth, being convinced, agreed. And on that same day the Deer who had spoken set forward, the swift youth running by his side, toward the Lake of the Dead. On and on they sped, and as night was falling they came to the borders of that lake, and the lights were shining over its middle and the Gardens of the Sacred Dance. And the old Drama-woman and the old Drama-man were walking on its shores, back and forth, calling across to each other.

As the Deer neared the shore of the lake, he turned and said to his companion: "Step in boldly with me. Ladders of rushes will rise to receive you, and down underneath the waters into the great Halls of the Dead and of the Sacred Dance we will be borne gently and swiftly."

Then they stepped into the lake. Brighter and lighter it grew. Great ladders of rushes and flags lifted themselves from the water, and upon them the Deer and his companion were borne downward into halls of splendor, lighted by many lights and fires.

And in the largest chamber the gods were sitting in council silently. Páutiwa, the Sun-priest of the Sacred Drama (Kâkâ), Shúlawitsi (the God of Fire), with his torch of ever-living flame, and many others were there; and when the strangers arrived they greeted and were greeted, and were given a place in the light of the central fire.

And in through the doors of the west and the north and the east and the south filed long rows of sacred dancers, those who had passed through the Lake of the Dead, clad in cotton mantles, white as the daylight, finely embroidered, decked with many a treasure shell and turquoise stone. These performed their sacred rites, to the delight of the gods and the wonder of the Deer and his foster-brother.

And when the dancers had retired, Páutiwa, the Sun-priest of the Sacred Dance, arose, and said: "What would'st thou?"-though he knew full well beforehand. "What would'st thou, oh, Deer of the forest mesas, with thy companion, thy foster-brother; for not thinking of nothing would one visit the home of the Kâkâ."

Then the Deer lifted his head and told his story.

"It is well," said the gods.

"Appear, my faithful one," said Páutiwa to Shúlawitsi. And Shúlawitsi appeared and waved his flame around the youth, so that he became convinced of his mortal origin and of his dependence upon food prepared by fire. Then the gods who speak the speech of men gathered around and breathed upon the youth, and touched to his lips moisture from their own mouths, and touched the portals of his ears with oil from their own ears, and thus was the youth made acquainted with both the speech and the understanding of the speech of mortal man.

Then the gods called out, and there were brought before them fine garments of white cotton embroidered in many colors, rare necklaces of sacred shell with many turquoises and coral-like stones and shells strung in their midst, and all that the most beautifully clad of our ancients could have glorified their appearance with. Such things they brought forth, and, making them into a bundle, laid them at the feet of the youth.

Then they said: "Oh, youth, oh, brother and father, since thou art the child of the Sun, who is the father of us all, go forth with thy foster-brother to thy last meeting-place with him and with his people; and when on the day after the morrow hunters shall gather from around thy country, some of ye, oh, Deer," said he, turning to the Deer, "'yield thyselves up that ye may die as must thy kind ever continue to die, for the sake of this thy brother."

"I will lead them," simply replied the Deer.

"Thanks."

And Páutiwa continued: "Here full soon wilt thou be gathered in our midst, or with the winds and the mists of the air at night-time wilt sport, ever-living. Go ye forth, then, carrying this bundle, and, as ye best know how, prepare this our father and child for his reception among men. And, O son and father," continued the priest-god, turning to the youth, "Fear not! Happy wilt thou be in the days to come, and treasured among men.

Hence thy birth. Return with the Deer and do as thou art told to do. Thy uncle, leading his priest-youths, will be foremost in the hunt. He will pursue thee and thy foster-mother. Lead him far away; and when thou hast so led him, cease running and turn and wait, and peacefully go home whither he guides thee."

The sounds of the Sacred Dance came in from the outer apartments, and the youth and the Deer, taking their bundle, departed. More quickly than they had come they sped away; and on the morning when the hunters of Háwikuh were setting forth, the Deer gathered themselves in a vast herd on the southern mesa, and they circled about the youth and instructed him how to unloose the bundle he had brought.

Then closer and closer came the Deer to the youth and bade him stand in his nakedness, and they ran swiftly about him, breathing fierce, moist breaths until hot steam enveloped him and bathed him from head to foot, so that he was purified, and his skin was softened, and his hair hung down in a smooth yet waving mass at the back of his head.

Then the youth put on the costume, one article after another, he having seen them worn by the Gods of the Sacred Dance, and by the dancers; and into his hair at the back, under the band which he placed round his temples, he thrust the glowing feathers of the macaw which had been given him. Then, seeing that there was still one article left, --a little string of conical shells, --he asked what that was for; and the Deer told him to tie it about his knee.

The Deer gathered around him once more, and the old chief said: "Who among ye are willing to die?" And, as if it were a festive occasion to which they were going, many a fine Deer bounded forth, striving for the place of those who were to die, until a large number were gathered, fearless and ready. Then the Deer began to move.

Soon there was an alarm. In the north and the west and the south and the east there was cause for alarm. And the Deer began to scatter, and then to assemble and scatter again. At last the hunters with drawn bows came running in, and soon their arrows were flying in the midst of those who were devoted, and Deer after Deer fell, pierced to the heart or other vital part.

At last but few were left, --amongst them the kind old Deer-mother and her two children; and, taking the lead, the glorious youth, although encumbered by his new dress, sped forth with them. They ran and ran, the fleetest of the tribe of Háwikuh pursuing them; but all save the uncle and his brave sons were soon left far behind. The youth's foster-brother was soon slain, and the youth, growing angry, turned about; then bethinking himself of the words of the gods, he sped away again. So his foster-sister, too, was killed; but he kept on, his old mother alone running behind him.

At last the uncle and his sons overtook the old mother, and they merely caught her and turned her away, saying: "Faithful to the last she has been to this youth." Then they renewed the chase for the youth; and he at last, pretending weariness, faced about and stood like a stag at bay. As soon as they approached, he dropped his arms and lowered his head. Then he said: "Oh, my uncle" (for the gods had told who would find him) --" Oh, my uncle, what wouldst thou? Thou hast killed my brothers and sisters; what wouldst thou with me?

The old man stopped and gazed at the youth in wonder and admiration of his fine appearance and beautiful apparel. Then he said: "Why dost thou call me uncle?"

"Because, verily," replied the youth, "thou art my uncle, and thy niece, my maiden-mother, gave birth to me and cast me away upon a dust-heap; and then my noble Deer found me and nourished me and cherished me."

The uncle and his sons gazed still with wonder. Then they thought they saw in the youth's clear eyes and his soft, oval face a likeness to the mother, and they said: "Verily, this which he says is true." Then they turned about and took him by the hands gently and led him toward Háwikuh, while one of them sped forward to test the truth of his utterances.

When the messenger arrived at Háwikuh he took his way straight to the house of the priest, and told him what he had heard. The priest in anger summoned the maiden.

"Oh, my child," said he, "hast thou done this thing which we are told thou hast done?" And he related what he had been told.

"Nay, no such thing have I done," said she.

"Yea, but thou hast, oh, unnatural mother! And who was the father?" demanded the old priest with great severity.

Then the maiden, thinking of her Sun-lover, bowed her head in her lap and rocked herself to and fro, and cried sorely. And then she said: "Yea, it is true; so true that I feared thy Wrath, oh, my father! I feared thy shame, oh, my mother! and what could I do?" Then she told of her lover, the Sun, --with tears she told it, and she cried out: "Bring back my child that I may nurse him and love but him alone, and see him the father of children!"

By this time the hunters arrived, some bringing game, but others bringing in their midst this wondrous youth, on whom each man and maiden in Háwikuh gazed with delight and admiration.

They took him to the home of his priest-grandfather; and as though he knew the way he entered the apartment of his mother, and she, rising and opening wide her arms, threw herself on his breast and cried and cried. And he laid his hand on her head, and said: "Oh, mother, weep not, for I have come to thee, and I will cherish thee.

So was the foster-child of the Deer restored to his mother and his people.

Wondrously wise in the ways of the Deer and their language was he--so much so that, seeing them, he understood them. This youth made little ado of hunting, for he knew that he could pay those rites and attentions to the

Deer that were most acceptable, and made them glad of death at the hand of the hunter. And ere long, so great was his knowledge and success, and his preciousness in the eyes of the Master of Life, that by his will and his arm alone the tribe of Háwikuh was fed and was clad in buckskins.

A rare and beautiful maiden he married, and most happy was he with her.

It was his custom to go forth early in the morning, when the Deer came down to drink or stretch themselves and walk abroad and crop the grass; and, taking his bow and quiver of arrows, he would go to a distant mesa, and, calling the Deer around him, and following them as swiftly as they ran, he would strike them down in great numbers, and, returning, say to his people: "Go and bring in my game, giving me only parts of what I have slain and taking the rest yourselves."

So you can readily see how he and his people became the greatest people of Háwikuh. Nor is it marvelous that the sorcerers of that tribe should have grown envious of his prosperity, and sought to diminish it in many ways, wherein they failed.

At last one night the Master of Sorcerers in secret places raised his voice and cried "Weh-h-h-h! Weh-h-h-h-h-h!" And round about him presently gathered all the sorcerers of the place, and they entered into a deep cavern, large and lighted by green, glowing fires, and there, staring at each other, they devised means to destroy this splendid youth, the child of the Sun.

One of their number stood forth and said: "I will destroy him in his own vocation. He is a hunter, and the Coyote loves well to follow the hunter." His words were received with acclamation, and the youth who had offered himself sped forth in the night to prepare, by incantation and with his infernal appliances, a disguise for himself.

On the next morning, when the youth went forth to hunt, an old Coyote sneaked behind him after he reached the mesas, and, following stealthily, waited his throwing down of the Deer; and when the youth had called and killed a number of Deer and sat down to rest on a fallen tree, the Coyote sneaked into sight. The youth, looking at him, merely thought: "He seeks the blood of my slain Deer," and he went on with his prayers and sacrifices to the dead of the Deer. But soon, stiffening his limbs, the Coyote swiftly scudded across the open, and, with a puff from his mouth and nostrils like a sneeze toward the youth, threw himself against him and arose a man, --the same man who had offered his services in the council of the wizards--while the poor youth, falling over, ran away, a human being still in heart and mind, but in form a coyote.

Off to the southward he wandered, his tail dragging in the dust; and growing hungry he had naught to eat; and cold on the sides of the mesas he passed the night, and on the following morning wandered still, until at last, very hungry, he was fain even to nip the blades of grass and eat the berries of the juniper. Thus he became ill and worn; and one night as he was seeking a warm place to lay him down and die, he saw a little red light glowing from the top of a hillock. Toward this light he took his way, and when he came near he saw that it was shining up through the sky hole of someone's house. He peered over the edge and saw an old Badger with his grizzly wife, sitting before a fire, not in the form of a badger but in the form of a little man, his badger-skin hanging beside him. Then the youth raid to himself I will cast myself down into their house, thus showing them my miserable condition." And as he tried to step down the ladder, he fell, teng, on the floor before them.

The Badgers were disgusted. They grabbed the Coyote, and hauling him up the ladder, threw him into the plain, where, toonoo, he fell far away and swooned from loss of breath. When he recovered his thoughts he again turned toward the glowing skyhole, and, crawling feebly back, threw himself down into the room again. Again he was thrown out, but this time the Badger said: "It is marvelously strange that this Coyote, the miserable fellow, should insist on coming back, and coming back."

"I have heard," said the little old Badger-woman, "that our glorious beloved youth of Háwikuh was changed some time ago into a Coyote. It may be he. Let us see when he comes again if it be he. For the love of mercy, let us see!"

Ere long the youth again tried to clamber down the ladder, and fell with a thud on the floor before them. A long time he lay there senseless, but at last opened his eyes and looked about. The Badgers eagerly asked if he were the same who had been changed into a Coyote, or condemned to inhabit the form of one. The youth could only move his head in acquiescence.

Then the Badgers hastily gathered an emetic and set it to boil, and when ready they poured the fluid down the throat of the seeming Coyote, and tenderly held him and pitied him. Then they laid him before the fire to warm him. Then the old Badger, looking about in some of his burrows, found a sacred rock crystal, and heating it to glowing heat in the fire, he seared the palms of the youth's hands, the soles of his feet, and the crown of his head, repeating incantations as he performed this last operation, whereupon the skin burst and fell off, and the youth, haggard and lean, lay before them. They nourished him as best they could, and, when well recovered, sent him home to join his people again and render them happy. Clad in his own fine garments, happy of countenance and handsome as before, and, according to his regular custom, bearing a Deer on his back, returned the youth to his people, and there he lived most happily.

As I have said, this was in the days of the ancients, and it is because this youth lived so long with the Deer and became acquainted with their every way and their every word, and taught all that he knew to his children and to others whom he took into his friendship, that we have today a class of menthe Sacred Hunters of our tribe, --who surpassingly understand the ways and the language of the Deer.

Thus shortens my story.

Treat the earth well.
It was not given to you by your parents,
it was loaned to you by your children.
We do not inherit the Earth from our Ancestors,
we borrow it from our Children.

Ancient Indian Proverb

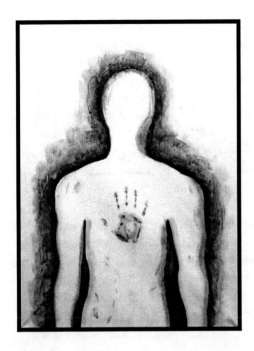

The Ice Man

A Cherokee Legend
Myths of the
Cherokee, James
Mooney, 1900

Once when the people were burning the woods in the fall the blaze set fire to a poplar tree, which continued to burn until the fire went down into the roots and burned a great hole in the ground.

It burned and burned, and the hole grew constantly larger, until the people became frightened and were afraid it would burn the whole world. They tried to put out the fire, but it had gone too deep, and they did not know what to do.

At last some one said there was a man living in a house of ice far in the north who could put out the fire, so messengers were sent, and after traveling a long distance they came to the ice house and found the Ice Man at home. He was a little fellow with long hair hanging down to the ground in two plaits.

The messengers told him their errand and he at once said, "O yes, I can help you," and began to unplait his hair. When it was all unbraided he took it up in one band and struck it once across his other hand, and the messengers felt a wind blow against their cheeks. A second time he struck his hair across his hand, and a light rain began to fall.

The third time he struck his hair across his open hand there was sleet mixed with the raindrops, and when he struck the fourth time great hailstones fell upon the ground, as if they had come out from the ends of his hair. "Go back now," said the lee Man, "and I shall be there to-morrow." So the messengers returned to their people, whom they found still gathered helplessly about the great burning pit.

The next-day while they were all watching about the fire there came a wind from the north, and they were afraid, for they knew that it came from the lee Man. But the wind only made the fire blaze up higher. Then a light rain began to fall, but the drops seemed only to make the fire hotter. Then the shower turned to a heavy rain, with sleet and hail that killed the blaze and made clouds of smoke and steam rise from the red coals.

The people fled to their homes for shelter, and the storm rose to a whirlwind that drove the rain into every burning crevice and piled great hailstones over the embers, until the fire was dead and even the smoke ceased.

When at last it was all over and the people returned they found a lake where the burning pit had been, and from below the water came a sound as of embers still crackling.

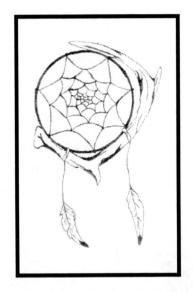

The Return of Ice Man

A Cherokee Legend
Myths of the Cherokee,
James Mooney, 1900

When the first man was created and a mate was given to him, they lived together very happily for a time, but then began to quarrel.

At last the woman left her husband and started off toward the Sun Land (Nundagunyi) in the east.

The man followed alone and grieving, but the woman kept on steadily ahead and never looked behind, until "Unelanunhi," the great Apportioner (The Sun), took pity on him and asked him if he was still angry with his wife.

He said he was not, and "Unelanunhi" then asked him if he would like to have her back again, to which he eagerly answered yes.

So "Unelanunhi" caused a patch of the finest ripe huckleberries to spring up along the path in front of the woman, but she passed by without paying any attention to them. Farther on he put a clump of blackberries, but these also she refused to notice. Other fruits, one, two, and three, and then some trees covered with beautiful red service berries, were placed beside the path to tempt her, but she went on until suddenly she saw in front a patch of large ripe strawberries, the first ever known.

She stooped to gather a few to eat, and as she picked them she chanced to turn her face to the west, and at once the memory of her husband came back to her and she found herself unable to go on.

She sat down, but the longer she waited the stronger became her desire for her husband, and at last she gathered a bunch of the finest berries and started back along the path to give them to him. He met her kindly and they went home together.

Native American Ten Commandments

Treat the Earth and all that dwell therein with respect
Remain close to the Great Spirit
Show great respect for your fellow beings
Work together for the benefit of all Mankind
Give assistance and kindness wherever needed
Do what you know to be right
Look after the well-being of Mind and Body
Dedicate a share of your efforts to the greater Good
Be truthful and honest at all times
Take full responsibility for your actions

The First War

A Jicarilla Apache Legend
Pliny E. Goddard, Anthropological Papers of the American Museum of Natural History, Vol. VIII

Raven divined to see whether people would die. First, he threw in the stick over which the skins are stretched in dressing.

When this came to the top of the water he tried again by throwing the stone muller. It did not come to the surface and the people began to die.

The people moved away in four directions but they could not sleep. The old couple of the lower world to whom they came back gave them four lice, two of which were placed in their hair, and two in their clothes. When they lay down they were all very sleepy. It was the biting of the lice that made them sleep.

Some of the people occupied the country near the head of the Arkansas River; others, were living along the Sangro de Cristo Range; and the remainder on the west side of the Rio Grande. There were two chiefs of those on the east side of the river named, Indayedittsitdn, and Indakadigadn.

The first named chief made a corral and gave a feast to which he invited all the people. Indakadigadn, alone, of all the people, refused to attend. After being repeatedly called by name, he finally came, holding an arrow in place on his stretched bow, saying, "Why did you call my name?"

"I did not call it for any particular purpose," the other replied. "I thought you called it for some reason," said the first, from whom the people were going away, because he was making motions as if to shoot. He shot an arrow to the feathers through Indayedittsitdn's arm and then went home.

The wounded chief sent word to the one who had shot him asking him to come quickly and take the arrow out. When he refused, he sent to him again, saving "Hurry, come and take the arrow out."

Neither this, nor a third message to the same effect, had any result. The fourth time he instructed the messenger to say, "Do not be afraid, come to me, and bring some medicine." Then Indakadigadn quickly took up his medicine bag, looked inside, and selected the required herb. When he came to the wounded man he found the arm badly swollen. "My grandchild, I did not intend to shoot you." He then cut into the outside of the arm, took out the arrow, and applied the medicine. "The swelling will be gone in four days," he told him. He was well in four days and became the grandson of the chief who had shot him.

Having moved the camp to the east side of the river, Indakadigadn, brought together five hundred men and started away to fight with the enemy. He took along ten horses for his own use in battle. When they came to the enemy and were surrounded by them, the chief said, "Wait until to-morrow and you will have some fun. Keep away from me."

The next morning, the chief said, "Now, we are ready."
There were many arrows ready for his use. He selected four
men, who, remaining out of the battle, should carry home
the report of the outcome.

"Who is chief?" asked one of the enemy.

"I am the only chief," replied Indakadigadn.

"Who is your chief?" he asked of the enemy. There were
four chiefs of the enemy. Indakadigadn rode his horse
toward the enemy and commenced the fighting. A number
of men were killed on both sides. When the chief's horse
was killed under him, he jumped on another and continued
fighting.

He continued to do this as his people decreased in numbers
until five horses had been killed under him. When he had
mounted the sixth horse and his people had all been killed
the enemy pulled him to the ground and killed him with a
knife.

The four men who had been selected for the purpose went
back to their country and reported, "Our people are all
dead." When Indayedittsitdn had received the message he
cut off his hair saying, "My grandson has been killed, I will
mourn for him properly."

Marriage of the North and the South

A Cherokee Legend
Mooney, Report of
the Bureau of
American Ethnology,
xix, 32-2, No. 70

The North went
traveling, and after
going far and
meeting many
different tribes he
finally fell in love with the daughter of the South and
wanted to marry her.

The girl was willing, but her parents objected and said,
"Ever since you came, the weather has been cold, and if
you stay here we may all freeze to death."

The North pleaded hard, and said that if they would let him
have their daughter he would take her back to his own
country, so at last they consented. They were married and
he took his bride to his own country, and when she arrived
there she found the people all living in ice houses.

The next day, when the sun rose, the houses began to leak,
and as it climbed higher they began to melt, and it grew
warmer and warmer, until finally the people came to the
young husband and told him he must send his wife home
again, or the weather would get so warm that the whole
settlement would be melted.

He loved his wife and so held out as long as he could, but as the sun grew hotter the people were more urgent, and at last he had to send her home to her parents.

The people said that as she had been born in the South, and nourished all her life upon food that grew in the same climate, her whole nature was warm and unfit for the North.

"The idea of full dress for preparation for a battle comes not from a belief that it will add to the fighting ability. The preparation is for death, in case that should be the result of conflict. Every Indian wants to look his best when he goes to meet the great Spirit, so the dressing up is done whether in imminent danger is an oncoming battle or a sickness or injury at times of peace."

Wooden Leg (late 19th century) Cheyenne

The Quill-Work Girl and Her Seven Brothers

A Cheyenne Legend

Hundreds of years ago there was a girl who was very good at quill work, so good that she was the best among all the tribes everywhere. Her designs were radiant with color, and she could decorate anything -- clothing, pouches, quivers, even tipi's.

One day this girl sat down in her parents' lodge and began to make a man's outfit of white buckskin -- war shirt, leggings, moccasins, gauntlets, everything. It took her weeks to embroider them with exquisite quill work and fringes of buffalo hair marvelous to look at. Though her mother said nothing, she wondered. The girl had no brothers, nor was a young man courting her, so why was she making a man's outfit?

As if life wasn't strange enough, no sooner had she finished the first outfit than she began working on a second, then on a third. She worked all year until she had made and decorated seven complete sets of men's clothes, the last a very small one. The mother just watched and kept wondering. At last after the girl had finished the seventh outfit, she spoke to her mother. "Someplace, many days' walk from here, lives seven brothers," she said. "Someday all the world will admire them. Since I am an only child, I want to take them for my brothers, and these clothes are for them."

"It is well, my daughter," her mother said. "I will go with you."

"This is too far for you to walk," said the girl.

"Then I will go part of the way," said her mother.

They loaded their strongest dogs with the seven bundles and set off toward the north. "You seem to know the way," said the mother.

"Yes, I don't know why, but I do," answered the daughter.

"And you seem to know all about these seven young men and what makes them stand out from ordinary humans."

"I know about them," said the girl, "though I don't know how."

Thus they walked, the girl seeming sure of herself. At last the mother said, "This is as far as I can go." They divided the dogs, the girl keeping two for her journey, and took leave of each other. Then the mother headed south back to her village and her husband, while her daughter continued walking into the north.

At last the daughter came to a lone, painted, and very large tipi which stood near a wide stream. The stream was shallow and she waded across it, calling: "It is I, the young-girl-looking-for-brothers, bringing gifts."

At that a small boy about ten years old came out of the tipi. "I am the youngest of seven brothers," he told the girl. "The others are out hunting buffalo, but they'll come back after a while. I have been expecting you. But you'll be a surprise to my brothers, because they don't have my special gifts of `No Touch'."

"What is the gift of no touch?" asked the girl.

"Sometime you'll find out. Well, come into the tipi."

The girl gave the boy the smallest outfit, which fitted him perfectly and delighted him with its beautiful quill work.

"I shall take you all for my brothers," the girl told him.

"And I am glad to have you for a sister," answered the boy.

The girl took all the other bundles off her two dogs' backs and told them to go back to her parents, and at once the dogs began trotting south.

Inside the tipi were seven beds of willow sticks and sage. The girl unpacked her bundles and put a war shirt, a pair of leggings, a pair of moccasins, and a pair of gauntlets upon each of the older brothers' beds. Then she gathered wood and built a fire. From her packs she took dried meat, choke cherries, and kidney fat, and cooked a meal for eight.

Toward evening just as the meal was ready, the six older brothers appeared laden with buffalo meat. The little boy ran outside the lodge and capered, kicking his heels and jumping up and down, showing off his quilled buckskin outfit.

"Where did you get these fine clothes?" the brothers asked.

"We have a new sister," said the child. "She's waiting inside, and she has clothes for you too. She does the most wonderful quill work in the world. And she's beautiful herself!"

The brothers greeted the girl joyfully. They were struck with wonder at the white buckskin outfits she had brought as gifts for them. They were as glad to have a sister to care for as she was to have brothers to cook and make clothes for. Thus they lived happily.

One day after the older brothers had gone out to hunt, a light-colored buffalo- calf appeared at the tipi and scratched and knocked with his hoof against the entrance flap. The boy came out and asked it what it wanted.

"I am sent by the buffalo nation," said the calf. "We have heard of your beautiful sister, and we want her for our own."

"You can't have her," answered the boy. "Go away."

"Oh well, then somebody bigger than I will come," said the calf and ran off jumping and kicking its heels.

The next day when the boy and the sister were alone again, a young heifer arrived, lowing and snorting, rattling the entrance flap of the tipi.

Once more the child came out to ask what she wanted.

"I am sent by the buffalo nation," said the heifer. "We want your beautiful sister for ourselves."

"You can't have her," said the boy. "Go away!"

"Then somebody bigger than I will come," said the heifer, galloping off like the calf before her.

On the third day a large buffalo cow, grunting loudly, appeared at the lodge. The boy came out and asked, "Big buffalo cow, what do you want?"

"I am sent by the buffalo nation," said the cow. "I have come to take your beautiful sister. We want her."

"You can't have her," said the boy. "Go away!"

"Somebody very big will come after me," said the buffalo cow, "and he won't come alone. He'll kill you if you don't give him your sister." With these words the cow trotted off.

On the fourth day the older brothers stayed home to protect the girl. The earth began to tremble a little, then to rock and heave. At last appeared the most gigantic buffalo bull in the world, much larger than any you see now. Behind him came the whole buffalo nation, making the earth shudder. Pawing the ground, the huge bull snorted and bellowed like thunder. The six older brothers, peering out through the entrance hole, were very much afraid, but the little boy stepped boldly outside. "Big, oversized buffalo bull, what do you want from us?" he asked.

"I want your sister," said the giant buffalo bull. "If you won't give her to me, I'll kill you all."

The boy called for his sister and older brothers to come out. Terrified, they did so.

"I'll take her now," growled the huge bull.

"No," said the boy, "she doesn't want to be taken. You can't have her. Go away!"

"In that case I'll kill you now," roared the giant bull. "I'm coming!"

"Quick, brother, use your special medicine!" the six older brothers cried to the youngest.

"I am using it," said he. "Now all of you, catch hold of the branches of this tree. Hurry!" He pointed to a tree growing by the tipi. The girl and the six brothers jumped up into its branches. The boy took his bow and swiftly shot an arrow into the tree's trunk, then clasped the trunk tightly himself. At once the tree started to grow, shooting up into the sky in no time at all. It all happened much, much quicker than it can be told.

The brothers and the girl were lifted up in the tree branches, out of reach of the buffalo. They watched the herd of angry animals grunting and snorting, milling around the tree far below.

"I'll chop the tree down with my horns!" roared the giant buffalo. He charged the tree, which shook like a willow and swayed back and forth. Trying not to fall off, the girl and the brothers clutched the branches. The big bull had gouged a large piece of wood from the trunk.

The little boy said, "I'd better use one more arrow." He shot another arrow high into the treetop, and again the tree grew, shooting up another thousand feet or so, while the seven brothers and the girl rose with it.

The giant buffalo bull made his second charge. Again his horns stabbed into the tree and splintered wood far and wide. The gash in the trunk had become larger.

The boy said, "I must shoot another arrow." He did, hitting the treetop again, and quick as a flash the tree rose another thousand feet.

A third time the bull charged, rocking the tree, making it sway from side to side so that the brothers and the girl almost tumbled out of their branches. They cried to the boy to save them. The child shot a fourth arrow into the tree, which rose again so that the seven young men and the girl disappeared into the clouds. The gash in the tree trunk had become dangerously large.

"When that bull charges again, he will shatter this tree," said the girl. "Little brother, help us!"

Just as the bull charged for the fourth time, the child let loose a single arrow he had left, and the tree rose above the clouds.

"Quick, step out right on the clouds. Hurry!" cried the little boy. "Don't be afraid!"

The bull's head hit the tree trunk with a fearful impact. His horns cut the trunk in two, but just as the tree slowly began to topple, the seven brothers and the girl stepped off its branches and into the sky.

There the eight of them stood. "Little brother, what will become of us now? We can never return to earth; we're up too high. What shall we do?"

"Don't grieve," said the little boy, "I'll turn us into stars."

At once the seven brothers and the girl were bathed in radiant light. They formed themselves into what the white men call the Big Dipper. You can see them there now. The brightest star is the beautiful girl, who is filling the sky with glimmering quill work, and the star twinkling at the very end of the Dipper's handle is the little boy. Can you see him?

May the stars carry your sadness away,
May the flowers fill your heart with beauty,
May hope forever wipe away your tears,
And, above all, may silence make you strong.

Chief Dan George

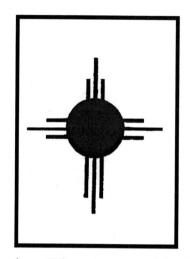

The Sun Tests His Son-in-law

A Bella Coola Legend
Boas, Jesup North Pacific
Expedition, i, 73

In a place on Bella Coola River, there used to be a salmon-weir. A chief and his wife lived at this place. One day the wife was cutting salmon on the bank of the river. When she opened the last salmon, she found a small boy in it.

She took him out and washed him in the river. She placed him near by, entered the house, and said to the people, "Come and see what I have found in my salmon!" She had a child in her house, which was still in the cradle.

The little boy whom she had found was half as long as her fore-arm. She carried him into the house, and the people advised her to take good care of him. She nursed him with her own baby.

When the people were talking in the house, the baby looked around as though he understood what they were saying. On the following day the people were surprised to see how much he had grown, and in a few days he was as tall as any ordinary child. Her own baby also grew up with marvelous rapidity. She gave each of them one breast. After a few days they were able to walk and to talk.

The two young men were passing by the houses, and looked into the doorways. There was a house in the center of this town; there they saw a beautiful girl sitting in the middle of the house. Her hair was red, and reached down to the floor. She was very white. Her eyes were large, and as clear as rock crystal. The boy fell in love with the girl. They went on, but his thoughts were with her.

The Salmon boy said, "I am going to enter this house. You must watch closely what I do, and imitate me. The Door of this house tries to bite every one who enters." The Door opened, and the Salmon jumped into the house. Then the Door snapped, but missed him. When it opened again, the boy jumped into the house. They found a number of people inside, who invited them to sit down. They spread food before them, but the boy did not like their food. It had a very strong smell, and looked rather curious. It consisted of algae that grow on logs that lie in the river.

When the boy did not touch it, one of the men said to him, "Maybe you want to eat those two children. Take them down to the river and throw them into the water, but do not look."

The two children arose, and he took them down to the river. Then he threw them into the water without looking at them. At the place where he had thrown them down, he found a male and a female Salmon. He took them up to the house and roasted them.

The people told him to preserve the intestines and the bones carefully. After he had eaten, one of the men told him to carry the intestines and the bones to the same place where he had thrown the children into the water. He carried them in his hands, and threw them into the river without looking. When he entered the house, he heard the children following him. The girl was covering one of her eyes with her hands.

The boy was limping, because he had lost one of his bones. Then the people looked at the place where the boy had been sitting, and they found the eye, and a bone from the head of the male salmon. They ordered the boy to throw these into the water. He took the children and the eye and the bone, and threw them into the river. Then the children were hale and well.

After a while the youth said to his Salmon brother, "I wish to go to the other house where I saw the beautiful girl." They went there, and he said to his Salmon brother, "Let us enter. I should like to see her face well."

They went in. Then the man arose, and spread a caribou blanket for them to sit on, and the people gave them food. Then he whispered to his brother, "Tell the girl I want to marry her." The Salmon boy told the girl, who smiled, and said, "He must not marry me. Whoever marries me must die. I like him, and I do not wish to kill him; but if he wishes to die, let him marry me.

The woman was the Salmon-berry Bird. After one day she gave birth to a boy, and on the following day she gave birth to a girl. She was the daughter of the Spring Salmon.

After a while the girl's father said, "Let us launch our canoe, and let us carry the young man back to his own people." He sent a messenger to call all the people of the village; and they all made themselves ready, and early the next morning they started in their canoes. The young man went in the canoe of the Spring Salmon, which was the fastest.

The canoe of the Sock-eye Salmon came next. The people in the canoe of the Calico Salmon were laughing all the time. They went up the river; and a short distance below the village of the young man's father they landed, and made fast their canoes. Then they sent two messengers up the river to see if the people had finished their salmon-weir.

Soon they returned with information that the weir had been finished. Then they sent the young man and his wife, and they gave them a great many presents for the young man's father.

The watchman who was stationed at the salmon-weir saw two beautiful salmon entering the trap. They were actually the canoes of the salmon; but they looked to him like two salmon. Then the watchman put the traps down over the weir, and he saw a great many fish entering them. He raised the trap when it was full, and took the fish out.

The young man thought, "I wish he would treat me and my wife carefully", and his wish came true. The man broke the heads of the other salmon, but he saved the young man and his wife. Then he carried the fish up to the house, and hung them over a pole.

During the night the young man and his wife resumed their human shape. The youth entered his father's house. His head was covered with eagle-down. He said to his father, "I am the fish whom you caught yesterday. Do you remember the time when you lost me? I have lived in the country of the Salmon. The Salmon accompanied me here. They are staying a little farther down the river. It pleases the Salmon to see the people eating fish." And, turning to his mother, he continued, "You must be careful when cutting Salmon.

Never break any of their bones, but preserve them, and throw them into the water." The two children of the young man had also entered into the salmon-trap. He put some leaves on the ground, placed red and white cedar-bark over them, and covered them with eagle-down, and he told his mother to place the Salmon upon these.

As soon as he had given these instructions, the Salmon began to come up the river. They crossed the weir and entered the traps. They went up the river as far as Stuick, and the people dried the Salmon according to his instructions. They threw the bones into the water, and the Salmon returned to life, and went back to their own country, leaving their meat behind.

The Cohoes Salmon had the slowest canoe, and therefore he was the last to reach the villages. He gave many presents to the Indians. He gave them many-colored leaves, and thus caused the leaves of the trees to change color in the autumn.

Now all the Salmon had returned. The Salmon-berry Bird and her children had returned with them. Then the young man made up his mind to build a small hut, from which he intended to catch eagles. He used a long pole, to which a noose was attached. The eagles were baited by means of Salmon. He spread a mat in his little house, and when he had caught an eagle he pulled out its down.

He accumulated a vast amount of down. Then he went back to his house and asked his younger brother to accompany him. When they came to the hut which he had used for catching eagles, he gave the boy a small staff. Then he said to him, "Do not be sorry when I leave you. I am going to visit the Sun. I am not going to stay away a long time. I staid long in the country of the Salmon, but I shall not stay long in heaven.

I am going to lie down on this mat. Cover me with this down, and then begin to beat time with your staff. You will

see a large feather flying upward, then stop." The boy
obeyed, and everything happened as he had said.

The boy saw the feather flying in wide circles. When it
reached a great height, it began to soar in large circles, and
finally disappeared in the sky. Then the boy cried, and went
back to his mother. The young man who had ascended to
heaven found there a large house. It was the House of
Myths. There he resumed his human shape, and peeped in
at the door. Inside he saw a number of people who were
turning their faces toward the wall. They were sitting on a
low platform in the rear of the house. In the right-hand
corner of the house he saw a large fire, and women sitting
around it.

He leaned forward and looked into the house. An old
woman discovered him, and beckoned him to come to her.
He stepped up to her, and she warned him by signs not to
go to the rear of the house. She said, "Be careful!

The men in the rear of the house intend to harm you." She
opened a small box, and gave him the bladder of a
mountain-goat, which contained the cold wind. She told
him to open the bladder if they should attempt to harm him.
She said that if he opened it, no fire could burn him. She
told him that the men were going to place him near the fire,
in order to burn him; that one of them would wipe his face,
then fire would come forth from the floor, scorching
everything.

The old woman told him everything that the people were
going to do. Now the man in the rear of the house turned
round. He was the Sun himself. He was going to try the
strength of the visitor. When he saw the young man, he said
to the old woman, "Did anybody come to visit you? Let the
young man come up to me. I wish him to sit down near

me." The young man stepped up to the Sun, and as soon as he had sat down, the Sun wiped his face and looked at the young man (he had turned his face while he was wiping it).

Then the young man felt very hot. He tied his blanket tightly round his body, and opened the bladder which the woman had given him. Then the cold wind that blows down the mountains in the winter was liberated, and he felt cool and comfortable. The Sun had not been able to do him any harm. The old man did not say anything, but looked at his visitor.

After a while he said, "I wish to show you a little underground house that stands behind this house." They both rose and went outside. The small house had no door. Access was had to it by an opening in the center of the roof, through which a ladder led down to the floor. Not a breath of air entered this house. It was made of stone. When they had entered, the Sun made a small fire in the middle of the house; then he climbed up the ladder and closed the door, leaving his visitor inside. The Sun pulled up the ladder, in order to make escape impossible. Then the house began to grow very hot.

When the boy felt that he could not stand the heat any longer, he opened the bladder, and the cold wind came out; snow began to fall on the fire, which was extinguished; icicles began to form on the roof, and it was cool and comfortable inside. After a while the Sun said to his four daughters, "Go to the little underground house that stands behind our house, and sweep it," meaning that they were to remove the remains of the young man whom he believed to be burned.

They obeyed at once, each being eager to be the first to enter. When they opened the house, they were much surprised to find icicles hanging down from the roof.

When they were climbing down the ladder, the youth arose and scratched them. The youngest girl was the last to step down. The girls cried when the youth touched them, and ran away. The Sun heard their screams, and asked the reason.

He was much surprised and annoyed to hear that the young man was still alive. Then he devised another way of killing his visitor. He told his daughters to call him into his house. They went, and the young man re-entered the House of Myths. In the evening he lay down to sleep.

Then the Sun said to his daughters, "Early tomorrow morning climb the mountain behind our house. I shall tell the boy to follow you." The girls started while the visitor was still asleep. The girls climbed up to a small meadow which was near a precipice. They had taken the form of mountain-goats. When the Sun saw his daughters on the meadow, he called to his visitor, saying, "See those mountain-goats!" The young man arose when he saw the mountain-goats.

He wished to kill them. The Sun advised him to walk up the right-hand side of the mountain, saying that the left-hand side was dangerous. The young man carried his bow and arrow.

The Sun said, "Do not use your own arrows! Mine are much better." Then they exchanged arrows, the Sun giving him four arrows of his own. The points of these arrows were made of coal.

Now the young man began to climb the mountain. When he came up to the goats, he took one of the arrows, aimed it, and shot. It struck the animals, but fell down without killing it. The same happened with the other arrows. When he had spent all his arrows, they rushed up to him from the four sides, intending to kill him. His only way of escape was in the direction of the precipice. They rushed up to him, and pushed him down the steep mountain.

He fell headlong, but when he was halfway down he transformed himself into a ball of bird's down. He alighted gently on a place covered with many stones. There he resumed the shape of a man, arose, and ran into the house of the Sun to get his own arrows. He took them, climbed the mountain again, and found the mountain-goats on the same meadow. He shot them and killed them, and threw them down the precipice; then he returned. He found the goats at the foot of the precipice, and cut off their feet. He took them home.

He found the Sun sitting in front of the house. He offered him the feet, saying, "Count them, and see how many I have killed." The Sun counted them and now he knew that all his children were dead. Then he cried, "You killed my children!"

Then the youth took the bodies of the goats, fitted the feet on, and threw the bodies into a little river that was running past the place where they had fallen down. Thus they were restored to life.

He had learned this art in the country of the Salmon. Then he said to the girls, "Now run to see your father! He is wailing for you." They gave him a new name, saying, "He has restored us to life." The boy followed them. Then the Sun said, when he entered, "You shall marry my two eldest daughters."

On the next morning the people arose. Then the Sun said to them, "What shall I do to my son-in-law?" He called him, and said, "Let us raise the trap of my salmon-weir." They went up to the river in the Sun's canoe. The water of the river was boiling. The youth was in the bow of the canoe, while the Sun was steering. He caused the canoe to rock, intending to throw the young man into the water. The water formed a small cascade, running down over the weir. He told the young man to walk over the top of the weir in order to reach the trap.

He did so, walking over the top beam of the weir. When he reached the baskets, the beam fell over, and he himself fell into the water. The Sun saw him rise twice in the whirlpool just below the weir. When he did not see him rise again, he turned his canoe, and thought, "Now the boy has certainly gone to Nuskyakek." The Sun returned to his house, and said to his daughters, "I lost my son-in-law in the river. I was not able to find him." Then his daughters were very sad.

When the boy disappeared in the water, he was carried to Nuskyakek; and he resumed the shape of a salmon while in the water, and as soon as he landed he resumed human shape and returned to his wife. The Sun saw him coming, and was much surprised. In the evening they went to sleep. On the following morning the Sun thought, "How can I kill my son-in-law?" After a while he said to him, " Arise! We will go and split wood for fuel."

He took his tools. They launched their canoe, and went down the river to the sea. When they reached there, it was perfectly calm. There were many snags embedded in the mud in the mouth of the river, some of which were only half submerged. They selected one of these snags a long distance from the shore, and began to split it. Then the Sun

intentionally dropped his hammer into the water, and
thought at the same time, "Do not fall straight down, but
fall sideways, so that he will have much difficulty in
finding you." Then he sat down in his canoe, and said, "Oh!
I lost my old hammer. I had it at the time when the Sun was
created." He looked down into the water, and did not say a
word.

After a while he said to the young man, "Do you know how
to dive? Can you get my hammer? The water is not very
deep here."

The young man did not reply. Then the Sun continued, "I
will not go back without my hammer." Then the boy said,
"I know how to dive. If you so wish, I will try to get it."

The Sun promised to give him supernatural power if he was
able to bring the hammer back. The youth jumped into the
water, and then the Sun ordered the sea to rise, and he
called the cold wind to make the water freeze. It grew so
cold that a sheet of ice a fathom thick was formed at once
on top of the sea.

"Now," he thought, "I certainly have killed you!" He left
his canoe frozen up in the ice, and went home. He said to
his daughters, "I have lost my son-in-law. He drifted away
when the cold winds began to blow down the mountains. I
have also lost my little hammer."

But when he mentioned his hammer, his daughters knew at
once what had happened. The young man found the
hammer, and after he had obtained it he was going to return
to the canoe, but he struck his head against the ice, and was
unable to get out. He tried everywhere to find a crack.
Finally, he found a very narrow one. He transformed
himself into a fish, and came out of the crack. He jumped

about on the ice in the form of a fish, and finally resumed his own shape.

He went back to the Sun's house, carrying the hammer. The Sun was sitting in front of the fire, his knees drawn up, and his legs apart. His eyes were closed, and he was warming himself. The young man took his hammer and threw it right against his stomach, saying, "Now take better care of your treasures."

The young man scolded the Sun, saying, "Now stop trying to kill me. If you try again, I shall kill you. Do you think I am an ordinary man? You cannot conquer me." The Sun did not reply.

In the evening he said to his son-in-law, "I hear a bird singing, which I should like very much to have."

The young man asked, "What bird is it?"

The Sun replied, "I do not know it. Watch it early to-morrow morning." The young man resolved to catch the bird. Very early in the morning he arose, then he heard the bird singing outside. He knew at once that it was the ptarmigan. He left the house, and thought, "I wish you would come down!" Then the bird came down, and when it was quite near by he shot it. He hit one of its wings, intending to catch it alive.

He waited for the Sun to arise. The bird understood what the young man said, who thus spoke: "The chief here wishes to see you. Do not be afraid, I am not going to kill you. The chief has often tried to kill me, but he has been unable to do so.

You do not need to be afraid." The young man continued, "When it is dark I shall tell the Sun to ask you to sit near

him, and when he is asleep I want you to peck out his
eyes." When the Sun arose, the youth went into the house
carrying the bird, saying, "I have caught the bird; now I
hope you will treat it kindly. It will awaken us when it is
time to arise. When you lie down, let it sit down near you,
then it will call you in the morning."

In the evening the Sun asked the bird to sit down next to his
face. When he was asleep, the bird pecked out his eyes
without his knowing it. Early in the morning he heard the
bird singing. He was going to open his eyes, but he was not
able to do so. Then he called his son, saying, "The bird has
blinded me."

The young man jumped up and went to his father-in-law,
and said, "Why did you wish for the bird? Do you think it
is good? It is a bad bird. It has pecked out your eyes." He
took the bird and carried it outside, and thanked it for
having done as it was bidden. Then the bird flew away.

When it was time for the Sun to start on his daily course, he
said, "I am afraid I might fall, because I cannot see my
way." For four days he stayed in his house. He did not eat;
he was very sad. Then his son-in-law made up his mind to
cure him. He did not do so before, because he wanted to
punish him for his badness.

He took some water, and said to his father-in-law, "I will
try to restore your eyesight." He threw the water upon his
eyes, and at once his eyes were healed and well.

He said, "Now you can see what power I have. The water
with which I have washed my face has the power to heal
diseases. While I was in the country of the Salmon, I
bathed in the water in which the old Salmon bathed, in
order to regain youth, therefore the water in which I wash

makes everything young and well."

From this time on, the Sun did not try to do any harm to the young man.

Finally, he wished to return to his father's village. He left the house, and jumped down through the hole in heaven. His wife saw him being transformed into a ball of eagle-down, which floated down gently. Then her father told her to climb as quickly as she could down his eyelashes. She did so, and reached the ground at the same time as her husband. He met his younger brother, who did not recognize him. He had been in heaven for one year.

"We, the great mass of the people think only of the love we have for our land, we do love the land where we were brought up. We will never let our hold to this land go, to let it go it will be like throwing away (our) mother that gave (us) birth.".

Letter from Aitooweyah to John Ross, Principal Chief of the Cherokee.

Untsaiyi', The Gambler

A Cherokee Legend
Myths of the Cherokee, James Mooney, 1900

Thunder lives in the west, or a little to the south of west, near the place where the sun goes down behind the water. In the old times he sometimes made a journey to the east, and once after he had come back from one of these journeys a child was born in the east who, the people said, was his son.

As the boy grew up it was found that he had scrofula sores all over his body, so one day his mother said to him, "Your father, Thunder, is a great doctor. He lives far in the west, but if you can find him he can cure you."

So the boy set out to find his father and be cured. He traveled long toward the west, asking of every one he met where Thunder lived, until at last they began to tell him that it was only a little way ahead.

He went on and came to Ûñ'tiguhï', on Tennessee, where lived Ûñtsaiyï' "Brass." Now a Ûñtsaiyï' was a great gambler, and made his living that way. It was he who invented the gatayûstï game that we play with a stone wheel and a stick.

He lived on the south side of the river, and everybody who came that way he challenged to play against him. The large flat rock, with the lines and grooves where they used to roll the wheel, is still there, with the wheels themselves and the stick turned to stone. He won almost every time, because he was so tricky, so that he had his house filled with all kinds of fine things.

Sometimes he would lose, and then he would bet all that he had, even to his own life, but the winner got nothing for his trouble, for Ûñtsaiyï' knew how to take on different shapes, so that he always got away.

As soon as Ûñtsaiyï' saw him he asked him to stop and play a while, but the boy said he was looking for his father, Thunder, and had no time to wait. "Well," said Ûñtsaiyï', "he lives in the next house; you can hear him grumbling over there all the time"--he meant the Thunder--"so we may as well have a game or two before you go on."

The boy said he had nothing to bet. "That's all right," said the gambler, "we'll play for your pretty spots." He said this to make the boy angry so that he would play, but still the boy said he must go first and find his father, and would come back afterwards.

He went on, and soon the news came to Thunder that a boy was looking for him who claimed to be his son. Said Thunder, "I have traveled in many lands and have many children. Bring him here and we shall soon know."

So they brought in the boy, and Thunder showed him a seat and told him to sit down. Under the blanket on the seat were long, sharp thorns of the honey locust, with the points all sticking up, but when the boy sat down they did not hurt him, and then Thunder knew that it was his son. He asked the boy why he had come. "I have sores all over my body, and my mother told me you were my father and a great doctor, and if I came here you would cure me. "Yes," said his father, "I am a great doctor, and I'll soon fix you."

There was a large pot in the corner and he told his wife to fill it with water and put it over the fire. When it was boiling, he put in some roots, then took the boy and put him in with them. He let it boil a long time until one would have thought that the flesh was boiled from the poor boy's bones, and then told his wife to take the pot and throw it into the river, boy and all. She did as she was told, and threw it into the water, and ever since there is an eddy there that we call Ûñ'tiguhǐ', "Pot-in-the-water."

A service tree and a calico bush grew on the bank above. A great cloud of steam came up and made streaks and blotches on their bark, and it has been so to this day. When the steam cleared away she looked over and saw the boy clinging to the roots of the service tree where they hung down into the water, but now his skin was all clean. She helped him up the bank, and they went back to the house.

On the way she told him, "When we go in, your father will put a new dress on you, but when he opens his box and tells you to pick out your ornaments be sure to take them from the bottom. Then he will send for his other sons to play ball against you. There is a honey-locust tree in front of the house, and as soon as you begin to get tired strike at that and your father will stop the play, because he does not want to lose the tree."

When they went into the house, the old man was pleased to see the boy looking so clean, and said, "I knew I could soon cure those spots. Now we must dress you."

He brought out a fine suit of buck-kin, with belt and headdress, and had the boy put them on. Then he opened a box and said, "Now pick out your necklace and bracelets."

The boy looked, and the box was full of all kinds of snakes gliding over each other with their heads up. He was not afraid, but remembered what the woman had told him, and plunged his hand to the bottom and drew out a great rattlesnake and put it around his neck for a necklace. He put down his hand again four times and drew up four copperheads and twisted them around his wrists and ankles.

Then his father gave him a war club and said, "Now you must play a ball game with your two elder brothers. They live beyond here in the Darkening land, and I have sent for them" He said a ball game, but he meant that the boy must fight for his life. The young men came, and they were both older and stronger than the boil, but he was not afraid and fought against them.

The thunder rolled and the lightning flashed at every stroke, for they were the young Thunders, and the boy himself was Lightning. At last he was tired from defending himself alone against two, and pretended to aim a blow at the honey-locust tree. Then his father stopped the fight, because he was afraid the lightning would split the tree, and he saw that the boy was brave and strong.

The boy told his father how Ûñtsaiyï' had dared him to play, and had even offered to play for the spots on his skin. "Yes," said Thunder, "he is a great gambler and makes his living that way, but I will see that you win." He brought a small climbing gourd with a hole bored through the neck, and tied it on the boy's wrist. Inside the gourd there was a string of beads, and one end hung out from a hole in the top, but there was no end to the string inside.

"Now," said his father, go back the way you came, and as soon as he sees you he will want to play for the beads. He is very hard to beat, but this time he will lose every game.

When he cries out for a drink, you will know he is getting discouraged, and then strike the rock with your war club and water will come, so that you can play on without stopping.

At last he will bet his life, and lose. Then send at once for your brothers to kill him, or he will get away, he is so tricky."

The boy took the gourd and his war club and started east along the road by which he had come. As soon as Ûñtsai'yĭ saw him he called to him, and when he saw the gourd with the bead string hanging out he wanted to play for it.

The boy drew out the string. but there seemed to be no end to it, and he kept on pulling until enough had come out to make a circle all around the playground. "I will play one game for this much against your stake," said the boy, "and when that is over we can have another game."

They began the game with the wheel and stick and the boy won. Ûñtsai'yĭ did not know what to think of it, but he put up another stake and called for a second game. The boy won again, and so they played on until noon, when Ûñtsai'yĭ had lost nearly everything he had and was about discouraged.

It was very hot, and he said, "I am thirsty," and wanted to stop long enough to get a drink.

"No," said the boy, and struck the rock with his club so that water came out, and they had a drink. They played on until Ûñtsai'yĭ had lost all his buckskins and beaded work, his eagle feathers and ornaments, and at last offered to bet his wife.

They played and the boy won her. Then Ûñtsai'yĭ was

desperate and offered to stake his life. "If I win I kill you, but if you win you may kill me." They played and the boy won.

"Let me go and tell my wife," said Ûñtsai'yï, "so that she will receive her new husband, and then you may kill me." He went into the house, but it had two doors, and although the boy waited long Ûñtsai'yï did not come back. When at last he went to look for him he found that the gambler had gone out the back way and was nearly out of sight going east.

The boy ran to his father's house and got his brothers to help him. They brought their dog--the Horned Green Beetle--and hurried after the gambler. He ran fast and was soon out of sight, and they followed as fast as they could. After a while they met an old woman making pottery and asked her if she had seen Ûñtsai'yï and she said she had not.

"He came this way," said the brothers.

"Then he must have passed in the night," said the old woman, "for I have been here all day."

 They were about to take another road when the Beetle, which had been circling about in the air above the old woman, made a dart at her and struck her on the forehead, and it rang like brass--ûñtsai'yï! Then they knew it was Brass and sprang at him, but he jumped up in his right shape and was off, running so fast that he was soon out of sight again. The Beetle had struck so hard that some of the brass rubbed off, and we can see it on the beetle's forehead yet.

They followed and came to an old man sitting by the trail, carving a stone pipe. They asked him if he had seen Brass pass that way and he said no, but again the Beetle-which could know Brass under any shape--struck him on the forehead so that it rang like metal, and the gambler jumped up in his right form and was off again before they could hold him.

He ran east until he came to the great water; then he ran north until he came to the edge of the world, and had to turn again to the west. He took every shape to throw them off the track, but the Green Beetle always knew him, and the brothers pressed him so hard that at last he could go no more and they caught him just as he reached the edge of the great water where the sun goes down.

They tied his hands and feet with a grapevine and drove a long stake through his breast, and planted it far out in the deep water. They set two crows on the end of the pole to guard it and called the place Kâgûñ'yï, "Crow place." But Brass never died, and cannot die until the end of the world, but lies there always with his face up. Sometimes he struggles under the water to get free, and sometimes the beavers, who are his friends, come and gnaw at the grapevine to release him. Then the pole shakes and the crows at the top cry Ka! Ka! Ka! and scare the beavers away.

The Moon and The Thunders

A Cherokee Legend
Myths of the
Cherokee, James
Mooney, 1900

The Sun was a young woman and lived in the East, while her brother, the Moon. lived in the West. The girl had a lover who used to come every month in the dark of the moon to court her. He would come at night, and leave before daylight.

Although she talked with him she could not see his face in the dark, and he would not tell her his name, until she was wondering all the time who it could be.

At last she hit upon a plan to find out, so the next time he came, as they were sitting together in the dark of the âsi, she slyly dipped her hand into the cinders and ashes of the fireplace and rubbed it over his face, saying, "Your face is cold; you must have suffered from the wind," and pretending to be very sorry for him, but he did not know that she had ashes on her hand.

After a while he left her and went away again.

The next night when the Moon came up in the sky his face was covered with spots, and then his sister knew he was the one who had been coming to see her. He was so much ashamed to have her know it that he kept as far away as he could at the other end of the sky all the night. Ever since he tries to keep a long way behind the Sun, and when he does sometimes have to come near her in the west he makes himself as thin as a ribbon so that he can hardly be seen.

Some old people say that the moon is a ball which was thrown up against the sky in a game a long time ago.

They say that two towns were playing against each other, but one of them had the best runners and had almost won the game, when the leader of the other side picked up the ball with his hand--a thing that is not allowed in the game-- and tried to throw it to the goal, but it struck against the solid sky vault and was fastened there, to remind players never to cheat.

When the moon looks small and pale it is because some one has handled the ball unfairly, and for this reason they formerly played only at the time of a full moon.

When the sun or moon is eclipsed it is because a great frog up in the sky is trying to swallow it.

Everybody knows this, even the Creeks and the other tribes, and in the olden times, eighty or a hundred years ago, before the great medicine men were all dead, whenever they saw the sun grow dark the people would come together and fire guns and beat the drum, and in a little while this would frighten off the great frog and the sun would be all right again.

The common people call both Sun and Moon Nûñdä, one being "Nûñdä that dwells in the day" and the other "Nûñdä that dwells in the night," but the priests call the Sun Su'tälidihï', "Six-killer," and the Moon Ge"yägu'ga, though nobody knows now what this word means, or why they use these names. Sometimes people ask the Moon not to let it rain or snow.

The great Thunder and his sons, the two Thunder boys, live far in the west above the sky vault. The lightning and the rainbow are their beautiful dress. The priests pray to the Thunder and call him the Red Man, because that is the brightest color of his dress.

There are other Thunders that live lower down, in the cliffs and mountains, and under waterfalls, and travel on invisible bridges from one high peak to another where they have their town houses. The great Thunders above the sky are kind and helpful when we pray to them, but these others are always plotting mischief. One must not point at the rainbow, or one's finger will swell at the lower joint.

What is life?
It is the flash of a firefly in the night.
It is the breath of a buffalo in the wintertime.
It is the little shadow which runs across
the grass and loses itself in the sunset.

Crowfoot, Blackfoot warrior and orator 1830 - 1890

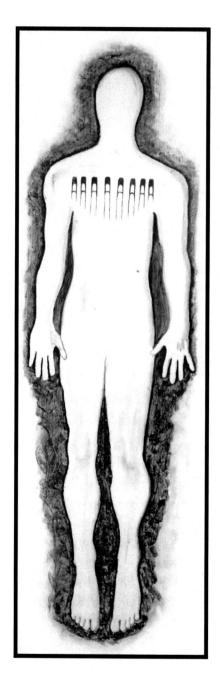

The Spirit Defenders of Nikwasi'

A Cherokee Legend
Myths of the Cherokee,
James Mooney, 1900

Long ago a powerful unknown tribe invaded the country from the southeast, killing people and destroying settlements wherever they went. No leader could stand against them, and in a little while they had wasted all the lower settlements and advanced into the mountains.

No leader could stand against them, and in a little while they had wasted all the lower settlements and advanced into the mountains.

The warriors of the old town of Nikwasi', on the head of Little Tennessee, gathered their wives and children

into the townhouse and kept scouts constantly on the
lookout for the presence of danger. One morning just
before daybreak the spies saw the enemy approaching and
at once gave the alarm.

The Nikwasi' men seized their arms and rushed out to meet
the attack, but after a long, hard fight they found
themselves overpowered and began to retreat, when
suddenly a stranger stood among them and shouted to the
chief to call off his men and he himself would drive back
the enemy. From the dress and language of the stranger the
Nikwasi' people thought him a chief who had come with
reinforcements from the Overhill settlements in Tennessee.

They fell back along the trail, and as they came near the
townhouse they saw a great company of warriors coming
out from the side of the mound as through an open
doorway. Then they knew that their friends were the
Nûñnë'hï, the Immortals, although no one had ever heard
before that they lived under Nikwasi' mound.

The Nûñnë'hï poured out by hundreds, armed and painted
for the fight, and the most curious thing about it all was that
they became invisible as soon as they were fairly outside of
the settlement, so that although the enemy saw the glancing
arrow or the rushing tomahawk, and felt the stroke, he
could not see who sent it.

Before such invisible foes the invaders soon had to retreat,
going first south along the ridge to where joins the main
ridge which separates the French Broad from the
Tuckasegee, and then turning with it to the northeast. As
they retreated they tried to shield themselves behind rocks
and trees, but the Nûñnë'hï arrows went around the rocks
and killed them from the other side, and they could find no
hiding place.

All along the ridge they fell, until when they reached the head of Tuckasegee not more than half a dozen were left alive, and in despair they sat down and cried out for mercy. Ever since then the Cherokee have called the place Dayûlsûñ'yï, "Where they cried."

Then the Nûñnë'hï chief told them they had deserved their punishment for attacking a peaceful tribe, and he spared their lives and told them to go home and take the news to their people. This was the Indian custom, always to spare a few to carry back the news of defeat. They went home toward the north and the Nûñnë'hï went back to the mound.

And they are still there, because, in the last war, when a strong party of Federal troops came to surprise a handful of Confederates posted there they saw so many soldiers guarding the town that they were afraid and went away without making an attack.

"When a white army battles Indians and wins, it is called a great victory, but if they lose it is called a massacre."

Chiksika, Shawnee

The Search for the Corn Maidens

A Zuni Legend
Katharine Berry Judson,
Myths and Legends of
California and the Old
Southwest, 1912

The people in their trouble called the two Master-Priests and said: "Who, now, think ye, should journey to seek our precious Maidens? Bethink ye! Who amongst the Beings is even as ye are, strong of will and good of eyes?"

Then they added, "There is our great elder brother and father, Eagle, he of the floating down and of the terraced tail-fan. Surely he is enduring of will and surpassing of sight."

"Yea. Most surely," said the fathers. "Go ye forth and beseech him."

Then the two sped north to Twin Mountain, where in a grotto high up among the crags, with his mate and his young, dwelt the Eagle of the White Bonnet.

They climbed the mountain, but behold! Only the eaglets were there. They screamed lustily and tried to hide themselves in the dark recesses. "Pull not our feathers, ye of hurtful touch, but wait. When we are older we will drop them for you even from the clouds."

"Hush," said the warriors. "Wait in peace. We seek not ye but thy father."

Then from afar, with a frown, came old Eagle. "Why disturb ye my featherlings?" he cried.

"Behold! Father and elder brother, we come seeking only the light of thy favor. Listen!"

Then they told him of the lost Maidens of the Corn, and begged him to search for them.

"Be it well with thy wishes," said Eagle. "Go ye before contentedly."

So the warriors returned to the council. But Eagle winged his way high into the sky. High, high, he rose, until he circled among the clouds, small-seeming and swift, like seed-down in a whirlwind. Through all the heights, to the north, to the west, to the south, and to the east, he circled and sailed. Yet nowhere saw he trace of the Corn Maidens.

Then he flew lower, returning. Before the warriors were rested, people heard the roar of his wings. As he alighted, the fathers said, "Enter thou and sit, oh brother, and say to us what thou hast to say." And they offered him the cigarette of the space relations.

When they had puffed the smoke toward the four points of the compass, and Eagle had purified his breath with smoke, and had blown smoke over sacred things, he spoke.

"Far have I journeyed, scanning all the regions. Neither bluebird nor woodrat can hide from my seeing," he said, snapping his beak. "Neither of them, unless they hide under bushes. Yet I have failed to see anything of the Maidens ye seek for. Send for my younger brother, the Falcon. Strong of flight is he, yet not so strong as I, and nearer the ground he takes his way ere sunrise."

Then the Eagle spread his wings and flew away to Twin Mountain. The Warrior-Priests of the Bow sped again fleetly over the plain to the westward for his younger brother, Falcon.

Sitting on an ant hill, so the warriors found Falcon. He paused as they approached, crying, "If ye have snare strings, I will be off like the flight of an arrow well plumed of our feathers! "

"No," said the priests. "Thy elder brother hath bidden us seek thee."

Then they told Falcon what had happened, and how Eagle had failed to find the Corn Maidens, so white and beautiful.

"Failed!" said Falcon. "Of course he failed. He climbs aloft to the clouds and thinks he can see under every bush and into every shadow, as sees the Sunfather who sees not with eyes. Go ye before."

Before the Warrior-Priests had turned toward the town, the Falcon had spread his sharp wings and was skimming off over the tops of the trees and bushes as though verily seeking for field mice or birds' nests. And the Warriors returned to tell the fathers and to await his coming.

But after Falcon had searched over the world, to the north and west, to the east and south, he too returned and was received as had been Eagle. He settled on the edge of a tray before the altar, as on the ant hill he settles today. When he had smoked and had been smoked, as had been Eagle, he told the sorrowing fathers and mothers that he had looked behind every copse and cliff shadow, but of the Maidens he had found no trace.

"They are hidden more closely than ever sparrow hid," he said. Then he, too, flew away to his hills in the west.

"Our beautiful Maiden Mothers," cried the matrons. "Lost, lost as the dead are they!"

"Yes," said the others. "Where now shall we seek them? The far-seeing Eagle and the close-searching Falcon alike have failed to find them."

"Stay now your feet with patience," said the fathers. Some of them had heard Raven, who sought food in the refuse and dirt at the edge of town, at daybreak.

"Look now," they said. "There is Heavy-nose, whose beak never fails to find the substance of seed itself, however little or well-hidden it be. He surely must know of the Corn Maidens. Let us call him."

So the warriors went to the river side. When they found Raven, they raised their hands, all weaponless.

"We carry no pricking quills," they called. "Blackbanded father, we seek your aid. Look now! The Mother-maidens of Seed whose substance is the food alike of thy people and our people, have fled away. Neither our grandfather the Eagle, nor his younger brother the Falcon, can trace them. We beg you to aid us or counsel us."

"Ka! ka!" cried the Raven. "Too hungry am I to go abroad fasting on business for ye. Ye are stingy! Here have I been since perching time, trying to find a throatful, but ye pick thy bones and lick thy bowls too clean for that, be sure."

"Come in, then, poor grandfather. We will give thee food to

cat. Yea, and a cigarette to smoke, with all the ceremony."

"Say ye so?" said the Raven. He ruffled his collar and opened his mouth so wide with a lusty kaw-la-ka- that he might well have swallowed his own head. "Go ye before," he said, and followed them into the court of the dancers.

He was not ill to look upon. Upon his shoulders were bands of white cotton, and his back was blue, gleaming like the hair of a maiden dancer in the sunlight. The Master-Priest greeted Raven, bidding him sit and smoke.

"Ha! There is corn in this, else why the stalk of it?" said the Raven, when he took the cane cigarette of the far spaces and noticed the joint of it. Then he did as he had seen the Master-Priest do, only more greedily.

He sucked in such a throatful of the smoke, fire and all, that it almost strangled him. He coughed and grew giddy, and the smoke all hot and stinging went through every part of him. It filled all his feathers, making even his brown eyes bluer and blacker, in rings. It is not to be wondered at, the blueness of flesh, blackness of dress, and skinniness, yes, and tearfulness of eye which we see in the Raven to-day. And they are all as greedy of corn food as ever, for behold! No sooner had the old Raven recovered than he espied one of the ears of corn half hidden under the mantle-covers of the trays.

He leaped from his place laughing. They always laugh when they find anything, these ravens. Then he caught up the ear of corn and made off with it over the heads of the people and the tops of the houses, crying.

"Ha! ha! In this wise and in no other will ye find thy Seed Maidens."

But after a while he came back, saying, "A sharp eye have I for the flesh of the Maidens. But who might see their breathing-beings, ye dolts, except by the help of the Father of Dawn-Mist himself, whose breath makes breath of others seem as itself." Then he flew away cawing.

Then the elders said to each other, "It is our fault, so how dare we prevail on our father Paiyatuma to aid us? He warned us of this in the old time."

Suddenly, for the sun was rising, they heard Paiyatuma in his daylight mood and transformation. Thoughtless and loud, uncouth in speech, he walked along the outskirts of the village. He joked fearlessly even of fearful things, for all his words and deeds were the reverse of his sacred being. He sat down on a heap of vile refuse, saying he would have a feast.

"My poor little children," he said. But he spoke to aged priests and white-haired matrons.

"Good-night to you all," he said, though it was in full dawning. So he perplexed them with his speeches.

"We beseech thy favor, oh father, and thy aid, in finding our beautiful Maidens." So the priests mourned.

"Oh, that is all, is it? But why find that which is not lost, or summon those who will not come?"

Then he reproached them for not preparing the sacred plumes, and picked up the very plumes he had said were not there.

Then the wise Pekwinna, the Speaker of the Sun, took two plumes and the banded wing-tips of the turkey, and approaching Paiyatuma stroked him with the tips of the feathers and then laid the feathers upon his lips.

Then Paiyatuma became aged and grand and straight, as is a tall tree shorn by lightning. He said to the father:

"Thou are wise of thought and good of heart. Therefore, I will summon from Summer-land the beautiful Maidens that ye may look upon them once more and make offering of plumes in sacrifice for them, but they are lost as dwellers amongst ye."

Then he told them of the song lines and the sacred speeches and of the offering of the sacred plume wands, and then turned him about and sped away so fleetly that none saw him.

Beyond the first valley of the high plain to the southward Paiyatuma planted the four plume wands. First he planted the yellow, bending over it and watching it. When it ceased to flutter, the soft down on it leaned northward but moved not. Then he set the blue wand and watched it; then the white wand. The eagle down on them leaned to right and left and still northward, yet moved not.

Then farther on he planted the red wand, and bending low, without breathing, watched it closely. The soft down plumes began to wave as though blown by the breath of some small creature. Backward and forward, northward and southward they swayed, as if in time to the breath of one resting.

"'T is the breath of my Maidens in Summer-land, for the plumes of the southland sway soft to their gentle breathing. So shall it ever be. When I set the down of my mists on the plains and scatter my bright beads in the northland, summer shall go thither from afar, borne on the breath of the Seed

Maidens. Where they breathe, warmth, showers, and fertility shall follow with the birds of Summer-land, and the butterflies, northward over the world."

Then Paiyatuma arose and sped by the magic of his knowledge into the countries of Summer-land, -fled swiftly and silently as the soft breath he sought for, bearing his painted flute before him. And when he paused to rest, he played on his painted flute and the butterflies and birds sought him. So he sent them to seek the Maidens, following swiftly, and long before he found them he greeted them with the music of his song sound, even as the People of the Seed now greet them in the song of the dancers.

When the Maidens heard his music and saw his tall form in their great fields of corn, they plucked ears, each of her own kind, and with them filled their colored trays and over all spread embroidered mantles, - embroidered in all the bright colors and with the creature-songs of Summer-land. So they sallied forth to meet him and welcome him. Then he greeted them, each with the touch of his hands and the breath of his flute, and bade them follow him to the northland home of their deserted children.

So by the magic of their knowledge they sped back as the stars speed over the world at night time, toward the home of our ancients. Only at night and dawn they journeyed, as the dead do, and the stars also. So they came at evening in the full of the last moon to the Place of the Middle, bearing their trays of seed.

Glorious was Paiyatuma, as he walked into the courts of the dancers in the dusk of the evening and stood with folded arms at the foot of the bow-fringed ladder of priestly council, he and his follower Shutsukya. He was tall and beautiful and banded with his own mists, and carried the banded wings of the turkeys with which he had winged his flight from afar, leading the Maidens, and followed as by his own shadow by the black being of the corn-soot, Shutsukya, who cries with the voice of the frost wind when the corn has grown aged and the harvest is taken away.

And surpassingly beautiful were the Maidens clothed in the white cotton and embroidered garments of Summer-land.

Then after long praying and chanting by the priests, the fathers of the people, and those of the Seed and Water, and the keepers of sacred things, the Maiden-mother of the North advanced to the foot of the ladder. She lifted from her head the beautiful tray of yellow corn and Paiyatama took it. He pointed it to the regions, each in turn, and the Priest of the North came and received the tray of sacred seed.

Then the Maiden of the West advanced and gave up her tray of blue corn. So each in turn the Maidens gave up their trays of precious seed. The Maiden of the South, the red seed; the Maiden of the East, the white seed; then the Maiden with the black seed, and lastly, the tray of all-color seed which the Priestess of Seed-and-All herself received.

And now, behold! The Maidens stood as before, she of the North at the northern end, but with her face southward far looking; she of the West, next, and lo! so all of them, with the seventh and last, looking southward.

And standing thus, the darkness of the night fell around them. As shadows in deep night, so these Maidens of the Seed of Corn, the beloved and beautiful, were seen no more of men.

And Paiyatuma stood alone, for Shutsukya walked now

behind the Maidens, whistling shrilly, as the frost wind whistles when the corn is gathered away, among the lone canes and dry leaves of a gleaned field.

When all the trees have been cut down,
when all the animals have been hunted,
when all the waters are polluted,
when all the air is unsafe to breathe,
only then will you discover you cannot eat money.

Cree Prophecy

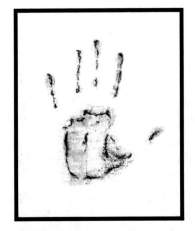

The Jealous Father

A Cree Legend
Skinner, Anthropological
Papers of the American
Museum of Natural History,
ix, 92

Once there was an old man named Aioswé who had two wives. When his son by one of these women began to grow up, Aioswé became jealous of him.

One day, he went off to hunt and when he came back, found marks on one of the women (the co-wife with his son's mother) which proved to him that his son had been on terms of intimacy with her.

One day the old man and the boy went to a rocky island to hunt for eggs. Wishing to get rid of his son, the old man persuaded him to gather eggs farther and farther away from the shore. The young man did not suspect anything until he looked up and saw his father paddling off in the canoe. "Why are you deserting me, father? "he cried.

"Because you have played tricks on your stepmother," answered the old man.

When the boy found that he was really left behind, he sat there crying hour after hour. At last, Walrus appeared. He came near the island and stuck his head above the water. "What are you crying for, my son?" said Walrus.

"My father has deserted me on this island and I want to get

home to the mainland. Will you not help me to get ashore?" the boy replied.

Walrus said that he would do so willingly. "Get on my back," said Walrus, "and I will take you to the mainland." Then Walrus asked Aioswé's son if the sky was clear. The boy replied that it was, but this was a lie, for he saw many clouds. Aioswé's son said this because he was afraid that Walrus would desert him if he knew it was cloudy. Walrus said, "If you think I am not going fast enough, strike on my horns [tusks] and let me know when you think it is shallow enough for you to get ashore, then you can jump off my back and walk to the land."

As they went along, Walrus said to the boy, "Now my son, you must let me know if you hear it thunder, because as soon as it thunders, I must go right under the water." The boy promised to let Walrus know. They had not gone far, when there came a peal of thunder. Walrus said, "My son, I hear thunder." "Oh, no, you are mistaken," said the boy who feared to be drowned, "what you think is thunder is only the noise your body makes going so quickly through the water." Walrus believed the boy and thought he must have been wrong.

Some time later, there came another peal of thunder and this time, Walrus knew he was not mistaken, he was sure it was thunder. He was very angry and said he would drop Aioswé's son there, whether the water was shallow or not. He did so but the lad had duped Walrus with his lies so that he came where the water was very shallow and the boy escaped, but Walrus was killed by lightning before he could reach water deep enough to dive in. This thunderstorm was sent to destroy Walrus by Aioswé's father, who conjured for it. Walrus, on the other hand, was the result of conjuring by his mother, who wished to save her son's life.

When Aioswé's son reached the shore, he started for home, but he had not gone far before he met an old woman, who had been sent as the result of a wish for his safety by his mother (or was a wish for his safety on his mother's part, personified). The old woman instructed the lad how to conduct himself if he ever expected to reach his home and mother again. "Now you have come ashore there is still a lot of trouble for you to go through before you reach home," said she, and she gave him the stuffed skin of an ermine (weasel in white winter coat). "This will be one of your weapons to use to protect yourself," were her words as she tendered him this gift, and she told him what dangers he would encounter and what to do in each case.

Then the son of Aioswé started for his home once more. As he journeyed through the forest he came upon a solitary wigwam inhabited by two old blind hags, who were the result of an adverse conjuration by his father. Both of these old women had sharp bones like) daggers; protruding from the lower arm at the elbow." They were very savage and used to kill everybody they met. When Aioswé's son approached the tent, although the witches could not see him, they knew from their magic powers that he was near. They asked him to come in and sit down, but he was suspicious, for he did not like the looks of their elbows.

He thought of a plan by which he might dupe the old women into killing each other. Instead of going himself and sitting between them he got a large parchment and fixing it to the end of a pole, he poked it in between them. The old women heard it rattle and thought it was the boy himself coming to sit between them.

Then they both turned their backs to the skin and began to hit away at it with their elbows. Every time they stabbed the skin, they cried out, " I am hitting the son of Aioswé!

I've hit him! I've hit him!" At last, they got so near each other that they began to hit one another, calling out all the time, "I am hitting the son of Aioswé!" They finally stabbed each other to death and the son of Aioswé escaped this danger also.

When the young man had vanquished the two old women he proceeded on his journey. He had not gone very far when he came to a row of dried human bones hung across the path so that no one could pass by without making them rattle. Not far away, there was a tent full of people and big dogs. Whenever they heard anyone disturb the bones, they would set upon him and kill him. The old woman who had advised Aioswé's son told him that when he came to this place he could escape by digging a tunnel in the path under the bones.

When he arrived at the spot he began to follow her advice and burrow under. He was careless and when he was very nearly done and completely out of sight, he managed to rattle the bones. At once, the dogs heard and they cried out, "That must be Aioswé's son." All the people ran out at once, but since Aioswé's son was under ground in the tunnel they could not see him, so after they had searched for a while they returned. The dogs said, "We are sure this is the son of Aioswé," and they continued to search.

At length, they found the mouth of the hole Aioswé's son had dug. The dogs came to the edge and began to bark till all the people ran out again with their weapons. Then Aioswé's son took the stuffed ermine skin and poked its head up. All the people saw it and thought it was really ermine. Then they were angry and killed the dogs for lying.

Aioswé's son escaped again and this time he got home. When he drew near his father's wigwam, he could hear his mother crying, and as he approached still closer he saw her. She looked up and saw him coming. She cried out to her husband and co-wife, "My son has come home again."

The old man did not believe it. "It is not possible," he cried. But his wife insisted on it. Then the old man came out and when he saw it was really his son, he was very much frightened for his own safety. He called out to his other wife, "Bring some caribou skins and spread them out for my son to walk on." But the boy kicked them away. "I have come a long way," said he, "with only my bare feet to walk on."

That night, the boy sang a song about the burning of the world and the old man sang against him but he was not strong enough. "I am going to set the world on fire," said the boy to his father, "I shall make all the lakes and rivers boil." He took up an arrow and said, "I am going to shoot this arrow into the woods; see if I don't set them on fire." He shot his arrow into the bush and a great blaze sprang up and all the woods began to burn.

"The forest is now on fire," said the old man, "but the water is not yet burning." "I'll show you how I can make the water boil also," said his son. He shot another arrow into the water, and it immediately began to boil. Then the old man who wished to escape said to his son, "How shall we escape?" The old man had been a great bear hunter and had a large quantity of bear's grease preserved in a bark basket. "Go into your fat basket," said his son, "you will be perfectly safe there."

Then he drew a circle on the ground and placed his mother there. The ground enclosed by the circle was not even scorched, but the wicked old man who had believed he would be safe in the grease baskets, was burned to death.

Aioswé's son said to his mother, "Let us become birds. What will you be?" "I'll be a robin," said she. "I'll be a whisky jack (Canada jay)," he replied. They flew off together.

Before our white brothers arrived to make us civilized men,
we didn't have any kind of prison.
Because of this, we had no delinquents.
Without a prison, there can be no delinquents.
We had no locks nor keys and therefore among us there were no thieves.
When someone was so poor that he couldn't afford a horse, a tent or a blanket, he would, in that case, receive it all as a gift.
We were too uncivilized to give great importance to private property.
We didn't know any kind of money and consequently, the value of a human being was not determined by his wealth.
We had no written laws laid down, no lawyers, no politicians, therefore, we were not able to cheat and swindle one another.
We were really in bad shape before the white men arrived and I don't know how to explain how we were able to manage without these fundamental things that (so they tell us) are so necessary for a civilized society.

John (Fire) Lame Deer
Sioux Lakota - 1903-1976

Mudjikiwis

A Cree Legend
Skinner, Journal of
American Folk-Lore,
xxix, 353, No. 3

Once upon a time the
Indians were camping.
They had ten lodges.
There were ten of
them; and the eldest
brother, Mudjikiwis,
was sitting in the
doorway.

It was winter, and all the Indians had their side-bags on;
and every day they went off and hunted in the direction
which they faced as they sat. Mudjikiwis always took the
lead, and the others followed.

Once when he came home to his camp, he saw smoke just
as he crossed the last hill. When he approached the lodge,
he saw a pile of wood neatly stacked by the door. He
himself had always cooked the dinner; and when he saw it
ready, he was very glad. "There is surely a girl here!" he
thought. "There must be some one who has done this."

He had many brothers younger than himself. "Maybe some
one is trying to marry them, or some girl wants me!"

When he arrived at the lodge, he saw a girl's pigeon-toed
tracks, and he was delighted. "It is a girl!" he cried, and he
rushed in to see her, but there was no one there. The fire
was just started, the meat cooked and ready, and water had
been drawn. Some one had just finished work when he
came.

There were even ten pairs of moccasins hanging up. "Now, at last, there is some one to sew for us! Surely one of us will get married!" he thought, and he also thought that he would be the fortunate one. He did not touch anything, but left everything as he had found it for his brothers to see.

After a while the brother next to him in age came in. He looked up and saw all the moccasins, and he too was very glad. Then Mudjikiwis said, "I do not know which of us is going to be married. A girl has just left here, but I cannot tell who she is, and there are ten of us. One of us is loved by some one!"

They soon were joined by the third, and then by the fourth brother, and the fire was out by that time. The youngest brother was the most handsome one of the family. "If one of us should marry, Mudjikiwis, we shall have to hunt hard and not let our sister-in-law hunger or be in need," he said. "I shall be very glad if we have a sister-in-law. Don't let her chop wood; she cannot attend to all of us. We just want her to cook and mend our clothes."

At night they were all crying, "He, he, he!" until dark came, because they were so glad. "I cannot attend to all my brothers, and I do not need to do so any more!" cried Mudjikiwis. The next day nine went off, and left the youngest brother on guard to see the girl. Mudjikiwis came back first, and found that the tenth boy had not been taken. "Oh, well! leave our ninth brother next time, "he said "Then we will try it once more with our eighth brother."

Three of them then kept house in succession, but the woman did not come. They then left the fifth one, and said, "If no one comes, make dinner for us yourself." Soon after they had left, some one came along making a noise like a rattle, for she had bells on her leggings.

"Oh, she shall not know me!" said the youth. "I shall be a bit of eagle-down," and he flew up between the canvas and the poles of the lodge. Presently the girl entered. She had very long hair, and was very pretty. She took the axe and went out to cut wood, and soon brought in four armfuls. Then she made the fire, took down the kettles, and prepared dinner. When she had done so she melted some snow, took another armful of wood, and started another fire.

After she had finished she called to the youth to come down from his hiding-place. "Maybe you think I don't know you are up there," she said. So he came down and took a seat with her by the fire.

When Mudjikiwis came home, he saw another big pile of wood. When he came near, he cried, "He, he, he!" to show that he was well pleased. "I could not attend to the needs of my brothers," he shouted, "I could not cook for them, and I could not provide my relatives with moccasins!" He entered the door and bent down, for Mudjikiwis had on a fisher-skin head-band with an eagle-quill thrust in behind. As he came in, he saw a pretty girl sitting there. When he sat down, he said, "Hai, hai, hai! The girl is sitting like her mother."

He pulled off his shoes and threw them to his youngest brother, and received a fine pair of moccasins from his sister-in-law. He was delighted, and cried, "Hai, hai, hai!" Soon all the other brothers came back, all nine of them, and each received new moccasins.

Mudjikiwis said, "I have already advised you. Do not let our sister-in-law chop wood or do any hard work. Hunt well, and do not let her be hungry." Morning came, and Mudjikiwis was already half in love with his sister-in-law. He started out, pretending that he was going to hunt, but he only went over a hill and stopped there. Then he wrapped his blanket around himself. It was winter, and he took some mud from under the snow and rubbed it over his forehead and on his hat-band. He had his ball-headed club with him, which had two eyes that winked constantly. Soon he saw his sister-in-law, who came out to chop wood.

He went to speak to her, but the girl had disappeared. Soon she came back. There was one pile of wood here, and one there. Mudjikiwis stopped at the one to the west. He had his bow, his arrows, and his club with him. He held his club on the left arm, and his bow and arrow on the right arm, folded his arms across his breast, and was smiling at her when she came up. "O my brother-in-law! I don't want to do that," she cried.

Then Mudjikiwis was angry because she scorned him. He took an arrow and shot her in the leg, and fled off to hunt. That night he returned late, last of all. As he came close to the lodge, he called out, "Yoha, yoha! what is wrong with you? You have done some kind of mischief. Why is there no wood for our sister-in-law?" He went in. "What is wrong with our sister-in-law, that she is not home?" he demanded. His brother then said, "Why are you so late? You used to be the first one here."

Mudjikiwis would not speak in reply. The married brother came in last. The young brother was tired of waiting, and asked each, "You did not see your sister-in-law, did you?" The others replied, "Mudjikiwis came very late. He never did so before."

"I shall track my wife," said the husband. So he set off in pursuit of her. He tracked her, and found that she had brought one load of wood. Her second trail ended at a little lodge of willows that she had made, and where she was.

She cried to him, "Do not come here! Your brother Mudjikiwis has shot me. I told him I did not want to receive him, and then he shot me down. Do not come here. You will see me on the fourth night. If you want to give me food, put it outside the door and go away, and I shall get it."

Her husband went home, as she commanded. After that the youth would bring her food, after hunting, every night. "It is well. Even though our brother shot my wife, I shall forgive him, if I can only see her after four nights," he said. The third night he could hardly stay away, he wanted to see her so badly. The fourth day at dawn he went to the lodge; and as he drew near, she cried, "Do not come!" but he went in, anyway, and saw her there. "I told you not to come, but you could not restrain yourself. When your brothers could not attend to themselves, I wished to help them," she cried. So he went home satisfied, since he had seen her.

They breakfasted, and he started out again with food for her. She had gone out, for he found her tracks, little steps, dabbled with blood. Then he went back home, and said to his brothers, "My brothers, I am going to go after my wife."

He dressed, and followed her footprints. Sometimes he ran, and at sunset he wanted to camp. So he killed a rabbit; and as he came out of the brush, he saw a lodge. "He, my grandchild!" called a voice, "You are thinking of following your wife. She passed here at dawn. Come in and sit down! Here is where she sat before you." He entered, and found an old woman, who told him to sit in the same place where his wife had sat.

He gave her the rabbit he had shot, as he was really hungry. "Oh, my grandchild must be very hungry!" she cried, " so I shall cook for him," said the old crone. Her kettle was no larger than a thimble. She put in one morsel of meat and one little berry. The youth thought that was a very small allowance, when he was really hungry.

"O my grandchild!" the old woman said aloud in answer to his thoughts, "no one has ever eaten all my kettle holds. You are wrong if you think you won't get enough of this."

But he still thought so, and did not believe her. After the food was cooked, she said, "Eat, nosis!" and gave him a spoon. He took out the piece of meat and the berry; but when he had eaten it, the kettle was still full. He did this many times over. When he had finished, he had not eaten it all, yet he had enough. Then the grandmother told him that he had married one of ten sisters.

"They are not real people," she said, "they are from way up in the skies. They have ten brothers. There are three more of your grandmothers on the road where you are going. Each will tell you to go back, as I advised you; but if you insist, I will give you two bones to help you climb over the mountains."

Now, this old woman was really a moose, and not a human grandmother at all. "If you get into difficulties, you must cry, 'Where is my grandmother?' and use these two front shin-bones of the moose that I gave you." He slept there, and in the morning she gave him breakfast from the same kettle. When he was through she said, "Do not walk fast. Even if you rest on the way, you will reach your next grandmother in the evening. If you walk as fast as you can, you will get there at night."

He followed the trail as fast as he could, for he did not believe his grandmother. In the evening he killed a rabbit; and when he came out of the brush, there stood another lonely lodge, as before.

"O my grandchild! there is room in here for you to come in," cried a voice. "Your wife passed here early yesterday morning." Yet he had traveled two days. "She came in here!"

The old woman cooked for him in the same way as his other grandmother had done. Again he did not believe in her kettle, for he had already forgotten about his first grandmother. This grandmother was older than the first one whom he had left, and who was the youngest of the four grandmothers he was to meet. They were all sisters. "Why did you not believe my sister when she told you to go slowly? When you go fast, you make the trail longer. Hau, nosis! it is a difficult country where you are going," she cried. She gave him a squirrel-skin, saying, "Use this, nosis, whenever you are in difficulties. 'Where is my grandmother?' you shall say. This is what makes everything easy. You will cry, and you will throw it away. You will not leave me till the morning."

So very early next day he started off. He went very slowly; and in a few minutes it was night, and he killed another rabbit. When he came out of the brush, he saw another lodge, a little nearer than the others, and less ragged.

The old woman said to him, "Your wife passed here the same morning that she left up there"; and this grandmother made supper for him, as the others had done. This time the food was corn. "Nosis, your last grandmother, who is my sister, will give you good advice. Your wife has had a child already. Go very slowly, and you will reach there at night; it is not far from here. It is a very difficult country where you are going. Maybe you will not be able to get there."

She gave him a stuffed frog and some glue. "Whenever the mountains are too steep for you to climb, cry, 'Where is my grandmother?' put glue on your hands, and climb, and you will stick to the rocks. When you reach your next grandmother, she will advise you well. Your child is a little boy."

In the morning he had breakfast, and continued on the trail. He went on slowly, and it was soon night, and he killed another rabbit. When he reached the next lodge, nearer than all the rest, his grandmother said, "They have been saying you would be here after your wife; she passed here four days ago at dawn."

The youth entered the tent, and found that this grandmother was a fine young girl in appearance. She said, "To-morrow at noon your wife is going to be married, and the young men will all sit in a circle and pass your child around. The man upon whom he urinates will be known as his father, and she will marry him." The old woman took off her belt, rolled it up nicely, and gave it to him. "This is the last one that you will use," she said, "When you are in trouble, cry out, 'Where is my grandmother?' and throw the belt out, and it will stick up there, so you can climb up to the top. Before noon you will reach a perpendicular precipice like a wall. Your wife is not of our people. She is one of the Thunderers."

That night the youth camped there. In the morning he had food. "If you manage to climb the mountain somehow," his grandmother said to him before he started, "you will cross the hill and see a steep slope, and there you will find a nest. There is one egg in it. That is a Thunderer's nest. As you come down, you will strike the last difficult place. There is a large log across a river.

The river is very deep, and the log revolves constantly. There you will find a big camp, headed by your father-in-law, who owns everything there. There is one old woman just on this side. She is one of us sisters; she is the second oldest of us. You will see bones strewn about when you get there. Many young men go there when they are looking for their wives, and their bones you will see lying about. The Thunderer destroys everything. Some have been cut in halves when they tried to get over the cut-knife mountain."

When the youth came to the mountain, he took first the two bones, and cried, "O grandmother! where are you?" and as he cried, she called from far off, "He, nosis, do not get into trouble!" He drove the bones into the mountain and climbed up hand over hand, driving them in as he climbed.

The bones pierced the rock. When he looked back, he saw that he was far up. He continued until the bones began to grow short, and at last he had to stop. Then he took out the squirrel-hide, called upon his grandmother for help, and threw the skin ahead. He went up in the air following it. All at once he stopped, and his nails wore out on the rock as he slipped back. Then he took the glue out of its bundle.

He cried for his grandmother, and heard her answer. She had told him that he would find a hollow at one place, and there he rested on a ledge when his glue gave out. Then he called for his next grandmother, heard her answer, and cast out his belt, unrolling it. Then he climbed up the sharp summit. He felt of the edge, which was very sharp indeed. Then he became a piece of eagle-down. "The eagle-down loved me once. I shall be it, and blow over the ledge," he cried.

When he got across, he saw the Thunderer's nest and the two Thunderers and their egg. He found a trail from there

on, until he came to the rolling log that lay across the deep
river. Then he became down again, and blew across; and
though many others had been drowned there, he crossed
alive. He went on, and at last saw a small, low lodge with a
little stone beside it. His last grandmother had told him to
enter, as this was the abode of one of her sisters. So he
went in.

"Ha, ha, ha, nosis!" she cried, "They said a long time ago
that you were following your wife. She is to be married
right now."--"Yes," he said. The marriage was to be in a
lodge. He went there, peeped in, and a man saw him, who
said, "Are you coming in? Our chief says he will pass the
child about and he on whose breast it urinates shall marry
its mother."

So he went in. The girl saw him, and told her mother. "Oh,
that is the one I married."

When he arrived there, Mudjikiwis (not the youth's brother,
but another one, a Thunderer) was there too. They took the
child, and one man passed it. Mudjikiwis, the Thunderer,
held some water in his mouth. He seized the child, crying,
"Come here, nosis!" and spat the water over himself; but,
when he tried to claim the child, all the others laughed, as
they had seen his trick. When the child's real father took it
up, it urinated on him. Then all went out. The chief said,
"Do not let my son-in-law walk about, because he is really
tired. He shall not walk for ten days."

His father-in-law would go off all day. Hanging in the
lodge the youth saw his brother's arrow, with which his
wife had been shot. The father-in-law would burn sweet-
grass for the arrow at the rare intervals when he came back,
for he would be off for days at a time. On the fifth night the
youth felt rested, and could walk a little. Then he asked his

wife, "Why does your father smoke that arrow?" and she answered, "Oh, we never see those things up here. It is from below, and he thinks highly of it; therefore, he does so."

On the sixth night he was able to walk around in the brush; and he came to a spring, where he found, on the surface of the water, a rusty stain with which he: painted his face. He returned, and, as he was entering, his father-in-law cried, "Oh, that is why I want a son-in-law that is a human being! Where did he kill that bear? He is covered with blood.

Go and dress it," he ordered. The youth was frightened, as he had not seen any bear at all. "You people that live below," his wife said, "call them Giant Panthers. Show your brothers-in-law where it is." The youth took his brother-in-law to the spring. "Here is where I found the Panther," he said.

The ten Thunderers came up and struck the spring, and killed something there. After that the youth looked for springs all the time, and it came to pass that he found a number. One day he asked his wife, "Why does your father go away for whole days at a time?" and his wife said, "There is a large lake up here, and he hunts for fish there. He kills one every day, seldom two. He is the only one that can kill them."

The next morning the youth went to the lake, and found his father-in-law sitting by the shore fishing. The old man had a peculiar spear, which was forked at the end. The youth took it, and put barbs on it, so that the old man was able to catch a number of fish quickly. Then they went home.

When they arrived, his father-in-law said, "My son-in-law has taken many of them. I myself can only kill one, and sometimes two."

So he told all the people to go and get fish and eat them
freely. On the following day, the young man, according to
his mother-in-law's wish, took his wife to fish. They took
many fish, and carried them home. The father-in-law knew,
before they returned, that they had caught many.

The old man had had a dream. When he saw how the youth
prepared the spear which his daughter had given him, he
said, referring to his dream, "My dream was wrong, I
thought the youngest of the ten liked me the best. I made
the spear in the way I saw it, not as this one has shown me.
It is due to my dream that it is wrong. Your nine brothers
are having a hard time. Now, my sons, your sisters are
going away soon to be married."

For nine nights the youth saw a dim light at a distance. The
father-in-law said to him, " Do not go there, for a powerful
being lives there." The tenth night, however, the youth
disobeyed this injunction.

When he reached there, he saw a tall tree, and a huge
porcupine that was burrowing at the foot of the tree. The
porcupine struck the tree, and tried to kill it by shooting its
quills into it. After the porcupine had shot off all its quills,
the youth knocked it on the head, took two long quills from
the tree, and carried them home.

Even before he got there, his father-in-law knew what had
happened. They were delighted, for they said that the
porcupine would kill the Thunderers when they tried to
attack it. The father-in-law went out, and called to his sons
to go and dress the porcupine that the youth had killed. The
latter gave the two quills to his wife, though his father-in-
law wanted them. The father-in-law said, "My children, this

porcupine killed all our friends when they went to war against it. My sons-in-law below are miserable and lonely." The eldest of the daughters, who was called Mudjikiskwe'wic, was delighted at the news. "You will marry the oldest one, Mudjikiwis," she was told. They were all to be married in order, the eldest girl to the eldest brother, the youngest to the youngest one. The old man said, "Mudjikiskwe'wic shall take her brother-in-law with her when she goes down to the earth." The young women went down. Sh-swsh! went Mudjikiskwe'wic (the girl) with her dress.

They reached the steep place, and the married woman said to her husband that they would fly around. " If you do not catch me when I fly past, you will be killed here."

The women went off a little ways, and a heavy thunderstorm arose, big black clouds and lightning, yet he saw Mudjikiskwe'wic in it. She was green, and so was the sun; and as they passed she shouted once, then again a little nearer, and again close by.

Then he jumped off and caught her by the back. He closed his eyes as he did so, and did not open them until the Thunderer wife said, "Now let go!"

Then he found himself at home. He left the girls behind, and went to the lodge and opened the door a little.

Tolowim Woman and Butterfly Man

Maidu
Based on a tale reported by
Roland Dixon in 1904.

A Tolowim woman went out to gather food. She took her child with her, and while she worked, she stuck the point of the cradleboard in the ground and left the child alone. A large butterfly flew past, and she started after it and chased it for a long time. She would almost catch it, and then just miss. She thought, "Perhaps I can't run fast enough because of this heavy thing," and she threw away her deerskin robe. But still she never could quite overtake the creature. Finally, she threw away her apron too and hurried on, chasing the butterfly til night came. Then, her child forgotten, she lay down under a tree and went to sleep.

When she awoke in the morning, she found a man lying beside her. He said, "You have followed me this far; perhaps you would like to follow me always. If so, you must pass through a lot of my people." Without thinking of her child at all, the woman rose and followed the butterfly man. By and by they came to a large valley, whose southern side was full of butterflies. When the two reached the edge of the valley, the man said, "No one has ever before come through this valley alive. But you'll be safe if you don't lose sight of me. Follow closely."

They traveled for a long time. "Keep tight hold of me; don't let go," the butterfly man said again and again. When they come halfway through the valley, other butterflies swarmed about them in great numbers. They flew every way, all around the couple's heads and in their faces, for they wanted to get the Tolowim woman for themselves. She watched them for a long time, holding tightly to her new husband. But at last, unable to resist, she let go of him and reached out to seize one of the others. She missed that one and she tried to grab now one, now the other, but always failed, and so she wandered in the valley forever, dazed and lost.

She died there, and the butterfly man she had lost went on through the valley to his home. And now when people speak of the olden times: they say that this woman lost her lover, and tried to get others but lost them, and went crazy and died.

Cherokee Prayer Blessing

May the Warm Winds of Heaven
Blow softly upon your house.
May the Great Spirit
Bless all who enter there.
May your Moccasins
Make happy tracks
in many snows,
and may the Rainbow
Always touch your shoulder.

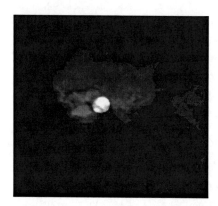

The Man Who Married the Moon

Isleta Pueblo
Published by Charles F. Lummis in St. Nicholas Magazine in 1897.

Long before the first Spaniards came to New Mexico, Isleta stood where it stands today--on a lava ridge that defies the gnawing current of the Rio Grande. In those far days, Nah-chu-ru-chu, "The Bluish Light of Dawn," dwelt in Isleta, and was a leader of his people. A weaver by trade, his rude loom hung from the dark rafters of his room; and in it he wove the strong black mantas or robes like those which are the dress of Pueblo women to this day.

Besides being very wise in medicine, Nah-chu-ru-chu was young, and tall, and strong, and handsome. All the girls of the village thought it a shame that he did not care to take a wife. For him the shyest dimples played, for him the whitest teeth flashed out, as the owners passed him in the plaza; but he had no eyes for them. Then, in the custom of the Tiwa, bashful fingers worked wondrous fringed shirts of buckskin, or gay awl sheaths, which found their way to his house by unknown messengers.

But Nah-chu-ru-chu paid no more attention to the gifts than to the smiles, and just kept weaving and weaving such mantas as were never seen in the land of the Tee-wahn before or since.

Two of his admirers were sisters who were called, in Tiwa language, Ee-eh-ch-choo-ri-ch'ahm-n- the Yellow Corn Maidens. They were both young and pretty, but they "had the evil road," or were witches, possessed of a magic power which they always used for ill. When all the other girls gave up, discouraged at Nah-chu-ru-shu's indifference, the Yellow Corn Maidens kept coming day after day, trying to win his notice. At last the matter became so annoying to Nah-chu-ru-chu that he hired the deep-voiced town crier to go through all the streets and announce that in four days Nah-chu-ru-chu would choose a wife.

For dippers to take water from the big earthen jars, the Tiwa used then, as they use to-day, queer little omates made of a gourd. But Nahchu-ru-chu, being a great medicine man and very rich, had a dipper of pure pearl, shaped like the gourds, but wonderfully precious.

"On the fourth day," proclaimed the crier, "Nah-chu-ru-chu will hang his pearl omate at his door, when every girl who will may throw a handful of cornmeal at it. And she whose meal is so well ground that it sticks to the omate, she shall be the wife of Nah-chu-ru-chu!"

When this strange news came rolling down the still evening air, there was a great scampering of little moccasined feet. The girls ran out from hundreds of gray adobe houses to catch every word; and when the crier had passed on, they ran back into the storerooms and began to ransack the corn bins for the biggest, evenest, and most perfect ears. Shelling the choicest, each took her few handfuls of kernels to the sloping metate, and with the mano, or hand stone, scrubbed the blue grist up and down and up and down till the hard corn was a soft blue meal. All the next day, and the next, and the next, they ground it over and over again, until it grew finer than ever flour was before; and every girl felt sure that her meal would stick to the omate of the handsome young weaver. The Yellow Corn Maidens worked hardest of all; day and night for four days they ground and ground, with all the magic spells they knew.

Now, in those far-off days the moon had not gone into the sky to live, but was a maiden of Isleta. And a very beautiful girl she was, but blind of one eye. She had long admired Nah-chu-ru-chu, but was always too maidenly to try to attract his attention as the other girls had done; and at the time when the crier made his proclamation, she happened to be away at her father's ranch. It was only upon the fourth day that she returned to town, and in a few moments the girls were to go with their meal to test it upon the magic dipper. The two Yellow Corn Maidens were just coming from their house as she passed, and they told her what was to be done. They were very confident of success, and hoped to pain her. They laughed derisively as she went running to her home.

By this time a long file of girls was coming to Nah-chu-ru-chu's house, outside whose door hung the pearl omate. Each girl carried in her hand a little jar of meal. As they passed the door, one by one, each took from the jar a handful and threw it against the magic dipper. But each time the meal dropped to the ground, and left the pure pearl undimmed and radiant as ever.

At last came the Yellow Corn Maidens, who had waited to watch the failure of the others. As they came where they could see Nah-chu-ru-chu sitting at his loom, they called: "Ah! here we have the meal that will stick!" and each threw a handful at the omate. But it did not stick at all; and still from his seat Nah-chu-ru-chu could see, in the shell's mirror like surface, all that went on outside.

The Yellow Corn Maidens were very angry, and instead of passing on as the others had done, they stood there and kept throwing and throwing at the omate, which smiled back at them with undiminished luster.

Just then, last of all, came the moon, with a single handful of meal which she had hastily ground. The two sisters were in a fine rage by this time, and mocked her, saying:

"Hoh! Pah-hlee-oh, Moon, you poor thing, we are very sorry for you! Here we have been grinding our meal for four days and still it will not stick, and we did not tell you till today. How then can you ever hope to win Nah-chu-ru-chu? Puh, you silly little thing!"

But the moon paid no attention whatsoever to their taunts. Drawing back her little dimpled hand, she threw the meal gently against the pearl omate, and so fine was it ground that every tiniest bit of it clung to the polished shell, and not a particle fell to the ground!

When Nah-chu-ru-chu saw that, he rose up quickly from his loom and came and took the moon by the hand, saying: "You are she who shall be my wife. You shall never want for anything, since I have very much." And he gave her many beautiful mantas, and cotton wraps, and fat boots of buckskin that wrap round and round, that she might dress as the wife of a rich chief. But the Yellow Corn Maidens, who had seen it all, went away vowing vengeance on the moon.

Nah-chu-ru-chu and his sweet moon-wife were very happy together. There was no other such housekeeper in all the pueblo as she, and no other hunter brought home so much buffalo meat from the vast plains to the east, nor so many antelopes, and black-tailed deer, and jack rabbits from the

Manzanos, as did Nah-chu-ru-chu. But constantly he was saying to her:

"Moon-wife, beware of the Yellow Corn Maidens, for they have the evil road and will try to do you harm; but you must always refuse to do whatever they propose."

And always the young wife promised.

One day the Yellow Corn Maidens came to the house and said: "Friend Nah-chu-ru-chu, we are going to the llano, the plain, to gather amole." (Amole is a soapy root the Pueblos use for washing.) "Will you not let your wife go with us?"

"Oh, yes, she may go," said Nah-chu-ru-chu. But taking her aside, he said: "Now be sure that while you are with them, you refuse whatever they may propose. "

The moon promised, and started away with the Yellow Corn Maidens.

In those days there was only a thick forest of cottonwoods where now the smiling vineyards, gardens, and orchards of Isleta are spread, and to reach the llano the three women had to go through the forest. In the very center of it they came to a deep pozo-a square well, with steps at one side leading down to the water's edge.

"Ay!" said the Yellow Corn Maidens, "How hot and thirsty is our walk! Come, let us get a drink of water."

But the moon, remembering her husband's words, said politely that she did not wish to drink. They urged in vain, but at last, looking down into the pozo, they called:

Oh, moon-friend, moon-friend! Come and look in this still water, and see how pretty you are!"

The moon, you must know, has always been just as fond of looking at herself in the water as she is to this very day; and forgetting Nahchu-ru-chu's warning, she came to the brink and looked down upon her fair reflection. But at that very moment the two witch sisters pushed her head foremost into the pozo, and drowned her; and then they filled the well with earth, and went away as happy as wicked hearts can be.

As the sun crept along the adobe floor, closer and closer to his seat, Nah-chu-ru-chu began to look oftener from his loom to the door. When the shadows were very long, he sprang suddenly to his feet, and walked to the house of the Yellow Corn Maidens with long, long strides.

"Yellow Corn Maidens," he asked them very sternly, "where is my little wife?" "Why, isn't she at home?" asked the wicked sisters, as if greatly surprised. "She got enough amole long before we did." "Ah," groaned Nah-chu-ru-chu within himself, "it is as I thought they have done her ill." But without a word to them he turned on his heel and went away.

From that hour all went wrong at Isleta; for Nah-chu-ru-chu held the well-being of all his people, even unto life and death. Paying no attention to what was going on about him, he sat motionless upon the topmost crosspiece of the estufa (the kiva, or sacred council chamber ladder the highest point in all the town) with his head bowed upon his hands. There he sat for days, never speaking, never moving. The children who played along the streets looked up with awe to the motionless figure, and ceased their boisterous play. The old men shook their heads gravely, and muttered: 'We are in evil times, for Nah-chu-ru-chu is mourning, and will not be comforted; and there is no more rain, so that our crops are dying in the fields. What shall we do?"

At last all the councilors met together, and decided that there must be another effort made to find the lost wife. It was true that the great Nah-chu-ru-chu had searched for her in vain, and the people had helped him; but perhaps someone else might be more fortunate. So they took some of the sacred smoking weed wrapped in a corn husk and went to the eagle, who has the sharpest eyes in all the world. Giving him the sacred gift, they said:

"Eagle-friend, we see Nah-chu-ru-chu in great trouble, for he has lost his moon-wife. Come, search for her, we pray you, to discover if she be alive or dead."

So the eagle took the offering, and smoked the smoke prayer; and then he went winging upward into the sky. Higher and higher he rose, in great upward circles, while his keen eyes noted every stick, and stone, and animal on the face of all the world. But with all his eyes, he could see nothing of the lost wife; and at last he came back sadly, and said:

"People-friends, I went up to where I could see the whole world, but I could not find her."

Then the people went with an offering to the coyote, whose nose is sharpest in all the world, and besought him to try and find the moon. The coyote smoked the smoke prayer, and started off with his nose to the ground, trying to find her tracks. He trotted all over the earth; but at last he too came back without finding what he sought.

Then the troubled people got the badger to search, for he is the best of all the beasts at digging (it was he whom the Trues employed to dig the caves in which the people first dwelt when they came to this world). The badger trotted and pawed, and dug everywhere, but he could not find the moon; and he came home very sad.

Then they asked the osprey, who can see furthest under water, and he sailed high above the lakes and rivers in the world, till he could count the pebbles and the fish in them, but he too failed to discover the lost moon.

By this time the crops were dead and sere in the fields, and thirsty animals walked crying along the river. Scarcely could the people themselves dig deep enough to find water to keep them alive. They were at a loss, but at last they thought: We will go now to the P'ah-ku-ee-teh-aydeh (the water-goose grandfather, which means turkey buzzard), who can find the dead-for surely she is dead, or the others would have found her.

So they went to him, and besought him. The turkey buzzard wept when he saw Nah-chu-ru-chu still sitting there upon the ladder, and said: "Truly it is sad for our great friend; but for me, I am afraid to go, since they who are more mighty than I have already failed. Yet I will try." And spreading his broad wings, he went climbing up the spiral ladder of the sky. Higher he wheeled, and higher, till at last not even the eagle could see him. Up and up, till the sun began to singe his head, and not even the eagle had ever been so high. He cried with pain, but still he kept mounting-until he was so close to the sun that all the feathers were burned from his head and neck. But he could see nothing, and at last, frantic with the burning, he came wheeling downward. When he got back to the estufa where all the people were waiting, they saw that his head and neck had been burned bare of feathers-and from that day to this the feathers would never grow out again.

"And did you see nothing?" they all asked, when they had bathed his burns.

"Nothing," he answered, "except that when I was halfway down, I saw in the middle of yon cottonwood forest a little mound covered with all the beautiful flowers in the world."

"Oh!" cried Nah-chu-ru-chu, speaking for the first time, "Go, friend, and bring me one flower from the very middle of the mound."

Off flew the buzzard, and in a few minutes returned with a little white flower. Nah-chu-ru-chu took it and, descending from the ladder in silence, walked solemnly to his house, while all the wondering people followed.

When Nah-chu-ru-chu came inside his home once more, he took a new manta and spread it in the middle of the room. Laying the wee white flower tenderly in its center, he put another manta above it. Then, dressing himself in the splendid buckskin suit that the lost wife had made him, and taking in his right hand the sacred guaje, rattle, he seated himself at the head of the mantas and sang:

"Shu-nah, shu-nah! Ai-ay, ai-ay, ai-ay-ay. Seeking her, seeking her! There-away, there-away."

When he had finished the song, all could see that the flower had begun to grow, so that it lifted the upper manta a little. Again he sang, shaking his gourd; and still the flower kept growing.

Again and again he sang; and when he had finished for the fourth time, it was plain to all that a human form lay between the two mantas. And when he sang his song the fifth time, the form sat up and moved. Tenderly he lifted away the upper cloth; and there sat his sweet moon-wife, fairer than ever, and alive as before!

For four days the people danced and sang in the public square. Nahchu-ru-chu was happy again; and now the rain began to fall. The choked earth drank and was glad and green, and the dead crops came to life.

When his wife told him what the witch sisters had done, he was very angry; and that day he made a beautiful hoop to play the hoop game. He painted it, and put many strings across it, and decorated it with beaded buckskin.

"Now," said he, "the wicked Yellow Corn Maidens will come to congratulate you, and will pretend not to know where you were. You must not speak of that, but invite them to go out and play a game with you."

In a day or two the witch sisters did come, with deceitful words; and the moon invited them to go out and play a game. They went up to the edge of the llano, and there she let them get a glimpse of the pretty hoop.

"Oh, give us that, moon-friend," they teased. But she refused. At last, however, she said: "Well, we will play the hoop game. I will stand here, and you there; and if, when I roll it to you, you catch it before it falls upon its side, you may have it."

So the witch sisters stood a little way down the hill, and she rolled the bright hoop. As it came trundling to them, both grasped it at the same instant; and lo! instead of the Yellow

Corn Maidens, there were two great snakes, with tears rolling down ugly faces. The moon came and put upon their heads a little of the pollen of the corn blossom (still used by Pueblo snake charmers) to tame them, and a pinch of sacred meal for their food.

"Now," she said, "you have the reward of treacherous friends. Here shall be your home among these rocks and cliffs forever, but you must never be found upon the prairie; and you must never bite a person. Remember you are women, and must be gentle."

And then the moon went home to her husband, and they were very happy together. As for the sister snakes, they still dwell where she bade them, and never venture away; though sometimes the people bring them to their houses to catch mice, for these snakes never hurt a person.

"Give thanks for unknown blessings
already on their way."

Native American Saying

A Legend of Multnomah Falls

Multnomah
Reported by Ella Clark
in 1953.

Many years ago the head chief of the Multnomah people had a beautiful young daughter. She was especially dear to her father because he had lost all his sons in fighting, and he was now an old man. He chose her husband with great care - a young chief from his neighbors, the Clatsop people. To the wedding feast came many people from tribes along the lower Columbia and south of it.

The wedding feast was to last for several days. There were swimming races and canoe races on the river. There would be bow-and-arrow contests, horse racing, dancing, and feasting. The whole crowd was merry, for both the maiden and the young warrior were loved by their people.

But without warning the happiness changed to sorrow. A sickness came over the village.

Children and young people were the first victims; then strong men became ill and died in one day. The wailing of women was heard throughout the Multnomah village and the camps of the guests.

"The Great Spirit is angry with us," the people said to each other. The head chief called together his old men and his warriors for counsel and asked gravely, 'What can we do to soften the Great Spirit's wrath?"

Only silence followed his question. At last one old medicine man arose. "There is nothing we can do. If it is the will of the Great Spirit that we die, then we must meet our death like brave men. The Multnomah have ever been a brave people."

The other members of the council nodded in agreement - all except one, the oldest medicine man. He had not attended the wedding feast and games, but he had come in from the mountains when he was called by the chief. He rose and, leaning on his stick, spoke to the council. His voice was low and feeble.

"1 am a very old man, my friends; 1 have lived a long, long time. Now you will know why. I will tell you a secret my father told me. He was a great medicine man of the Multnomah, many summers and many snows in the past.

"When he was an old man, he told me that when I became old, the Great Spirit would send a sickness upon our people. All would die, he said, unless a sacrifice was made to the Great Spirit. Some pure and innocent maiden of the tribe, the daughter of a chief, must willingly give her life for her people. Alone, she must go to a high cliff above Big River and throw herself upon the rocks below. If she does this, the sickness will leave us at once."

Then the old man said, "I have finished; my father's secret is told. Now I can die in peace."

Not a word was spoken as the medicine man sat down. At last the chief lifted his head. "Let us call in all the maidens whose fathers or grandfathers have been headmen."

Soon a dozen girls stood before him, among them his own loved daughter. The chief told them what the old medicine man had said. "I think his words are the words of truth," he added.

Then he turned to his medicine men and his warriors, "Tell our people to meet death bravely. No maiden shall be asked to sacrifice herself. The meeting has ended."

The sickness stayed in the village, and many more people died. The daughter of the head chief sometimes wondered if she should be the one to give her life to the Great Spirit. But she loved the young warrior she wanted to live.

A few days later she saw the sickness on the face of her lover. Now she knew what she must do. She cooled his hot face, cared for him tenderly, and left a bowl of water by his bedside. Then she slipped away alone, without a word to anyone.

All night and all the next day she followed the trail to the great river. At sunset she reached the edge of a cliff overlooking the water. She stood there in silence for a few moments, looking at the jagged rocks far below. Then she turned her face toward the sky and lifted up her arms. She spoke aloud to the Great Spirit.

"You are angry with my people. Will you make the sickness pass away if I give you my life? Only love and peace and purity are in my heart. If you will accept me as a sacrifice for my people, let some token hang in the sky. Let me know that my death will not be in vain and that the sickness will quickly pass."

Just then she saw the moon coming up over the trees across the river. It was the token. She closed her eyes and jumped from the cliff.

Next morning, all the people who had expected to die that day arose from their beds well and strong. They were full of joy. Once more there was laughter in the village and in the camps of the guests.

Suddenly someone asked, "What caused the sickness to pass away? Did one of the maidens-?"

Once more the chief called the daughters and granddaughters of the headmen to come before him. This time one was missing.

The young Clatsop warrior hurried along the trail which leads to Big River. Other people followed. On the rocks below the high cliff they found the girl they all loved. There they buried her.

Then her father prayed to the Great Spirit, "Show us some token that my daughter's spirit has been welcomed into the land of the spirits."

Almost at once they heard the sound of water above. All the people looked up to the cliff. A stream of water, silvery white, was coming over the edge of the rock. It broke into floating mist and then fell at their feet. The stream continued to float down in a high and beautiful waterfall. For many summers the white water has dropped from the cliff into the pool below. Sometimes in winter the spirit of the brave and beautiful maiden comes back to see the waterfall. Dressed in white, she stands among the trees at one side of Multnomah Falls. There she looks upon the place where she made her great sacrifice and thus saved her lover and her people from death.

We do not want schools....
they will teach us to have churches.
We do not want churches....
they will teach us to quarrel about God.
We do not want to learn that.
We may quarrel with men sometimes
about things on this earth,
but we never quarrel about God.
We do not want to learn that.

Heinmot Tooyalaket (Chief Joseph), Nez Perce Leader

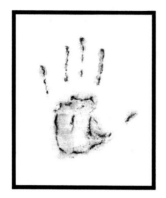

The False Bride Groom

A Gros Ventre Legend
Kroeber, Anthropological
Papers of the American
Museum of Natural History, i,
108, No. 28

There were two girls, sisters.
The older sister said, "We will go to look for Shell-Spitter." There was a man who was poor and who lived alone with his old mother. He was the Loon and his mother was Badger-Woman.

He heard that two girls were looking for Shell-Spitter. He went to the children of the camp, and took their shells away from them. The girls arrived, and asked for Shell-Spitter's tent. It was shown them, and they went to it. There stood the Loon. "What are you girls looking for?" he said. "We are looking for Shell-Spitter." "I am he." "Let us see you spit shells."

He had filled his mouth with shells, and now spit them out. The two girls stooped, and hastily picked them up, each trying to snatch them before the other. Then he took them to his tent. His tent was old and poor. His mother was gray-headed. He said to them, "I have another tent. It is fine and large. I have brought you here because there is more room to sleep." The girls went inside.

Soon some one called to the Loon, "Come over! they are making the sun-dance!" "Oh!" he said. "Now I have to sit in the middle again, and give away presents. I am tired of it. For once they ought to get some one else. I am to sit on the chief's bed in the middle of the lodge."

He told his mother, "Do not let these women go out." Then
he went out, and the old woman guarded the door. When
she was asleep, one of the girls said, "I will go out to look."
She stepped over the old woman, and went to the dance-
lodge. Looking in, she saw the people dancing on the
Loon's rump. On the bed in the middle sat a fine man.
Whenever he spit, he spit shells. The ground all around him
was covered with them.

Then the girl went back, and called to her sister, "Come
out! They are dancing on this man; but the one who spits
shells sits in the middle of the lodge." Then they both went
to the lodge. They went inside and sat down behind Shell-
Spitter.

Then the man on the ground, on whom the people were
dancing, saw them. He jumped up. He killed Shell-Spitter,
and ran out. He said to his mother, "I told you to watch, and
not to let those women out." Then he told her, "Dig a hole
quickly!" She quickly dug a hole inside the tent. He entered
it, and then she followed him. The people came, but could
do nothing. When they stopped trying to shoot, Badger-
Woman came out of the hole, singing in ridicule of Shell-
Spitter's death. Before the people could reach her she
dropped into the hole again. She did this repeatedly.

The Alligator That Stole a Man

A Hitchiti Legend
John R. Swanton, Myths and Tales
of the Southeastern Indians, 1929

A man was out hunting and made a camp at night. He got a log and lay down, using it as a pillow. While he was lying there an alligator crept up to him and seized him.

But when it was taking him off it carried him through some thick bushes and he held on to them so firmly that it could not get along well with him and laid him down. The man looked around to see which way to go and when the alligator was some distance away he ran off.

Then he returned to his camp, brought in a log, wrapped a blanket around it, laid it down and waited at, a little distance.

He stood by a tree holding his gun. Now the alligator came back again and acted as before, taking the log in its mouth. The man aimed at its mouth, and, when he fired, it ran away.

Then he went off and slept. In the morning he came back. When he went to look for the alligator he came to a pond near which was a nest.

He saw the alligator lying bent over the nest dead

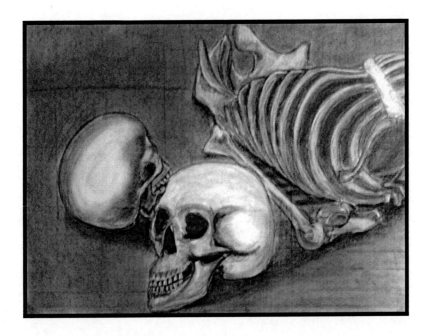

The Man Who Was Afraid of Nothing

Brule Sioux
Told by Lame Deer, and recorded by Richard Erdoes.

Now, there were four ghosts sitting together, talking, smoking ghost smoke, having a good time, as far as it's possible for ghosts to have a good time. One of them said: "I've heard of a young man nothing can scare. He's not afraid of us, so they say."

The second ghost said: "I bet I could scare him." The third ghost said: "We must try to make him shiver and run and hide." The fourth ghost said: "Let's bet; let's make a wager. Whoever can scare him the most, wins." And they agreed to bet their ghost horses.

So this young man who was never afraid came walking along one night. The moon was shining. Suddenly in his path the first ghost materialized, taking the form of a skeleton. "Hou, friend," said the ghost, clicking his teeth together, making a sound like a water drum.

"Hou, cousin," said the young man, "you're in my way. Get off the road and let me pass." "Not until we have played the hoop-and-stick game. If you lose, I'll make you into a skeleton like me."

The young man laughed. He bent the skeleton into a big hoop, tying it with some grass. He took one of the skeleton's leg bones for his game stick and rolled the skeleton along, scoring again and again with the leg bone. "Well, I guess I won this game," said the young man. "How about some shinny ball?"

The young man took the skeleton's skull and used the leg bone to drive it ahead of him like a ball.

"Ouch!" said the skull. "You're hurting me; you're giving me a headache."

"Well, you asked for it. Who proposed this game, you or me? You're a silly fellow." The young man kicked the skull aside and walked on.

Further on he met the second ghost also in the form of a skeleton, who jumped at him and grabbed him with bony hands. "Let's dance, friend," the skeleton said.

"A very good idea, cousin ghost," said the young man. "What shall we use for a drum and drumstick? I know!" Taking the ghost's thighbone and skull, the young man danced and sang, beating on the skull with the bone.

"Stop, stop!" cried the skull. "This is no way to dance. You're hurting me; you're giving me a headache."

"You're lying, ghost," said the young man. "Ghosts can't feel pain."

"I don't know about other ghosts," said the skull, "but me, I'm hurting."

"For a ghost you're awfully sensitive," said the young man. "Really, I'm disappointed. There we were, having a good time, and you spoiled my fun with your whining. Groan somewhere else."

 The young man kicked the skull aside and scattered the rest of the bones all over.

"Now see what you've done," complained the ghost, "it will take me hours to get all my bones together. You're a bad man." "Stop your whining," said the young man. "It gives you something to do." Then he went on. Soon he came upon the third ghost, another skeleton. "This is getting monotonous," said the young man. "Are you the same as before? Did I meet you further back?"

"No," Said the ghost. "Those were my cousins. They're soft. I'm tough. Let's wrestle. If I win, I'll make you into a skeleton like me."

"My friend," said the young man, "I don't feel like wrestling with you, I feel like sledding. There's enough snow on the hill for that. I should have buffalo ribs for it, but your rib cage will go."

The young man took the ghost's rib cage and used it as a sled. "This is fun!" he said, whizzing down the hill.

"Stop, stop," cried the ghost's skull "You're breaking my ribs!"

The young man said: "Friend, you look funny without a rib cage. You've grown so short. Here!" And he threw the ribs into a stream. "Look what you've done! What can I do without my ribs? I need them."

"Jump in the water and dive for them," said the young man. "You look as if you need a bath. It'll do you good, and your woman will appreciate it."

'What do you mean? I am a woman!" said the ghost, insulted.

"With skeletons I can't tell, you pretty thing," he said, and walked on.

Then he came upon the chief ghost, a skeleton riding a skeleton horse. "I've come to kill you," said the skeleton.

The young man made faced at the ghost. He rolled his eyes; he showed his teeth; he gnashed them; he made weird noises. "I'm a ghost myself, a much more terrible ghost than you are," he said.

The skeleton got scared and tried to turn his ghost horse, but the young man seized it by the bridle. "A horse is just what I want," he said. 'I've walked enough. Get off!" He yanked the skeleton from its mount and broke it into pieces. The skeleton was whimpering, but the young man mounted the skeleton horse and rode it into camp. Day was just breaking, and some women who were up early to get water saw him and screamed loudly. They ran away while the whole village was awakened by their shrieking. The people looked out of their tipis and became frightened when they saw him on the ghost horse. As soon as the sun appeared, however, the skeleton vanished. The young man laughed.

The story of his ride on the skeleton horse was told all through the camp. Later he joined a group of men and started to brag about putting the four skeleton ghosts to flight. People shook their heads, saying, "This young man is really brave. Nothing frightens him. He is the bravest man who ever lived."

Just then a tiny spider was crawling up this young man's sleeve. When someone called his attention to it, he cried, "Eeeeech! Get this bug off me! Please, someone take it off, I can't stand spiders! Eeeeeeech!" He shivered, he writhed, he carried on. A little girl laughed and took the spider off him.

"We are now about to take our leave and kind farewell to our native land, the country the Great Spirit gave our Fathers, we are on the eve of leaving that country that gave us birth, it is with sorrow we are forced by the white man to quit the scenes of our childhood...we bid farewell to it and all we hold dear." –

Charles Hicks, Tsalagi (Cherokee) Vice Chief speaking of the Trail of Tears, November 4, 1838

The Deer Women

A Hitchiti Legend
John R. Swanton, Myths
and Tales of the
Southeastern Indians,
1929

A man wanted two young women. Those women went to the dances but always disappeared immediately afterwards, and he could not find where they went.

After things had gone on in this way for some time, at one of the dances that man fastened a string to the dresses of those young women. He held the string in his hand. He followed them about and when they started off he still followed, holding the string. The women discovered that he was following them.

When they said to him, "What do you want?" he answered, "I want to go with you," and they said "All right," and set forward.

"Near our home there is a big hole. We are going to jump into it and you jump in with us," they said to him. When they got to the place it was as he had been told and they jumped down into the hole, the man still with them. Then they went on again.

Before they had gone far they came to a large cavern where there were many deer. That is where the deer came from. When the three got there the old Bucks said to him, "What are you doing here?"

When they asked him that, he said, "I came because I want to marry these women."

"Well, wait and it will soon be time to go out. When that time comes, they will go out and you can have the women."

So the man waited. While he was sitting there the time to go out came, and when they went out he went with them. He went out and walked around covered with a deerskin, and he chased the female deer.

While he was there, the old Bucks said, "You must travel about very carefully. Red-feet travel about. They must be watched very closely. Soup-eaters are also about but they are not dangerous."

It was just as they had told him, and presently he was killed. Then he went back and they dressed him up in another deerskin. The fourth time one is killed it is the last, and that man then disappeared for good.

This is how it has been told.

The Transformed Grandmother

Pima Papago
Based on a tale collected
by Lucy Howard.

An old woman lived with her two grandchildren in a lonely place near a high, steep mountain.

One day she told the children that a plant which the Indians use for food grows on the mountains, and that she had made up her mind to gather some of it.

She started toward the mountain nearby, and when she got to the foot of it, she could not see the top. Yet she was determined to climb it. She took her cane in one hand, and, singing her song, began to clamber up.

She grew weary, sat down, and looked up, but the top did not seem any nearer. She began climbing again.

She had to rest many times before she could even see the summit, and it was evening before she arrived there. She had suffered all the way, and her feet were bleeding from rocks and thorns.

At last, however, she stood before the plant itself and began pulling it out of the ground. But she pulled it too hard, and away she rolled down the mountainside, the plant with her.

Great stones and rocks rolled over her before her body reached the bottom. She was killed on the way, but it was said that the bones picked themselves up and started toward home, singing a song.

In the meantime, the children had begun to feel anxious for her. As they sat around the little fire they had built, they heard someone singing or talking far away. Nearer and nearer the sound came, and the younger one asked what was making the noise. The older one recognized the voice of her grandmother, but knew from its strangeness that her grandmother was no longer living. She told the younger one that they must go into the house and close the doorway with a "mine," a kind of blanket that is made from a weed woven like a basket.

They went inside and held the mine over the door, so that the woman might not enter. At last she came and ran around the house many times, singing as she ran. The children wondered what they would do if she should break through the door. The girl said she would turn into a blue stone, and her little brother said he would turn into a stick burning at one end. So they dropped the mine they held in their hands, and when the woman entered, there was nobody to be seen-only the blue stone and the burning stick. She stood calling, but no answer came.

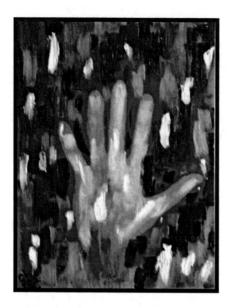

Big Eater's Wife

Pequod
Retold from several
nineteenth-century
sources.

Big Eater ate and ate.
He never stopped
eating. He had his
wigwam and two
canoes on an island
close to the mainland
shore. Big Eater was
powerful, but
sometimes an evil ghost woman can defeat the most powerful man.

One-day Big Eater was looking across the water, and there
on the opposite shore he saw a beautiful young woman
digging clams. How could he know that she was a ghost-
witch? He hailed her across the water: "Beautiful girl, come
live with me. Sleep with me!"

"No," she said. "Yes-No. yes. No. Yes, yes, yes! Well, all
right."

Big Eater got in one of his two canoes and paddled over.
The woman was even more beautiful close up. All right,
pretty one, step into the canoe."

"Yes, but first I must get my things." Soon the girl came
back with a mortar and pestle and some eggs. She put them
in the canoe, and Big Eater paddled her over.

They ate. The beautiful woman said: "Oh my, what great heaps of food you can eat!" "Yes, I'm powerful that way." They went to bed. "Oh my, how often you can do it" "Yes, I'm powerful that way." "You sure are." So they lived happily for a long time.

But after a while this girl got tired of Big Eater. She thought, "He's fat, he's not young. I want a change; I want to have a young, slim man loving me. I'll leave."

So when Big Eater went out fishing in one of his canoes, the girl made a doll, a large doll, large as a grown woman. She placed the doll in her bed, took her mortar, pestle, and eggs, put them in Big Eater's second canoe, and paddled off.

Big Eater came home early from fishing. Thinking it was his wife he was climbing in with, he got into bed. He touched the doll, and the doll began to scream and shriek. "Wife," he said, "stop this big noise or I'm going to beat you." Then he saw that it was a doll lying in bed with him.

Big Eater jumped up and looked around. The mortar and pestle and eggs were gone. He ran down to the shore, got into the remaining canoe, and paddled furiously after his wife.

Soon he saw her, also paddling hard. But he was stronger than she and pulled closer and closer. He drew up behind her canoe until both almost touched. "Now I'll catch her," he thought.

Then the woman threw her mortar out of the canoe over the stem. At once all the water around him turned into mortars, and Big Eater was stuck. He couldn't paddle until at last he lifted his canoe and carried it over the mortars. By the time he gained clear water again, his wife was a long way off.

Again he paddled furiously. Again he gained on her. Again he almost caught her. Then she threw her pestle out over the stem, and at once the water turned into pestles. Again Big Eater was stuck, trying to paddle through this sea of pestles but unable to. He had to carry his canoe over them, and when he hit open water again, his wife was far distant.

Again Big Eater drove through the water with all his strength. Again he gained on her; again he almost caught her. Then from the stem of her canoe the woman threw the eggs out. At once the water turned into eggs, and once more Big Eater was stuck. The eggs were worse than the mortar and pestle, because Big Eater couldn't carry his canoe over them. Then he hit the eggs, smashing them one by one and cleaving a path through the gooey mess. He hit clear water, and his wife's canoe was only a little dot on the horizon.

Again he paddled mightily. Slowly he gained on her again. It took a long time, but finally he was almost even with her. "This time I'll catch you!" he shouted. "You have nothing left to throw out."

But his wife just laughed. She pulled out a long hair from her head, and at once it was transformed into a lance. She stood up and hurled this magic hair lance at Big Eater. It hit him square in the chest, piercing him through and through. Big Eater screamed loudly and fell down dead. That's what can happen to a man if he marries a ghost-witch.

The Orphan and The Owl

A Hitchiti Legend John R. Swanton, Myths and Tales of the Southeastern Indians, 1929

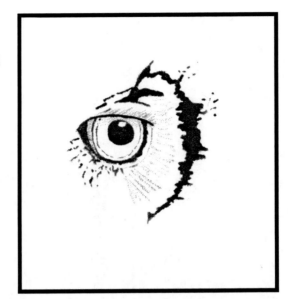

Some men started off hunting. They traveled along and camped at a certain place. They had an orphan boy to look after their camp. Just before light they started out hunting, and while the orphan still sat in camp an Owl sitting on the top of a tree said, "A bear is hidden in the ăsawe tree standing there. Tell the man who is good to you; let him kill it and eat." After the Owl had gone away the orphan sat about until the hunters came back one by one, but that one that liked him had not come.

He came back last, and the orphan said to him, "An Owl came and said to me, 'A bear is hidden close by. Let him kill it for you and then you eat it.'" So they two started out When they reached the place the bear was there as had been foretold, and the man killed it and skinned it, and they brought it back.

When they got to camp they had a quantity of meat.

That night the Owl came again and sat on a tree. When it made a noise, one of the hunters said, "What does he say?"

That orphan boy said to him, "He says to you 'Someone else is going with your wife.'" That is what he told him.

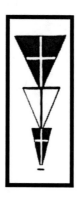

There is a road in the hearts of all of us, hidden and seldom traveled,
which leads to an unkown, secret place.
The old people came literally to love the soil,
and they sat or reclined on the ground with a feeling of
being close to a mothering power.
Their teepees were built upon the earth
and their altars were made of earth.
The soul was soothing, strengthening, cleansing and healing.
That is why the old Indian still sits upon the earth instead of
propping himself up and away from its life giving forces.
For him, to sit or lie upon the ground is to be able to think more deeply
and to feel more keenly. He can see more clearly into the mysteries of
life and come closer in kinship to other lives about him.

Chief Luther Standing Bear

The Wanderings of the Bear Clan

A Hopi Legend
H. R. Voth, The Traditions of the Hopi, Field Columbian Museum Anthropological Series, 1905

After we had left the sípahpuni the Bear people separated and went ahead of the others. First they came somewhere near the present site of Phoenix, and stayed there awhile.

They remained for or shorter or longer periods at many different places. Finally, they came to the Little Colorado River, and about there it was where they assumed the clan name, but just exactly where the place was nobody can tell. Their forefathers say that the party once came upon a dead bear that they looked at, and from that they were called forever afterwards the Bear clan. Another party that traveled with them took the hide of the bear, of which the hair had already been removed by little animals (Mû'yi. Pl. Mû'mutyu), who use hair or wool for their nests or burrows.

These people took the skin and cut from it carrying straps (piqö'sha), from which they were called Piqö'sha clan. Another party came upon the bear at just this time and were called Mû'yi clan, after the small mice mentioned before.

These three clans arrived there just about the same time, and hence are considered as closely related to one another.

Shortly after another party passed by and found many bluebirds sitting upon the cadaver eating from it; so they were called the Bluebird clan (Chórzh-ñamu). Still later another party, came upon the scene and found the remains of the cadaver full of spider web, so this party was called Spider (Kóhk'ang) clan. By and by a sixth migrating party came along.

By this time the bones of the bear were bleached already. They took the skull, tied yucca leaves to it and carried it along as a drinking vessel in the manner in which the chief's or priest's jugs (móngwikurus) are carried at the present time, and from this. that party was called the jug (Wíkurzh) clan. Finally, a seventh party came along and found the place where the bear had been killed swarming with ants, so they were called the Ant (Ánñamu) clan.

These seven clans have derived their names from the same origin, and are now considered as being related to one another. The Bear clan is also said to have halted at various places along the Little Colorado River. From there they moved eastward, stopping for some time at a place called Badger Spring (Honánva).

From this place they again moved eastward, stopped at a place called Mákwutavi, and from here they finally moved to Matö'ví, a large spring a number of miles south of Shongópavi. At this place they also remained for a considerable length of time, but finally they moved northward to the present site of Shongópavi, where they remained. They being the first to arrive at this place, they have ever since considered themselves to be the leading clan in the village, the village chief having also been chosen from their clan.

A few persons of the Bear clan moved from here to Oraíbi, where the chieftainship of the so-called Liberal or Friendly faction is still held by that clan, the Conservative or Hostile faction of that village selecting their chief from the Spider clan. Two of this clan moved to the villages of Shupaúlavi and Mishóngnovi, where the office of the village chief has also remained in this clan to the present day.

The Bear clan brought with them the altar paraphernalia, song, etc., of the Blue Flute cult. When they stopped and planted anywhere they would perform the Blue Flute ceremony and sing the songs, and their crop would then grow and mature very quickly, so that they would have something to eat. They also brought with them the Hû Katcina, the Bear (Hon) Katcina, the Â'ototo Natácka, his wife Cóoyok Wuhti, and finally the Cóoyoko Táhaam.

Later on other clan and migrating parties arrived at Shongópavi asking of the Bear clan admission to the village. If proper arrangements could be made with the Bear clan they remained; if not, they moved on. Many of the large and small ruins with which the country is covered date back to the time of the migration of these different clans, showing the places where they made stays of shorter or longer duration.

The Two War Gods and the Two Maidens

A Hopi Legend
H. R. Voth, The
Traditions of the Hopi,
Field Columbian Museum
Anthropological Series,
1905

A long time ago Pöokónghoya and his little brother Balö'ngahoya lived north of the village at the shrine of the Achámali. One day they heard that two beautiful maidens were watching some fields west of the village of Hû'ckovi, of which the ruins may still be seen a few miles north-west of Oraíbi. They concluded that they would go hunting and at the same time visit those two maidens.

When they arrived there the maidens joyfully greeted them and they were joking and teasing each other. The maidens believed that the two brothers had come with the intention to marry them, and they said, in a half-jesting manner, to their suitors: "We will cut off an arm from each one of you, and if you do not die you may own us."

The younger brother was at once willing, saying to his elder brother: "They are beautiful; let us not be afraid of having our arm cut off." The elder brother hesitated, saying, that that would hurt. So the younger brother said, "I am willing," laid his right arm over the edge of the mealing trough at which the maidens had been working, and one of the maidens struck the arm with the upper mealing stone and cut it off, the arm dropping into the trough or bin. His elder brother hereupon laid his arm over the edge of the bin, which consisted of a thin, sharp slab, and the other maiden also cut his arm off with her mealing stone. Now the two brothers said: "If we recover, we shall come after you. Hand us our arm, now." The maidens did so and the two brothers left, each one carrying his severed arm, arriving at their home north of Oraíbi, they told their grandmother what had happened.

"There," she said, "you have been in something again and have done some mischief."

"Yes," they said, "We met two beautiful maidens and liked them very much, and so we allowed them to cut off our arms. "Very well, she said, "I am going to set you right again." So she asked them to lay down north of the fireplace.

She placed the two arms by their sides, covered them up, whereupon she commenced to sing a song. When she was through singing, she told them now to get up. They did so and found their arms healed. The next day they proceeded to the house of the maidens, who were surprised to see them fully recovered. The older of the two sisters was the prettier one and Pöokónghoya wanted to choose that one. His younger brother protested, saying: "Yesterday you were not willing to have your arm cut off, as you were then afraid, and now you want to have the first choice. I had my arm cut off first and I am going to choose first," to which his elder brother finally consented. They slept with the maidens that night and then left them and returned to their home north of Oraíbi.

Dug-From Ground

A Hupa Legend
Goddard, University of Cal. Publications in American
Archaeology & Ethnology, i, 146, No. 2

An old woman was living with her granddaughter, a virgin.
The girl used to go to dig roots and her grandmother used
to say to her, "You must not dig those with two stocks."
The girl wondered why she was always told that.

One morning she thought, "I am going to dig one," so she
went across the river and began digging. She thought, "I am
going to take out one with a double stock." When she had
dug it out she heard a baby cry. She ran back to the river,
and when she got there she heard someone crying "mother"
after her.

She jumped into the boat and pushed it across. When she
got across, the baby had tumbled down to the other shore.
She ran up to the house and there she heard it crying on that
side. She ran into the house, then she heard it crying back
of the house.

At once she sat down and then she heard it tumble on the
roof of the house. The baby tumbled through the smoke-
hole and then rolled about on the floor. The old woman
jumped up and put it in a baby basket. The young woman
sat with her back to the fire and never looked at the child.

The old woman took care of the baby alone. After a time, it

commenced to sit up and finally to walk. When he was big enough to shoot, the old woman made a bow and he began to kill birds. Afterward he killed all kinds of game; and, because his mother never looked at him, he gave whatever he killed to his grandmother.

Finally, he became a man. The young woman had been in the habit of going out at dawn and not returning until dark. She brought back with her acorns as long as her finger. One time the young man thought "I am going to watch and see where she goes."

The young woman had always said to herself, "If he will bring acorns from the place I bring them, and if he will kill a white deer, I will call him my son."

Early one morning the son saw his mother come out of the house and start up the ridge. He followed her and saw her go along until she came to a dry tree. She climbed this and it grew with her to the sky. The young man then returned saying, "Tomorrow I am going up there." The woman came home at night with the usual load of long acorns.

The next morning the man went the way his mother had gone, climbed the tree as he had seen her do, and it grew with him to the sky. When he arrived there he saw a road. He followed that until he came to an oak, which he climbed, and waited to see what would happen. Soon he heard laughing girls approaching.

They came to the tree and began to pick acorns from allotted spaces under it.

The young man began to throw down acorns. "That's right, Blue jay," said one of the girls. Then another said, "It might be Dug-from-the-ground. You can hardly look at him, they say, he is so handsome."

Two others said, "Oh, I can look at him, I always look at this walking one (pointing to the sun); that is the one you can hardly look at." He came down from the tree and passed between the girls. The two who had boasted they could look at him, turned their faces to the ground. The other two who had thought they could not look him in the face were able to do so.

The young man killed the deer, the killing of which the mother had made the second condition for his recognition as a son. He then filled the basket from his mother's place under the tree and went home. When the woman saw him with the acorns as long as one's finger, she called him her son.

After a time, he said, "I am going visiting." "All right," said the grandmother, and then she made for him a bow and arrows of blue-stone, and a shiny stick and sweat-house wood of the same material. These he took and concealed by putting them under the muscles of his forearm.

He dressed himself for the journey and set out. He went to the home of the immortals at the edge of the world toward the east. When he got down to the shore on this side they saw him. One of them took out the canoe of red obsidian and stretched it until it was the proper size. He launched it and came across for him.

When he had landed, the young man placed his hand on the bow and as he did so, the boat gave a creak, he was so strong. When they had crossed he went to the village. In the middle of it he saw a house of blue-stone with a pavement in front of black obsidian.

He went in and heard one say, "It is my son-in-law for whom I had expected to be a long time looking."

When the sun had set there came back from different places ten brothers. Some had been playing kiñ, some had been playing shinny, some had been hunting, some spearing salmon, and others had been shooting at a mark.

Eagle and Panther were both married to daughters of the family. They said to him, "You here, brother-in-law?" "Yes," he said, "I came a little while ago." When it was supper time they put in front of him a basket of money's meat, which mortal man cannot swallow.

He ate two baskets of it and they thought he must be a smart man. After they had finished supper they all went to the sweathouse to spend the night. At midnight the young man went to the river to swim. There he heard a voice say, "The sweathouse wood is all gone." Then Mink told him that men could not find sweat-house wood near by, but that some was to be found to the southeast.

They called to him for wood from ten sweat-houses and he said "Yes" to all. Mink told him about everything they would ask him to do.

He went back to the sweat-house and went in. When the east whitened with the dawn, he went for sweat-house wood as they had told him. He came to the place where the trail forks and one of them turns to the northeast and the other to the southeast. There he drew out from his arm the wood his grandmother had provided him with and split it fine.

He made this into ten bundles and carried them back to the village. When he got there he put them down carefully but the whole earth shook with the shock. He carried a bundle to each sweat-house.

They all sweated themselves. He spent the day there and at evening went again to the sweat-house. When he went to the river to swim, Mink met him again and told him that the next day they would play shinny.

After they were through breakfast the next morning, they said, "Come, brother-in-law, let us go to the place where they play shinny." They all went and after placing their bets began to play. Twice they were beaten. Then they said, "Come, brother-in-law, play." They passed him a stick.

He pressed down on it and broke it. "Let me pick up something," he said. He turned about and drew out his concealed shinny stick and the balls. Then he stepped out to play and Wildcat came to play against him. The visitor made the stroke and the balls fell very near the goal.

Then he caught Wildcat, smashing his face into its present shape, and threw the ball over the line. He played again, this time with Fox.

Again he made the stroke and when he caught Fox he pinched his face out long as it has been ever since. He then struck the ball over the line and won. The next time he played against Earthquake.

The ground opened up a chasm but he jumped over it. Earthquake threw up a wall of blue-stone but he threw the ball through it. "Dol" it rang as it went through. Then he played with Thunder. It rained and there was thunder.

It was the running of that one which made the noise. It was then night and he had won back all they had lost. There were ten strings of money, besides otterskins, fisherskins, and blankets.

The next day they went to shoot at the white bird which Indians can never hit. The others commenced to shoot and then they said to their guest, "Come, you better shoot." They gave him a bow, which broke when he drew it.

Then he pulled out his own and said, "I will shoot with this although the nock has been cut down and it is not very good." They thought, "He can't hit anything with that." He shot and hit the bird, and dentalia fell all about. They gathered up the money and carried it home.

The Hupa man went home to his grandmother. As many nights as it seemed to him he had spent, so many years he had really been away. He found his grandmother lying by the fire. Both of the women had been worried about him. He said to them, "I have come back for you." "Yes," they said, "we will go." Then he repaired the house, tying it up anew with hazel withes. He poked a stick under it and away it went to the end of the world toward the east, where he had married. They are living there yet.

The Jealous Uncle

A Kodiak Legend
Golder, Journal of American Folk-Lore, xvi, 90, No. 8

In a village lived a man, known to his neighbors as "Unnatural Uncle." When his nephews became a few years old, he would kill them. Two had already suffered death at his hands.

After the second had disappeared, his wife went to the mother of the boys, and said: "Should another boy be born to you, let us conceal the fact from my husband, and make him believe the child a girl. In that case he will not harm him, and we may succeed in bringing him up."

Not long after the above conversation another nephew was born. Unnatural Uncle, hearing that a child was born, sent his wife to ascertain the sex of the child. She, as had been agreed upon, reported the child a girl. "Let her live," he said.

The two women tended and dressed the boy as if he were a girl. When he grew older, they told him to play with the girls, and impressed upon him that he should at all times imitate the ways, attitudes, and postures of the girls, especially when attending to the calls of nature. Unnatural Uncle watched the boy as he was growing up, and often wondered at his boyish looks. One day the boy, not knowing that his uncle was about and observing him, raised up his parka, and so exposed his body.

"Ah," said Unnatural Uncle to his wife, on reaching home, "this is the way you have fooled me. But I know everything now. Go and tell my nephew I wish to see him." With tears in her eyes the poor woman delivered the message to the nephew, told him of the disappearance of his brothers, and of his probable fate. The father and mother of the boy wept bitterly, for they were certain he would never return. The boy himself, although frightened, assured his parents to the contrary, and begged them not to worry, for he would come back safe and sound.

"Did my brothers have any playthings?" he asked before going. He was shown to a box where their things were kept. In it he found a piece of a knife, some eagle-down, and a sour cranberry. These he hid about his person, and went to meet his uncle. The latter greeted him, and said: "Nephew, let us go and fetch some wood."

When they came to a large forest, the boy remarked: "Here is good wood; let us take some of it, and go back." "Oh, no! There is better wood farther on," said the uncle.

From the forest they stepped into a bare plain. "Let us go back. There is no wood here," called the boy. But the uncle motioned to him to come on, telling him that they would soon find better wood. A little later they came to a big log. "Here is what I want," exclaimed the uncle, and began splitting it. "Here, nephew, jump in, and get that wedge out," called the uncle to the boy, as one of the wedges fell in. When the boy did so, the man knocked out the other wedges; the log closed in on the boy, and held him fast. "Stay there!" said Unnatural Uncle, and walked off.

For some time, the boy remained in this helpless condition, planning a means of escape. At last he thought of his sour cranberry, and, taking it in his hand, he rubbed with it the interior of the log from edge to edge. The sourness of the berry caused the log to open its mouth, thus freeing him.

On his way back to the village, he gathered a bundle of wood, which he left at his uncle's door, announcing the fact to him: "Here, uncle, I have brought you the wood." The latter was both surprised and vexed at his failure, and determined more than ever to kill the boy. His wife, however, warned him: "You had better not harm the boy; you have killed his brothers, and if you hurt him, you will come to grief."

"I will kill him, too," he savagely replied.

When the boy reached his father's home, he found them weeping and mourning. "Don't weep!" he pleaded. "He cannot hurt me; no matter where he takes me, I will always come back." In the morning he was again summoned to appear at his uncle's. Before going, he entreated his parents not to feel uneasy, assuring them that no harm would befall him, and that he would be back. The uncle called the boy to go with him after some ducks and eggs.

They passed several places abounding in ducks and eggs, and each time that the boy suggested, "Let us take these and go back," the uncle replied: "Oh, no! There are better ducks and eggs farther on." At last they came to a steep bluff, and, looking down, saw a great many ducks and eggs. "Go down carefully, nephew, and gather those ducks and eggs. Be quick, and come back as soon as you can.

The boy saw the trap at a glance, and prepared for it by taking the eagle-down in each hand, between thumb and finger. As the boy took a step or two downward, the uncle gave him a push, causing him to lose his footing. "He will never come back alive from here," smiled the uncle to himself, as he walked back. If he had remained awhile longer and looked down before going, he would have seen the boy descending gently instead of falling.

The eagle-down kept him up in the air, and he lighted at his own pleasure safe and sound. After gathering all the ducks and eggs he wanted, he ascended by holding up the down, as before, and blowing under it. Up, up he went, and in a short time stood on the summit. It was night before he sighted his uncle's home. At the door he deposited the birds and eggs, and shouted: "Here, uncle, are the ducks and eggs."

"What! back again!" exclaimed the man very much mortified. His wife again pleaded with him to leave the boy in peace. "You will come to grief, if you don't," she said. "No; he cannot hurt me," he replied angrily, and spent the remainder of the night thinking and planning. Although he assured them that he would return, the boy's parents did not have much faith in it; for he found them on his return weeping for him. This grieved him. "Why do you weep?" he said. "Didn't I say I would come back? He can take me to no place from which I cannot come back."

In the evening of the third day the aunt appeared and said that her husband wished the boy. He told his parents not to be disturbed, and promised to come back soon. This time the uncle invited him to go with him after clams. The clams were very large, large enough to enclose a man. It was ebb tide, and they found plenty of clams not far from the beach.

The boy suggested that they take these and go back, but the uncle put him off with, "There are better clams farther out." They waded into the water, and then the man noticed an extraordinarily large clam. "Take him," he said, but when the boy bent over, the clam took him in. So confident was Unnatural Uncle of his success this time that he uttered not a word, but with a triumphant grin on his face and a wave of his hand he walked away.

The boy tried to force the valves apart, but not succeeding, he cut the ligament with his piece of a knife, compelling the clam to open up little by little until he was able to hop out. He gathered some clams, and left them at his uncle's door as if nothing had happened.

The man, on hearing the boy's voice outside, was almost beside himself with rage. His wife did not attempt to pacify him. "I will say nothing more," she said. "I have warned you, and if you persist in your ways, you will suffer."

The next day Unnatural Uncle was busy making a box.

"What is it for?" asked his wife.

"A plaything for our nephew," he replied.

In the evening the boy was sent for. On leaving his parents he said: "Do not feel uneasy about my absence. This time I may be away a long time, but I will come back nevertheless."

"Nephew, here is something to amuse you," said his uncle. "Get inside of it, so that I may see whether it fits you." It fitted him; so did the lid the box; and the rope the lid. He felt himself borne along, and from the noise of the waves he knew it was to the sea.

The box was lowered, and with a shove it was set adrift. It was stormy, the waves beat over the box, and several times he gave himself up as lost. How long he drifted he had no idea; but at last he heard the waves dashing against the beach, and his heart rejoiced.

Louder, and louder did the joyful peal sound. He gathered himself together for the sudden stop which soon came, only to feel himself afloat again the next moment. This experience he went through several times, before the box finally stopped and he realized he was on land once more.

As he lay there, many thoughts passed through his mind; where was he? was any one living there? would he be saved? or would the flood tide set him adrift again? what were his people at home doing? These, and many other thoughts passed through his brain, when he was startled by hearing voices, which he recognized, a little later, as women's. This is what he heard:

"I saw the box first," said one.

"No, I saw it first," said the other.

"I am sure I saw it before you," said the first speaker again, "and, therefore, it is mine."

"Well, you may have the box, but its contents shall belong to me," replied the other.

They picked up the box, and began to carry it, but finding it somewhat heavy and being anxious to know what it contained, they stopped to untie it.

"If there are many things in there, I shall have some of them," said the first speaker, who rued her bargain. The other one said nothing. Great was their surprise on beholding him. He was in turn surprised to see two such beautiful girls, the large village, the numerous people, and their peculiar appearance, for he was among the Eagle people in Eagle land.

The full grown people, like the full grown eagles, had white faces and heads, while those of the young people, like those of young eagles, were dark. Eagle skins were hanging about all over the village; and it amused him to watch some of the people put on their eagle skins and change to eagles, and after flying around, take them off and become human beings again.

The girls, being the daughters of the village chief, led the boy to their father, each claiming him. When he had heard them both, the chief gave the boy to the older girl (the second speaker). With her he lived happily, but his thoughts would very often wander back to his former home, the people there, his parents; and the thought of his uncle's cruelty to them would make his heart ache. His wife noted these spells of depression, and questioned him about them until he told her of his parents and uncle.

She, like a good wife, bade him cheer up, and then went to have a talk with her father. He sent for his son-in-law, and advised him to put on his (chief's) eagle skin, soar up high until he could see his village, fly over there, visit his parents, and bring them back with him. He did as he was told, and in a short time found himself in the village. Although he could see all other people, his parents were not in sight. This was in the evening. During the night he went out to sea, brought back a large whale, and placed it on the beach, knowing that all the villagers would come out for the meat. The first person to come to the village beach in the morning was Unnatural Uncle; and when he saw the whale, he aroused the village, and a little later all, except the boy's father and mother, were there, cutting and storing up the whale.

His parents were not permitted to come near the whale, and when some of the neighbors left some meat at their house, Unnatural Uncle scolded, and forbade it being done again. "I can forgive him the killing of my brothers, the attempts on my life, but I will revenge his treatment of my parents." With these thoughts in his mind, the eagle left his perch, and flew over to the crowd. He circled over its head a little while, and then made a swoop at his uncle. "Ah, he knows that I am chief, and the whale is mine, and he asks me for a piece of meat." Saying this, he threw a piece of meat at the eagle.

The second time the eagle descended it was still nearer the man's head, but he tried to laugh it off, and turn it to his glory. The people, however, did not see it that way, and warned him to keep out of the eagle's clutches, for the eagle meant mischief. When the eagle dropped the third time, it was so near his head that he fell on his face. The fourth time the eagle swooped him, and flew off with him.

Not far from the shore was a high and steep rock, and on its summit the eagle put down the man, placing himself opposite. When he had taken off the skin, and disclosed himself, he said to his trembling uncle: "I could have forgiven you the death of my brothers, the four attempts on my life, but for the cruel treatment of my parents you shall pay.

The whale I brought was for my parents and others, and not for you alone; but you took entire possession of it, and would not allow them even to approach it. I will not kill you without giving you a chance for your life. Swim back to the shore, and you shall be spared." As he could not swim, Unnatural Uncle supplicated his nephew to take him back, but the latter, putting on the eagle skin, and hardening his eagle heart, clutched him, and from a dizzy height in the air dropped him into the sea.

From the beach the crowd watched the fatal act, understood and appreciated it, and, till it was dark, continued observing, from the distance, the eagle. When all had retired, he pulled off the skin, and set out for his father's barrabara. He related to his parents his adventures, and invited them to accompany him to his adopted land, to which they gladly consented. Early in the morning he put on again his skin, and, taking a parent in each claw, flew with them to Eagle land, and there they are living now.

"The land is sacred. These words are at the core of your being. The land is our mother, the rivers our blood. Take our land away and we die. That is, the Indian in us dies."

Mary Brave Bird, Lakota

The Man in the Moon

A Lillooet Legend
Teit, Journal of American Folk-Lore, xxv, 298, No. 3

The three Frog sisters had a house in a swamp, where they lived together. Not very far away lived a number of people in another house. Among them were Snake and Beaver, who were friends.

They were well-grown lads, and wished to marry the Frog girls.

One-night Snake went to Frog's house, and, crawling up to one of the sisters, put his hand on her face. She awoke, and asked him who he was. Learning that he was Snake, she said she would not marry him, and told him to leave at once. She called him hard names, such as, "slimy-fellow," "small-eyes," etc. Snake returned, and told his friend of his failure.

Next night Beaver went to try, and, crawling up to one of the sisters, he put his hand on her face. She awoke, and, finding out who he was, she told him to be gone. She called him names, such as, "short-legs," "big-belly," "big-buttocks." Beaver felt hurt, and, going home, began to cry. His father asked him what the matter was, and the boy told him. He said, "That is nothing. Don't cry! It will rain too much." But young Beaver said, "I will cry."

As he continued to cry, much rain fell, and soon the swamp where the Frogs lived was flooded. Their house was under the water, which covered the tops of the tall swamp-grass. The Frogs got cold, and went to Beaver's house, and said to him, "We wish to marry your sons." But old Beaver said, "No! You called us hard names."

The water was now running in a regular stream. So the Frogs swam away downstream until they reached a whirlpool, which sucked them in, and they descended to the house of the Moon. The latter invited them to warm themselves at the fire; but they said, "No. We do not wish to sit by the fire. We wish to sit there," pointing at him.

He said, "Here?" at the same time pointing at his feet. They said, "No, not there." Then he pointed to one part of his body after another, until he reached his brow. When he said, "Will you sit here?" they all cried out, "Yes," and jumped on his face, thus spoiling his beauty. The Frog's sisters may be seen on the moon's face at the present day.

The Hunting of the Great Bear
An American Indian Legend - Nation Unknown

There were four hunters who were brothers. No hunters were as good as they at following a trail. They never gave up once they began tracking their quarry.

One day, in the moon when the cold nights return, an urgent message came to the village of the four hunters. A great bear, one so large and powerful that many thought it must be some kind of monster, had appeared. The people of the village whose hunting grounds the monster had invaded were afraid. The children no longer went out to play in the woods. The long houses of the village were guarded each night by men with weapons, who stood by the entrances.

Each morning, when the people went outside, they found the huge tracks of the bear in the midst of their village. They knew that soon it would become even bolder.

Picking up their spears and calling to their small dog, the four hunters set forth for that village, which was not far away. As they came closer they noticed how quiet the woods were. There were no signs of rabbits or deer and even the birds were silent. On a great pine tree, they found the scars where the great bear had reared up on hind legs and made deep scratches to mark its territory. The tallest of the brothers tried to touch the highest of the scratch marks with the tip of his spear. "It is as the people feared," the first brother said. "This one we are to hunt is Nyah-gwaheh, a monster bear."

"But what about the magic that the Nyah-gwaheh has?" said the second brother.

The first brother shook his head. "That magic will do it no good if we find its track."

"That's so," said the third brother. "I have always heard that from the old people. Those creatures can only chase a hunter who has not yet found its trail. When you find the track of the Nyah-gwaheh and begin to chase it, then it must run from you."

"Brothers," said the fourth hunter who was the fattest and laziest, "did we bring along enough food to eat? It may take a long time to catch this big bear. I'm feeling hungry."

Before long, the four hunters and their small dog reached the village. It was a sad sight to see. There was no fire burning in the center of the village and the doors of all the long houses were closed. Grim men stood on guard with clubs and spears and there was no game hung from the racks or skins stretched for tanning. The people looked hungry.

The elder sachem of the village came out and the tallest of the four hunters spoke to him.

"Uncle," the hunter said, "we have come to help you get rid of the monster."

Then the fattest and laziest of the four brothers spoke. "Uncle," he said, "is there some food we can eat? Can we find a place to rest before we start chasing this big bear? I'm tired."

The first hunter shook his head and smiled. "My brother is only joking, Uncle." he said. " We are going now to pick up the monster bear's trail."

"I am not sure you can do that, Nephews," the elder sachem said. "Though we find tracks closer and closer to the doors of our lodges each morning, whenever we try to follow those tracks they disappear."

The second hunter knelt down and patted the head of their small dog. "Uncle," he said, that is because they do not have a dog such as ours." He pointed to the two black circles above the eyes of the small dog. "Four-Eyes can see any tracks, even those many days old."

"May Creator's protection be with you," said the elder sachem.

"Do not worry. Uncle," said the third hunter, "Once we are on a trail we never stop following until we've finished our hunt," the fourth hunter said. "That's why I think we should have something to eat first." But his brothers did not listen. They nodded to the elder sachem and began to leave. Sighing, the fattest and laziest of the brothers lifted up his long spear and trudged after them.

They walked, following their little dog. It kept lifting up its head, as if to look around with its four eyes. The trail was not easy to find.

"Brothers," the fattest and laziest hunter complained, "don't you think we should rest. We've been walking a long time." But his brothers paid no attention to him. Though they could see no tracks, they could feel the presence of the Nyah-gwaheh. They knew that if they did not soon find its trail, it would make its way behind them. Then they would be the hunted ones.

The fattest and laziest brother took out his pemmican pouch. At least he could eat while they walked along. He opened the pouch and shook out the food he had prepared so carefully by pounding together strips of meat and berries with maple sugar and then drying them in the sun. But instead of pemmican, pale squirming things fell out into his hands. The magic of the Nyah-gwaheh had changed the food into worms.

"Brothers," the fattest and laziest of the hunters shouted, "Let's hurry up and catch that big bear! Look what it did to my pemmican. Now I'm getting angry!"

Meanwhile, like a pale giant shadow, the Nyah-gwaheh was moving through the trees close to the hunters. Its mouth was open as it watched them and its huge teeth shone, its eyes flashed red. Soon it would be behind them and on their trail.

Just then, though, the little dog lifted its head and yelped. "Eh-heh!" the first brother called.

"Four-Eyes has found the trail," shouted the second brother.

"We have the track of the Nyah-gwaheh," said the third brother.

"Big Bear," the fattest and laziest one yelled, "we are after you, now!"

Fear filled the heart of the great bear for the first time and it began to run. As it broke from the cover of the pines, the four hunters saw it, a gigantic white shape, so pale as to appear almost naked. With loud hunting cries, they began to run after it. The great bear's strides were long and it ran more swiftly than a deer. The four hunters and their little dog were swift also though and they did not fall behind. The trail led through the swamps and the thickets. It was easy to read, for the bear pushed everything aside as it ran, even knocking down big trees. On and on they ran, over hills and through valleys. They came to the slope of a mountain and followed the trail higher and higher, every now and then catching a glimpse of their quarry over the next rise. Now though the lazy hunter was getting tired of running. He pretended to fall and twist his ankle.

"Brothers," he called, "I have sprained my ankle. You must carry me."

So his three brothers did as he asked, two of them carrying him by turns while the third hunter carried his spear. They ran more slowly now because of their heavy load, but they were not falling any further behind. The day had turned now into night, yet they could still see the white shape of the great bear ahead of them. They were at the top of the mountain now and the ground beneath them was very dark as they ran across it. The bear was tiring, but so were they. It was not easy to carry their fat and lazy brother. The little dog, Four-Eyes, was close behind the great bear, nipping at its tail as it ran.

"Brothers," said the fattest and laziest one. "Put me down now. I think my leg has gotten better."

The brothers did as he asked. Fresh and rested, the fattest and laziest one grabbed his spear and dashed ahead of the others. Just as the great bear turned to bite at the little dog, the fattest and laziest hunter leveled his spear and thrust it into the heart of the Nyah-Gwaheh. The monster bear fell dead.

By the time the other brothers caught up, the fattest and laziest hunter had already built a fire and was cutting up the big bear.

"Come on, brothers," he said. "Let's eat. All this running has made me hungry!"

So they cooked the meat of the great bear and its fat sizzled as it dripped from their fire. They ate until even the fattest and laziest one was satisfied and leaned back in contentment. Just then, though, the first hunter looked down at his feet.

"Brothers," he exclaimed, "look below us!"

The four hunters looked down. Below them were thousands of small sparkling lights in the darkness which. They realized, it was all around them.

"We aren't on a mountain top at all," said the third brother. "We are up in the sky." And it was so. The great bear had indeed been magical. Its feet had taken it high above the earth as it tried to escape the four hunters. However, their determination not to give up the chase had carried them up that strange trail.

Just then their little dog yipped twice.

"The great bear!" said the second hunter. "Look!"

The hunters looked. There, where they had piled the bones of their feast the Great Bear was coming back to life and rising to its feet. As they watched, it began to run again, the small dog close on its heels.

"Follow me," shouted the first brother. Grabbing up their spears, the four hunters again began to chase the great bear across the skies.

So it was, the old people say, and so it still is. Each autumn the hunters chase the great bear across the skies and kill it. Then, as they cut it up for their meal, the blood falls down from the heavens and colors the leaves of the maple trees scarlet. They cook the bear and the fat dripping from their fire turns the grass white.

If you look carefully into the skies as the seasons change, you can read that story. The great bear is the square shape some call the bowl of the Big Dipper. The hunters and their small dog (which you can just barely see) are close behind, forming the dipper's handle. When autumn comes and that constellation turns upside down, the old people say. "Ah, the lazy hunter has killed the bear." But as the moons pass and the sky moves once more towards spring, the bear slowly rises back on its feet and the chase begins again.

Iktomi

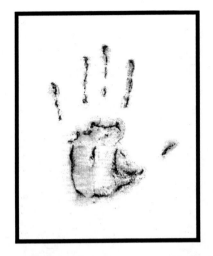

Iktomi

A Lakota Legend
Zitkala Sa, Old Indian
Legends, 1901

Iktomi is a spider fairy. He wears brown deerskin leggings with long soft fringes on either side, and tiny beaded moccasins on his feet.

His long black hair is parted in the middle and wrapped with red, red bands. Each round braid hangs over a small brown ear and falls forward over his shoulders.

He even paints his funny face with red and yellow, and draws big black rings around his eyes. He wears a deerskin jacket, with bright colored beads sewed tightly on it. Iktomi dresses like a real Lakota brave. In truth, his paint and deerskins are the best part of him--if ever dress is part of man or fairy.

Iktomi is a wily fellow. His hands are always kept in mischief. He prefers to spread a snare rather than to earn the smallest thing with honest hunting. Why! he laughs outright with wide open mouth when some simple folk are caught in a trap, sure and fast.

He never dreams another lives so bright as he. Often his own conceit leads him hard against the common sense of simpler people. Poor Iktomi cannot help being a little imp. And so long as he is a naughty fairy, he cannot find a single friend.

No one helps him when he is in trouble. No one really loves him. Those who come to admire his handsome beaded jacket and long fringed leggings soon go away sick and tired of his vain, vain words and heartless laughter.

Thus Iktomi lives alone in a cone-shaped wigwam upon the plain.

"Our land is everything to us... I will tell you one of the things we remember on our land. We remember that our grandfathers paid for it - with their lives."

John Wooden Leg, Cheyenne

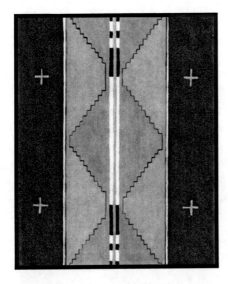

Iktomi's Blanket

A Lakota Legend
Zitkala Sa, Old Indian
Legends, 1901

Alone within his teepee sat Iktomi. The sun was but a hands breadth from the western edge of land. "Those, bad, bad gray wolves! They ate up all my nice fat ducks!" muttered he, rocking his body to and fro. He was cuddling the evil memory he bore those hungry wolves.

At last he ceased to sway his body backward and forward, but sat still and stiff as a stone image. "Oh! I'll go to Inyan, the great-grandfather, and pray for food!" he exclaimed. At once he hurried forth from his teepee and, with his blanket over one shoulder, drew nigh to a huge rock on a hillside. With half-crouching, half-running strides, he fell upon Inyan with outspread hands.

"Grandfather! pity me. I am hungry. I am starving. Give me food. Great-grandfather, give me meat to eat!" he cried. All the while he stroked and caressed the face of the great stone god.

The all-powerful Great Spirit, who makes the trees and grass, can hear the voice of those who pray in many varied ways. The hearing of Inyan, the large hard stone, was the one most sought after. He was the great-grandfather, for he had sat upon the hillside many, many seasons. He had seen

the prairie put on a snow-white blanket and then change it
for a bright green robe more than a thousand times.

Still unaffected by the myriad moons he rested on the
everlasting hill, listening to the prayers of Indian warriors.
Before the finding of the magic arrow he had sat there.
Now, as Iktomi prayed and wept before the great-
grandfather, the sky in the west was red like a glowing
face. The sunset poured a soft mellow light upon the huge
gray stone and the solitary figure beside it. It was the smile
of the Great Spirit upon the grandfather and the wayward
child.

The prayer was heard. Iktomi knew it.

"Now, grandfather, accept my offering; 'tis all I have," said
Iktomi as he spread his half-worn blanket upon Inyan's cold
shoulders. Then Iktomi, happy with the smile of the sunset
sky, followed a footpath leading toward a thicketed ravine.
He had not gone many paces into the shrubbery when
before him lay a freshly wounded deer!

"This is the answer from the red western sky!" cried Iktomi
with hands uplifted. Slipping a long thin blade from out his
belt, he cut large chunks of choice meat. Sharpening some
willow sticks, he planted them around a wood-pile he had
ready to kindle. On these stakes he meant to roast the
venison.

While he was rubbing briskly two long sticks to start a fire,
the sun in the west fell out of the sky below the edge of
land. Twilight was over all. Iktomi felt the cold night air
upon his bare neck and shoulders. "Ough!" he shivered as
he wiped his knife on the grass.

Tucking it in a beaded case hanging from his belt, Iktomi

stood erect, looking about. He shivered again.

"Ough! Ah! I am cold. I wish I had my blanket!" whispered he, hovering over the pile of dry sticks and the sharp stakes round about it. Suddenly he paused and dropped his hands at his sides.

"The old great-grandfather does not feel the cold as I do. He does not need my old blanket as I do. I wish I had not given it to him. Oh! I think I'll run up there and take it back!" said he, pointing his long chin toward the large gray stone.

Iktomi, in the warm sunshine, had no need of his blanket, and it had been very easy to part with a thing which he could not miss. But the chilly night wind quite froze his ardent thank-offering. Thus running up the hillside, his teeth chattering all the way, he drew near to Inyan, the sacred symbol.

Seizing one corner of the half-worn blanket, Iktomi pulled it off with a jerk. "Give my blanket back, old grandfather! You do not need it. I do!"

This was very wrong, yet Iktomi did it, for his wit was not wisdom. Drawing the blanket tight over his shoulders, he descended the hill with hurrying feet. He was soon upon the edge of the ravine.

A young moon, like a bright bent bow, climbed up from the southwest horizon a little way into the sky. In this pale light Iktomi stood motionless as a ghost amid the thicket. His woodpile was not yet kindled. His pointed stakes were still bare as he had left them. But where was the deer - the venison he had felt warm in his hands a moment ago?

It was gone.

Only the dry rib bones lay on the ground like giant fingers from an open grave. Iktomi was troubled. At length, stooping over the white dried bones, he took hold of one and shook it. The bones, loose in their sockets, rattled together at his touch. Iktomi let go his hold. He sprang back amazed. And though he wore a blanket his teeth chattered more than ever.

Then his blunted sense will surprise you, little reader; for instead of being grieved that he had taken back his blanket, he cried aloud, "Hin-hin-hin! If only I had eaten the venison before going for my blanket!"

Those tears no longer moved the hand of the Generous Giver. They were selfish tears. The Great Spirit does not heed them ever.

I do not think the measure of a civilization
is how tall its buildings of concrete are,
But rather how well its people have learned to relate
to their environment and fellow man.

Sun Bear of the Chippewa Tribe

Iktomi and the Coyote

A Lakota Legend
Zitkala Sa, Old Indian
Legends, 1901

Afar off upon a large level land, a summer sun was shining bright. Here and there over the rolling green were tall bunches of coarse gray weeds. Iktomi in his fringed buckskins walked alone across the prairie with a black bare head glossy in the sunlight.

He walked through the grass without following any well-worn footpath. From one large bunch of coarse weeds to another he wound his way about the great plain. He lifted his foot lightly and placed it gently forward like a wildcat prowling noiselessly through the thick grass. He stopped a few steps away from a very large bunch of wild sage.

From shoulder to shoulder he tilted his head. Still farther he bent from side to side, first low over one hip and then over the other. Far forward he stooped, stretching his long thin neck like a duck, to see what lay under a fur coat beyond the bunch of coarse grass. A sleek gray-faced prairie wolf!

His pointed black nose tucked in between his four feet drawn snugly together; his handsome bushy tail wound over his nose and feet; a coyote fast asleep in the shadow of a bunch of grass! - this is what Iktomi spied.

Carefully he raised one foot and cautiously reached out
with his toes. Gently, gently he lifted the foot behind and
placed it before the other. Thus he came nearer and nearer
to the round fur ball lying motionless under the sage grass.
Now Iktomi stood beside it, looking at the closed eyelids
that did not quiver the least bit.

Pressing his lips into straight lines and nodding his head
slowly, he bent over the wolf. He held his ear close to the
coyote's nose, but not a breath of air stirred from it.
"Dead!" said he at last. "Dead, but not long since he ran
over these plains! See! there in his paw is caught a fresh
feather. He is nice fat meat!"

Taking hold of the paw with the bird feather fast on it, he
exclaimed, "Why, he is still warm! I'll carry him to my
dwelling and have a roast for my evening meal. Ah-ha!" he
laughed, as he seized the coyote by its two fore paws and
its two hind feet and swung him over head across his
shoulders.

The wolf was large and the teepee was far across the
prairie. Iktomi trudged along with his burden, smacking
his hungry lips together. He blinked his eyes hard to keep
out the salty perspiration streaming down his face. All the
while the coyote on his back lay gazing into the sky with
wide open eyes. His long white teeth fairly gleamed as he
smiled and smiled. "To ride on one's own feet is tiresome,
but to be carried like a warrior from a brave fight is great
fun!" said the coyote in his heart."

He had never been borne on any one's back before and the
new experience delighted him. He lay there lazily on
Iktomi's shoulders, now and then blinking blue winks. Did
you never see a birdie blink a blue wink? This is how it
first became a saying among the plains people.

When a bird stands aloof watching your strange ways, a thin bluish white tissue slips quickly over his eyes and as quickly off again; so quick that you think it was only a mysterious blue wink. Sometimes when children grow drowsy they blink blue winks, while others who are too proud to look with friendly eyes upon people blink in this cold bird-manner.

The coyote was affected by both sleepiness and pride. His winks were almost as blue as the sky. In the midst of his new pleasure the swaying motion ceased. Iktomi had reached his dwelling place.

The coyote felt drowsy no longer, for in the next instant he was slipping out of Iktomi's hands. He was falling, falling through space, and then he struck the ground with such a bump he did not wish to breathe for a while. He wondered what Iktomi would do, thus he lay still where he fell. Humming a dance-song, one from his bundle of mystery songs, Iktomi hopped and darted about at an imaginary dance and feast.

He gathered dry willow sticks and broke them in two against his knee. He built a large fire out of doors. The flames leaped up high in red and yellow streaks. Now Iktomi returned to the coyote who had been looking on through his eyelashes.

Taking him again by his paws and hind feet, he swung him to and fro. Then as the wolf swung toward the red flames, Iktomi let him go. Once again the coyote fell through space. Hot air smote his nostrils. He saw red dancing fire, and now he struck a bed of cracking embers. With a quick turn he leaped out of the flames. From his heels were scattered a shower of red coals upon Iktomi's bare arms and shoulders.

Dumbfounded, Iktomi thought he saw a spirit walk out of his fire. His jaws fell apart. He thrust a palm to his face, hard over his mouth!

He could scarce keep from shrieking. Rolling over and over on the grass and rubbing the sides of his head against the ground, the coyote soon put out the fire on his fur. Iktomi's eyes were almost ready to jump out of his head as he stood cooling a burn on his brown arm with his breath.

Sitting on his haunches, on the opposite side of the fire from where Iktomi stood, the coyote began to laugh at him. "Another day, my friend, do not take too much for granted. Make sure the enemy is stone dead before you make a fire!"

Then off he ran so swiftly that his long bushy tail hung out in a straight line with his back.

Iktomi and the Ducks

A Lakota Legend
Zitkala Sa, Old Indian Legends, 1901

One day Iktomi sat hungry within his teepee. Suddenly he rushed out, dragging after him his blanket. Quickly spreading it on the ground, he tore up dry tall grass with both his hands and tossed it fast into the blanket.

Tying all the four corners together in a knot, he threw the light bundle of grass over his shoulder. Snatching up a slender willow stick with his free left hand, he started off with a hop and a leap. From side to side bounced, the bundle on his back, as he ran light-footed over the uneven ground.

Soon he came to the edge of the great level land. On the hilltop he paused for breath. With wicked smacks of his dry parched lips, as if tasting some tender meat, he looked straight into space toward the marshy river bottom. With a thin palm shading his eyes from the western sun, he peered far away into the lowlands, munching his own cheeks all the while.

"Ah-ha!" grunted he, satisfied with what he saw. A group of wild ducks were dancing and feasting in the marshes. With wings outspread, tip to tip, they moved up and down in a large circle. Within the ring, around a small drum, sat the chosen singers, nodding their heads and blinking their eyes.

They sang in unison a merry dance-song, and beat a lively tattoo on the drum. Following a winding footpath near by, came a bent figure of a Lakota brave. He bore on his back a very large bundle. With a willow cane he propped himself up as he staggered along beneath his burden.

"Ho! who is there?" called out a curious old duck, still bobbing up and down in the circular dance. Hereupon the drummers stretched their necks till they strangled their song for a look at the stranger passing by.

"Ho, Iktomi! Old fellow, pray tell us what you carry in your blanket. Do not hurry off! Stop! halt!" urged one of the singers.

"Stop! stay! Show us what is in your blanket!" cried out other voices.

"My friends, I must not spoil your dance. Oh, you would not care to see if you only knew what is in my blanket. Sing on! dance on! I must not show you what I carry on my back," answered Iktomi, nudging his own sides with his elbows.

This reply broke up the ring entirely.

Now all the ducks crowded about Iktomi. "We must see what you carry! We must know what is in your blanket!"

they shouted in both his ears. Some even brushed their wings against the mysterious bundle.

Nudging himself again, wily Iktomi said, "My friends, 't is only a pack of songs I carry in my blanket."

"Oh, then let us hear your songs!" cried the curious ducks.

At length Iktomi consented to sing his songs. With delight all the ducks flapped their wings and cried together, "Hoye! hoye!" Iktomi, with great care, laid down his bundle on the ground. "I will build first a round straw house, for I never sing my songs in the open air," said he.

Quickly he bent green willow sticks, planting both ends of each pole into the earth. These he covered thick with reeds and grasses. Soon the straw hut was ready. One by one the fat ducks waddled in through a small opening, which was the only entranceway. Beside the door Iktomi stood smiling, as the ducks, eying his bundle of songs, strutted into the hut.

In a strange low voice Iktomi began his queer old tunes. All the ducks sat round-eyed in a circle about the mysterious singer. It was dim in that straw hut, for Iktomi had not forgot to cover up the small entrance way. All of a sudden his song burst into full voice. As the startled ducks sat uneasily on the ground, Iktomi changed his tune into a minor strain. These were the words he sang:

"Istokmus wacipo, tuwayatunwanpi kinhan ista nishashapi kta," which is, "With eyes closed you must dance. He who dares to open his eyes, forever red eyes shall have."

Up rose the circle of seated ducks and holding their wings close against their sides began to dance to the rhythm of

Iktomi's song and drum. With eyes closed they did dance!
Iktomi ceased to beat his drum. He began to sing louder
and faster. He seemed to be moving about in the center of
the ring.

No duck dared blink a wink. Each one shut his eyes very
tight and danced even harder. Up and down! Shifting to the
right of them they hopped round and round in that blind
dance. It was a difficult dance for the curious folk.

At length one of the dancers could close his eyes no longer!
It was a Skiska who peeped the least tiny blink at Iktomi
within the center of the circle. "Oh! oh!" squawked he in
awful terror! "Run! fly! Iktomi is twisting your heads and
breaking your necks! Run out and fly! fly!" he cried.
Hereupon the ducks opened their eyes.

There beside Iktomi's bundle of songs lay half of their
crowd - flat on their backs. Out they flew through the
opening Skiska had made as he rushed forth with his alarm.
But as they soared high into the blue sky they cried to one
another: "Oh! your eyes are red-red!" "And yours are red-
red!" For the warning words of the magic minor strain had
proven true.

"Ah-ha!" laughed Iktomi, untying the four corners of his
blanket, "I shall sit, no more hungry within my dwelling."
Homeward he trudged along with nice fat ducks in his
blanket. He left the little straw hut for the rains and winds
to pull down. Having reached his own teepee on the high
level lands, Iktomi kindled a large fire out of doors. He
planted sharp-pointed sticks around the leaping flames. On
each stake he fastened a duck to roast. A few he buried
under the ashes to bake.

Disappearing within his teepee, he came out again with

some huge seashells. These were his dishes. Placing one
under each roasting duck, he muttered, "The sweet fat
oozing out will taste well with the hard-cooked breasts."

Heaping more willows upon the fire, Iktomi sat down on
the ground with crossed shins. A long chin between his
knees pointed toward the red flames, while his eyes were
on the browning ducks. Just above his ankles he clasped
and unclasped his long bony fingers. Now and then he
sniffed impatiently the savory odor.

The brisk wind which stirred the fire also played with a
squeaky old tree beside Iktomi's wigwam. From side to side
the tree was swaying and crying in an old man's voice,
"Help! I'll break! I'll fall!"

Iktomi shrugged his great shoulders, but did not once take
his eyes from the ducks. The dripping of amber oil into
pearly dishes, drop by drop, pleased his hungry eyes.

Still the old tree man called for help. "He! What sound is it
that makes my ear ache!" exclaimed Iktomi, holding a hand
on his ear. He rose and looked around. The squeaking came
from the tree. Then he began climbing the tree to find the
disagreeable sound. He placed his foot right on a cracked
limb without seeing it. Just then a whiff of wind came
rushing by and pressed together the broken edges. There in
a strong wooden hand Iktomi's foot was caught.

"Oh! my foot is crushed!" he howled like a coward. In vain
he pulled and puffed to free himself.

While sitting a prisoner on the tree he spied, through his
tears, a pack of gray wolves roaming over the level lands.
Waving his hands toward them, he called in his loudest
voice, "He! Gray wolves! Don't you come here! I'm caught

fast in the tree so that my duck feast is getting cold. Don't you come to eat up my meal."

The leader of the pack upon hearing Iktomi's words turned to his comrades and said: "Ah! hear the foolish fellow! He says he has a duck feast to be eaten! Let us hurry there for our share!"

Away bounded the wolves toward Iktomi's lodge. From the tree Iktomi watched the hungry wolves eat up his nicely browned fat ducks. His foot pained him more and more. He heard them crack the small round bones with their strong long teeth and eat out the oily marrow.

Now severe pains shot up from his foot through his whole body. "Hin-hin-hin!" sobbed Iktomi. Real tears washed brown streaks across his red-painted cheeks.

Smacking their lips, the wolves began to leave the place, when Iktomi cried out like a pouting child, "At least you have left my baking under the ashes!"

"Ho! Po!" shouted the mischievous wolves; "he says more ducks are to be found under the ashes! Come! Let us have our fill this once!" Running back to the dead fire, they pawed out the ducks with such rude haste that a cloud of ashes rose like gray smoke over them.

"Hin-hin-hin!" moaned Iktomi, when the wolves had scampered off. All too late, the sturdy breeze returned, and, passing by, pulled apart the broken edges of the tree. Iktomi was released. But alas! he had no duck feast.

Native American Prayer

Oh, Great Spirit
Whose voice I hear in the winds,
And whose breath gives life to all the world,
hear me, I am small and weak,
I need your strength and wisdom.
Let me walk in beauty and make my eyes ever behold
the red and purple sunset.
Make my hands respect the things you have
made and my ears sharp to hear your voice.
Make me wise so that I may understand the things
you have taught my people.
Let me learn the lessons you have
hidden in every leaf and rock.
I seek strength, not to be greater than my brother,
but to fight my greatest enemy - myself.
Make me always ready to come to you
with clean hands and straight eyes.
So when life fades, as the fading sunset,
my Spirit may come to you without shame.

(translated by Lakota Sioux Chief Yellow Lark in 1887)
published in Native American Prayers - by the Episcopal
Church.

Iktomi and the Fawn

A Lakota Legend
Zitkala Sa, Old Indian Legends, 1901

In one of his wanderings through the wooded lands, Iktomi saw a rare bird sitting high in a tree-top. Its long fan-like tail feathers had caught all the beautiful colors of the rainbow. Handsome in the glistening summer sun sat the bird of rainbow plumage.

Iktomi hurried hither with his eyes fast on the bird. He stood beneath the tree looking long and wistfully at the peacock's bright feathers.

At length he heaved a sigh and began: "Oh, I wish I had such pretty feathers! How I wish I were not I! If only I were a handsome feathered creature how happy I would be! I'd be so glad to sit upon a very high tree and bask in the summer sun like you!" said he suddenly, pointing his bony finger up toward the peacock, who was eying the stranger below, turning his head from side to side.

"I beg of you make me into a bird with green and purple feathers like yours!" implored Iktomi, tired now of playing the brave in beaded buckskins. The peacock then spoke to Iktomi: "I have a magic power. My touch will change you in a moment into the most beautiful peacock if you can keep one condition."

"Yes! yes!" shouted Iktomi, jumping up and down, patting his lips with his palm, which caused his voice to vibrate in a peculiar fashion.

"Yes! yes! I could keep ten conditions if only you would change me into a bird with long, bright tail feathers. Oh, I am so ugly! I am so tired of being myself! Change me! Do!"

Hereupon the peacock spread out both his wings, and scarce moving them, he sailed slowly down upon the ground. Right beside Iktomi he alighted. Very low in Iktomi's ear the peacock whispered, "Are you willing to keep one condition, though hard it be?"

"Yes! yes! I've told you ten of them if need be!" exclaimed Iktomi, with some impatience.

"Then I pronounce you a handsome feathered bird. No longer are you Iktomi the mischief-maker." saying this the peacock touched Iktomi with the tips of his wings. Iktomi vanished at the touch.

There stood beneath the tree two handsome peacocks. While one of the pair strutted about with a head turned aside as if dazzled by his own bright-tinted tail feathers, the other bird soared slowly upward.

He sat quiet and unconscious of his gay plumage. He seemed content to perch there on a large limb in the warm sunshine. After a little while the vain peacock, dizzy with his bright colors, spread out his wings and lit on the shame branch with the elder bird. "Oh!" he exclaimed, "how hard to fly! Brightly tinted feathers are handsome, but I wish they were light enough to fly!"

Just there the elder bird interrupted him. "That is the one condition. Never try to fly like other birds. Upon the day you try to fly you shall be changed into your former self."

"Oh, what a shame that bright feathers cannot fly into the sky!" cried the peacock. Already he grew restless. He longed to soar through space. He yearned to fly above the trees high upward to the sun.

"Oh, there I see a flock of birds flying thither! Oh! oh!" said he, flapping his wings, "I must try my wings! I am tired of bright tail feathers. I want to try my wings."

"No, no!" clucked the elder bird. The flock of chattering birds flew by with whirring wings.

"Oop! Oop!" called some to their mates.

Possessed by an irrepressible impulse the Iktomi peacock called out, "He! I want to come! Wait for me!" and with that he gave a lunge into the air. The flock of flying feathers wheeled about and lowered over the tree whence came the peacock's cry.

Only one rare bird sat on the tree, and beneath, on the ground, stood a brave in brown buckskins. "I am my old self again!" groaned Iktomi in a shad voice.

"Make me over, pretty bird. Try me this once again!" he pleaded in vain.

"Old Iktomi wants to fly! Ah! We cannot wait for him!"
sang the birds as they flew away.

Muttering unhappy vows to himself, Iktomi had not gone
far when he chanced upon a bunch of long slender arrows.
One by one they rose in the air and shot a straight line over
the prairie. Others shot up into the blue sky and were soon
lost to sight.

Only one was left. He was making ready for his flight when
Iktomi rushed upon him and wailed, "I want to be an
arrow! Make me into an arrow! I want to pierce the blue
Blue overhead. I want to strike yonder summer sun in its
center. Make me into an arrow!"

"Can you keep a condition? One condition, though hard it
be?" the arrow turned to ask.

"Yes! Yes!" shouted Iktomi, delighted.

Hereupon the slender arrow tapped him gently with his
sharp flint beak. There was no Iktomi, but two arrows stood
ready to fly.

"Now, young arrow, this is the one condition. Your flight
must always be in a straight line. Never turn a curve nor
jump about like a young fawn," said the arrow magician.
He spoke slowly and sternly. At once he set about to teach
the new arrow how to shoot in a long straight line. "This is
the way to pierce the Blue overhead," said he; and off he
spun high into the sky.

While he was gone a herd of deer came trotting by. Behind
them played the young fawns together. They frolicked
about like kittens. They bounced on all fours like balls.
Then they pitched forward, kicking their heels in the air.

The Iktomi arrow watched them so happy on the ground. Looking quickly up into the sky, he said in his heart, "The magician is out of sight. I'll just romp and frolic with these fawns until he returns. Fawns! Friends, do not fear me. I want to jump and leap with you. I long to be happy as you are," said he.

The young fawns stopped with stiff legs and stared at the speaking arrow with large brown wondering eyes.

"See! I can jump as well as you!" went on Iktomi. He gave one tiny leap like a fawn. All of a sudden the fawns snorted with extended nostrils at what they beheld. There among them stood Iktomi in brown buckskins, and the strange talking arrow was gone.

"Oh! I am myself. My old self!" cried Iktomi, pinching himself and plucking imaginary pieces out of his jacket. "Hin-hin-hin! I wanted to fly!"

The real arrow now returned to the earth. He alighted very near Iktomi. From the high sky he had seen the fawns playing on the green. He had seen Iktomi make his one leap, and the charm was broken. Iktomi became his former self. "Arrow, my friend, change me once more!" begged Iktomi.

"No, no more," replied the arrow. Then away he shot through the air in the direction his comrades had flown.

By this time the fawns gathered close around Iktomi. They poked their noses at him trying to know who he was.

Iktomi's tears were like a spring shower. A new desire dried them quickly away. Stepping boldly to the largest fawn, he looked closely at the little brown spots all over the furry face.

"Oh, fawn! What beautiful brown spots on your face!
Fawn, dear little fawn, can you tell me how those brown
spots were made on your face?"

"Yes," said the fawn. "When I was very, very small, my
mother marked them on my face with a red hot fire. She
dug a large hole in the ground and made a soft bed of grass
and twigs in it. Then she placed me gently there. She
covered me over with dry sweet grass and piled dry cedars
on top.

From a neighbor's fire she brought hither a red, red ember.
This she tucked carefully in at my head. This is how the
brown spots were made on my face."

"Now, fawn, my friend, will you do the same for me?
Won't you mark my face with brown, brown spots just like
yours?" asked Iktomi, always eager to be like other people.

"Yes. I can dig the ground and fill it with dry grass and
sticks. If you will jump into the pit, I'll cover you with
sweet smelling grass and cedar wood," answered the fawn.

"Say," interrupted Iktomi, "will you be sure to cover me
with a great deal of dry grass and twigs? You will make
sure that the spots will be as brown as those you wear."

"Oh, yes. I'll pile up grass and willows once oftener than
my mother did."

"Now let us dig the hole, pull the grass, and gather sticks,"
cried Iktomi in glee.

Thus with his own hands he aids in making his grave. After
the hole was dug and cushioned with grass, Iktomi,
muttering something about brown spots, leaped down into
it. Lengthwise, flat on his back, he lay.

While the fawn covered him over with cedars, a far-away voice came up through them, "Brown, brown spots to wear forever!" A red ember was tucked under the dry grass. Off scampered the fawns after their mothers; and when a great distance away they looked backward.

They saw a blue smoke rising, writhing upward till it vanished in the blue ether.

"Is that Iktomi's spirit?" asked one fawn of another.

"No! I think he would jump out before he could burn into smoke and cinders," answered his comrade.

"A very great vision is needed and the man who has it must follow it as the eagle seeks the deepest blue of the sky."

Crazy Horse, Sioux Chief

What's This? My Balls for Dinner?

White River Sioux
Told by one of the Left Handed Bull
family in White River, Rosebud
Indian Reservation, and recorded by
Richard Erdoes

Iktome, the wicked Spider Man, and Shunk-Manitou, Coyote, are two no-good loafers. They lie, they steal, they are greedy, they are always after women. Maybe because they are so very much alike, they are friends, except when they try to trick each other.

One day Iktome invited Coyote for dinner at his lodge. Ikto told his wife: "Old Woman, here are two fine, big buffalo livers for my friend Coyote and myself. Fry them up nicely, the way I like them. And get some timpsila, some wild turnips, on the side, and afterwards serve us up some wojapi, some berry soup. Use chokecherries for that. Coyote always likes something sweet after his meal."

"Is that all?" asked Iktome's wife.

"I guess so; I can't think of anything else."

"There's no third liver for me?" the wife inquired.

"You can have what's left after my friend Coyote and I have eaten," said Iktome. "Well, I'll go out for a while; maybe I can shoot a fine, plump duck too. Coyote always stuffs himself, so one liver may not be enough for him. But watch this good friend of mine; don't let him stick his hands under your robe. He likes to do that. Well, I go now. Have everything ready for us; Coyote never likes to wait."

Iktome left and his old woman got busy cooking. "I know who's always stuffing himself," she thought. "I know whose hands are always busy feeling under some girl's robe. I know who can't wait - it's that no-good husband of mine."

The fried livers smelled so wonderful that the wife said to herself: "Those greedy, stingy, overbearing men! I know them; they'll feast on these fine livers, and a few turnips will be all they leave for me. They have no consideration for a poor woman. Oh, that liver here looks so good, smells so good; I know it tastes good. Maybe I'll try a little piece, just a tiny one. They won't notice."

So the wife tasted a bit of the liver, and then another bit, and then another, and in no time at all that liver was gone. "I might as well eat the other one too," the wife said to herself, and she did.

"What will I do now?" she thought. "When Iktome finds out, he'll surely beat me. But it was worth it!"

Just then Coyote arrived. He had dressed himself up in a fine beaded outfit with fringed sleeves. "Where is my good friend Iktome?" he asked. "What's he up to? Probably nothing good."

"How are you, friend?" said the woman, "My husband, Iktome, is out taking care of some business. He'll be back soon. Sit down; be comfortable."

"Out on business-you don't say!" remarked Coyote, quickly sticking his hand under the woman's robe and between her legs.

"Iktome told me you'd try to do that. He told me not to let you."

"Oh, Iktome and I are such good friends," said Coyote, "we share everything." He joked, he chucked the woman under the chin, he tickled her under the arms, and pretty soon he was all the way in her; way, way up inside her.

"It feels good," said the woman, "but be quick about it. Iktome could be back any time now."

"You think he'd mind, seeing we are such good friends?"

"I'm sure he would. You'd better stop now."

"Well, all right. It smells very good here, but I see no meat cooking, just some timpsila. Meat is what I like."

"And meat is what you'll get. One sees this is the first time that you've come here for dinner; otherwise you'd know what you'll get. We always serve a guest the same thing. Everybody likes it."

"Is it really good?"

"It's more than good. It's lila washtay, very good."

Coyote smacked his lips, his mouth watering. "I can't wait. What is it? Tell me!"

"Why, your itka, your susu, your eggs, your balls, your big hairy balls! We always have the balls of our guests for dinner."

"Oh my! This must be a joke, a very bad joke."

"It's no joke at all. And I'd better cut them off right now with my big skinning knife, because it's getting late. Ikto gets mad when I don't have his food ready-he'll beat me.

And there I was, fooling around with you instead of doing my cooking. I'll do it right now; drop your breechcloth. You won't feel a thing; I do this so fast. I have practice."

The woman came after Coyote with the knife in her hand.

"Wait a bit," said Coyote. "Before you do this, let me go out and make some water. I'll be right back," and saying this, he ran out of the lodge. But he didn't come back. He ran and ran as fast as his feet would carry him.

Just then Iktome came back without any ducks; he had caught nothing. He saw Coyote running away and asked, "Old Woman, what's the matter with that crazy friend of mine? Why is he running off like that?"

"Your good friend is very greedy. He doesn't have the sharing spirit," his wife told Iktome. "Never invite him again. He has no manners. He doesn't know how to behave. He saw those two fine buffalo livers, which I cooked just as you like them, and didn't want to share them with you. He grabbed both and made off with them. Some friend!"

Iktome rushed out of the lodge in a frenzy, running after Coyote as fast as he could, shouting: "Coyote! Kola! Friend! Leave me at least one! Leave one for me! For your old friend Iktome!"

Coyote didn't stop. He ran even faster than Ikto. Running, running, he looked back over his shoulder and shouted: "Cousin, if you catch me, you can have both of them!"

Creation Tales

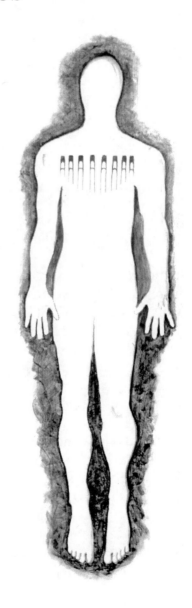

Creation
Hopi

In the beginning there were only two: Tawa, the Sun God, and Spider Woman, the Earth Goddess. All the mysteries and power in the Above belonged to Tawa, while Spider Woman controlled the magic of the Below. In the Underworld, abode of the Gods, they dwelt and they were All. There was neither man nor woman, bird nor beast, no living thing until these Two willed it to be.

In time it came to them that there should be other Gods to share their labors. So Tawa divided himself and there came Muiyinwuh, God of All Life Germs; Spider Woman also divided herself so that there was Huzruiwuhti, Woman of the Hard Substances, the Goddess of all hard ornaments of wealth such as coral, turquoise, silver and shell.

Huzruiwuhti became the always-bride of Tawa. They were the First Lovers and of their union there came into being those marvelous ones the Magic Twins -- Puukonhoya, the Youth, and Palunhoya, the Echo. As time unrolled there followed Hicanavaiya, Ancient of Six (the Four World Quarters, the Above and Below), Man-Eagle, the Great Plumed Serpent and many others. But Masauwhu, the Death God, did not come of these Two but was bad magic, who appeared only after the making of creatures.

And then it came about that these Two had one Thought and it was a mighty Thought -- that they would make the Earth to be between the Above and the Below where now lay shimmering only the Endless Waters. So they sat them side by side, swaying their beautiful bronze bodies to the pulsing music of their own great voices, making the First Magic Song, a song of rushing winds and flowing waters, a song of light and sound and life.

"I am Tawa," sang the Sun God. "I am Light. I am Life. I am Father of all that shall ever come."

"I am Kokyanwuhti," the Spider Woman crooned. "I receive Light and nourish Life. I am Mother of all that shall ever come."

"Many strange thoughts are forming in my mind -- beautiful forms of birds to float in the Above, of beasts to move upon the Earth and fish to swim in the Waters," intoned Tawa.

"Now let these things that move in the Thought of Tawa appear," chanted Spider Woman, while with her slender fingers she caught up clay from beside her and made the Thoughts of Tawa take form. One by one she shaped them and laid them aside -- but they breathed not nor moved.

"We must do something about this," said Tawa. "It is not good that they lie thus still and quiet. Each thing that has a form must also have a spirit. So now, my beloved, we must make a mighty Magic."

They laid a white blanket over the many figures, a cunningly woven woolen blanket, fleecy as a cloud, and made a mighty incantation over it, and soon the figures stirred and breathed.

"Now, let us make ones like unto you and me, so that they may rule over and enjoy these lesser creatures," sang Tawa, and Spider Woman shaped the Thoughts into woman and man figures like unto their own. But after the blanket magic had been made, the figures remained inert. So Spider Woman gathered them all in her arms and cradled them, while Tawa bent his glowing eyes upon them. The two now sang the magic Song of Life over them, and at last each human figure breathed and lived.

"Now that was a good thing and a mighty thing," said Tawa. "So now all this is finished, and there shall be no new things made by us. Those things we have made shall multiply. I will make a journey across the Above each day to shed my light upon them and return each night to Huzruiwuhti. And now I shall go to turn my blazing shield upon the Endless Waters, so that the Dry Land may appear. And this day will be the first day upon Earth."

"Now I shall lead all these created beings to the land that you shall cause to appear above the waters," said Spider Woman. Then Tawa took down his burnished shield from the turquoise wall of the kiva and swiftly mounted his glorious way to the Above. After Spider Woman had bent her wise, all-seeing eyes upon the thronging creatures about her, she wound her way among them, separating them into groups.

"Thus and thus shall you be and thus shall you remain each one in her own tribe forever. You are Zunis, you are Kohoninos, you are Pah-Utes...." The Hopis, all, all people were named by Kokyanwuhti then.

Placing her Magic Twins beside her, Spider Woman called all the people to follow where she led. Through all the Four Great Caverns of the Underworld she led them until they finally came to an opening, a sipapu, which led above. This came out at the lowest depth of the Pisisbaiya (the Colorado River) and was the place where the people were to come to gather salt. So lately had the Endless Waters gone down that the Turkey, Koyona, pushing early ahead, dragged its tail feathers in the black mud where the dark bands were to remain forever.

Mourning Dove flew overhead, calling to some to follow, and those who followed where his sharp eyes had spied out springs and built beside them were called "Huwinyamu" after him. So Spider Woman chose a creature to lead each clan to a place to build their house. The Puma, the Snake, the Antelope, the Deer, and other Horn creatures, each led a clan to a place to build their house. Each clan henceforth bore the name of the creature who had led them.

The Spider Woman spoke to them thus: "The woman of the clan shall build the house, and the family name shall descend through her. She shall be house builder and homemaker. She shall mold the jars for the storing of food and water. She shall grind the grain for food and tenderly rear and teach the young. The man of the clan shall build kivas of stone under the ground. In these kivas the man shall make sand pictures as altars. Of colored sand shall he make them, and they shall be called 'ponya.' The man too shall weave the clan blankets with their proper symbols. The man shall fashion himself weapons and furnish his family with game."

Stooping down, she gathered some sand in her hand, letting it run out in a thin, continuous stream. "See the movement of the sand? That is the life that will cause all things therein to grow. The Great Plumed Serpent, Lightning, will rear and strike the earth to fertilize it; Rain Cloud will pour down waters, and Tawa will smile upon it so that green things will spring up to feed my children."

Her eyes now sought the Above where Tawa was descending toward his western kiva in all the glory of red and gold. "I go now, but have no fear, for we Two will be watching over you. Look upon me now, my children, ere I leave. Obey the words I have given you, and all will be well. If you are in need of help, call upon me, and I will send my sons to your aid."

The people gazed wide-eyed upon her shining beauty. Her woven upper garment of soft white wool hung tunic-wise over a blue skirt. On its left side was woven a band bearing the Butterfly and Squash Blossom, in designs of red and yellow and green with bands of black appearing in between. Her neck was hung with heavy necklaces of turquoise, shell and coral, and pendants of the same hung from her ears. Her face was fair, with warm eyes and tender lips, and her form most graceful. Upon her feet were skin boots of gleaming white, and they now turned toward where the sand spun about in whirlpool fashion. She held up her right hand and smiled upon them, then stepped upon the whirling sand. Wonder of wonders, before their eyes the sands seemed to suck her swiftly down until she disappeared entirely from their sight.

Legend of the Cherokee Creation

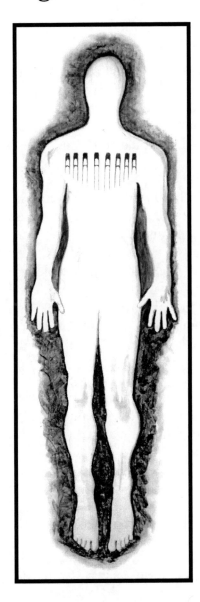

Earth is floating on the waters like a big island, hanging from four rawhide ropes fastened at the top of the Sacred four directions. The ropes are tied to the ceiling of the sky, which is made of hard rock crystal. When the ropes break, this world will come tumbling down, and all living things will fall with it and die. Then everything will be as if the earth had never existed, for water will cover it. Maybe the white man will bring this about.

Well, in the beginning also, water covered everything. Though living creatures existed, their home was up there, above the rainbow, and it was crowded. "We are all jammed together," the animals said. "We need more room." Wondering what was under the water, they sent Water Beetle to look around.

Water Beetle skimmed over the surface but couldn't find any solid footing, so he dived to the bottom and brought up a little dab of soft mud. Magically the mud spread out in the four directions and became this island we are living on – this Earth. Someone powerful then fastened it to the sky ceiling with ropes.

In the beginning the Earth was flat, soft, and moist. All the animals were eager to live on it, and they kept sending down birds to see if the mud had dried and hardened enough to take their weight. But the birds flew back and said that there was still no spot they could perch on.

Then the animals sent Grandfather Buzzard down. He flew very close and saw that the Earth was still soft, but when he glided low over what would become Cherokee country, he found that the mud was getting harder. By that time Buzzard was tired and dragging. When he flapped his wings down they made a valley where they touched the earth; when he swept them up, they made a mountain. The animals watching from above the rainbow said, "If he keeps on, there will only be mountains," and they made him come back. That's why we have so many mountains in Cherokee land.

At last the earth was hard and dry enough, and the animals descended. They couldn't see very well because they had no sun or moon, and someone said, "Let's grab Sun from up there behind the rainbow! Let's get him down too!" Pulling Sun down, they told him, "Here's a road for you," and showed him the way to go.... from east to west.

Now they had light, but it was much too hot, because Sun was too close to the earth. The crawfish had his back sticking out of a stream, and Sun burned it red. His meat was spoiled forever, and the people still won't eat crawfish.

Everyone asked the sorcerers, the shamans, to put Sun higher. They pushed him up as high as a man, but it was still too hot. So they pushed him farther, but it wasn't far enough. They tried four times, and when they had Sun up to the height of four men, he was just hot enough. Everyone was satisfied, so they left him there.

Before making humans, Someone Powerful had created plants and animals and had told them to stay awake and watch for seven days and seven nights. (This is just what young men do today when they fast and prepare for a ceremony). But most of the plants and animals couldn't manage it, some fell asleep after one day, some after two days.

Among the trees and other plants, only the cedar, pine, holly, and laurel were still awake on the eighth morning. Someone Powerful said to them: "Because you watched and stayed awake as you had been told, you will not lose your hair in the winter." So these plants stay green all the time.

After creating plants and animals, Someone Powerful made man and his sister. The man poked her with a fish and told her to go give birth. After seven days she had a baby, and after seven more days she had another, and every seven days another came. The humans increased so quickly that Someone Powerful, thinking there would soon be no more room on this earth, arranged things so that a woman could have only one child every year. And that's how it was.

Now, there is still another world under the one we live on. You can reach it by going down a spring, a water hole; but you need underworld people to be your scouts and guide you. The world under our earth is exactly like ours, except that it's winter down there when its summer up here. We can see that easily, because spring water is warmer than the air in winter and cooler than the air in summer.

When the World was Young

A Blackfoot Legend

When the world was young, Old Man and Old Woman Coyote were walking around. "Let us decide how things will be," Old Man Coyote Said.

"That would be good," said Old Woman Coyote. "How shall we do it?"

"It was my idea so I'll have the first say" said Old Man Coyote.

"That is fine," said Old Woman Coyote. "Just as long as I have the last say."

So for a while they walked around looking at things. Finally, Old Man Coyote said something. "The men will be the hunters. Any time they want to shoot an animal they will call it and it will come."

"I too think men should be the hunters," said Old Woman Coyote. "But if the animals come so easily then life will be too easy for the people. The animals shall run away and hide. This will make it harder for the hunters but it will make them smarter and stronger."

"You have the last say," said Old Man Coyote.

They walked around some more and again Old Man Coyote said something. "I've been thinking about how people will look. They will have eyes on one side of their face and their mouth on the other. Their mouths will go up and down. They will have ten fingers on each hand."

"I too think that people should have their eyes and their mouth on their faces, but their eyes will be at the top of their face and their mouth at the bottom and they will be across from each other." Said Old Woman Coyote "and I agree they should have fingers, but ten on each hand will be too awkward. They will have 5 fingers on each hand."

"You have the last say," said Old Man Coyote.

They continued to walk and finally they were by the river when Old Man Coyote spoke. "Let us decide about life and death. I will do it this way. I will throw this buffalo chip into the river. If it floats, then when people die they will come back to life after 4 days and live forever."

Old Man Coyote threw the chip in and it floated.

"I too think we should decide this way," Old Woman Coyote said. "But we will use a stone instead of a buffalo chip. I will throw this stone in the river. If it floats, then people will come back in 4 days and live forever. If it sinks, then people will not come back to life after they die."

Old Woman Coyote threw the stone in the river and it sank.

"That is the way it should be," Old Woman Coyote said. "If people lived forever the Earth would get to crowded and there would not be enough food. This way people will learn compassion."

Old Man Coyote said nothing.

Some time passed. Old Woman Coyote had a child. She and Old Man Coyote loved the child a lot and they were happy.

One day, the child became ill and died. Then Old Woman Coyote went to Old Man Coyote.

"Let us have our say again about death," she said.

But Old Man Coyote shook his head." NO, you had the last say."

"I am a red man. If the Great Spirit had desired me to be a white man he would have made me so in the first place. He put in your heart certain wishes and plans, in my heart he put other and different desires. Each man is good in his sight. It is not necessary for Eagles to be Crows. We are poor... but we are free. No white man controls our footsteps. If we must die...we die defending our rights."

Sitting Bull, Hunkpapa Sioux

Children of the Sun

Osage
From Alice Fletcher and Francis Lafleche, who recorded this myth in 1911.

Way beyond the earth, a part of the Osage lived in the sky. They wanted to know where they came from, so they went to the sun. He told them that they were his children. Then they wandered still farther and came to the moon. She told them that she gave birth to them, and that the sun was their father. She said that they must leave the sky and go down to live on earth. They obeyed, but found the earth covered with water. They could not return to their home in the sky, so they wept and called out, but no answer came from anywhere. They floated about in the air, seeking in every direction for help from some god; but they found none.

The animals were with them, and of these the elk inspired all creatures with confidence because he was the finest and most stately. The Osage appealed to the elk for help, and he dropped into the water and began to sink. Then he called to the winds, and they came from all quarters and blew until the waters went upward in mist.

At first only rocks were exposed, and the people traveled on the rocky places that produced no plants to eat. Then the waters began to go down until the soft earth was exposed. When this happened, the elk in his joy rolled over and over, and all his loose hairs clung to the soil. The hairs grew, and from them sprang beans, corn, potatoes, and wild turnips, and then all the grasses and trees.

Earth, Teach Me

Earth teach me quiet ~ as the grasses are still with new light.
Earth teach me suffering ~ as old stones suffer with memory.
Earth teach me humility ~ as blossoms are humble with beginning.
Earth teach me caring ~ as mothers nurture their young.
Earth teach me courage ~ as the tree that stands alone.
Earth teach me limitation ~ as the ant that crawls on the ground.
Earth teach me freedom ~ as the eagle that soars in the sky.
Earth teach me acceptance ~ as the leaves that die each fall.
Earth teach me renewal ~ as the seed that rises in the spring.
Earth teach me to forget myself ~ as melted snow forgets its life.
Earth teach me to remember kindness ~ as dry fields weep with rain.

- An Ute Prayer

The Tower of Babel

A Choctaw Legend
Bushnell, Bulletin of the Bureau of American Ethnology, xlviii, 30

Many generations ago Aba, the good spirit above, created many men, all Choctaw, who spoke the language of the Choctaw, and understood one another.

These came from the bosom of the earth, being formed of yellow clay, and no men had ever lived before them. One day all came together and, looking upward, wondered what the clouds and the blue expanse above might be. They continued to wonder and talk among themselves and at last determined to endeavor to reach the sky.

So they brought many rocks and began building a mound that was to have touched the heavens. That night, however, the wind blew strong from above and the rocks fell from the mound. The second morning they again began work on the mound, but as the men slept that night the rocks were again scattered by the winds.

Once more, on the third morning, the builders set to their

task. But once more, as the men lay near the mound that night, wrapped in slumber, the winds came with so great force that the rocks were hurled down on them.

The men were not killed, but when daylight came and they made their way from beneath the rocks and began to speak to one another, all were astounded as well as alarmed they spoke various languages and could not understand one another.

Some continued thenceforward to speak the original tongue, the language of the Choctaw, and from these sprung the Choctaw tribe. The others, who could not understand this language, began to fight among themselves. Finally, they separated.

The Choctaw remained the original people; the others scattered, some going north, some east, and others west, and formed various tribes. This explains why there are so many tribes throughout the country at the present time.

The Sun Dance Wheel

An Arapaho Legend

At one time the whole world was covered with water. It was everywhere, no matter where one looked.

The water did not stop a man carrying Flat Pipe, his companion and counselor, from walking across the waters for four days and nights. The man wanted to treat his pipe in the best way, so he gave much thought to this subject. He thought for six days and finally decided that in order to provide a good home for Flat Pipe there should be land and the good company of creatures.

So on the seventh day the man set out to find land among all the water, calling to the four directions as he went. From the four directions came many animal helpers, and with their help man found a land home. He put the Four Old Men in each of the four directions to control the winds. Now, the land would also provide a place for a Sun Dance of ceremony and thanksgiving every year.

A garter snake came to the man, and the man said "Oh, you will be a great comfort to the people and have a great place in the Sun Dance as the Sacred Wheel to represent the waters that surround this earth."

He then looked again to all around him for help and many offered. Long Stick, a bush with flexible limbs and dark bark, came and said "I offer myself for the wheel for the good of all." All approved so Long Stick was made into the ring of the Sacred Wheel, representing the circle that is the Sun.

The eagle soared by and said "My strength is great enough to carry me above the earth and water as I fly on the winds of the four directions. Please take my feathers to represent the Four Old Men."

The man was pleased, and told all that four bunches of eagle feathers would forever be tied to the wheel to honor the desire of the eagle and anyone who would ever offer an eagle feather as a gift.

Once the man shaped the Sacred Wheel he painted it in the image of garter snake and placed the feathers in the position of the Four Old Men - Northwest, Northeast, Southeast and Southwest - who rule the directions and control the winds and to represent the Thunderbird who brings the rain. To further enhance the wheel, the man added groups of stars, painting special images of the Sun, the Moon and the Milky Way. Blue beads tied on represented the sky.

When finished, the man thanked garter snake for serving his people in this way with the creation of the wheel that symbolizes all creation.

How the Milky Way Came to Be
A Cherokee Legend

Long ago when the world was young, there were not many stars in the sky.

In those days the people depended on corn for their food. Dried corn could be made into corn meal by placing it inside a large hollowed stump and pounding it with a long wooden pestle. The cornmeal was stored in large baskets. During the winter, the ground meal could made into bread and mush.

One morning an old man and his wife went to their storage basket for some cornmeal. They discovered that someone or something had gotten into the cornmeal during the night. This upset them very much for no one in a Cherokee village stole from someone else.

Then they noticed that the cornmeal was scattered over the ground. In the middle of the spilt meal were giant dog prints. These dog prints were so large that the elderly couple knew this was no ordinary dog.

They immediately alerted the people of the village. It was decided that this must be a spirit dog from another world. The people did not want the spirit dog coming to their village. They decided to get rid of the dog by frightening it so bad it would never return. They gathered their drums and turtle shell rattles and later that night they hid around the area where the cornmeal was kept.

Late into the night they heard a whirring sound like many bird wings. They look up to see the form of a giant dog swooping down from the sky. It landed near the basket and then began to eat great mouthfuls of cornmeal.

Suddenly the people jumped up beating and shaking their noise makers. The noise was so loud it sounded like thunder. The giant dog turned and began to run down the path. The people chased after him making the loudest noises they could. It ran to the top of a hill and leaped into the sky, the cornmeal spilling out the sides of its mouth.

The giant dog ran across the black night sky until it disappeared from sight. But the cornmeal that had spilled from its mouth made a path way across the sky. Each gain of cornmeal became a star.

The Cherokees call that pattern of stars, gi li' ut sun stan un' yi (gil-LEE-oot-soon stan-UNH-yee), "the place where the dog ran."

And that is how the Milky Way came to be.

Strange Tales

The Destruction of the Bear

A Jicarilla Apache Legend
Frank Russell, Myths of the
Jicarilla Apaches, 1898

An Apache boy, while playing with his comrades, pretended to be a bear, and ran into a hole in the hillside. When he came out his feet and hands had been transformed into bear's paws. A second time he entered the den, and his limbs were changed to the knees and elbows.

Four times he entered the den, and then came forth the voracious cac-tla-yæ that devoured his former fellow-beings. One day the bear met a fox in the mountains. "I am looking for a man to eat," said Bear.

"So am I," said Fox, "but your legs are so big and thick you cannot run very fast to catch them. You ought to allow me to trim down those posts a little, so you can run as swift as I."

Bear consented to have the operation performed, and Fox not only cut the flesh from the legs of Bear, but also broke the bones with his knife, thus killing the dreaded man-eater. Taking the leg bones of Bear with him, he went to the home of the bear family, and there found two other bears.

These monsters preyed upon the people, who were unable to kill them, as they left their hearts at home when off on their marauding expeditions.

Fox remained in hiding until the bears went away. When they ran among the Indians, Fox responded to the cries for assistance, not by flying to attack the bears, but by hastening to cut their hearts in two.

The bears were aware that their hearts had been tampered with, and rushed with all speed to rescue them, but fell dead just before they reached Fox.

Thus Fox destroyed one of the most dreaded of man's enemies of that primeval time.

O' Great Spirit
help me always
to speak the truth quietly,
to listen with an open mind
when others speak,
and to remember the peace
that may be found in silence.

Cherokee Prayer

The Killing of the Monsters

A Jicarilla Apache Legend
Pliny E. Goddard,
Anthropological Papers of the
American Museum of Natural
History, Vol. VIII

Naiyenesgani came where Elk had been killing people. He could not get near it although he tried to approach it from every side. Then another person came to him to be his partner. "My companion," he said, "I will gnaw off the hair on his breast for you." Having done this, he returned, saying, "Now go to him."

Naiyenesgani went to him, made motions four times, and then shot him. He hid in one of the holes that his partner had made. The elk broke out the uppermost hole. Naiyenesgani went into the next hole. The elk broke that out also.

He then went into mother which Elk also broke out.

He went into the bottom tunnel; just as Elk broke this out he fell down dead. The partner then came up to him and said, "The breast will be mine."

Naiyenesgani skinned it and took the hide. He also chopped off one of the horns. He filled two of the blood vessels with blood and spread out the hide in the sun until it was dry.

He started away toward the eagle. When he came to him he wrapped the elk hide about himself and went out into an open place. The eagle, when he swooped down, attempted to drive his talons into him but could not penetrate the hide.

He flew up without getting hold of him. He came to him again but failed to get his talons in.

He flew up again. He came back and having failed, flew away again. Then he came back and drove in his talons. He flew away to his home with the man. He brought him to his young. When they bent their heads down over him he said, "Sst."

"Father, when we put our heads down to it, it says 'sst,'" one of them said. "Do not mind it; go ahead and eat. It is the air coming out of the wound that makes that noise." Then the blood flowed through the opening. The old eagle flew away.

Naiyenesgani came up to them holding the horn in his hand. "When your father comes home, on what rock does he sit?" he asked.

"He sits on yonder point of rock," one of them told him. Naiyenesgani sat there with eagle's children until the father came again bringing with him a pretty dead girl which he threw down. Making motions four times, Naiyenesgani struck him and he fell into the canyon. He heard him burst as he struck. "When your mother comes back, where does she sit?" he asked.

"She sit, here," one of them said. The mother came back. Naiyenesgani making motions four times, struck her, throwing her into the canyon.

Then he said to the young eagles, "You will be just as large as you are now. People will like your feathers."

"Those who take them will have their muscles draw up."

"You shall not talk," he said. Then they ceased talking.

In the distance, his grandmother (bat) was coming into the open from the timber. She walked along carrying a basket.

Then he shouted to her, "Grandmother, take me down," but she did not hear. He shouted to her again and then she heard. Then his grandmother came near him. "I shouted to you, 'take me down, grandmother,'" he said.

"Come up to me and take me down," he told her. Then she climbed up to him, carrying her basket. "Grandmother, this carrying rope on your basket is very small."

"Why, grandson, I carry very heavy things with this. Fill it with stones and see if it breaks."

When he had filled it she jumped with it. Then she took the stones out again and he got in. "Shut your grandson."

She started to go down with him. "Do not open your eyes, grandson," she cautioned him, the rock is sheer. We are falling, grandson, do not open your eyes. We are down." When they were at the foot of the cliff, Naiyenesgani said, "Grandmother, I have killed something, let us go to it."

When they came there he said, "Now, grandmother, I will give you some good property. Put down your basket here." He then filled it with feathers. "Now, you may carry it away but do not go along the hillside, go along the top of the hills," he told her.

She carried it away along the hillside, and the birds came and took away the feathers. She came back to him and he filled her basket again. "Do not carry the basket on the hillside," he told her.

Again, she carried it along the side of the hill and the birds came and took away all the feathers. She came back to him again and he filled the basket for her. "'Do not carry it along the sloping places,' I told you," he said. Then they took the feathers away front her. When she came back to him this time he said, "You do not want to possess this good property which I have been giving you. For that reason, your feathers will be poor. You will live in the clefts of the rocks and will use bark for your house. Your garments will be poor. You do not want things that are good. You will not have a shirt."

He went again where there was something bad. When he came among the people there they said to him, "If you have supernatural power, take out our people from the marsh where they have sunk."

"Very well," he said, "I will take them out for you." When he came to the place he stood first at the east, then at the south, then at the west, and finally at the north. Then the water disappeared of itself and he went to the entrance and went in.

"I have come for the people you have taken away," he said, "bring them to me. Do not bring me just one."

"There are no people," replied the monster. "Just bring them to me, do not talk." Then he brought them to him. "Just one sits there," he said.

"I did not come for one," he told him. Then he sent one out to him.

"Are there many people where you are staying?" he asked.

"There are many people there," he said.

"Bring them all out," Naiyenesgani called. The people all began to crowd outside. Then they went up to the surface of the ground. "You may just stay in the marsh," he said to the monster. When all the people had come out he spoke to him (the monster), "You must not do it any time. Just soft mud does not talk. It must not speak words." Then he went out away from him and came where the people were.

"Four of you take charge of your people," he said. "Do not go close in among the houses." Then four of them came there. Now pick out your own people and go home with them," he told them.

"Now you pick your people," he said to another. Then that one picked out his people. Then he went to another place, "You pick out your people," he told the third."

That one selected his relatives. Then he called to another in the same manner and he picked out his folks. Then they were all satisfied. Naiyenesgani was sitting there. "I just speak to you," he said, "select for me four pretty girls. I wish to go with them."

Then he went away with them toward the west. At Kagodjae he left one; at Tsosbai, another; and at Becdelkai, the third. With the other one he went to the west where they remain forever.

Case of the Severed Head

A Cheyenne Legend
Based on an account by
George Bird Grinnell
in 1903.

Once in a lonely lodge there lived a man, his wife, and two children – a girl and a boy. In front of the lodge, not far off, was a great lake, and a plain trail leading from the lodge down to the shore where the family used to go for water.

Every day the man went hunting, but before starting he would paint the woman red all over, coating her face, her arms, and her whole body with this sacred medicine to protect her from harm.

After he departed, she would leave the children alone in the lodge and go for water; when she returned with it, the red paint was always gone and her hair was un-braided. She would manage to get back with her water just before her husband arrived. Not being a good hunter, he never brought any meat.

Though he asked her no questions, her husband thought it strange that every night the paint he had put on his wife in the morning had disappeared. One day he said to his daughter, "What does your mother do every day? When I go out, I paint her, and when I get back, she has no paint on."

The girl replied, "Whenever you start out hunting, she goes for water, and she is usually away for a long time."

The next day, the man painted his wife as usual and then took his bow and arrows and left the lodge.

But instead of going off hunting, he went down to the lake shore, dug a hole in the sand, and buried himself, leaving a little place where he could look out.

The man had not been hidden long when he saw his wife coming with a bucket. When she was near the water's edge, she slipped off her dress, un-braided her hair, sat down on the shore, and said, "Na shu eh', I am here."

Soon the man saw the water begin to move, and a mih'ni, a water spirit, rose from it, crawled out on the land, crept up to the woman, wrapped itself about her, and licked off all the red paint that was on her body.

The man emerged from his hiding place and rushed down to the pair. With his knife he cut the monster to pieces and cut off his wife's head.

The pieces of the monster crept and rolled back into the water and were never seen again. The man cut off the woman's arms at the elbow and her legs at the knees. Saying, "Take your wife!" he threw these pieces and her head into the water. Then he opened the body, extracted a side of her ribs, and skinned it.

Returning to the lodge, he said, "Ah, my little children, I have had good luck; I have killed an antelope and brought back some of the meat. Where is your mother?"

The children answered, "Our mother has gone to bring water."

"Well," he said, "since I killed my meat sooner than I thought, I carried it back to camp. Your mother will be here pretty soon. In the meantime, I'll cook something for you to eat before I go out again."

He cooked a kettle of meat and took it to the children, who both ate. The little boy, who was the younger and the last one to suckle, said to his sister, "This tastes like mother!"

"Oh," said his sister, "keep still; this is antelope meat."

After the children had finished, the little girl saved some of the meat for the mother to eat when she returned.

The father got his moccasins and other things together and started off, intending never to come back. He was going to look for his tribe's camp.

After he had gone, the children were sitting in the lodge, the girl making moccasins and putting porcupine quills on them.

Suddenly they heard a voice outside say, "I love my children, but they don't love me; they have eaten me!"

The girl said to her brother, "Look out the door and see who is coming."

The boy looked out and then cried, very much frightened, "Sister, here comes our mother's head!"

"Shut the door," cried the girl. The little boy did so. The girl picked up her moccasins and her quills - red, white, and yellow — rolled them up, and seized her root digger.

Meanwhile the head had rolled against the door. "Daughter, open the door," it called.

The head would strike the door, roll part way up the lodge, and then fall back again.

The girl and her brother ran to the door, pushed it open, and stood to the side. The head rolled into the lodge and clear across to the back.

The girl and boy jumped out, the girl closed the door, and both children ran away as fast as they could. As they ran, they heard the mother calling to them from the lodge.

They ran, and they ran, and at last the boy called, "sister, I'm tired; I can't run any longer." The girl took his robe and carried it for him, and they ran on.

At last they reached the top of the divide, they looked back, and there they could see the head coming, rolling over the prairie.

Somehow it had gotten out of the lodge. The children kept running, but at last the head had almost overtaken them. The little boy was frightened nearly to death, as well as exhausted. The sister said, "This running is almost killing my brother. When I was a little girl playing, sometimes the prickly pears were so thick on the ground that I couldn't get through them."

As she said this, she scattered behind her a handful of the yellow porcupine quills. At once there appeared a great bed of tall prickly pears with great yellow thorns. This cactus patch was strung out for a long way in both directions across the trail they had made.

When the head reached that place, it rolled up on the prickly pears and tried to roll over them, but kept getting caught in the thorns. For a long time it kept trying and trying to work its way through, and at last it did get loose from the thorns and passed over. But by this time the girl and the boy had gone a long distance.

After a while, however, they looked back and again saw the head coming. The little boy almost fainted. He kept calling out, "Sister, I'm tired; I can't run any longer."

When the sister heard him, she said while she was running, "When I was a little girl, I often used to find the bullberry bushes very thick."

As she said this, she threw behind her a handful of the white quills, and where they touched the ground a huge grove of thick, thorny bullberry bushes grew up. They blocked the way, and the head stopped there for a long time, unable to pass through the bushes.

The children ran on and on, toward the place where the tribe had last been camped. But at length they looked back and saw the head coming again.

The little boy called out, "Sister, I'm tired; I can't run any longer."

Again the girl threw quills behind - this time the red ones - and a great thicket of thorny rosebushes sprang up and stopped the head.

Again the children went a long way, but at last they saw the head coming, and the boy called out: "Sister, I'm tired."

Then the sister said, "When I was a little girl playing, I often came to small ravines that I couldn't cross."

She stopped and drew the point of her root digger over the ground in front of her. This made a little groove in the dirt, and she placed the root digger across the groove.

Then she and her brother walked over on the root digger, and when they had crossed, the furrow became wider and wider and deeper and deeper.

Soon it was a great chasm with cut walls, and at the bottom they could see a little water trickling. "Now," said the girl, "we will run no longer; we will stay here."

"No, no," said the boy, "let's run."

"No," said the girl, "I will kill our mother here."

Presently the head came rolling up to the edge of the ravine and stopped.

"Daughter," it said, "where did you cross? Place your root digger on the ground so that I can cross too."

The girl attempted to do so, but the boy pulled her back every time. At last she managed to lay the root digger down, and the head began rolling over. But when it was halfway across, the girl tipped the stick, the head fell into the ravine, and the ravine closed on it.

After this the children started on again to look for the people. At last they found the camp and drew near it. Before they arrived, however, they heard a man's loud voice. As they came closer, they saw that it was their father speaking. He was walking about the camp and telling everyone that while he was out hunting, his two children had killed and eaten their mother. He warned the people that if the children came to the camp, they should not be allowed to enter.

When they heard this, the children were frightened. Still, they didn't know what else to do but go on into the camp.

The people immediately caught them and tied their hands and feet. And the next day the whole tribe moved away and left the children there, still tied.

In the camp there was an old, old dog who knew what had happened and took pity on the children. The night of their arrival, she went into a lodge, stole some sinew, a knife, and an awl, and took them into a hole where she had her pups.

The next day after all the people had gone, the children heard a dog howling. Presently the old, old dog approached them. "Grandchildren," she said, "I pity you and have come to help you."

The girl said, "Untie me first, and I can untie my brother."

So the old dog began to gnaw at the rawhide strings around the girl's hands. The animal had no teeth and could not cut the cords, but they became wet and began to slip.

The girl kept working her hands and at last got them free. She untied her legs and then freed her brother.

That evening they walked about through the camp and picked up old moccasins to wear. Both children were crying, and so was the dog.

They all sat on the hill near the camp and cried bitterly, for they had nothing to eat, no place to sleep, and nothing to cover themselves with, and winter was coming. The girl and the dog sat weeping with their heads hanging down, but the boy was looking about. Presently he said, "Sister, see that wolf; it's coming straight toward us!"

"It's useless for me to look," said the girl. "I couldn't kill him by looking at him, so we can't eat him."

"But look, Sister," said the boy, "he's coming right up to us."

At last the girl raised her head, and when she looked at the wolf, it fell dead. Then the dog brought the tools that she had stolen before the tribe left. With the knife they cut the wolf up, and from its skin they made a bed for the dog.

The children stayed in the abandoned camp, living well now, while the people in the new camp were starving. The children kept a large fire burning day and night and used big logs so that it never went out.

But after they had eaten the wolf, they began to feel hungry again. The girl became very unhappy, and one day as she sat crying, with the dog sitting beside her and the boy standing and looking about, he said, "Sister, look at that antelope coming!"

"No," said the girl, "it's useless for me to look; looking will do no good."

"But look even so," said the boy. "Perhaps it will do as the wolf did."

The girl looked, and as with the wolf, the antelope fell dead.

They cut it up and used its skin to make a bed for themselves. They ate the flesh and fed the old dog on the liver. The girl would chew pieces up fine for the toothless animal.

At last the antelope was all eaten, and again they grew hungry. Again the boy saw a strange-looking animal - this time an elk, which fell dead before the girl's look. She stretched the elk hide, which they used for a shelter. With the sinews the dog had stolen, they sewed their moccasins and mended their clothing.

When the elk ran out, the boy saw a buffalo coming straight to their shelter, and the girl killed it by a look. They cut up the meat and used the hide to make a larger and better shelter, where they stayed until winter came and snow began to fall.

One night when the girl went to bed, she said, "I wish that I might see a lodge over there in that sheltered place in the morning. I could sleep there with my brother and the dog, on a bed in the back of the lodge. I could make a bow and some arrows, so that my brother could kill the buffalo close to the camp when they gather in the underbrush during bad weather." She also wished that her brother might become a young man, and that they might have meat racks in the camp and meat on them.

In the morning when the boy got up and looked out, he said, "Sister, our lodge is over there now." It was in the very place the girl had wished. They moved their possessions and their fire over to it, and when the boy entered the lodge, he was a young man. That winter he killed many buffalo and they had plenty of meat.

One night as she was going to bed, the girl made another wish. "Brother," she said, "our father has treated us very badly. He caused us to eat our mother, and he had us tied up and deserted by the people. I wish we knew how to get word to the camp, and I wish that we had two bears that we could tell to eat our father."

Next morning when the girl got up, two bears were sitting in the lodge on either side of the door. "Hello, my animals," she said. "Arise and eat."

After giving them food, she went out to one of the meat racks and pulled off a piece of bloody fat. She called to a raven that was sitting in a tree nearby: "Come here; I want to send you on an errand."

When the raven had flown to her, she said, "Go and look for the camp of my people. Fly about among the lodges and call them. And when the people come out and ask each other, `What's that raven doing? And what is he carrying?' drop this piece of fat into the thick of the crowd. Then tell them that the people you came from have great scaffolds of meat."

The raven took the piece of fat in his bill and flew away. He found the camp and flew about, calling and calling, and a number of men sitting here and there began to say to each other, "What's that raven carrying?"

The raven dropped the meat, and someone who picked it up said, "why, it's fresh fat." Then the raven said, "Those people whom you threw away are still in the old camp, and they have scaffolds of meat like this." Then the raven flew back to the girl.

An old man began crying out to the people as he walked through the camp: "Those children whom we threw away have plenty of meat! They are in the old camp, and now we must move back to it as quickly as we can."

The people tore down their lodges, packed up, and started back. Some of the young men went ahead in little groups of threes and fours, and when they reached the children's camp, the girl fed them and gave them meat to carry back to the others. All the trees about the lodge were covered with meat, and buffalo hides were stacked in great piles.

After a while the whole village arrived and camped not far from the children's lodge, and everyone began to come to the lodge for food. The girl sent word to her father to hold off until all the rest had been fed, so that he could come and take his time instead of eating in a hurry. She said to the bears, "I'm going to send for your food last. After that person gets here and has eaten, I'll say, `There's your food,' as he goes out of the lodge. Then you may eat him up."

In the evening when the last of the people was leaving the lodge, she said to her brother, "Tell everyone not to come anymore tonight; it is my father's turn now."

When the father came and they fed him, he said happily, "Oh, my children, you're living well here; you have plenty of meat and tongues and back fat."

He did not eat everything his daughter had set before him. "I'll take all this home for my breakfast," he said.

After he had left the lodge, the girl said to the bears, "There's your food; eat him up!" The bears sprang after the father and pulled him down. He called to his daughter to take her animals away, but they killed him and began to drag him back to the lodge.

The girl said, "Take him off somewhere else and eat him, and what you don't eat, throw into the stream."

What the bears did not eat they threw into the creek, and then they washed their hands, and no one ever knew what had become of the father. Since that time, bears have eaten human flesh when they could.

The boy and the girl returned to the camp, and always afterward lived well there.

Little People of the Cherokee

A Cherokee Legend
James Mooney,
History, Myths and
Sacred Formulas of
the Cherokee, 1891

The Little People of
the Cherokee are a
race of Spirits who
live in rock caves on
the mountain side.
They are little fellows and ladies reaching almost to your
knees. They are well shaped and handsome, and their hair
so long it almost touches the ground.

They are very helpful, kind-hearted, and great wonder
workers. They love music and spend most of their time
drumming, singing, and dancing. They have a very gentle
nature, but do not like to be disturbed.

Sometimes their drums are heard in lonely places in the
mountains, but it is not safe to follow it, for they do not like
to be disturbed at home, and they will throw a spell over
the stranger so that he is bewildered and loses his way, and
even if he does at last get back to the settlement he is like
one dazed ever after.

Sometimes, also, they come near a house at night and the
people inside hear them talking, but they must not go out,
and in the morning they find the corn gathered or the field
cleared as if a whole force of men had been at work. If

anyone should go out to watch, he would die.

When a hunter finds anything in the woods, such as a knife or a trinket, he must say, 'Little People, I would like to take this' because it may belong to them, and if he does not ask their permission they will throw stones at him as he goes home.

Some Little People are black, some are white and some are golden like the Cherokee.

Sometimes they speak in Cherokee, but at other times they speak their own 'Indian' language. Some call them "Brownies".

Little people are here to teach lessons about living in harmony with nature and with others.

There are three kinds of Little People: the Laurel People, the Rock People, and the Dogwood People.

The Rock People are the mean ones who practice "getting even" who steal children and the like. But they are like this because their space has been invaded.

The Laurel People play tricks and are generally mischievous. When you find children laughing in their sleep - the Laurel People are humorous and enjoy sharing joy with others.

Then there are the Dogwood People who are good and take care of people.

The lessons taught by the Little People are clear. The Rock People teach us that if you do things to other people out of meanness or intentionally, it will come back on you. We must always respect other people's limits and boundaries.

The Laurel People teach us that we shouldn't take the world too seriously, and we must always have joy and share that joy with others. The lessons of the Dogwood People are simple - if you do something for someone, do it out of goodness of your heart. Don't do it to have people obligated to you or for personal gain.

In Cherokee beliefs, many stories contain references to beings called the Little People. These people are supposed to be small mythical characters, and in different beliefs they serve different purposes.

"There are a lot of stories and legends about the Little People. You can see the people out in the forest. They can talk and they look a lot like Indian people except they're only about two feet high, sometimes they're smaller. Now the Little People can be very helpful, and they can also play tricks on us, too.

And at one time there was a boy. This boy never wanted to grow up. In fact, he told everyone that so much that they called him "Forever Boy" because he never wanted to be grown. When his friends would sit around and talk about: 'Oh when I get to be a man, and when I get to be grown I'm gonna be this and I'm gonna go here and be this,' he'd just go off and play by himself.

He didn't even want to hear it, because he never wanted to grow up. Finally, his father got real tired of this, and he said,' Forever Boy, I will never call you that again. From now on you're going to learn to be a man, you're going to take responsibility for yourself, and you're going to stop playing all day long. You have to learn these things. Starting tomorrow you're going to go to your uncle's, and he's going to teach you everything that you are going to need to know.'

Forever Boy was broken hearted at what his father told him, but he could not stand the thought of growing up. He went out to the river and he cried. He cried so hard that he didn't see his animal friends gather around him. And they were trying to tell him something, and they were trying to make him feel better, and finally he thought he understood them say, 'Come here tomorrow, come here early.' Well, he thought they just wanted to say goodbye to him. And he drug his feet going home. He couldn't even sleep he was so upset.

The next morning, he went out early, as he had promised, to meet his friends. And he was so sad, he could not bear the thought of telling them goodbye forever. Finally, he began to get the sense that they were trying to tell him something else, and that is to look behind him.

As he looked behind him, there they were, all the Little People. And they were smiling at him and laughing and running to hug him. And they said, 'Forever Boy you do not have to grow up. You can stay with us forever.

You can come and be one of us and you will never have to grow up...we will ask the Creator to send a vision to your parents and let them know that you are safe and you are doing what you need to do.'

Forever Boy thought about it for a long time. But that is what he decided he needed to do, and he went with the Little People.

And even today when you are out in the woods and you see something, and you look and it is not what you really thought it was, or if you are fishing and you feel something on the end of your line, and you think it is the biggest trout ever, and you pull it in, and all it is, is a stick that got tangled on your hook, that is what the Little People are doing.

They are playing tricks on you so you will laugh and keep young in your heart. Because that is the spirit of Little People, and Forever Boy, to keep us young in our hearts."

And while I stood there
I saw more than I can tell,
and I understood more than I saw;
for I was seeing in a sacred manner
the shapes of things in the spirit,
and the shape of all shapes as they must
live together like one being.

Black Elk, Black Elk Speaks

The Eye Juggler

A Cheyenne Legend
Kroeber, Journal of American Folk-Lore, xiii, 168, No. 11

There was a man that could send his eyes out of his head, on the limb of a tree, and call them back again, by saying "Eyes hang upon a branch."

White-man saw him doing this, and came to him crying; he wanted to learn this too.

The man taught him, but warned him not to do it more than four times in one day. White-man went off along the river. When he came to the highest tree he could see, he sent his eyes to the top. Then he called them back. He thought he could do this as often as he wished, disregarding the warning.

The fifth time his eyes remained fastened to the limb. All day he called, but the eyes began to swell and spoil, and flies gathered on them. White-man grew tired and lay down, facing his eyes, still calling for them, though they never came; and he cried. At night he was half asleep, when a mouse ran over him. He closed his lids that the mice would not see he was blind, and lay still, in order to catch one.

At last one sat on his breast. He kept quiet to let it become used to him, and the mouse went on his face, trying to cut his hair for its nest. Then it licked his tears, but let its tail hang in his mouth. He closed it, and caught the mouse. He seized it tightly, and made it guide him, telling him of his misfortune. The mouse said it could see the eyes, and they had swelled to an enormous size. It offered to climb the tree and get them for him, but White-man would not let it go. It tried to wriggle free, but he held it fast. Then the mouse asked on what condition he would release it, and White-man said, only if it gave him one of its eyes. So it gave him one, and he could see again, and let the mouse go. But the small eye was far back in his socket, and he could not see very well with it.

A buffalo was grazing near by, and as White-man stood near him crying, he looked on and wondered. White-man said: "Here is a buffalo, who has the power to help me in my trouble." So the Buffalo asked him what he wanted. White-man told him he had lost his eye and needed one. The buffalo took out one of his and put it in White-man's head. Now White-man could see far again. But the eye did not fit the socket; most of it was outside. The other was far inside. Thus he remained.

The Serpent of the Sea

A Zuni Legend
Frank Hamilton Cushing,
Zuni Folk Tales, 1901

In the times of our forefathers, under Thunder Mountain was a village called K'iákime ("Home of the Eagles"). It is now in ruins; the roofs are gone, the ladders have decayed, the hearths grown cold.

But when it was all still perfect, and, as it were, new, there lived in this village a maiden, the daughter of the priest-chief. She was beautiful, but possessed of this peculiarity of character: There was a sacred spring of water at the foot of the terrace whereon stood the town.

We now call it the Pool of the Apaches; but then it was sacred to Kólowissi (the Serpent of the Sea). Now, at this spring the girl displayed her peculiarity, which was that of a passion for neatness and cleanliness of person and clothing.

She could not endure the slightest speck or particle of dust or dirt upon her clothes or person, and so she spent most of her time in washing all the things she used and in bathing herself in the waters of this spring.

Now, these waters, being sacred to the Serpent of the Sea, should not have been defiled in this way.

As might have been expected, Kólowissi became troubled

and angry at the sacrilege committed in the sacred waters
by the maiden, and he said: "Why does this maiden defile
the sacred waters of my spring with the dirt of her apparel
and the dun of her person? I must see to this."

So he devised a plan by which to prevent the sacrilege and
to punish its author.

When the maiden came again to the spring, what should
she behold but a beautiful little child seated amidst the
waters, splashing them, cooing and smiling. It was the Sea
Serpent, wearing the semblance of a child, --for a god may
assume any form at its pleasure, you know. There sat the
child, laughing and playing in the water.

The girl looked around in all directions--north, south, east,
and west--but could see no one, nor any traces of persons
who might have brought hither the beautiful little child.

She said to herself: "I wonder whose child this may be! It
would seem to be that of some unkind and cruel mother,
who has deserted it and left it here to perish. And the poor
little child does not yet know that it is left all alone. Poor
little thing! I will take it in my arms and care for it."

The maiden then talked softly to the young child, and took
it in her arms, and hastened with it up the hill to her house,
and, climbing up the ladder, carried the child in her arms
into the room where she slept.

Her peculiarity of character, her dislike of all dirt or dust,
led her to dwell apart from the rest of her family, in a room
by herself above all of the other apartments.

She was so pleased with the child that when she had got
him into her room she sat down on the floor and played

with him, laughing at his pranks and smiling into his face; and he answered her in baby fashion with cooings and smiles of his own, so that her heart became very happy and loving. So it happened that thus was she engaged for a long while and utterly unmindful of the lapse of time.

Meanwhile, the younger sisters had prepared the meal, and were awaiting the return of the elder sister.

"Where, I wonder, can she be?" one of them asked.

"She is probably down at the spring," said the old father; "she is bathing and washing her clothes, as usual, of course! Run down and call her."

But the younger sister, ongoing, could find no trace of her at the spring. So she climbed the ladder to the private room of this elder sister, and there found her, as has been told, playing with the little child. She hastened back to inform her father of what she had seen. But the old man sat silent and thoughtful. He knew that the waters of the spring were sacred.

When the rest of the family were excited, and ran to behold the pretty prodigy, he cried out, therefore: "Come back! come back! Why do you make fools of yourselves? Do you suppose any mother would leave her own child in the waters of this or any other spring? There is something more of meaning than seems in all this."

When they again went and called the maiden to come down to the meal spread for her, she could not be induced to leave the child.

"See! it is as you might expect," said the father. "A woman will not leave a child on any inducement; how much less her own."

The child at length grew sleepy. The maiden placed it on a
bed, and, growing sleepy herself, at length lay by its side
and fell asleep. Her sleep was genuine, but the sleep of the
child was feigned. The child became elongated by degrees,
as it were, fulfilling some horrible dream, and soon
appeared as an enormous Serpent that coiled itself round
and round the room until it was full of scaly, gleaming
circles. Then, placing its head near the head of the maiden,
the great Serpent surrounded her with its coils, taking
finally its own tail in its mouth.

The night passed, and in the morning when the breakfast
was prepared, and yet the maiden did not descend, and the
younger sisters became impatient at the delay, the old man
said: "Now that she has the child to play with, she will care
little for aught else. That is enough to occupy the entire
attention of any woman."

But the little sister ran up to the room and called. Receiving
no answer, she tried to open the door; she could not move
it, because the Serpent's coils filled the room and pressed
against it. She pushed the door with all her might, but it
could not be moved. She again and again called her sister's
name, but no response came. Beginning now to be
frightened, she ran to the skyhole over the room in which
she had left the others and cried out for help.

They hastily joined her, --all save the old father, --and
together were able to press the door sufficiently to get a
glimpse of the great scales and folds of the Serpent. Then
the women all ran screaming to the old father. The old man,
priest and sage as he was, quieted them with these words:
"I expected as much as this from the first report which you
gave me.

It was impossible, as I then said, that a woman should be so foolish as to leave her child playing even near the waters of the spring. But it is not impossible, it seems, that one should be so foolish as to take into her arms a child found as this one was."

Thereupon he walked out of the house, deliberately and thoughtful, angry in his mind against his eldest daughter. Ascending to her room, he pushed against the door and called to the Serpent of the Sea: "Oh, Kólowissi! It is I, who speak to thee, O Serpent of the Sea I, thy priest. Let, I pray thee, let my child come to me again, and I will make atonement for her errors. Release her, though she has been so foolish, for she is thine, absolutely thine. But let her return once more to us that we may make atonement to thee more amply." So prayed the priest to the Serpent of the Sea.

When he had done this the great Serpent loosened his coils, and as he did so the whole building shook violently, and all the villagers became aware of the event, and trembled with fear.

The maiden at once awoke and cried piteously to her father for help.

"Come and release me, oh, my father! Come and release me!" she cried.

As the coils loosened she found herself able to rise. No sooner had she done this than the great Serpent bent the folds of his large coils nearest the doorway upward so that they formed an arch. Under this, filled with terror, the girl passed. She was almost stunned with the dread din of the monster's scales rasping past one another with a noise like the sound of flints trodden under the feet of a rapid runner, and once away from the writhing mass of coils, the poor maiden ran like a frightened deer out of the doorway, down the ladder and into the room below, casting herself on the breast of her mother.

But the priest still remained praying to the Serpent; and he ended his prayer as he had begun it, saying: "It shall be even as I have said; she shall be thine!"

He then went away and called the two warrior priest-chiefs of the town, and these called together all the other priests in sacred council. Then they performed the solemn ceremonies of the sacred rites--preparing plumes, prayer-wands, and offerings of treasure.

After four days of labor, these things they arranged and consecrated to the Serpent of the Sea. On that morning the old priest called his daughter and told her she must make ready to take these sacrifices and yield them up, even with herself, --most precious of them all, --to the great Serpent of the Sea; that she must yield up also all thoughts of her people and home forever, and go hence to the house of the great Serpent of the Sea, even in the Waters of the World. "For it seems," said he, "to have been your desire to do thus, as manifested by your actions.

You used even the sacred water for profane purposes; now this that I have told you is inevitable. Come; the time when you must prepare yourself to depart is near at hand."

She went forth from the home of her childhood with sad cries, clinging to the neck of her mother and shivering with terror. In the plaza, amidst the lamentations of all the people, they dressed her in her sacred cotton robes of ceremonial, embroidered elaborately, and adorned her with earrings, bracelets, beads, --many beautiful, precious things.

They painted her cheeks with red spots as if for a dance; they made a road of sacred meal toward the Door of the Serpent of the Sea--a distant spring in our land known to this day as the Doorway to the Serpent of the Sea--four steps toward this spring did they mark in sacred terraces on the ground at the western way of the plaza.

And when they had finished the sacred road, the old priest, who never shed one tear, although all the villagers wept sore, --for the maiden was very beautiful, --instructed his daughter to go forth on the terraced road, and, standing there, call the Serpent to come to her.

Then the door opened, and the Serpent descended from the high room where he was coiled, and, without using ladders, let his head and breast down to the ground in great undulations. He placed his head on the shoulder of the maiden, and the word was given-the word: "It is time"--and the maiden slowly started toward the west, cowering beneath her burden; but whenever she staggered with fear and weariness and was like to wander from the way, the Serpent gently pushed her onward and straightened her course.

Thus they went toward the river trail and in it, on and over the Mountain of the Red Paint; yet still the Serpent was not all uncoiled from the maiden's room in the house, but continued to crawl forth until they were past the mountain-- when the last of his length came forth. Here he began to draw himself together again and to assume a new shape. So that ere long his serpent form contracted, until, lifting his head from the maiden's shoulder, he stood up, in form a beautiful youth in sacred gala attire! He placed the scales of his serpent form, now small, under his flowing mantle, and called out to the maiden in a hoarse, hissing voice: "Let us speak one to the other. Are you tired, girl?" Yet she never moved her head, but plodded on with her eyes cast down.

"Are you weary, poor maiden?"--then he said in a gentler voice, as he arose erect and fell a little behind her, and wrapped his scales more closely in his blanket--and he was now such a splendid and brave hero, so magnificently dressed! And he repeated, in a still softer voice: "Are you still weary, poor maiden?"

At first she dared not look around, though the voice, so changed, sounded so far behind her and thrilled her wonderfully with its kindness. Yet she still felt the weight on her shoulder, the weight of that dreaded Serpent's head; for you know after one has carried a heavy burden on his shoulder or back, if it be removed he does not at once know that it is taken away; it seems still to oppress and pain him. So it was with her; but at length she turned around a little and saw a young man-a brave and handsome young man.

"May I walk by your side?" said he, catching her eye. "Why do you not speak with me?"

"I am filled with fear and sadness and shame," said she.

"Why?" asked he. "What do you fear?"

"Because I came with a fearful creature forth from my home, and he rested his head upon my shoulder, and even now I feel his presence there," said she, lifting her hand to the place where his head had rested, even still fearing that it might be there."

"But I came all the way with you," said he, "and I saw no such creature as you describe."

Upon this she stopped and turned back and looked again at him, and said: "You came all the way? I wonder where this fearful being has gone!"

He smiled, and replied: "I know where he has gone."

"Ah, youth and friend, will he now leave me in peace," said she, "and let me return to the home of my people?"

"No," replied he, "because he thinks very much of you."

"Why not? Where is he?"

"He is here," said the youth, smiling, and laying his hand on his own heart. "I am he."

"You are he?" cried the maiden. Then she looked at him again, and would not believe him. "Yea, my maiden, I am he!" said he. And he drew forth from under his flowing mantle the shriveled serpent scales, and showed them as proofs of his word. It was wonderful and beautiful to the maiden to see that he was thus, a gentle being; and she looked at him long.

Then he said: "Yes, I am he. I love you, my maiden! Will you not haply come forth and dwell with me? Yes, you will go with me, and dwell with me, and I will dwell with you, and I will love you. I dwell not now, but ever, in all the Waters of the World, and in each particular water. In all and each you will dwell with me forever, and we will love each other."

Behold! As they journeyed on, the maiden quite forgot that she had been sad; she forgot her old home, and followed and descended with him into the Doorway of the Serpent of the Sea and dwelt with him ever after.

It was thus in the days of the ancients. Therefore, the ancients, no less than ourselves, avoided using springs,

except for the drinking of their water; for to this day we
hold the flowing springs the most precious things on earth,
and therefore use them not for any profane purposes
whatsoever.

Thus shortens my story

Lakota Prayer

Wakan Tanka, Great Mystery,
teach me how to trust
my heart,
my mind,
my intuition,
my inner knowing,
the senses of my body,
the blessings of my spirit.
Teach me to trust these things
so that I may enter my Sacred Space
and love beyond my fear,
and thus Walk in Balance
with the passing of each glorious Sun.

.

Sedna, Mistress of the Underworld

An Eskimo Legend
Boas, Report of the Bureau
of American Ethnology, vi,
583

Once upon a time there lived on a solitary shore an Inung with his daughter Sedna. His wife had been dead for some time and the two led a quiet life.

Sedna grew up to be a handsome girl and the youths came from all around to sue for her hand, but none of them could touch her proud heart. Finally, at the breaking up of the ice in the spring a fulmar flew from over the ice and wooed Sedna with enticing song. "Come to me," it said; "come into the land of the birds, where there is never hunger, where my tent is made of the most beautiful skins. You shall rest on soft bearskins.

My fellows, the fulmars, shall bring you all your heart may desire; their feathers shall clothe you; your lamp shall always be filled with oil, your pot with meat."

Sedna could not long resist such wooing and they went together over the vast sea. When at last they reached the country of the fulmar, after a long and hard journey, Sedna discovered that her spouse had shamefully deceived her. Her new home was not built of beautiful pelts, but was covered with wretched fishskins, full of holes, that gave free entrance to wind and snow. Instead of soft reindeer skins her bed was made of hard walrus hides and she had to live on miserable fish, which the birds brought her.

Too soon she discovered that she had thrown away her opportunities when in her foolish pride she had rejected the Inuit youth. In her woe she sang: "Aja. O father, if you knew how wretched I am you would come to me and we would hurry away in your boat over the waters.

The birds look unkindly upon me the stranger; cold winds roar about my bed; they give me but miserable food. O come and take me back home. Aja."

When a year had passed and the sea was again stirred by warmer winds, the father left his country to visit Sedna. His daughter greeted him joyfully and besought him to take her back home. The father, hearing of the outrages wrought upon his daughter, determined upon revenge. He killed the fulmar, took Sedna into his boat, and they quickly left the country which had brought so much sorrow to Sedna.

When the other fulmars came home and found their companion dead and his wife gone, they all flew away in search of the fugitives. They were very sad over the death of their poor murdered comrade and continue to mourn and cry until this day.

Having flown a short distance, they discerned the boat and stirred up a heavy storm. The sea rose in immense waves that threatened the pair with destruction. In this mortal peril the father determined to offer Sedna to the birds and flung her overboard. She clung to the edge of the boat with a death grip. The cruel father then took a knife and cut off the first joints of her fingers.

Falling into the sea they were transformed into whales, the

nails turning into whalebone.

Sedna holding on to the boat more tightly, the second finger joints fell under the sharp knife and swam away as seals; when the father cut off the stumps of the fingers they became ground seals.

Meantime the storm subsided, for the fulmars thought Sedna was drowned. The father then allowed her to come into the boat again. But from that time she cherished a deadly hatred against him and swore bitter revenge.

After they got ashore, she called her dogs and let them gnaw off the feet and hands of her father while he was asleep.

Upon this he cursed himself, his daughter, and the dogs which had maimed him; whereupon the earth opened and swallowed the hut, the father, the daughter, and the dogs. They have since lived in the land of Adlivun, of which Sedna is the mistress.

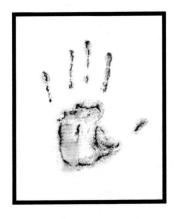

The Pookonghoyas and the Cannibal Monster

A Hopi Legend
H. R. Voth, The Traditions of
the Hopi, Field Columbian
Museum Anthropological
Series, 1905

A very long time ago a large monster, whom our forefathers called Shíta, lived somewhere in the west, and used to come to the village of Oraíbi and wherever it would find children it would devour them.

Often also grown people were eaten by the monster. The people became very much alarmed over the matter, and especially the village chief was very much worried over it. Finally, he concluded to ask the Pöokónghoyas for assistance. These latter, namely Pöokónghoya and his younger brother Balö'ngahoya, lived north of and close to the village of Oraíbi. When the village chief asked them to rid them of this monster they told him to make an arrow for each one of them. He did so, using for the shaft feathers, the wing feathers of the bluebird. These arrows he brought to the little War Gods mentioned.

They said to each other: "Now let us go and see whether such a monster exists and whether we can find it." So they first went to Oraíbi and kept on the watch around the village.

One time, when they were on the east side of the village at the edge of the mesa, they noticed something approaching from the west side. They at once went there and saw that it was the monster that they were to destroy. When the monster met the two brothers it said to them: "I eat you" (Shíta). Both brothers objected.

The monster at once swallowed the older one and then the other one. They found that it was not dark inside of the monster, in fact, they found themselves on a path which the younger brother, who had been swallowed last, followed, soon overtaking his older brother.

The two brothers laughed and said to each other: "So this is the way we find it here. We are not going to die here."

They found that the path on which they were going was the esophagus of the monster, which led into its stomach. In the latter they found a great many people of different nationalities which the monster had devoured in different parts of the earth; in fact, they found the stomach to be a little world in itself, with grass, trees, rock, etc.

Before the two brothers had left their home on their expedition to kill the monster, if possible, their grandmother had told them that in case the monster should swallow them too, to try to find its heart; if they could shoot into the heart the monster would die. So they concluded that they would now go in search of the heart of the monster.

They finally found the path which led out of the stomach, and after following that path quite a distance they saw way above them hanging something which they at once concluded must be the heart of the monster. Pöokónghoya at once shot an arrow at it, but failed to reach it, the arrow dropping back. Hereupon his younger brother tried it and his arrow pierced the heart, whereupon the older brother also shot his arrow into the heart. Then it became dark and, the people noticed that the monster was dying.

The two brothers called all the people together and said to them: "Now let us get out." They led them along the path to the mouth of the monster, but found that they could not get out because the teeth of the monster had set firmly in death. They tried in vain to open the mouth but finally discovered a passage leading up into the nose. Through this they then emerged.

It was found that a great many people assembled there north of the village. The village chief had cried out that a great many people had arrived north of the village and asked his people to assemble there too. They did so and many found their children and relatives that had been carried off by the monster, and were very glad to have them back again.

The two brothers then said to the others that they should now move on and try to find their own homes where they had come from, which they did, settling down temporarily at different places, which accounts for the many small ruins scattered throughout the country The old people say that this monster was really a world or a country, as some call it, similar to the world that we are living in.

Ghost Tales

The Ghosts' Buffalo
A Blackfoot Legend

A long time ago there were four Blackfeet, who went to war against the Crees. They traveled a long way, and at last their horses gave out, and they started back toward their homes. As they were going along they came to the Sand Hills; and while they were passing through them, they saw in the sand a fresh travois trail, where people had been travelling.

One of the men said: "Let us follow this trail until we come up with some of our people. Then we will camp with them." They followed the trail for a long way, and at length one of the Blackfeet, named E-kus'-kini, a very powerful person, said to the others: "Why follow this longer? It is just nothing." The others said: "Not so. These are our people. We will go on and camp with them." They went on, and toward evening, one of them found a stone maul and a dog travois. He said: "Look at these things. I know this maul and this travois. They belonged to my mother, who died. They were buried with her. This is strange." He took the things. When night overtook the men, they camped.

Early in the morning, they heard, all about them, sounds as if a camp of people were there. They heard a young man shouting a sort of war cry, as young men do; women chopping wood; a man calling for a feast, asking people to come to his lodge and smoke, all the different sounds of the camp. They looked about, but could see nothing; and then they were frightened and covered their heads with their robes. At last they took courage, and started to look around and see what they could learn about this strange thing. For a little while they saw nothing, but pretty soon one of them said: "Look over there. See that pis'kun. Let us go over and

look at it." As they were going toward it, one of them
picked up a stone pointed arrow. He said: "Look at this. It
belonged to my father. This is his place." They started to go
on toward the pis'kun, but suddenly they could see no
pis'kun. It had disappeared all at once.

A little while after this, one of them spoke up, and said:
"Look over there. There is my father running buffalo.
There! he has killed. Let us go over to him." They all
looked where this man pointed, and they could see a person
on a white horse, running buffalo. While they were looking,
the person killed the buffalo, and got off his horse to
butcher it. They started to go over toward him, and saw him
at work butchering, and saw him turn the buffalo over on
its back; but before they got to the place where he was, the
person got on his horse and rode off, and when they got to
where he had been skinning the buffalo, they saw lying on
the ground only a dead mouse. There was no buffalo there.
By the side of the mouse was a buffalo chip, and lying on it
was an arrow painted red. The man said: "That is my
father's arrow. That is the way he painted them." He took it
up in his hands; and when he held it in his hands, he saw
that it was not an arrow but a blade of spear grass. Then he
laid it down, and it was an arrow again.

Another Blackfoot found a buffalo rock, I-nis'-kim.

Some time after this, the men got home to their camp. The
man who had taken the maul and the dog travois, when he
got home and smelled the smoke from the fire, died, and so
did his horse. It seems that the shadow of the person who
owned the things was angry at him and followed him home.
Two others of these Blackfeet have since died, killed in
war; but E-kus'-kini is alive yet. He took a stone and an
iron arrow point that had belonged to his father, and always
carried them about with him. That is why he has lived so

long. The man who took the stone arrow point found near the pis'kun, which had belonged to his father, took it home with him. This was his medicine. After that he was badly wounded in two fights, but he was not killed; he got well.

The one who took the buffalo rock, I-nis'-kim, it afterward made strong to call the buffalo into the pis'kun. He would take the rock and put it in his lodge close to the fire, where he could look at it, and would pray over it and make medicine. Sometimes he would ask for a hundred buffalo to jump into the pis'kun, and the next day a hundred would jump in. He was powerful.

If the white man wants to live in peace with the Indian, he
can live in peace...
Treat all men alike.
Give them all the same law.
Give them all an even chance to live and grow.
All men were made by the same Great Spirit Chief.
They are all brothers.
The Earth is the mother of all people, and all people should
have equal rights upon it....
Let me be a free man, free to travel, free to stop, free to
work, free to trade where I choose my own teachers, free to
follow the religion of my fathers, free to think and talk and
act for myself, and I will obey every law, or submit to the
penalty.

Heinmot Tooyalaket (Chief Joseph), Nez Perce Leader

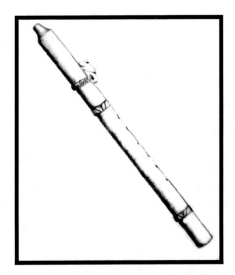

Two Ghostly Lovers

Brule, Sioux
Told by Lame Deer at
Winner Rosebud
Indian Reservation,
South Dakota, 1970.
Recorded by Richard
Erdoes

Long ago her lived a young, good-looking man whom no woman could resist. He was an elk charmer--a man who had elk medicine, which carries love power. When this man played the *siyotanka*, the flute, it produced a magic sound. At night a girl hearing it would just get up and go to him, forsaking her father and mother, her own lover, or husband. Maybe her mind told her to stay, but her heart was already beating faster and her feet were running.

Yet the young man, the elk charmer himself, was a lover with a stone heart. He wanted only to conquer women, the way a warrior conquers an enemy. After they came to him once, he had no more use for them. So in spite of his wonderful powers, he did not act as a young man should and was not well liked.

One day when the elk charmer went out to hunt buffalo, he did not return to the village. His parents waited for him day after day, but he never came back. At last they went to a special kind of medicine man who has "finding stones" that give him the power to locate lost things and lost people.

After this holy man had used his finding stones, he told the parents: "I have sad news for you. Your son is dead, and not from sickness or an accident. He was killed. He is lying out there on the prairie."

The medicine man described the spot where they would find the body, it was as he had said. out on the prairie their son was lying dead, stabbed through the heart. Whether he had been killed by an enemy warrior, or a wronged husband from his own tribe, or even a discarded, thrown-away girl, no one ever knew.

His parents dressed him in his finest war shirt, which he had loved more than all his women, and in dead man's moccasins, whose soles are beaded with spirit-land designs. They put his body up on the funeral scaffold, and then the tribe left that part of the country. For it was a very bad thing, this killing which was probably within the tribe. It was, in fact, the very worst thing that could happen, even though everybody was thinking that the young man had brought it on himself.

One evening many days' ride away, when the people had already forgotten this sad happening and were feasting in their tipis, all the dogs in camp started howling. Then the coyotes in the hills took up their mournful cry. Nobody could discover the reason for all this yowling and yipping. But when it finally stopped, the people could hear the hooting of many owls, speaking of death and ghostly things. The laughter in the camp stopped. The fires were put out, and the entry flaps to the tipis were closed.

People tried to sleep, but instead they found themselves listening. They knew a spirit was coming. Finally, they heard the unearthly sounds of a ghost flute and a voice they knew very well--the voice of the dead young man with the elk medicine. They heard this voice singing:

Weeping I roam.
I thought I was the only one
Who had known many loves,
Many girls, many women,
Too many of them.
Now I am having a hard time.
I am roaming, roaming,
And I have to keep
roaming
As long as the world
stands.

After that night, the people heard the song many times. A lone girl coming home late from a dance, a young woman up before sunrise to get water from the stream, would hear the ghostly song mixed with the sound of the flute. And they would see the shape of a man wrapped in a gray blanket hovering above the ground, for even as a ghost this young man would not leave the girls alone.

Well, it happened long ago, but even now the old-timers at Rosebud, Pine Ridge, and Cheyenne River are still singing this ghost song.

Now, there was another young man who also had a cold heart. He too made love to too many girls and soon threw them away. he was a brave warrior though. He was out a few times with a girl who was in love with him, and he said he would marry her. But he didn't really mean it; he was like many other men who make the same promise only to get under a girl's blanket. One day he said: "I have to go away on a horse stealing raid, I'll be back soon, and then I'll marry you." She told him: "I'll wait for you forever!"

The young warrior went off and never came back; he forgot all about her. The girl, however, waited for a long time.

Well, this young man roamed about for years and had many loves. Then one time when he was hunting, he saw a fine tipi. It had a sun-and-moon design painted on it. He recognized it immediately: it was the tipi of the girl he had left long ago. "Is she still good-looking and loving?" he wondered. "I'll find out!"

He went inside, and there was the girl, lovelier than ever. She was dressed in a white, richly quilled buckskin dress. She smiled at him. "My lover, have you come back at last?"

After serving him a fine meal, she helped him take off his moccasins and his war shirt. She traced his scars from many fights with her fingers. "My warrior," she said, "lie down here beside me, on this soft, soft buffalo robe." He lay down and made love to her, and it was sweeter than he had ever experienced, sweeter than he could have imagined. Then she said: "Rest and sleep now."

The young man--though not very young anymore--woke up in the morning and saw the morning sun shining into the tipi. But the tipi was no longer bright and new; it was ragged and rotting. The buffalo robe under which they had slept was almost hairless and full of holes. He lifted the robe and pulled it aside to look at the girl, and instead of a living, beautiful woman, he found a skeleton. A few strands of black hair still adhered to the skull, which seemed to smile at him. They young girl had died there long ago, waiting for him to come back. He had made love to a spirit. He had embraced bones. He had kissed a skull. He had coupled with a skeleton!

As the thought sank in, the warrior cried aloud, jumped up, and began running in great fear running he knew not where. When he finally came to, he was *witko*, mad. He spoke in strange sounds. His eyes wandered. His thoughts went astray. he was never right in his mind again.

I am poor and naked, but I am the chief of the nation. We do not want riches but we do want to train our children right. Riches would do us no good. We could not take them with us to the other world. We do not want riches. We want peace and love.

Red Cloud

The Land of the Dead

Serrano
From a story reported by Ruth Benedict in 1926

A great hunter brought home a wife. They loved each other and were very happy. But the man's mother hated the young wife, and one day when the husband was out hunting, she put a sharp, pointed object in the wife's seat, and the woman sat down upon it and was killed.

The people immediately brought brush and piled it up. They put her body on it and burned it, and by the time her husband returned that night her body was consumed.

The man went to the burning place and stayed there motionless. Curls of dust rose and whirled about the charred spot. He watched them all night and all day. At evening they grew larger, and at last one larger than all the rest whirled round and round the burned spot. It set off

down the road and he set off after it. When it was quite
dark, he saw that the dust he was following was his wife,
but she would not speak to him.

She was leading him in the direction of the rock past which
all dead people go. If they have lived bad lives, the rock
falls on them and crushes them. When they came to it, she
spoke to her husband. "We are going to the place of dead
people," she told him. "I will take you on my back so that
you will not be seen and recognized as one of the living."

Thus they traveled on until they came to the river that the
dead have to ford. This was very dangerous for the man
because he was not dead, but the woman kept him on her
back, and they came through safely. The woman went
directly to her people, to her parents and brothers and
sisters who had died before. They were glad to see her, but
they did not like the man, for he was not dead. The woman
pleaded for him, however, and they let him stay. Special
food always had to be cooked for him, because he could not
eat what dead people live on. And in the daytime he could
see nothing, it was as if he were alone all day long; only in
the night did he see his wife and the other people.

When the dead were going hunting, they took him along
and stationed him on the trail the deer would take.
Presently he heard them shouting, "The deer, the deer!" and
he knew they were shouting to him that the deer were
coming in his direction. But he could see nothing. Then he
looked again and spotted two little black beetles, which he
knocked over. When the people had come up, they praised
him for his hunting.

After that the dead did not complain about his presence, but
they did feel sorry for him. "It's not time for him to die
yet," they said. "He has a hard time here. The woman ought

to go back with him." So they arranged for both of them to return, and they instructed the man and the woman to have nothing to do with each other for three nights after they were back on earth.

Three nights for the dead, however, meant three years for the living. Not aware of this, the husband and wife returned to earth and remained continent for three nights. The following evening, they embraced, and when the husband woke on the morning of the fourth day, he was alone.

Hold On

Hold on to what is good,
Even if it's a handful of earth.
Hold on to what you believe,
Even if it's a tree that stands by itself.
Hold on to what you must do,
Even if it's a long way from here.
Hold on to your life,
Even if it's easier to let go.
Hold on to my hand,
Even if someday I'll be gone away from you.

A Pueblo Indian Prayer

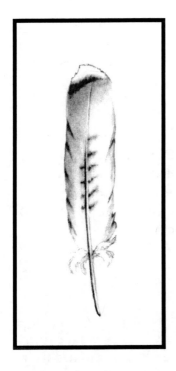

Blue Jay Visits Ghost Town

Chinook
Based on a tale reported by
Franz Boas in 1894.

One night the ghosts decided to go out and buy a wife. They chose a woman named Io'i, and gave her family dentalia as a dowry. They were married one night, and on the following morning Io'i disappeared.

Now Io'i had a brother named Blue Jay. For a year he waited to hear from her, then said, "I'll go and search for her." He asked all the trees, "Where do people go when they die?" They remained silent. He asked all the birds, but they did not tell him either. Then he asked an old wedge. It said, "Pay me and I'll carry you there." He did, and it took him to the ghosts.

The wedge and Blue Jay arrived near a large town, where they saw no smoke rising from any of the houses except the last one, a great edifice. Blue Jay went into it and found his elder sister, who greeted him fondly.

"Ah, my brother," she said, "where have you come from? Have you died?" "Oh, no," he said, "I am not dead at all. The wedge brought me here on his back." Then he went out and opened the doors to all the other houses. They were full of bones. He noticed a skull and bones lying near his sister, and when he asked her what she was doing with them, she replied: "That's your brother-in-law." "Pshaw! Io'i is lying all the time," he thought. "She says a skull is my brother-in-law!" But when it grew dark people arose from what had been just bones, and the house was suddenly full of activity.

When Blue Jay asked his sister about all the people, she laughed and replied, "Do you think they are people? These are ghosts!" Even hearing this, though, he resumed staying with his sister. She said to him, "Do as they do and go fishing with your dip net." "I think I will,". he replied. "Go with that boy," she said, pointing to a figure. "He is one of your brother-in-law's relations. But don't speak to him; keep quiet." These people always spoke in whispers, so that Blue Jay didn't understand them.

And so they started in their canoes. He and his guide caught up with a crowd of people who were going down the river, singing aloud as they paddled. When Blue Jay joined their song, they fell silent. Blue Jay looked back and saw that where the boy had been, there were now only bones in the stern of the canoe. They continued to go down the river, and Blue Jay kept quiet. Then he looked at the stern again, and the boy was sitting there. Blue Jay said in a low voice, "Where is your fish trap?" He spoke slowly, and the boy replied, "It's down the river." They paddled on. Then Blue Jay said in a loud voice, "Where is your trap?" This time he found only a skeleton in the stern. Blue Jay was again silent. He looked back, and the boy was sitting in the canoe. He lowered his voice and said, "Where is your trap?" "Here," replied the boy.

Now they fished with their dip nets. Blue Jay felt something in his net, lifted it, and found only two branches. He turned his net and threw them into the water. When he put his net again into the water, it soon became full of

leaves. He threw them back, but some fell into the canoe
and the boy gathered them up. Then Blue Jay caught
another branch and some more leaves and threw them back;
but again a few leaves fell into the canoe, and again the boy
gathered them up. As they continued fishing, Blue Jay
caught two more branches that he decided to take back to
Io'i for making a fire.

They arrived at home and went up to the house. Blue Jay
was angry that he had not caught anything, but the boy
brought up a mat full of trout, even though Blue Jay had
not seen him catch a single one in his net. While the people
were roasting them, the boy announced, "He threw most of
the catch out of the canoe. Our canoe would have been full
if he had not thrown so much away." His sister said to Blue
Jay: "Why did you throw away what you had caught?" "I
threw away nothing but branches and leaves." "That is our
food," she replied. "Did you think they were branches? The
leaves were trout, and the branches were fall salmon." He
said, "Well, I brought you two branches to use for making a
fire." So his sister went down to the beach and found two
fall salmon in the canoe. She carried them up to the house,
and Blue Jay said, "Where did you steal those salmon?"
She replied, "That's what you caught." "Io'i is always
lying," Blue Jay said.

The next day Blue Jay went to the beach. There lay the
canoes of the ghosts, now full of holes and covered with
moss. He went up to the house and said to his sister, "How
bad your husband's canoes are, Io'i!" "Oh, be quiet," she
said. "They'll become tired of you." "But the canoes of
these people are full of holes!" Exasperated, his sister
turned to him and said, "Are they people? Are they people?
Don't you understand? They are ghosts."

When it grew dark again, Blue Jay and the boy made themselves ready to go fishing again. This time he teased the boy: as they made their way down the river, he would shout, and only bones would be there. When they began fishing, Blue Jay gathered in the branches and leaves instead of throwing them away. When the ebb tide set in, their canoe was full. On the way home, he teased all the other ghosts. As soon as they met one he would shout out loud, and only bones would lie in the other canoe. They arrived at home, and he presented his sister with armfuls of fall salmon and silver-side salmon.

The next morning Blue Jay went into the town and waited for the dark, when the life came back. That evening he heard someone announce, "Ah, a whale has been found!" His sister gave him a knife and said, "Run! a whale has been found!" Anxious to gather meat, Blue Jay ran to the beach, but when he met one of the people and asked in a loud voice, "Where is the whale?" only a skeleton lay there. He kicked the skull and left it. A few yards away he met some other people, but again he shouted loudly, and again only skeletons lay there. Then he came to a large log with thick bark. A crowd of people were peeling off the bark, and Blue Jay shouted to them so that only skeletons lay there. The bark was full of pitch. He peeled off two pieces and carried them home on his shoulder.

He went home and threw the bark down outside the house. He said to his sister, "I really thought it was a whale. Look here: it's just bark from a fir." His sister said, "It's whale meat, it's whale meat; did you think it's just bark?" His sister went out and pointed to two cuts of whale meat lying on the ground. "It's good whale, and its blubber is very thick." Blue Jay stared down at the bark, astonished to find a dead whale lying there. Then he turned back, and when he saw a person carrying a piece of bark on his back, he shouted and nothing but a skeleton lay there. He grabbed the bark and carried it home, then went back to catch more ghosts. In the course of time he had many meals of whale meat.

The next morning, he entered a house and took a child's skull, which he put on a large skeleton. And he took a large skull and put it on that child's skeleton. He mixed up all the people like this, and when it grew dark the child rose to its feet. It wanted to sit up, but it fell down again because its head pulled it down. The old man arose. His head was too light! The next morning Blue Jay replaced the heads and switched around their legs instead. He gave small legs to an old man, and large legs to a child. Sometimes he exchanged a man's and a woman's legs.

In course of time Blue Jay's antics began to make him very unpopular. Io'i's husband said: "Tell him he must go home. He mistreats them, and these people don't like him." Io'i tried to stop her younger brother's pranks, but he would pay no attention. On the next morning he awoke early and found Io'i holding a skull in her arms. He tossed it away and asked, "Why do you hold that skull, Io'i? "Ah, you have broken your brother-in-Iaw's neck!" When it grew dark, his brother-in-law was gravely sick, but a shaman was able to make him well again.

Finally, Blue Jay decided it was time to go home. His sister gave him five buckets full of water and said, "Take care! When you come to burning prairies, save the water until you come to the fourth prairie. Then pour it out." "All right," replied Blue Jay. He started out and reached a prairie. It was hot. Red flowers bloomed on the prairie. He poured water on the prairie, using half of one of his buckets. He passed through a woods and reached another prairie, which was burning at its end. "This is what my sister told me about." He poured the rest of the bucket out on the trail. He took another bucket and poured, and when it was half empty he reached the woods on the other side of the prairie. He came to still another prairie, the third one. One half of it was burning strongly. He took a bucket and emptied it. He took another bucket and emptied half of it.

Then he reached the woods on the other side of the prairie.

Now he had only two and a half buckets left. He came to another prairie which was almost totally on fire. He took the half bucket and emptied it. He took one more bucket, and when he arrived at the woods at the far side of the prairie, he had emptied it. Now only one bucket was left. He reached another prairie which was completely ablaze. He eked out the last drop of water.

When he had gotten nearly across he had run out of water, so he took off his bearskin blanket and beat the fire. The whole bearskin blanket blazed up. Then his head and his hair caught fire and soon Blue Jay himself was burned to death.

Now when it was just growing dark Blue Jay returned to his sister. "Kukukukukuku, Io'i," he called. Mournfully his sister cried, "Ah, my brother is dead." His trail led to the water on the other side of the river. She launched her canoe to fetch him. Io'i's canoe seemed beautiful to him.

She said, "And you told me that my canoe was moss-grown!" "Ah, Io'i is always telling lies. The other ones had holes and were moss-grown, anyway." "You are dead now, Blue Jay, so you see things differently." But still he insisted, "Io'i is always telling lies."

Now she paddled her brother across to the other side. He saw the people. Some sang; some played dice with beaver teeth or with ten disks. The women played hoops. Farther along, Blue Jay heard people singing conjurers' songs and saw them dancing, kumm, kumm, kumm, kumm. He tried to sing and shout, but they all laughed at him.

Blue Jay entered his sister's house and saw that his brother-in-law was a chief, and a handsome one. She said, "And you broke his neck!" "Io'i is always telling lies. Where did these canoes come from? They're pretty." "And you said they were all moss-grown!" "Io'i is always telling lie.

The others all had holes. Parts of them were moss-grown." "You are dead now, and you see things differently," said his sister. "Io'i is always telling lies." Blue Jay tried to shout at the people, but they laughed at him. Then he gave it up and became quiet. Later when his sister went to look for him, he was standing near the dancing conjurors. He wanted their powers, but they only laughed at him. He pestered them night after night, and after five nights he came back to his sister's house. She saw him dancing on his head, his legs upward. She turned back and cried. Now he had really died. He had died a second time, made witless by the magicians.

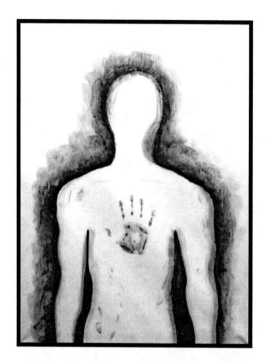

The Spirit Land

A Gallinomero Legend
Katharine Berry Judson, Myths and Legends of California and the Old Southwest, 1912

When the flames burn low on the funeral pyres of the Gallinomero, Indian mourners gather up handfuls of ashes and scatter them high in air. Thus the good mount up into the air, or go to the Happy Western Land beyond the Big Water.

But the bad Indians go to an island in the Bitter Waters, an island naked and barren and desolate, covered only with brine-spattered stone, swept with cold winds and the biting sea-spray.

Here they live always, breaking stone upon one another, with no food but the broken stones and no drink but the salt sea water.

The Skin Shifting Old Woman

A Wichita Legend
Dorsey, Publications of the Carnegie Institution, xxi, 124,
No. 17

In the story of Healthy-Flint-Stone-Man, it is told that he
was a powerful man and lived in a village and was a chief
of the place. He was not a man of heavy build, but was
slim.

Often when a man is of this type of build he is called
"Healthy-Flint-Stone-Man," after the man in the story.
Healthy-Flint-Stone-Man had parents, but at this time he
had no wife. Soon afterwards he married, and his wife was
the prettiest woman that ever lived in the village. When she
married Healthy-Flint-Stone-Man they lived at his home.

She was liked by his parents, for she was a good worker
and kind-hearted. As was their custom, the men of the
village came at night to visit Healthy-Flint-Stone-Man, and
his wife did the cooking to feed them, so that he liked her

all the more, and was kind to her.

Early in the morning a strange woman by the name of Little-Old-Woman came to their place and asked the wife to go with her to get wood. Out of kindness to Little-Old-Woman she went with her, leaving her husband at home. Little-Old-Woman knew where all the dry wood was to be found. When they reached the place where she thought there was plenty of wood they did not stop.

They went on past, although there was plenty of good dry wood. The wife began to cut wood for the old woman and some for herself. When she had cut enough for both she fixed it into two bundles, one for each. Little-Old-Woman knelt by her pile and waited for the wife to help her up. Little-Old-Woman then helped the wife in the same way, and they started toward their home. They talked on the way about their manner of life at home. Arrived at the village, the old woman went to her home. When the wife got home she began to do her work.

Again, the second time, the old woman came around and asked the wife to go with her to fetch wood. They started away together, and this time went farther than on the first time to get their wood, though they passed much good wood. The wife cut wood for both and arranged it in two piles, but this time she herself first knelt by her pile and asked the old woman to take hold of her hands and pull her up; then the wife helped the old woman with her load.

They returned home, and on the way the old woman said to the wife, "If you will go with me to fetch wood for the fourth time I shall need no more help from you." They again went far beyond where any other women had gone to get wood. When they got to the village they parted. The wife wondered why the old woman came to her for help.

She found the men passing the time talking of the past as usual. She kept on doing her duty day after day.

The third time the old woman came for the wife to ask her to help her fetch wood, as she was all out of it again. Again they went out, and this time they went still further for the wood, and now they were getting a long way from the village. The wife cut wood and arranged it in two bundles, one for each of them to carry. This time it was the old woman's turn first to be helped up with the wood.

They helped each other, and on the way home the old woman told the wife that they had only once more to go for wood, and the work would all be done. She always seemed thankful for the help she received. They reached the village and went to their homes. The wife found her men as usual, and commenced to do her work. After the men were through eating they went home, though some stayed late in the night.

Finally, the old woman came the fourth time to ask the wife to go with her and help her fetch some wood. This time they went about twice as far as they had gone the third time from the village. When the old woman thought they were far enough they stopped, and the wife began cutting wood for both of them. When she had cut enough she arranged it in two bundles. Now it was the wife's turn to be helped up with the wood, but the old woman refused to do it as usual and told her to go ahead and kneel by the bundle of wood. The wife refused.

Now, each tried to persuade the other to kneel first against the bundle of wood. The old woman finally prevailed, and the wife knelt against the wood, and as she put her robe around her neck the old woman seemed pleased to help her, but as the old woman was fixing the carrying ropes she tightened them, after slipping them around the wife's neck until the wife fell at full length, as though dying.

The old woman sat down to rest, as she was tired from choking the wife. Soon she got up and untied the wife. Now, they were in the thick timber, and there was flowing water through it. After the old woman had killed the wife she blew into the top of her head and blew the skin from her, hair and all. This she did because she envied the wife her good looks, since the wife was the best-looking woman in the village, and her husband was good-looking and well thought of by all the prominent men, and the old woman wanted to be treated as well as the wife had been treated.

Then the old woman began to put on the wife's skin, but the wife was a little smaller than the old woman, though the old woman managed to stretch the skin and drew it over her, fitting herself to it. Then she smoothed down the skin until it fitted her nicely. She took the wife's body to the flowing water and threw it in, having found a place that was never visited by anyone, and that had no trail leading to it. She then went to her pile of wood and took it to her home. She found the men visiting the chief.

The chief did not discover that she was not his wife. The old woman knew all about the former wife's ways, for she had talked much with her when they were coming home with the wood, and she had asked the wife all sorts of questions about her husband. She understood how the men carried on at the chief's place. The wife had told the chief that the old woman had said that they were to go for wood four different times, and the last time being the fourth time, he supposed it was all over and his wife had got through with the old woman. So, as the old woman was doing his wife's duty, he thought her to be his wife until the time came when the skin began to decay and the hair to come off. Still there were big crowds of men around, and the old woman began to be fearful lest they would find her out. So she made as if she were sick. The chief tried to get a man to doctor her, but she refused to be doctored. Finally, he hired a servant to doctor her. This was the man who always sat right by the entrance, ready to do errands or carry announcements to the people. His name was Buffalo-Crow-Man. He had a dark complexion. The old woman began to rave at his medicine working.

He began to tell who the old woman was, saying that there was no need of doctoring her; that she was a fraud and an evil spirit; and that she had become the wife of the chief through her bad deeds. The old woman told the chief not to believe the servant; and that he himself was a fraud and was trying to get her to do something wrong. The servant then stood at the feet of the old woman and began to sing.

Then over her body he went and jumped at her head. Then he commenced to sing again, first on her left side, then on her right. He sang the song four times, and while he was doing this the decayed hide came off from her. The servant told the men to take her out and take her life for what she had done to the chief's wife, telling how she had fooled the chief. They did as they were told.

The servant told the men he had suspected the old woman when she had come around to get the wife to go after wood with her; that when going after wood they always went a long distance, so that no one could observe them, but that he had always flown very high over them, so they could not see him, and had watched them; that on the fourth time they went for wood he had seen the old woman choke the wife with the wife's rope; how the old woman had secured the whole skin of the wife and had thrown her body into the flowing water. He told the men where the place was, and

directed them there the next day. The men went to their
homes, feeling very sad for the wicked thing the old
woman had done.

On the next day the chief went as directed, and he came to
a place where he found a pile of wood that belonged to his
former wife. He went to the place where he supposed his
wife to be. He sat down and commenced to weep. There he
stayed all night and the next day. He returned to his home,
but he could not forget the occurrence. So he went back
again and stayed another night and again returned home.

The chief was full of sorrow. He went back to the place the
third time, and when he got there he sat down and
commenced to weep. Again he stayed all night, and early
next morning it was foggy and he could not see far. While
he sat and wept he faced the east, and he was on the west
side of the flowing waters, so that he also faced the flowing
water wherein his wife's body was thrown.

He heard some one singing, but he was unable to catch the
sound so that he could locate the place where the sound
came from. He finally discovered that it came from the
flowing water. He went toward the place and listened, and
indeed it was his wife's voice, and this is what she sang:

Woman-Having-Powers-in-the-Water, Woman-Having-
Powers-in-the-Water, I am the one (you seek), I am here in
the water.

As he went near the river he saw in the middle of the water
his wife standing on the water. She told him to go back
home and tell his parents to clean their grass-lodge and to
purify the room by burning sage. She told her husband that
he might then return and take her home; that he should tell
his parents not to weep when she should return, but that

they should rejoice at her return to life, and that after that
he could take her home. So the man started to his home.

After he arrived he told his mother to clean and purify the
lodge; and that he had found his wife and that he was going
back again to get her. He told her that neither she nor any
of their friends should weep at sight of the woman. While
his mother was doing this cleaning he went back to the
river and stayed one more night, and early in the morning
he heard the woman singing again. He knew that he was to
bring his wife back to his home. When he heard her sing he
went straight to her.

She came out of the water and he met her. She began to tell
her husband about her troubles--how she met troubles and
how he was deceived. That day they went to their home,
and Flint-Stone-Man's parents were glad to see his wife
back once more. They lived together until long afterward.

"I have heard you intend to settle us on a reservation near
the mountains. I don't want to settle. I love to roam over the
prairies. There I feel free and happy, but when we settle
down we grow pale and die."

Satanta, Kiowa Chief

The Spirit Wife

Zuni
Retold from a nineteenth-century version.

A young man was grieving because the beautiful young wife whom he loved was dead. As he sat at the graveside weeping, he decided to follow her to the Land of the Dead. He made many prayer sticks and sprinkled sacred corn pollen. He took a downy eagle plume and colored it with red earth color. He waited until nightfall, when the spirit of his departed wife came out of the grave and sat beside him. She was not sad, but smiling. The spirit-maiden told her husband: "I am just leaving one life for another. Therefore, do not weep for me."

"I cannot let you go," said the young man, "I love you so much that I will go with you to the land of the dead."

The spirit-wife tried to dissuade him, but could not overcome his determination. So at last she gave in to his wishes, saying: "If you must follow me, know that I shall be invisible to you as long as the sun shines. You must tie this red eagle plume to my hair. It will be visible in daylight, and if you want to come with me, you must follow the plume."

The young husband tied the red plume to his spirit-wife's hair, and at daybreak, as the sun slowly began to light up the world, bathing the mountaintops in a pale pink light, the spirit-wife started to fade from his view. The lighter it became, the more the form of his wife dissolved and grew transparent, until at last it vanished altogether. But the red plume did not disappear. It waved before the young man, a mere arm's length away, and then, as if rising and falling on a dancer's head, began leading the way out of the village, moving through the streets out into the cornfields, moving through a shallow stream, moving into the foothills of the mountains, leading the young husband ever westward toward the land of the evening.

The red plume moved swiftly, evenly, floating without effort over the roughest trails, and soon the young man had trouble following it. He grew more and more tired and finally was totally exhausted as the plume left him farther behind. Then he called out, panting: "Beloved wife, wait for me. I can't run any longer."

The red plume stopped, waiting for him to catch up, and when he did so, hastened on. For many days the young man traveled, following the plume by day, resting during the nights, when his spirit-bride would sometimes appear to him, speaking encouraging words. Most of the time, however, he was merely aware of her presence in some mysterious way. Day by day the trail became rougher and rougher. The days were long, the nights short, and the young man grew wearier and wearier, until at last he had hardly enough strength to set one foot before the other.

One day the trail led to a deep, almost bottomless chasm, and as the husband came to its edge, the red plume began to float away from him into nothingness. He reached out to seize it, but the plume was already beyond his reach, floating straight across the canyon, because spirits can fly through the air.

The young man called across the chasm: "Dear wife of mine, I love you. Wait!"

He tried to descend one side of the canyon, hoping to climb up the opposite side, but the rock walls were sheer, with nothing to hold onto. Soon he found himself on a ledge barely wider than a thumb, from which he could go neither forward nor back. It seemed that he must fall into the abyss and be dashed into pieces. His foot had already begun to slip, when a tiny striped squirrel scooted up the cliff, chattering: "You young fool, do you think you have the wings of a bird or the feet of a spirit? Hold on for just a little while and I'll help you." The little creature reached into its cheek pouch and brought out a little seed, which it moistened with saliva and stuck into a crack in the wall. With his tiny feet the squirrel danced above the crack, singing: "Tsithl, tsithl, tsithl, tall stalk, tall stalk, tall stalk, sprout, sprout quickly." Out of the crack sprouted a long, slender stalk, growing quickly in length and breadth, sprouting leaves and tendrils, spanning the chasm so that the young man could cross over without any trouble.

On the other side of the canyon, the young man found the red plume waiting, dancing before him as ever. Again he followed it at a pace so fast that it often seemed that his heart would burst. At last the plume led him to a large, dark, deep lake, and the plume plunged into the water to disappear below the surface. Then the husband knew that the spirit land lay at the bottom of the lake. He was in despair because he could not follow the plume into the deep. In vain did he call for his spirit-wife to come back. The surface of the lake remained undisturbed and unruffled like a sheet of mica. Not even at night did his spirit-wife reappear. The lake, the land of the dead, had swallowed her up. As the sun rose above the mountains, the young man buried his face in his hands and wept.

Then he heard someone gently calling: "Hu-hu-hu," and felt the soft beating of wings on his back and shoulders. He looked up and saw an owl hovering above him. The owl said: "Young man, why are you weeping?"

He pointed to the lake, saying: "My beloved wife is down there in the land of the dead, where I cannot follow her."

"I know, poor man," said the owl. "Follow me to my house in the mountains, where I will tell you what to do. If you follow my advice, all will be well and you will be reunited with the one you love."

The owl led the husband to a cave in the mountains and, as they entered, the young man found himself in a large room full of owl-men and owl-women. The owls greeted him warmly, inviting him to sit down and rest, to eat and drink. Gratefully he took his seat.

The old owl who had brought him took his owl clothing off, hanging it on an antler jutting out from the wall, and revealed himself as a man-like spirit. From a bundle in the wall this mysterious being took a small bag, showing it to the young man, telling him: "I will give this to you, but first I must instruct you in what you must do and must not do."

The young man eagerly stretched out his hand to grasp the medicine bag, but the owl drew back. "Foolish fellow, suffering from the impatience of youth! If you cannot curb your eagerness and your youthful desires, then even this medicine will be of no help to you."

"I promise to be patient," said the husband.

"Well then," said the owl-man," this is sleep medicine. It will make you fall into a deep sleep and transport you to some other place. When you awake, you will walk toward the Morning Star.

Following the trail to the middle anthill, you will find your spirit-wife there. As the sun rises, so she will rise and smile at you, rise in the flesh, a spirit no more, and so you will live happily.

"But remember to be patient; remember to curb your eagerness. Let not your desire to touch and embrace her get the better of you, for if you touch her before bringing her safely home to the village of your birth, she will be lost to you forever."

Having finished this speech, the old owl-man blew some of the medicine on the young husband's face, who instantly fell into a deep sleep. Then all the strange owl-men put on their owl coats and, lifting the sleeper, flew with him to a place at the beginning of the trail to the middle anthill. There they laid him down underneath some trees.

Then the strange owl-beings flew on to the big lake at the bottom of which the land of the dead was located. The old owl-man's magic sleep medicine, and the feathered prayer sticks which the young man had carved, enabled them to dive down to the bottom of the lake and enter the land of the dead. Once inside, they used the sleep medicine to put to sleep the spirits who are in charge of that strange land beneath the waters. The owl-beings reverently laid their feathered prayer sticks before the altar of that netherworld, took up the beautiful young spirit-wife, and lifted her gently to the surface of the lake. Then, taking her upon their wings, they flew with her to the place where the young husband was sleeping.

When the husband awoke, he saw first the Morning Star, then the middle anthill, and then his wife at his side, still in deep slumber. Then she too awoke and opened her eyes wide, at first not knowing where she was or what had happened to her. When she discovered her lover right by her side, she smiled at him, saying: "Truly, your love for me is strong, stronger than love has ever been, otherwise we would not be here."

They got up and began to walk toward the pueblo of their birth. The young man did not forget the advice the old owl-man had given him, especially the warning to be patient and shun all desire until they had safely arrived at their home. In that way they traveled for four days, and all was well.

On the fourth day they arrived at Thunder Mountain and came to the river that flows by Salt Town. Then the young wife said: "My husband, I am very tired. The journey has been long and the days hot. Let me rest here awhile, let me sleep a while, and then, refreshed, we can walk the last short distance home together." And her husband said: "We will do as you say."

The wife lay down and fell asleep. As her lover was watching over her, gazing at her loveliness, desire so strong that he could not resist it overcame him, and he stretched out his hand and touched her.

She awoke instantly with a start, and, looking at him and at his hand upon her body, began to weep, the tears streaming down her face. At last she said: "You loved me, but you did not love me enough; otherwise you would have waited. Now I shall die again." And before his eyes her form faded and became transparent, and at the place where she had rested a few moments before, there was nothing. On a branch of a tree above him the old owl-man hooted mournfully: "Shame, shame, shame." Then the young man sank down in despair, burying his face in his hands, and ever after his mind wandered as his eyes stared vacantly.

If the young lover had controlled his desire, if he had not longed to embrace his beautiful wife, if he had not touched her, if he had practiced patience and self-denial for only a short time, then death would have been overcome. There would be no journeying to the land below the lake, and no mourning for others lost

But then, if there were no death, men would crowd each other with more people on this earth than the earth can hold. Then there would be hunger and war, with people fighting over a tiny patch of earth, over an ear of corn, over a scrap of meat. So maybe what happened was for the best.

Cheyenne Prayer for Peace

Let us know peace.
For as long as the moon shall rise,
For as long as the rivers shall flow,
For as long as the sun shall shine,
For as long as the grass shall grow,
Let us know peace.

Cheyenne Prayer

Earth Prayer

Grandfather, Great Spirit, once more behold me on earth
and lean to hear my feeble voice.
You lived first, and you are older than all need, older than
all prayer.
All things belong to you -- the two-legged, the four-legged,
the wings of the air, and all green things that live.
You have set the powers of the four quarters of the earth to
cross each other.
You have made me cross the good road and road of
difficulties, and where they cross, the place is holy.
Day in, day out, forevermore, you are the life of things.
Hey! Lean to hear my feeble voice.
At the center of the sacred hoop
You have said that I should make the tree to bloom.
With tears running, O Great Spirit, my Grandfather,
With running eyes I must say
The tree has never bloomed
Here I stand, and the tree is withered.
Again, I recall the great vision you gave me.
It may be that some little root of the sacred tree still lives.
Nourish it then
That it may leaf
And bloom
And fill with singing birds!
Hear me, that the people may once again
Find the good road
And the shielding tree.

Black Elk 3

CPSIA information can be obtained at www.ICGtesting.com
Printed in the USA
LVOW07s1510231015

459499LV00017B/528/P